8-16-19

G-2576
"
"
N 125.92

but dated
NR
1st ÷ 1st

VG
$ 24.95

Also by Sharon Cameron
The Dark Unwinding

A SPARK UNSEEN

Sharon Cameron

SCHOLASTIC PRESS • *New York*

Library of Congress Cataloging-in-Publication Data

Cameron, Sharon, 1970–
A spark unseen / Sharon Cameron. — 1st ed.
p. cm.
Summary: When Katharine Tulman foils an attempt to kidnap her Uncle Tully, she finds
herself caught up in international intrigue. Aware that there are people who want to turn
her uncle's mechanical fish into an explosive device, and unsure of who to trust, she decides
to fake her uncle's death and flee to Paris in search of Lane Moreau, her uncle's assistant.
ISBN 978-0-545-32813-5 (jacketed hardcover) 1. Eccentrics and eccentricities — Juvenile
fiction. 2. Uncles — Juvenile fiction. 3. Inventions — Juvenile fiction. 4. Detective and
mystery stories. 5. Paris (France) — History — 1848–1870 — Juvenile fiction.
6. France — History — Second Empire, 1852–1870 — Juvenile fiction. [1. Mystery and
detective stories. 2. Eccentrics and eccentricities — Fiction. 3. Uncles — Fiction.
4. Inventions — Fiction. 5. Paris (France) — Fiction. 6. France — History — Second
Empire, 1852–1870 — Fiction.] I. Title.
PZ7.C1438Sp 2013
813.6 — dc23
2012046637

10 9 8 7 6 5 4 3 2 1   13 14 15 16 17

Printed in the U.S.A.   23
First edition, October 2013
The text type was set in Goudy Old Style.
The display type was set in OPTI Ceasar.
Book design by Elizabeth B. Parisi

FOR MY FAMILY
AND THEIR QUEST FOR TRUTH DURING A
SUNDAY LUNCH

Spark Machine

Principal Constituent Parts of Apparatus

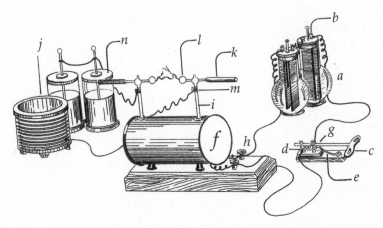

a. Grenet's cell	*h.* primary winding terminals
b. cell terminals	*i.* secondary winding stanchions
c. key	*j.* large coil
d. key stop adjustment	*k.* spark adjustment
e. spring	*l.* spark contacts
f. induction coil	*m.* secondary winding terminals
g. key contacts	*n.* Leyden jar

CHAPTER ONE

September 1854

I opened my eyes, the air in my bedchamber pulsing with the
kind of silence that only comes in the wake of sound — a sound
that never should have been there. I waited, listening. Shadows hid
the dressing table, my bookshelves, the roses on the wallpaper, each
window swathed in a shroud of black. But my room was empty. I felt
this as certainly as the satin coverlet clutched in my hand. And then
it came again. A soft clink of metal, and a creak of floorboard in the
hall. I watched a shaft of yellow light move across the crack beneath
my door.

I flung back the coverlet and ran, barefoot and noiseless, across
the carpet; all thought now narrowed to a single key that stood in the
lock on my door. The same key I had forgotten to turn before climbing into bed. My feet stopped of their own accord just before the door,
nightgown tangled about my knees, and quietly I pressed one cheek
against the cold mahogany while my left hand felt through the darkness, searching for the key. There was a low murmur in the corridor,
a man's timbre, and an answering grumble. Two of them. My fingers
found the key. I turned it, slowly, dreading its click. And just as slowly,

I felt the knob above my key begin to move, twisted by a hand from the other side. The door locked with an audible *thunk* as the knob gave a short rattle.

And then I fled, skirting around furniture I knew to be there but could not see, hair wild and unbraided, through the inner door, across the bathing room, and into Mary's little bedchamber. I passed her sleeping form and tried the latch of the door to my uncle's workshop. Locked. I let out my breath. The room we called the workshop also had a door to the corridor, the corridor that held at least two men trying to enter my bedchamber. But it was not me they wanted to find, or my maid; I was certain of that. How long before they discovered they had the wrong door? I hurried to the rumpled bed, Mary's face just visible in the red light of her stove's dying coals.

"Mary!" I whispered. "Wake up!"

Mary's breath went in and out, whistling.

"Mary!" I grabbed a candle, thrust the taper in the coals, and put the flaming wick to an oil lamp on the bedside table. Light bloomed across her dreaming face. I shook Mary hard, and when that didn't work, shook her violently. Heavy lids fluttered, her mouth opened, and I clamped a hand over it before any words could come out.

"Men in the corridor," I said, holding my voice low.

Mary's eyes focused, going large and wide above my knuckles.

"We must get Uncle Tully. Do you understand?"

She stared at me a moment longer, then nodded. I removed my hand and she clambered out of the bed, her nightcap askew. "Lord, Miss, but you gave me a fright!" she hissed. "I don't know what this house is coming to when —"

"Never mind," I said, pushing away her hands. She had been trying to stuff my arm into the sleeve of a dressing gown, as if I might be concerned at this moment with a lack of decency. "Where is the key? To the workshop?"

"On the table. But what about John George, Miss? Weren't it his night to be watching in the —"

"I don't know. I don't know where he is. We have to get Uncle . . ."

We froze at the same instant, Mary's gaze snapping up to find mine. There were voices in my bedchamber, echoing on the marble walls of the bathing room, no longer bothering with quiet. How could they have gotten through my locked door so quickly and without noise? The dressing gown slipped from Mary's hands, becoming a silken puddle on the carpet.

I flitted to the bathing-room door, shut it softly, and slid its bolt into place — no lock to turn here — while Mary shuffled through the things on her bedside table, searching for the key to the workshop. The door moved, and then rattled hard in its frame, caught against the bolt.

I took a step back, and Mary knocked the key off the table and into a basket of knitting.

One.

I counted the dull, slow thuds of a shoulder ramming against the door.

Two. Three.

I grabbed the oil lamp while Mary got to her knees, scrabbling for the key in a tangle of yarn.

Four. Five . . .

Mary pulled the key free.

Six. Seven. Eight . . . She thrust it into the keyhole, fumbling with the lock.

Nine.

Wood groaned, Mary coaxed the lock to turn, and then we were in the workshop, running the outlandish paths that snaked through the stacks of my uncle's inventions. My light slithered over cogs and wheels of brass, catching on the metallic under-webbing of a shin or cheek, or a disembodied leg, their gears exposed like sinew and bone. And then we heard the wounded door succumb, splintering around the bolt.

I pulled Mary to a stop. My uncle's bedchamber was in the gloom on the other end of the room; I could almost see his door from where I stood. But I would not be so foolish as to show it to them. Mary looked at me and understood. We turned together, the lamp shining out from my hand like a beacon, facing the pair of black shapes that now stood motionless in the doorway of the workshop.

We examined each other. Two against two, white nightgowns and yellow light against dark clothing and shadow. The door to the corridor was too far away, across a sea of humanlike machines, all eyeless, skinless, and unfinished; there had been no one here to give life to their expressions for a long time. And then I saw that the living shapes before me were also without faces. The two men wore masks. Mary's hand tightened on mine.

The larger one took a cautious step toward my light, and I could just make out the glint of eyes through the slits in the mask, searching for the path that would lead him to us. He focused on my face and began picking his way gingerly in the dim. The smaller of the two hung back, still and enigmatic. My eyes roved, seeking help that was not there.

"*Ne te déplace pas,*" said the large one softly, almost soothingly, as he moved. "*Ne bouge pas, Katharine.*"

My stomach twisted. He was speaking French, and he knew my name. I might not know what words he had used, but any doubt about why these men had come was now banished. I thought of my uncle Tully's door, hidden only by the darkness behind me; I had not the smallest hope it would be locked. The man reached out a hand as he came, beckoning, a gentle gesture, almost imploring. In his other hand was a dagger, twinkling in my light.

"*On n'a pas besoin d'avoir recours à la violence, Katharine,*" he said. "*Donne-moi Monsieur Tulman.*"

This time I understood my uncle's name and something about "violence." The other man stood silent, waiting behind his mask. "Mary," I said, hoping these men had no more English than I had French, "we will move toward the hall, away from . . . from . . ." I didn't want to say "Uncle Tully." Mary nodded, still gripping me hard. We took one small side step, together, toward the corridor.

"*Donnez-nous Tulman!*" the man said, voice now gruff. "*Maintenant!*" He waved the dagger.

"This way," I said, very loud and clear. I pushed Mary slightly, and we took another step toward the hall, and then another. I bumped my hip hard as I moved around a workbench, eyes on the arm with the dagger. *Sleep, Uncle Tully,* I begged silently. *Stay asleep. And where are you, John George? You were supposed to be watching the corridor. You should have been in the corridor. . . .* Mary whimpered, her fingers digging into my hand. "Mr. Tulman is this way," I said again.

The man shouted again, and we had taken three more steps before I realized that the silent one was moving, coming fast across the room. In one movement, he had vaulted the workbench between us and yanked Mary by the arm, tearing her away from me. A small pistol cocked, the muzzle disappearing into her tangle of braids.

Mary screamed, yelling as if she'd been shot already, and my arm moved instinctively, acting on an eruption of pure, unthinking fear. I threw the oil lamp.

It was a decent shot. The lamp hit the man and exploded, leaving lines of streaking flame as the base skipped across the carpet. Mary broke free, pushing herself away from the blaze, stumbling over backward as the man dropped the pistol; his arm was on fire. I reached out for Mary and was jerked from behind, cold metal touching the warm skin of my neck. I sucked in a gasp.

"Ne bouge pas ou je te coupe," said the man with the dagger, his breath hot in my ear.

I clutched at the viselike arm around my chest, pinning me from behind as the burning man struggled to rip off his jacket. The sharp point of the knife pressed into my throat. I squeezed my eyes closed, terror giving way to a sort of cold surprise. This was not how I'd thought I would die. Had not been part of my meticulous plans when I'd pulled on my nightgown and climbed into bed. There were this month's ledger books waiting on my desk, and the new plastering to start tomorrow in the ruined lower wing. That rent to be mended in my white stocking, and the walls of Uncle Tully's new workshop, rising stone by stone from the riverbank . . .

My eyes flew open, widening at the sting of the knifepoint as it entered my skin. Lane would come back to Stranwyne Keep, and I would not be here to meet him.

And then the mouth at my ear grunted, the body behind me jerked, and the knife fell away from my throat. I spun, hand on my bleeding neck, and saw the masked man folding in on himself, like badly starched laundry, crumpling to the floor with an almost imperceptible thud.

My gaze traveled up and found Mary, each freckle dark on her pale and sweating face. She had a hammer in her upraised hand, its blunt end bloody in a flickering orange light.

I coughed and looked behind me. The burning man was gone, the hall door open, the air a haze. The jacket blazed in a ball of fire on the carpet, the flames inching outward.

"Water, Mary!" I yelled, stumbling to the drapes, hearing her throw down the hammer as she ran for the bathing room. I ripped the rods from the windows, dragging the heavy cloth over tools and torsos of clockwork, knocking them to the floor until I could pile the drapes onto the fire on the carpet. Smoke billowed. I stomped, beating the fire beneath the drapes with bare feet as Mary threw water onto both the cloth and me before running for more.

A few minutes and the fire was gone, the air around us a poisonous fog. Mary's face was blackened, her watering eyes laying a white stripe on each cheek. She thrust a wet cloth into my face to breathe through as I staggered toward the naked window. I tried to turn the latch — an act that had likely not been attempted in more than two hundred years — and when it would not yield I picked up a metallic arm and smashed the windowpanes, sending sprays of glass down into the gardens below. The cool autumn night sucked at the smoke.

I took a breath of the purer air, the burn of it like fire itself, and turned away from the broken window, stumbling through the wreckage of machinery, past the twisted shape on the floor, a dark stain spreading halo-like from around his head. The soles of his shoes were smoldering. And then I broke into a run across the workshop, scattering a bucket of screws and tearing my gown on a jagged piece of iron before I burst through the door in a cloud.

"Uncle Tully!" I yelled. "Uncle!"

I searched the bare and tidy room with streaming eyes. But my uncle was not there.

CHAPTER TWO

$\mathcal{M}$rs. Cooper put a cup of boiling tea in front of me on the kitchen table. I was sitting in what I thought of as "my chair," the one I had claimed more than two years ago, the first day I'd stepped inside Stranwyne Keep. I felt much the same now as I had then: frightened, uncertain, and steaming with an anger that set the heat of my tea to shame — my inevitable reaction to anything beyond my control. But I was a different girl from the one who had sat here brazenly baiting Mrs. Cooper — Mrs. Jeffries, then — with a bravado that only partially covered my fear. I counted that day I'd come to Stranwyne as the first of my life, my real life; the person I'd been before it was hardly worth remembering. I held my anger in check.

Mrs. Cooper put another cup of tea in front of Mary, nattering on and on as she did it, calling her "duck" and "poppet" and a "right good girl," the rags tied in her hair fluttering like feathers above a white cotton nightgown. I was wearing her dressing gown, the faded blue she kept in the kitchen for baking, pulled close over my wet and sooty nightdress. I reached for the little jug in front of me.

"Cream, Mary?" I asked, steadying my hand.

She didn't answer, just stared stone-faced while I poured it, her unnatural silence hurting me so much more than the small, throbbing cut at the base of my throat. She should not go back upstairs tonight. Maybe she should go home with Mrs. Cooper, or to her mother's in the village. I smiled gamely at the still-blathering Mrs. Cooper, an expression I knew would give her comfort, and then my gaze lifted past them both, into the far corner of the room and another source of chatter. And like the cream pouring into my over-hot tea, my anger cooled, sweetened by an exquisite sense of relief.

My uncle sat cross-legged on the kitchen floor, his attention directed like a beam of light on a broken pocket watch, a trinket I had tucked away for just this purpose, to bring about distraction when needed. I had found him in his nightshirt, wandering in the ticks of his clock room, blissfully unaware of the goings-on in the upper reaches of Stranwyne. The bright eyes were innocent still, intent as he hunched over the watch, alternately listening and then peering at its innards.

"Would you like some tea, Uncle?"

"One, two, three, click," he muttered. "Spin, spin, four, five, click . . ."

"Or some milk?"

"Yes, yes. That is just so. Just so . . ."

I did not think he was speaking of milk. "Or . . ."

"I am not sleepy, Simon's baby!" The light of his attention had focused suddenly on me. "I am not sleepy. The clocks were ticking, but you came before they could tell me when." He cocked his head, accusations now over. "You know about the clocks, don't you, little niece? You like the ticks. You know how to listen to the when?"

"Yes, Uncle." I understood it perfectly. I smiled as his face relaxed in relief. How I wished I could go to him, give him one fierce hug to assure me of his safety. But only crisis or exhaustion had ever induced Uncle Tully to accept affection, and right now he was conscious of neither. He was sighing happily.

"My little niece knows. Lane knows what is right, and my little niece knows the when, and what we should do. This one does not tell me when. Right now, it cannot say. . . ."

His white beard moved with soft but incessant words, the intense gaze back on the watch, observing the machinations of tiny gears. He would solve the problem in his hand very soon, if he had not solved it already. It was for this that those men had come, for the strange and wonderful contents of my uncle's mind. And they could not have it. They would not have it.

Knuckles rapped at the door, and Mary started violently, knocking the contents of her cup into a brown, seeping streak across the table. Mrs. Cooper fell mercifully silent.

"Tea doesn't belong on tables," Uncle Tully stated. "No, no. Tea belongs in cups, pots, cupboards, cabinets, people, mugs, tins. . . ."

"Who's there?" I called.

The response from the corridor was muffled. "Only Matthew, Miss."

I breathed again, shaking my head at my foolishness as Mrs. Cooper moved to unlock the door. I doubted the man that had nearly shot Mary and run flaming from the workshop was likely to announce his presence with a polite knock. His companion would never knock again.

Matthew shambled into the room, a shy, retiring ox of a man whose unlikely occupation was filling in the tiny details of flowers and vines on the figurines produced by Stranwyne's pottery kilns. How his enormous fists did such fiddly work was a conundrum to me. I set down my cup.

"You found nothing of him?" I asked him.

"No, Miss."

"Then the man is likely several miles onto the moors by now. I will come upstairs and see what can be seen." I stood, glad of something to do. "Mrs. Cooper, lock the door behind me, just in case, and see that Mary has a place to lie down, or that she gets to her mother's, would you?" I saw Mary cross her arms at this, frowning at the table.

"Don't go for long, little niece," my uncle called, eyes on the watch. "Not for long! We are not sleepy, but it is the wrong time for kitchens. The wrong time. I can wait in the wrong time without my niece for twenty, and then we must be back in the right place for the right time. I can only wait for twenty."

"Of course, Uncle." I leaned close to Mrs. Cooper. "If the watch is repaired before I return, there is a broken clock on the top shelf of the sideboard."

Mrs. Cooper nodded unhappily, her round face like a worried dumpling. Water came unexpectedly to my eyes. "Don't worry, Aunt Bit," I said. "I'll be gone fifteen minutes, no more."

I kissed her wrinkled cheek before I went out the door.

Matthew waited for me in the kitchen corridor, hat in hands, brow troubled, his great weight shifting from foot to foot, making the floorboards squeak. He would not meet my eyes. "Miss," he said slowly, "I'm thinking there's no need of you going up. There's really . . ."

"Did Mr. Cooper allow Dr. Pruitt to finish his examination?" Dr. Pruitt was brought to Stranwyne's village nearly six months ago, a decent, highly trained, rather progressive physician, who had unfortunately lost his reputation the same day a prominent patient lost his life. Mr. Cooper had been in high dudgeon ever since.

"Yes, Miss. Dr. Pruitt says he was gone before he hit the floor, most likely. And Mr. Cooper agrees with him, for what that's worth. But I do think there's no need for you to be . . ."

My stony look must have quelled this last observation, which would no doubt have expressed reservations about a young lady going voluntarily into the presence of death. Even if she had been present when it happened. Matthew's mouth formed a straight line, his gaze fixed on a place somewhere about ten feet behind my left ear. Or, I thought suddenly, perhaps it was the nightgown. I pulled the blue dressing gown tighter as we started down the corridor.

"And have you found where John George has gotten to?" I had some particular words planned for the man I had assigned to stand guard in my corridor.

When Matthew remained silent, I looked up. His face informed me of the truth before his voice could. Shock stilled my feet, and then an abrupt conflagration of fury had me setting a brisk pace down the hall.

"How?" I asked him.

Matthew jogged to catch up. "His throat was cut, Miss."

I climbed the stone stairs that led to my wing of the house, to what had always been my inner sanctum. "Where was he?"

"In the chapel, Miss."

I reached the top of the stairs, the smell of burnt carpet wafting down the corridor, horror, indignation, fury, and sadness all at war inside me. I had liked John George. Had trusted him. What had he been doing in the chapel? Had he followed Uncle Tully? The clock room was adjoining, only one door away. I thought of how close I had been to my lifeless friend when finding my uncle. I thought of how close those two masked devils had been to my uncle when they poured that friend's life onto the chapel floor. How dare they? I threw open the door to the smoldering workshop, letting it bang hard against the wall.

The room flickered with candle glow. Dr. Pruitt and Mr. Cooper were crouched over the inert body, their two heads coming up to frown at my entrance, the shadowy, metallic body parts of my uncle's inventions glinting randomly in the light. I marched up to the thing lying on the carpet. Now that the candles were lit, I could see the man's mask was no more than a sack of dyed linen, crude holes cut for the eyes. I reached down and tugged at the cloth, jerking the lifeless head in a way that made Mr. Cooper wince. And when the mask came away, I saw gray-brown hair, skin paling beneath unshaven stubble, open eyes of a nondescript color. A complete stranger to me. The knife he had held at my throat lay on the carpet a few feet away. The blade was bloodstained, more blood than could have possibly been my own.

I ransacked the man's pockets, ignoring the *tut* of Mr. Cooper, and found one surprisingly clean and unmarked handkerchief, a shilling, two francs, and one pence, and a crumpled sheet of paper. I stood and smoothed the paper, holding it to the light, studying the penned squares and lines that took me several moments to recognize as a rough plan of Stranwyne Keep. The position of my corridor was marked with an X.

I turned away without a word, the crude map in my hand, and walked out the door to the hallway. I leaned against the corridor wall, well away from the workshop's light spill, and allowed the guilt to settle down on me, like snowflakes of iron, falling one by one, each adding their weight to my shoulders. The north wind came up, the ripping breeze that was as much a part of Stranwyne Keep as my Uncle Tully, and an unnatural, resonant wail began, the trogwynd, rising around the walls of the house, drowning out the low talk of the men in the workshop. I used its noise to move silently along the corridor, down the stairs, and out of my wing of the house.

Light showed from beneath the kitchen door, where my uncle was chattering, but I moved quickly past it, slipping instead into another door a little farther down the hall. There was no gaslight here, and I felt for the candle and matches I kept on the table. The matches were an extravagance, but I didn't want to bring a light in here with me; I didn't want anyone to know I came. The match struck, sizzling, and the plainest room in Stranwyne leapt into visibility. It was little more than a closet, a bed neat and unslept-in, the hooks for the clothes empty, a set of carving tools abandoned on a worktable. But Lane had wanted his room this way, small and with no fuss.

I sat on the edge of the bed and closed my eyes, blocking out the candlelight, breathing against the weight that sat on me. Lane's smell was here, though only just. It was one of the reasons I knew Mr. Wickersham's letter six weeks ago could not have been true, why I had thrown the paper on the coals and watched the ink burn. How could Lane be gone from the world — like the dead man upstairs and John George — and his scent still be in this room? The deepest part of me, a place that had nothing to do with logic, screamed that it could not be, that it was not possible, that therefore Lane must be somewhere.

I had nearly three minutes before I was late for my uncle, and therefore two minutes to let my tears flow, and to wonder if I could ever be the little niece that knew what we should do and when. Lane Moreau would have let me come in here to cry if I needed to, I knew that. I just didn't know why he had not come back to me.

CHAPTER THREE

$\mathcal{M}$r. Babcock leaned back in his chair as I finished my recitation, the buttons of his waistcoat straining. It was the second dawn since the Frenchman had died in my uncle's workshop, and the sun had only just crested the moors. But I had been prepared for one of Mr. Babcock's infamous early arrivals, the natural result of putting himself on a train as soon as my express could have arrived in his London offices. The story I told him had been clear and succinct, my manner calm, expression collected. In other words, I was an utter sham. I held my hands in my lap, watching the shrewd eyes of the Tulman family solicitor hood themselves into a familiar expression of deep contemplation. My gaze moved from Mr. Babcock to the settee, where I found Mr. Wickersham coolly regarding me.

Mr. Wickersham appeared exactly as he had the last time he'd dropped unexpectedly into my morning room, even down to the nameless companion who sat beside him, scribbling our words into a notebook. If it was not the same scribbling man, then it was another of the breed, showing the similar traits of too much ink and too little sun. But Mr. Wickersham was of a different variety, more farmhand than gentleman of vague position in the British government, with large, rough hands and a manner to match. A lump of coal broke in the fireplace, glittering, the nameless man's pen scratched across the paper, and I challenged Mr. Wickersham's gaze with growing dislike each passing second.

"Well, this is bad, my dear. Very bad," said Mr. Babcock eventually. I could not disagree with him. He drummed three fingers on his round belly. "I must say that I considered Mr. Wickersham's warnings last month to perhaps be a bit overcautious. But now I am inclined to believe that we have not been near cautious enough."

"I put men at the doors and in the corridor," I said, the weeping of John George's widow still fresh in my mind. "But my uncle will wander. Perhaps with a man at —"

"Tosh, Miss Tulman," Mr. Wickersham broke in. "This house is a sieve, and you know it."

My gaze went back to the settee. He was right, of course. I had seen the scratches on my lock, made by a thin tool used to turn my key from the outside, and we had also found where the two men had entered, a broken window in a lower storeroom, two floors and a dozen rooms away from any ears that could have detected the shattering glass. A house as vast and empty as Stranwyne Keep had to be vulnerable, but how I hated Mr. Wickersham for saying so. There was one empty room in Stranwyne for which I blamed him entirely.

I caught a glimpse of Mr. Babcock's eyes, now unhooded, lifted to my face and perceiving my anger. "Katharine, my child, there is common purpose here. We would do well to remember it."

I took his gentle admonishment and focused my attention on the matter at hand. "Mr. Wickersham, obviously you believe my uncle is not safe at Stranwyne. If we —"

"Do you not believe it yourself, Miss Tulman?"

"We would value your opinion on how to make him so, I'm sure," I replied, my voice crackling with ice. Mr. Babcock sighed while Mr. Wickersham eyed me from behind his bushy mustache.

"Miss Tulman, a child of only marginal intelligence could enter this house without being seen, and we are not dealing with children or stupidity." He held out a hand and the scratching of the pen instantly stopped, the nameless man's eyes seeking a portion of the carpet and remaining there, as if he were one of my uncle's clockwork machines that had suddenly wound down. I looked in surprise from the man back to Mr. Wickersham, who was leaning forward in his chair.

"England is at war in the Crimea, Miss Tulman, and with France as our ally against the Russian tsar. The —"

"We do get the newspapers at Stranwyne, Mr. Wickersham," I said, unable to help myself. The man was schooling me like a child. He smiled at my rudeness.

"What you perhaps do not know, Miss Tulman, is that the alliance between England and France is an uneasy one, one that will likely continue to be uneasy, no matter who wins this war or which country controls what in the Ottoman Empire. And the war does not go well. The Royal Navy has suffered a defeat at the hand of the Russians, a defeat so humiliating that the admiral in command shot himself in the hold of his own ship rather than face his government." I grimaced, but Mr. Wickersham took no notice. "It is the strength of our navies that will decide whether England or France is the supreme power in Europe. And the emperor has built ironclad batteries, floating arsenals impregnable to cannon that can bombard a shoreline, and ironclad ships powered by steam are not far behind them. These French ships will be fast and impervious to our weapons. They will be unstoppable, Miss Tulman."

"You seem rather certain of these doings by the Emperor Napoléon," I cut in. "Just where has all this information come from, Mr. Wickersham? From Lane Moreau, by any chance?"

"I will say to you again, Miss Tulman, that the late Mr. Moreau's doings in France had nothing to do with me or the British government."

Liar, I thought.

Mr. Wickersham leaned even farther toward me in his chair, the move almost a threat. "The only information I have of Mr. Moreau, Miss Tulman, is the notification of his demise six weeks ago."

If I could have flayed the man alive with my eyes, I would have. "Then perhaps you could provide me with this document, Mr. Wickersham? Or a certificate of death?" Mr. Babcock sighed heavily from his chair.

"I have no obligation to provide you with anything, young woman. But let us stick to the pertinent facts, shall we? We believe that guncotton is currently being manufactured by the French, the same explosive the man you knew as Ben Aldridge was testing for use in your uncle's mechanical fish. We . . ."

Instantly my mind went to my uncle's fish, swimming in a sleek metallic streak beneath the surface of the water, never sinking, never floating, holding its depth for reasons only Uncle Tully could fathom.

To him the fish had been a "toy," no different than the peacock that walked or his humanlike machines that played games or musical instruments. It was Ben Aldridge who had seen the great monetary advantage of handing France my uncle's fish filled with a powerful explosive. I felt a moment of grim happiness that Ben was dead. Then I realized Mr. Wickersham was still speaking and that his thoughts had been following my own.

". . . that your uncle's fish would become an exploding weapon that could sink the fastest, most unsinkable ship clad in iron. If the Emperor Napoléon acquires this weapon first, then the race to naval supremacy is over. France will rule the seas and, inevitably, will rule Britain. The emperor knows this well; the fact that two French-speaking men entered your house to take Mr. Tulman tells us so, and it tells us that the time for perfecting this crucial weapon grows short. But I also believe the attempt to take Mr. Tulman means that the French cannot make their version of his mechanical fish work."

I stared at Mr. Wickersham. Mr. Babcock's fingers drummed. "But how could the French even begin to make their own version?" I replied. "The only models of my uncle's fish were destroyed. And only Ben Aldridge had discovered how the device worked — if he even had — and he is long dead. There is no one to demonstrate, no model to refer —"

"Hence the difficulties, I'm sure!" Mr. Wickersham interrupted. "You know that we have long believed that Mr. Aldridge — or Mr. Arceneaux, to use his true name — had an accomplice, a contact on the French side. I believe that enough was known about the workings of the fish to attempt the creation of another, and that the attempt does not go well. It has not gone well for the British, and I am certain we began with more information than Napoléon did."

Mr. Babcock's mouth rounded in a silent "ahhh," as if Mr. Wickersham had spoken something he'd been waiting for, and the little fingers changed to a staccato rhythm.

"Do you mean to say," I asked, "that you have been trying to make one of Uncle Tully's fish as well, Mr. Wickersham?"

He smiled amiably. "France may be ahead of us in the race to an ironclad ship, Miss Tulman, but both countries shall certainly have them. It is the side that has the weapon to destroy an ironclad that will own the seas, and that is a prize that both Her Majesty Victoria and the Emperor Napoléon would very much like to reserve for themselves. England and France may march together in the Crimea, but do not forget that the first Napoléon Bonaparte ruled Europe and came close to defeating us. And now his nephew Napoléon the Third has dissolved the French parliament and crowned himself emperor. He is out to recapture the reign and glory of his family, Miss Tulman, make no mistake about that. And I, for one, would not like to see that much power fall back into the hands of a Bonaparte."

A small silence fell. Mr. Wickersham slapped his knees, and the limp man beside him seemed to wake up, immediately resuming the scratching of his pen. "So I am sure you will understand when I say that we expect your uncle in London as soon as is possible."

His words hit my mind like a physical slap. "I'm afraid I must have misunderstood you," I replied. Mr. Wickersham shook his head.

"You are no simpleton, Miss Tulman, and have better sense than to make an enemy of your own government. We will be prepared to collect Mr. Tulman by half past three on the day after tomorrow."

"But you cannot do that."

Mr. Wickersham smiled. "And why can we not?"

"Mr. Wickersham," I began as if speaking to a particularly slow child, "you do not understand. My uncle will not work or create on your command, no matter how much you might wish him to. If you forcibly remove him to unfamiliar surroundings, he may not even function. I have grave doubts that he would even survive the journey."

"And yet we cannot risk having him here, where the emperor can so easily snatch him. It would take half a legion of soldiers to secure this estate. We might as well telegraph our intentions to Paris. England is in need of this weapon, Miss Tulman, if only to hold the balance of power, no matter what the consequences. So to London he goes."

I balled up a piece of skirt in my hand. "So what you are saying, Mr. Wickersham, is that you consider this weapon to be worth more than the life of my uncle. Do I understand you correctly?"

"Katharine, my child," said Mr. Babcock softly, though there was steel in the little man's voice. I closed my mouth as he turned to Mr. Wickersham. "Miss Tulman is understandably distressed. I think a time of quiet in her own chamber, for refreshment and reflection, would be necessary for any young lady in her position. Do you not agree, Mr. Wickersham?"

Mr. Wickersham looked hard at the little lawyer and then at me. "You are quite right, I am sure," he said. He got to his feet, adjusting the position of his jacket sleeves. "But there is one more subject for Miss Tulman's necessary 'reflections.' Her Majesty's government is well aware that Mr. Tulman has . . . eccentricities, shall we say, and understands how necessary Miss Tulman's person is to his health and well-being. Therefore it is not only Mr. Tulman's presence that is required in London, but that of his niece as well."

The bushy mustache turned to face me directly. "We shall return at half past three on the day after tomorrow. Please have your affairs in order, Miss Tulman, and do be prepared for an extended stay." He gave us both a slight bow before he smiled. "And we will be setting a watch on both the road and the river. For Mr. Tulman's continued safety, of course. A good morning to you both."

The scribbling man hastily gathered up his things and followed Mr. Wickersham out through my morning-room door while Mr. Babcock sat quietly, lost in silent thought. I was too stunned for words. When their footsteps had faded, a voice spoke out from behind me.

"That man can't be having Mr. Tully. Or you neither, Miss!"

I turned to see Mary's head sticking in from around the opposite doorjamb, where she'd been eavesdropping.

"Of course he can't," Mr. Babcock and I said together. Mary stood upright and crossed her arms.

"And Lane Moreau is not dead," I added, just as stoutly.

To this, neither one of them answered.

It was after midnight when Mary and I finally saw Mr. Babcock to his carriage and came creeping back to our corridor, exhausted and with our throats hoarse from talking. It had been a day of whispered conversation — many whispered conversations — conducted around the strictures of my uncle's routine. After Uncle Tully was settled for the night, we'd followed Mr. Babcock to one of the deserted rooms in the lower wing, locked the door, and put the finishing touches to our plan amid the dirt and half-torn-out walls, the leftover casualties of the previous flood. Matthew was at the foot of my stairs when Mary and I arrived, a pistol thrust through his belt. He nodded to me once in affirmation that all was well, keeping any curiosity about where I'd been and what I'd been doing well away from his eyes.

I locked my door, but not before giving a quick glance to the portrait of Marianna, my grandmother, standing guard from her wall across the hallway. For the first time, I wondered how she could have failed me. I wondered how I could have failed them all. I removed the key to the bedside table this time, threw off my petticoats, put on a dressing gown, and dropped into my chair before a nonexistent fire, sliding the pins one by one from my hair. I felt so heavy, weighted in mind and body by all that had been decided and all that was now to come.

I pulled my stockinged feet up onto the edge of the cushion, closer to the warmth of my body, and settled my chin onto my knees. The chimney clock ticked. I remembered another night I had sat heavy before this hearth, two years earlier, Uncle Tully lying catatonic in my bed and my wretched aunt Alice lurking the lower floors, ready to rip all I'd so newly come to love away from me at the rising of the sun. Lane had come and sat vigil beside me, on the floor beside this chair, dark and silent, the two of us listening to the tick, tick, tick as the clock hands moved inexorably toward the morning. He reached out and took one of my hands, lifting it until his rough cheek lay against my wrist, and we'd sat that way, waiting, my pulse beating against his cheek, his breath warming my skin. . . .

Mary's voice beside my chair gave me a start. I opened my eyes to find my wrist pressed tight against my own cheek, and an unasked-for cup of tea in Mary's hand. I straightened up in the chair.

"Thank you, Mary," I said gratefully. I hoped she'd poured one for herself. She probably needed it just as much as I did. I took the first cautious sip, breathing in the fragrant steam. "Thank you, Mary," I said again. "For everything."

One side of her mouth quirked down, and I knew what thought was in her mind: a black linen mask, and the way a body folds when the life is out of it. Mary reached out, adjusting the vertical angle of a candle on the chimneypiece.

"Do you think we really can be doing it, Miss? Can we really be doing as Mr. Babcock says?"

"Of course we can," I replied, though my every fiber longed to deny it. "Or, at least, I must, Mary. You don't have to. I . . . I can hardly ask it of you." I noted the number of intervening heartbeats, watching Mary think, aching at the thought of being one step closer to alone. Mary lifted her chin, a gesture I recognized as my own.

"I'm thinking we must, Miss. That I must. For Mr. Tully."

She left the candle to its tilt and flounced defiantly back to her room while I breathed silent gratitude over the steaming tea. The room settled into quiet, and the clock on the chimneypiece ticked. What a strange sort of symmetry that I was here once more, only this time there was no Lane to help me watch the clock hands. The heaviness inside me tightened into a single, burning knot.

We had thirty-eight hours until Mr. Wickersham came.

CHAPTER FOUR

I am sleepy, Simon's baby! Sleepy! But it is not the right time to be sleepy. Not right! The wrong time . . ."

"I know it, Uncle," I whispered. He thrashed once in the little cot he preferred to a bed, threatening to knock the empty rose-striped teacup from the table. "But remember what I told you, that when you wake up, you will have done just as Marianna said to."

The usually bright, inquisitive eyes locked on to mine, searching my face for understanding. They were becoming dull and unfocused. "We should . . . always . . . do . . . always . . . remember what . . . Marianna . . . says. My little niece . . . knows. . . ."

I gave him a Judas-like smile and sat down on the edge of his cot, to be near, though not so near as to make him uncomfortable. If he could only be unafraid in these last few moments, it was all I could ask. Mary stood a few feet away, a sick expression on her face, hands behind her, staring at the far wall of Uncle Tully's bedchamber. I knew why she could not look. What we were doing went against every inclination of nature, like eating spoiled meat or slicing open one's own skin. But I had promised myself long ago that I would do anything for my uncle, that I would protect him at all costs, even if that protection was one he could never understand. I made no promise lightly.

Uncle Tully pulled fitfully at the blankets, his movements losing force. "Marianna . . . said . . . Niece said . . . She . . ." The rest of his words were unintelligible.

"Shhh, Uncle," I soothed, my lies very gentle. "Marianna says it is time to sleep."

Uncle Tully's eyelids fluttered shut, his breath coming slow. After a few moments, his hand fell limp on his chest, sliding down to rest at his side. The blankets did not move. We waited, holding our breath, listening to the quiet. Uncle Tulman lay peaceful, childlike, and very still on his little bed.

Mary moved first, dashing tears impatiently from her cheeks, and I stood, straightening my back, moving to the bedchamber door with the automatic precision of a piece of clockwork. Dr. Pruitt must have heard me coming because he was there when the door swung open, his forehead dotted with sweat.

"We are finished here," I told him. "Please call the village committee together and say that I regret to inform them that Mr. Frederick Tulman is dead."

I shut the door behind Dr. Pruitt and locked it, turning back to gaze at Mary. She was already in motion, smoothing the blanket, arranging my uncle's hair, liberties he would have never before allowed her.

I whispered into the silent room. "We have to move him, Mary. Now."

Two hours later I was in my bedchamber, comforting a nearly incoherent Mrs. Cooper. I had been dreading this moment, to the point of physical sickness, and now that the time was here it was infinitely worse than I'd imagined. I had been afraid I would be frosty and silent, an unfeeling statue in the face of the poor woman's grief, and instead I cried just as hard as she did, guilt and a horrible, hot shame pouring out with the water from my eyes. Despite my pet name of "aunt," Mrs. Cooper and I were of no relation, but she had lived a lifetime of loyalty to my uncle and for many months had been a kind of brusque and fussing mother to me. And we shared the same hurts, down to the length, shape, and maybe even depth of the wounds. We understood each other's losses, and now I had been the one to give her another.

"'Tis too much," she wheezed into her apron. "Too much. First Davy gone, and Lane leaving us, and now . . ."

I'd already been to Davy's grave that morning, in the little depression on top of the moor hill where Davy had always gone to play. Standing there beside the grassy mound, the wind lashing my back, I'd wished that the clocks' hands could turn the wrong way and that none of it had ever happened. That Davy would come, small and silent, and lean against the standing stone, trying to imitate Lane's lithe grace with a short body and a bunny in his lap. That we would all go rolling in the splendor of the ballroom. That Ben Aldridge had never laid eyes on Davy and that Lane had never blamed himself for failing to see how someone like Ben might have found such a child so easy to use and manipulate. That Davy had not been rescued from the workhouse only to come to Stranwyne and die. That Mr. Wickersham had never arrived on our doorstep, that this small grave on the moor hill — and the lack of one for Ben — might never have compelled Lane to leave in the first place. That Ben Aldridge had remained unborn. If any of that had been so, then the awful deeds of today would have never been necessary.

Mrs. Cooper was still crying, dabbing her eyes with an apron end. I gathered up the shreds of my courage. This would not do. I knew what was required of me. But still I could not speak. I put my gaze on the floor.

"Will you go with me, then?" she said. "Shall we go and be seeing Mr. Tully together?"

Another dagger of guilt went stabbing through my chest. We had gone together to see Davy's body when it was found, the first of our common hurts. But that could not be. Not this time. I straightened my back.

"I don't wish to see my uncle, Aunt Bit." I let the words sink in as she stared, shock actually stopping her tears. "I don't wish for anyone to see him. He . . . does not look well. And I will not have him remembered that way. I will not." I lifted my chin. "I won't have it."

Mrs. Cooper's astonishment gave way to a frown. "But . . ."

"I won't have it," I repeated.

"But, Katie, pet," she said, "who's to do the laying out, and —"

"Mary has already done it."

Mrs. Cooper sat back in her chair, her jaw unhinged.

"There will be a quiet burial tomorrow, with no fuss. Uncle Tully . . . he would not have wished for people or a commotion. You can see that, can't you?" Pooled tears went rolling down my cheeks; I could not help or heed them. "And, Aunt Bit, I have made another decision. I . . . I am leaving Stranwyne Keep. Immediately. And I expect that I shall be away . . . a longish time."

She sat perfectly still. I stared down at my two hands, firmly clasped on the black silk of my mourning dress. "Of course, you shall be in charge of the house. I could trust no one else, and the kitchen is yours, as always. But the rest of the house is to be shut up. Until needed again." I reached out to put a hand on hers. "This will always be your home. That does not change."

She removed her hand carefully from beneath mine. "But, Miss," she said slowly. I bled internally that I was no longer her "Katie." "Where will you be going?"

I put my hand back in my lap. "I have decided to spend some time in Paris. My grandmother had a house there. Mr. Babcock will act as steward for the estate, as he once did, and will help to . . . arrange things." I swallowed, my brief spurt of courage draining away.

"Paris?" she repeated. The ensuing pause was so long I was wondering if I should have clarified the city's location in France when Mrs. Cooper suddenly said, "This is 'cause of him, ain't it?"

I looked up. The usual good-willed — or not-so-good-willed — foolishness that was so much a part of Mrs. Cooper's features had been replaced with a flash of sharp penetration. She had no idea that Lane had gone to Paris, or why he had left Stranwyne in the first place. Stoicism not being one of Mrs. Cooper's many good qualities, I had taken my cue from Lane's secrecy and told her nothing about clandestine assignments from the British government, or the letter informing us of Lane's death. But Aunt Bit had perceived what I was trying to hide, or at least part of it, and she was entirely right. I was marching straight into the hornet's nest of Paris for no other reason than to find Lane Moreau. And I would find him and throw Mr. Wickersham's lies right back into his mustached face. Mrs. Cooper must have seen something of these thoughts in my expression because her eyebrows went up.

"When that boy is coming back, there will be a murder done," she pronounced, her tears beginning anew.

I could only believe that it hadn't been done already.

"The coffin is made, Miss, and Matthew is digging the grave, though I never knew a body to go so slow about a thing. I swear he —"

"Did the boxes go this afternoon, Mary? They need to be at the house in Paris when we arrive."

"Yes, Miss, two wagonloads. And didn't young Tom fuss about loading them, too? And he says there was a man up on the hill, Miss, away by the tunnel, watching the boxes go in —"

"Did you get the striped cups?"

"Of course I was getting them! What do you take me for, Miss? I swear the last —"

"Here, Mary," I said, shoving a wad of dark cloth quickly into her hands. "Press the lace on my black veil, would you?"

She went out the door, still muttering and shaking her head. I sank down onto a stool, head aching, looking at bits of torn paper and odd pins, the flotsam that was all that remained of my life in my grandmother's room. Now only my steamer trunk was left, ready for filling. Mary dealt with the pain of parting in words, but I needed quiet to let my own feelings writhe and fester. I picked up the silver swan from my dressing table, the gift Lane had made for me, its delicate wings uplifted. *"I can feel it trying to fly,"* I had told him, gazing at the swan balanced on my palm. *"You would like to fly, I think,"* the low voice had replied. *"That is why it's yours."* Now I did not wish to fly. I wanted nothing more than to stay at home.

The heavy knot in my middle pulled painfully tight, the silver swan warming to the heat of my hand. There were twenty-three hours until Mr. Wickersham came.

CHAPTER FIVE

he family cemetery was on a rise beyond the upper end of
Stranwyne, surrounded by a crumbling stone wall with a wrought-
iron railing rusting along its top. I did not come here often. Leaning
slabs of weather-washed stone rose irregularly from the ground, while
in some places nothing but a rectangular depression in the grass
marked the resting place of an ancestor. The monument to my grandmother, Marianna Louise Tulman, rose tall near one corner of the
enclosure, but I felt no real affinity with a granite obelisk, or even
the ground that held my grandmother's bones. It was her room, her
furniture, her clothes — the things of her life — that made her real
to me, and today I was leaving them. The wind on the high ground
whipped violently, as if it had taken a fancy to steal my black veil,
and the trogwynd sang low, a lament to my uncle. I put up a gloved
hand and held on to my bonnet.

". . . we commit his body to the ground . . ." said Parson Lowe.

Mrs. Cooper cried noisily beside me, and I took her hand in my
free one, wishing for comfort as much as I wanted to give it.

"Earth to earth, ashes to ashes . . ."

I met Mary's eyes over the hole in the ground. She was crying as well, though for different reasons, I knew, than Mrs. Cooper, and I was suddenly struck by the sight of her. She was the same Mary as always: large-eyed, freckled, with her upturned nose and wide mouth capable of speech in speeds and quantities that one could scarcely credit. And yet, in that sober dark dress with the fitted bodice, and with her hair tamed and twisted into a knot beneath her bonnet, she was not the gawking girl I had met when I first came to Stranwyne. She was, most assuredly, a young woman, one who would expertly assist in my most wild of schemes, and even, evidently, wield a hammer for my sake.

The parson nodded and the coffin hit the bottom of the grave hole with a hateful *thump*. The lowering ropes were pulled free, and Matthew, young Tom, and two other men from the village stepped up, hats or caps popping back onto their heads, shovels in their hands. The dirt hit Uncle Tully's coffin with dry, grating rasps, like when we'd buried John George the day before, like when Lane had buried Davy. The wind keened.

I looked away from the coffin, past Mary and down the slope to Stranwyne Keep, the jumble of brown stone and chimneys and roof tiles that was my home. And then I saw the carriage, just emerging from the tunnel through the moor hills, making its way at high and silent speed around the circular drive, the trogwynd snatching away the sound of its wheels. I turned my face back to the shovelers.

"Faster, please," I said crisply, causing both Mrs. Cooper and Parson Lowe to look at me and frown. But the effort to fill my uncle's grave was quickened. I saw Mary staring down the slope, her lips pressing tight.

Mr. Wickersham had arrived. Three hours and forty-two minutes early.

And he was in the drawing room when I entered it, his scribbling man perched on the settee, an ink pot and spare nibs spread out on the table. I gave them both a small curtsy. I had slept perhaps four of the past forty-eight hours, and my body felt the loss like a missing limb. But I smiled, laid the veiled bonnet carefully on the table, and prepared to do battle from the edge of a damask chair.

"Do sit, Mr. Wickersham. I'm so glad you did not stand on formality, and just let yourself in."

He did not sit. "Where is your uncle, Miss Tulman?"

"I . . . we . . ." My eyes filled, wetting my lashes. Tears were so close to the surface these days that they were extraordinarily easy to summon. "Have you had no letter, Mr. Wickersham? Mr. Babcock assured me that he would —"

"Yes, yes. I got the bloody letter. Caught me in Milton only just this morning." I thought I heard him grit his teeth. "I was not aware that your uncle suffered from any 'ailment of the heart.'"

"I'm afraid we were not aware of it either, Mr. Wickersham," I replied.

Mr. Wickersham thrust his hands in his pockets, blustering about the room while the inevitable pen scratched, cursing circumstance and lack of luck beneath his breath. My eyes narrowed.

"Your compassion and concern during this difficult time are truly admirable, Mr. Wickersham. I am very much comforted."

He stopped his pacing to look at me, my loss of temper somehow making his own relax. He smiled and sat down abruptly.

"Where is the body, Miss Tulman?"

"My uncle was laid to rest just a short time ago. Beside his mother."

"Quick work," he commented.

"It was not . . . convenient to wait longer. We have no undertaker here."

There was a small silence. "This will be a disappointment for Her Majesty's government," Mr. Wickersham continued. "The loss of Frederick Tulman is rather a blow to our plans. A sad loss for our plans." He leaned back in his chair, still grinning at me, a posture that was nothing like that of a gentleman. "Of course, you do understand, Miss Tulman, that you will still be required to accompany me to London."

I looked back at him steadily. "I certainly shall not."

"Oh, yes. You certainly shall."

"To what purpose?"

The pen wrote furiously. "To explain all and anything you might know about the workings of your uncle's inventions, of course, and their —"

"Mr. Wickersham," I interrupted, "do you truly believe that I can answer some riddle of genius that your scientific men are currently incapable of solving? Are you really so desperate that you would present to these men as a solution to their problems a mere girl, one whose entire qualifications rest on having once seen the invention in question? They will laugh in your face."

I was laying it on a bit thick, I thought, but it seemed to be working. The scribbling man's brows had gone up while Mr. Wickersham's went down. I moderated my tone.

"Mr. Wickersham, I am a person of independent means with no

pressing responsibilities." How I wished that were true. "And there are memories in this house that I find very painful. I plan to leave this afternoon, in less than an hour — thirty-eight minutes, as a matter of fact — and will travel until such a time as I choose to come back again. Most of my trunks have already gone."

Mr. Wickersham stroked his mustache thoughtfully. "I can easily have you taken to London, Miss Tulman, whether you choose it or no."

"And I can be extremely troublesome, and with the help of my solicitor, can promise to both legally and physically kick up such a fuss as you've never seen. Do you think me incapable of it?" We locked eyes, and after a moment I said, "Mr. Wickersham, I know nothing of my uncle's inventions. I have no idea how they worked or even what parts went together to make them. My uncle created nothing resembling his fish since the flood that destroyed his workshop two years ago. And as for his more recent workshop upstairs . . ." The man's gaze shot toward the ceiling. ". . . everything there has been removed to the foundry and melted."

I broke our gaze, dabbing again at my eyes. "I loved my uncle dearly and, as I said, the memories here are very painful."

The pen caught up to my last words with the result that I could hear the trogwynd howling very softly in the chimney. I looked up to see Mr. Wickersham giving me another smile.

"It seems you have thought of everything, Miss Tulman. Please accept my most sincere condolences. When do you sail?"

I hid my surprise behind the handkerchief. "I do not believe I mentioned sailing, Mr. Wickersham."

"Did you not, Miss Tulman? Dashed odd. Are you certain?" He leaned back again, ungentlemanly in his chair. "Then perhaps I just assumed that you were going to your grandmother's residence in Paris?"

I stared at him, rooted to my seat, watching his little eyes go dreamy.

"Rather a nice old place, though the neighborhood, I fancy, is not quite the fashion it was before the current emperor's reign. But still, I think you will enjoy it. The Reynoldses are in residence next door at the moment, a fine old family, fleeing the cholera in London, I believe, as are many. Do tell them I wish them well. As I do you, Miss Tulman." He stood and bowed, causing the scribbling man to leap to his feet. "Good-bye. Or maybe I should say *au revoir*? I think we may be seeing each other again very soon."

And once again Mr. Wickersham walked out my door, leaving me with nothing to say.

In reality, it was more than an hour before I said good-bye to Mrs. Cooper, and the clocks, and my grandmother's room, everything I had once been certain I would never leave. Marianna's portrait I carried out the front door with me, wrapped tight in a cloth. Mary climbed into the carriage, and I looked toward the tunnel and the moor hills surrounding us. I saw no sign of Mr. Wickersham's man, the one that young Tom had seen watching from the grasses, but that did not mean he wasn't there or that he was alone. I turned to the driver of the wagon that waited behind us, the last of the boxes, bags, and my steamer trunk lashed to its bed.

"You are certain all is secure?" I asked him. He nodded his assent. "Then we will drive as quickly as we are able. But keep out of the ruts as much as you can. I want nothing broken." He responded with a scant tip of his hat before handing me up the step.

Inside the carriage, Mary was not crying as I'd thought she might. She sat grim-faced in the green velvet interior, bonnet tied tight, her carpetbag of things perched primly on her knees. The pocket watch she wore pinned by a chain to her dress lay open on her palm.

"Will we be making the boat, Miss?" she asked as I settled the portrait into the seat beside me. I heard a chirrup to the horses and felt my body jerk backward. The carriage was rolling.

"It will be close, but I think we shall. Mr. Babcock should be there before us; he sent the other luggage on this morning, and I am in hopes that he can convince the captain to hold if we are delayed." What we would do if we missed that boat was more than I could fathom. "Mary . . ." Her round eyes darted to my face. She knew me well enough to know that her name in that tone meant nothing to our advantage. "Mr. Wickersham knew we were sailing. He knew what house we're going to, down to the names of the neighbors. We could have . . . visitors, I'm afraid. Much sooner than I'd planned."

Mary whistled beneath her breath, her face screwing up in thought for only a second or two before her eyes went round. "Miss! There's men up there, Miss!" The carriage was coming around the circular drive, giving us a view of the cemetery. "At Mr. Tully's grave! What can —"

"They're from the village, Mary. I sent them."

She squinted at me. "But why, Miss?"

"Because Mr. Wickersham will want proof. At some point he will want it, and he will come and try to get it."

Mary squinted even harder, her nose wrinkling before her eyes snapped open wide. "He wouldn't. He wouldn't dare, Miss. He wouldn't dare be digging up Mr. Tully!"

When I did not respond, Mary began a lengthy opinion on the morals, personal appearance, and maternal origins of Mr. Wickersham. I watched the neatly trimmed grasses of the lawn go by, and then the more wild, swaying stems, yellowing with the season, blowing on the hills that ringed the entrance to Stranwyne. We had need of speed, but it was all going too fast. Everything was passing me by, and it was too fast. I looked back, and could just see Aunt Bit, still standing at the front door.

The road dipped, the slopes and grasses disappearing into brief blackness before that, too, melted away into the soft glow of gaslight. We were in the tunnel. The air of the trogwynd shoved and harried us, shrieking, pushing me back toward the house. I counted the gas lamps as the carriage rocked, but I counted them backward, *three hundred and twenty-six, three hundred and twenty-five* . . . to *four, three, two,* and *one.* And then it was black again. The carriage tilted, and the wind sighed. I had left Stranwyne Keep.

CHAPTER SIX

We watered the horses and ourselves at Milton, I checked the security of our luggage in the wagon, and we did not stop again until the beasts were drooping and we were in Devonport. For a long time I had leaned against the threadbare velvet wall, suspended in a hazy mixture of waking and sleep, but I went bolt upright at the sudden stillness of the carriage. A set of iron gates blocked the road before us, rising up from wisps of trailing mist, illuminated by a lantern in the hand of a uniformed guard. Our driver appeared from the dark and I opened the carriage window, silently handing him a sealed paper that had arrived by express from Mr. Babcock the night before. I had no notion what promises Mr. Babcock might have made or what favors he might have called forth to gain the privileges this letter contained, but whatever they were, the paper seemed to work. The guard waved us through the gate. Mary rubbed her eyes and flipped open the pocket watch with a soft click, waiting for the light of a passing streetlamp to hold it up.

"'Tis past time, Miss," she whispered.

I bit my lip and looked out the window, craning my neck to see the wagon rattling over the road stones behind us. We were moving past buildings on both sides of the carriage now, almost military in their sameness and precision, and then the last remnants of haze lifted from my mind, burned away by the significance of the gate, the guard's uniform, and the port we were entering. We were driving through a Royal Navy base. I sat back against the seat cushion, the burning knot in my stomach twisting tight. Mr. Babcock had failed to mention this particular complication, but then again, what difference would it have made if he had? Devonport was the closest harbor, and everything depended on our speed.

I kept my eyes on the dark rows of naval barracks, waiting irrationally for armed marines to come pouring out after us in the fog, but then the barracks were gone and the street became more like a small city, lined with churches and taverns and other public buildings, most sleeping and dark. We were stopped by another set of gates, again produced Mr. Babcock's paper, and at last the carriage was rattling onto the docks. I sat forward, competing with Mary for the view.

Air blew soft from the still-open window, and with it came the smell of fish and the odor of something else, different from what I remembered of the Thames, not pleasant or unpleasant, but powerful. A bell tolled, and I could hear chains clink and the creak of stretching rope, while farther out, bobbing against the dark horizon, were huge, hulking silhouettes, spiderwebs of rope and mast lit by a quarter moon. Waves were out there in the spray of light, glinting beneath the thin, hovering mist, but beyond them was nothing but a vast expanse of water, melting black into the night.

"Lord," said Mary under her breath, sitting back to click open the pocket watch, but I had eyes only for the sea. Lane had always wanted to see the ocean. I wondered what he had thought of it. I half stood, sticking my head out the window.

"Wait . . ." I began.

"That ain't such a good idea, Miss, if you don't mind me saying," said Mary, frowning at the pocket watch.

"No, I mean, there's someone coming."

A shape was running toward us down the dock, short, squat legs pumping an uneven beat, arms flapping against the restraint of a long-tailed coat. It was Mr. Babcock.

"This way, this way!" he called, panting and, after a concurring nod from me, the driver slapped the reins and I pulled my head back through the window. We followed Mr. Babcock's frenzied gait down the dock, the wagon creeping behind us, Mary tapping a finger on the watch case. Mr. Babcock slowed, waving us repeatedly toward a boat slip.

A small vessel rose and fell gently behind him, its sails furled, a British flag ruffling in a slight gust of breeze, smoke billowing from a single stack. I could hear the steam engine thrumming, water slapping the sides of the boat. I leapt out of the carriage, heart hammering as I looked over my shoulder for the wagon. We truly were behind time. Mary scrambled out after me with her carpetbag, Mr. Babcock pecked my cheek and grabbed my arm, his other hand directing a pair of barefooted sailors toward our luggage as we hurried to the gangplank.

It took three trips to get our things unloaded, two straining men alone to carry the steamer trunk belowdecks. They set it with our other boxes in a dim, clammy room that stank of fish and the smoking oil lamp that swung from the ceiling, making their way out again while I fidgeted with impatience. There were no chairs here, only crates and our boxes, and I wondered if it was possible that any of this boat's cargo was legal, and if not, by which officer's underhanded arrangement it had come to be here in the first place.

Mary had the watch out, her freckles scrunched as she attempted to see its hands in the wavering light. As soon as the door was shut, I took several purposeful steps toward my trunk, but Mr. Babcock held up a hand.

"We are expecting a visit from our captain, my dears, such as he is. Tact was indeed part of our arrangement, but I am not at all certain how far his discretion might go."

"But we are behind time!" I said, voice rising. An uncharacteristic panic was taking hold of me. This entire idea had been madness, a crime against my own common sense. What had made any of us think it should be attempted? I felt Mary's hand on my shoulder.

"Mr. Babcock's right, Miss. What's done is done. Only a little time more. Sit on this now, Miss, but mind you don't dirty your dress, 'cause there's no knowing when the next cleaning might be, or how often them French people are even doing such things, if you know what I mean, and we wouldn't want you knocking on the door of your new house looking less than a lady, would we now? How would I be holding my head up in France if you was seen walking down the street with dirt on your dress, Miss?"

I sat, Mary's nonsense lashing me to reality just as firmly as the crate I was sitting on was tied to the floor. Mr. Babcock plopped down onto a similar perch, mopping his forehead with a handkerchief.

"That was a near thing, my dears, a near thing! The captain has a deadline that will brook no delay, a deadline that seems to involve tides and when the most recently bribed agent is scheduled for the customs shed. They are saying the wind will be against us in the Channel, and that we shan't make good time, and so the boat would have to sail by . . ."

As if to emphasize Mr. Babcock's words, I felt a jerk, and another, and then a pull, a smooth sense of movement more akin to rolling on skates than the trains and carriages to which I was accustomed. The floor dipped and rose back up again, the humming in the air increased to a vibration beneath my feet. I crossed my arms against the clench in my stomach.

"Lord!" exclaimed Mary. "Would you look at that?" Her nose was pressed against a small round window, the glass smeared by the smack of an occasional wave. "Who'd ever be thinking that much water could go and be getting so filthy, Miss!"

"In any case," Mr. Babcock continued, taking no notice of Mary, "our captain said he was leaving within the half hour, with or without you, which caused considerable unpleasantness all around." He sighed heavily. "And our packages? I assume they had a safe trip?"

I nodded, hanging on to the crate as the floor tilted, anxiety eating hot at my insides. "Mr. Wickersham came early," I told him, "just at the end of the funeral. I dealt with it, but it put us behind schedule."

Mr. Babcock's eyes went shrewd. "And how much did he guess?"

Before I could answer, knuckles rapped sharply on the door, and two men entered our fetid little room with a pomp more fitting to a grand hotel. The first had a dirty face, fraying cuffs, and a hat that managed to look both official and disreputable all at once; the second had the oily sort of smile that made me think instantly of a snake.

"Coo!" Mary said, whispering in my ear. "There's a pair of ne'er-do-wells if I ever saw them. Better be staying close to me, Miss." I would have comforted Mary, had her tone not been positively dripping with glee.

The official hat made a sweeping arc through the air, showing a balding pate as the captain bowed and began to speak rapidly in French. The reptilian man translated right on top of the words, his accent thick.

"If it pleases the guests," he said, "we leave Devonport and Plymouth, sail the coast, and with God's help will cross the Channel and stand in Le Havre before the noon. The captain asks . . ."

A dull, muffled *thump* came from somewhere off to my right, where my trunk was stowed. I blinked, laced my fingers together, and kept my eyes on the rambling captain.

". . . that you would stay below, please, for the avoiding of questions, and when Le Havre is reached if your baggage would stay below for the same reason, we would all be most happy."

Mr. Babcock inclined his head, and again a soft *thump*, with three more in quick succession, came from my right. I felt Mary tense. The captain was still speaking, gesticulating wildly with his hat, and the translator leaned outside the door and brought two metal bowls back in with him. With a brevity that seemed to have nothing whatsoever to do with the captain's unceasing speech, he said, "The captain says to give you these. For the . . ."

He paused, struggling for the correct word as the captain talked on and on. The soft thumping was continuous now, regular and rhythmic, though between the captain's babbling and the thoughtful scratching of the second man's head, neither seemed to notice. The translator finally gave up the linguistic fight, shrugged one shoulder, and said simply, "First the boat will be up, and then it will be down. Up and then down. Good night."

He gave us a grin that was long and narrow, the bowls went to the floor with a clatter, and the captain bowed himself out, words still flowing as the slippery translator shut the door after them.

The interior of the little room was suddenly quiet. The three of us remained still, the lamp above our heads making the shadows sway. The thumping had stopped. I listened to the scurry of feet and the shouting of men on the deck above, to the silence outside our door, counting eight terrified heartbeats before in unspoken agreement we all three leapt forward and ran to my trunk, the key already in my hand. I turned the lock and threw back the lid, tossing the top layer of dresses out onto the dirty floor.

My uncle lay curled in a nest of cushions, still and with his face pale, wrapped tightly in the blanket from his bed. Only his wild, white hair and unkempt beard disturbed what would have otherwise been the look of a dreaming child. Nothing moved. The hammering in my chest seemed to pause, then beat with a speed that stole my breath.

"Well?" said Mr. Babcock.

I reached a hand into the trunk and found my uncle's neck, feeling the skin with two fingers until I had located what I wanted: a pulse, very slow, but strong. Uncle Tully's chest rose up suddenly in a long, deep breath.

"Sleeping," I said weakly, and felt some of the collective tension release around me. I smoothed Uncle Tully's hair, damp with the stuffiness of my trunk, and carefully adjusted his legs and the cushions, making sure the small air holes drilled into the leather-covered wood were unobscured.

Uncle Tully breathed deeply once more, and then all at once he yelled loudly, kicking out hard against the side of the trunk. The cocoon of his blanket loosened as he flailed, shouting out nonsense. I held his head, eyes darting to the door as Mary knelt quickly beside me, taking one of the little brown bottles Dr. Pruitt had given us out of her carpetbag and holding it to my uncle's lips. He drank without ever opening his eyes, coughing and sputtering as he struggled, but after a long minute, a time when every sound pricked me with fear, the movement in the trunk quieted. Uncle Tully relaxed, his face going slack. I let go of his head and arranged the blankets, tucking him in tightly, as if he were in bed. Blood pounded in my ears.

"All well?" Mr. Babcock whispered, his ugly face creased.

"He should have had that dose nearly an hour ago," I said, "but Dr. Pruitt did say to wait as long as we could, that the less we gave him the better. . . ." I rubbed a finger over my throbbing temple. I felt ill, though whether from guilt or relief I wasn't sure. What would have happened if my uncle had shouted like that while those men were in the room? I doubted our captain's "tactful," tariff-free enterprise actually included sailing screaming men locked in trunks across the English Channel.

"Don't worry, Miss," Mary said. "It doesn't seem to have been doing him any harm."

My head nodded mechanically as I counted Uncle's Tully's breaths, watching them gradually slow. I trusted Dr. Pruitt. He was a good man, and I did not believe for a moment that he would give my uncle away. And he had assured me again and again that though experimental, he had used the contents of his little brown bottles many times with no ill effects. But this long, enforced sleep was so unnatural. I stroked my uncle's hair, trying to ignore the tightening pain in my middle.

Mr. Babcock had dropped himself back onto a crate, once again mopping at his brow. "You put men in the cemetery, I assume?"

I nodded in response, laying the discarded dresses carefully back on top of my uncle before shutting the lid and locking the trunk. Mr. Babcock *tsk*ed softly. I could guess what he was thinking. How many days before Mr. Wickersham or one of his men stood on the edge of my uncle's open grave, looking down into its contents? How many days before a dead man's face became unrecognizable? None of them had ever actually seen my Uncle Tulman, not to my knowledge, but how soon could a decaying man in his forties be mistaken for one in his sixties? Before a head wound given by the stroke of a hammer would not be so readily noticed?

The boat pitched, and my stomach went with it. I barely heard Mary's exclamation of "Lord!" before I vomited hard into the metal bowl she held out for me.

CHAPTER SEVEN

*I*t was an action I repeated many times over the next few hours, catching only snatches of sleep, curled between crates on two moth-eaten blankets we had found in a corner. Mary, to my shame, was not the slightest bit indisposed, and neither was Mr. Babcock. I could not crawl far from my bowl. As the rising sun lit the sea, it was Mary, her nose against the little window, who got our first glimpse of France.

When the boat docked and the engine thrum I'd forgotten I was hearing sputtered and stopped, I pushed against the floor and experimented with being upright. Seagulls were crying, bells clanging, and I could hear scurrying footsteps above us. Mary was instantly at my side, snapping shut the pocket watch.

"Now don't you worry, Miss. We've got to be staying right here until that captain has paid out the money Mr. Babcock was giving him. Then somebody will come and say we can be getting off. Mr. Tully's had another dose, and I've gotten his water down him, too, so there's no trouble there, and there's to be wagons or some such at the docks that will take us to a place called Rouen, though I never heard of such a name as that, and Mr. Babcock, he says there will be something to eat on them as we go. . . ."

"Nothing to eat," I whispered, "please, Mary." Though the uppermost thought trickling through my mind was the amazing power of Mr. Babcock to make impossible things happen. The man should have been prime minister. That would have settled Mr. Wickersham. And possibly the emperor of France.

". . . and there's a train here, too, he says, though he don't want us to be getting on it just yet, 'cause that's too easy." Mary began stuffing my wayward hair back into order. "And when you're on the train, you can rest proper, Miss — though I won't be resting 'cause having never been on a train, I ain't planning to miss a thing — and then we'll be in Paris in a snap, and we'll hire a carriage to be taking us to the new house. But Mr. Babcock, he says not to be looking worried or in a hurry when we get out there. To just be easy, like 'ladies on their way.' That's what he said to me, Miss, 'ladies on their way.' Ain't that kind of him to say such a thing? My mum, she would have said —"

"Where is Mr. Babcock?" I interrupted.

She pointed to the other end of our little room, even dingier now with the bit of sunlight that came through the porthole. Mr. Babcock lay on top of a crate, curled up like a bulldog, sleeping beneath his coat.

When all the proper bribery had been accomplished, and the captain had taken his incomprehensible leave, our items were unloaded and I stepped, squinting, onto the dock. The sun was hot and bright, welcome after the dim dampness of the boat, and a wagon was waiting. Mr. Babcock climbed into the back to sit with the steamer trunk and other luggage while Mary and I were squashed in beside the driver. He was an elderly man with a deeply tanned face, no English, and some sort of stinking tobacco that was as good for my delicate insides as the rutted roads outside the city.

We bounced and bruised against the hard wooden seat until Mr. Babcock leaned forward, tapping the driver on the back. He spoke gruffly in the man's native tongue, causing the driver to grumble, shrug, and avoid the potholes with more diligence. I looked over my shoulder at Mr. Babcock, one eyebrow raised.

"You speak French?"

"Passably, my dear, passably," he replied, settling his round little frame more deeply among the boxes.

"But you didn't tell the captain that. You let that grinning sailor say whatever he wanted."

Mr. Babcock smiled his steely smile, the one that was often dismissed, yet caused the wise to shake in their boots. "Sometimes it is best to keep one's advantages close," he said. "Those are words to live by, my child. This time it saved us five hundred francs."

I turned back in my seat to see Mary, large eyes on Mr. Babcock, drinking in these words like nectar. If Mr. Babcock should have been prime minister, then before this trip was over he was going to have Mary Brown fit for minister of war.

Endless fields in the midst of harvest gave way to a town again, a rail station with an enormous four-faced clock tower and great puffing engines that made Mary's eyes bulge, and then the noise, smoke, and blessed speed of the train. Mr. Babcock rode in the luggage car with the trunk. I was still weak from the Channel crossing, sick to death of movement and nearly comatose with fatigue, but before I'd even properly looked at the passing villages, we were in the bustle of a station — Gare Saint-Lazare, I heard it called, sooty from the trains and a nearby ironworks — then into a rocking carriage and onto the streets of Paris.

The road was narrow and congested. We stopped and started frequently, the inevitable wagon rolling along just behind us with the trunk and our luggage. Mary succumbed to sleep at last, and Mr. Babcock dozed, but I could not close my eyes. Not here. Rickety buildings rose upward on either side of the carriage, built in teetering overhangs that stretched toward one another, as if threatening to touch over our heads, or perhaps collapse on top of us, until we made a turn onto a wide boulevard. The sky opened out and the sun shone, and we rolled on smooth paving, newly planted trees lining the center of the street and both sidewalks. It was brighter here, both with light and color, and I could hear music from a passing café, just as foreign to me as the shouts from the sidewalks. The smells that had been penetrating the walls of the carriage — not quite as putrid as what I remembered of London — eased as well. Hammers banged, and I saw skeletal rows of newly erected timbers, piles of grubby stone and plaster being hauled away by the wagonload. Block after block, this scene was replayed. The old Paris was being replaced with the new, it seemed, entire streets' worth at a time.

But it was the people that were keeping my attention, standing about in front of stores and shops, crossing the boulevards through a maze of horse and omnibus; I realized I'd been involuntarily counting the number of tall, dark heads our carriage passed. The twenty-second of these had long hair, loose and almost shoulder length, and he was coming down the sidewalk at a slow stride, not three feet from my window, face downward, searching for something in a jacket pocket. A red cap was tugged down low on his forehead. I leaned forward, hand to the window glass, and a pale face, stubbled and with a hooked nose, suddenly jerked up and looked directly into my stare, as if I'd called to him. I sat back, air returning audibly to my lungs. It was not Lane Moreau. But it could have been.

I watched every face that passed by our carriage.

"Katharine, child, if you are not too indisposed, we need to discuss the situation with the house."

I started, prying my gaze from the window. I had not realized Mr. Babcock was awake. We were stopped, in any case, in a glut of carriages that appeared to be traveling at cross purposes, temporarily making the road impassable.

"Of course," I replied, scooting back into the space where Mary still slumped, though not so far as to obscure my view of the street. Mr. Babcock sat up against the cushion, adjusting his waistcoat. It was a horrible piece of finery, embroidered with many-colored flowers, but his gesture was one that I recognized. He was sliding into his official role of solicitor. I folded my hands.

"As I have explained before," he began, "the house has been empty and shut up for some time. But you should know that a family by the name of DuPont has been engaged for several years now to do the housekeeping. A rather easy income for them, merely coming in once a month or so to do a minimum of cleaning, and a letter to my offices should repairs be needed, et cetera. They have now been informed of your impending arrival by post, express post, and telegraph, but these communications may not have been received, or may not have been received in time to engage proper help. So I warn you that the house may not be in readiness."

"I daresay a bit of dust will not frighten me, Mr. Babcock," I said, smiling. Stranwyne Keep had been one great pile of dust and damp when I first came there; parts of it were little more still. Mr. Babcock acknowledged this with a chuckle before he continued.

"It is the . . . 'special' rooms that I need to discuss with you, my dear. How your grandmother came to know of them I could not tell you, though there were distant cousins living in Paris around the time of the Terror, I believe. Perhaps they knew of some unfortunate who had used the place to evade the guillotine. In any case, when it became evident that your uncle would not outgrow his oddities and that a removal from England might be someday necessary, Marianna acquired the house and had these secret rooms made ready."

"In what ways did she ready them, Mr. Babcock?"

"I know not. Only that there is a door behind a shelf in a room on the top floor for which I have the key. We can only hope the place is adequate, or is still adequate, after all this time."

My gaze went back to the window. We were moving again.

"All of this was long before Mr. and Mrs. DuPont were employed, of course, and with no permanent residents in the house, it is my hope the rooms are still hidden . . ."

I bit my lip. I had not even thought of this. What if the rooms had been discovered? What would we do with Uncle Tully then?

". . . and why it is absolutely essential that they remain so. This could require some ingenuity on your part, my dear."

I nodded again.

"You will need a housekeeper immediately. I would suggest one that is English speaking, who can procure a cook and as many staff as she deems necessary on your behalf. But none of these should sleep in the house. This is important, Katharine. Your help needs to be of the daytime variety. But this will be unusual, and cause for remark."

I pulled my eyes back to the little man, feeling a tiny frown wrinkle my forehead. "But, Mr. Babcock, who would possibly remark upon it?"

Mr. Babcock tugged on the hideous waistcoat. "Perhaps you are not aware, my dear, how much of our English society reside off and on in Paris? And there are even more at the moment, fleeing the cholera in London. You are a young heiress, coming unaccompanied to the city with no one but one maid and your solicitor. It will be talked of, and you should expect to be visited. You can reasonably plead mourning for a time, but you will be required to take a place in society."

I stared at him. My plans had centered solely on smuggling my uncle out of Stranwyne, keeping him happy and hidden from both the British and the French, and finding one young man in a city of thousands upon thousands. Teacups and pursed lips in a parlor I had not reckoned with. And why should I reckon with them? I opened my mouth, but Mr. Babcock cut short my protest.

"You must appear normal, Katharine. An unconventional or hermit-like existence can only increase the mystique, while also raising the suspicions of the already suspicious, like our friend Mr. Wickersham. For your uncle's sake, you must not draw untoward attention, which, ironically, is exactly what staying strictly at home would bring you. You must be a quiet English girl in mourning, beginning anew in a foreign land, wishing to live a dull, unremarkable life of purity and simplicity. That is the impression you must give."

I looked hard at Mr. Babcock. There was something in his tone, an extra layer of discomfort in this conversation that had fully awakened my faculties. I sat taller in the swaying carriage. "Explain what you mean by 'purity,' Mr. Babcock."

He returned my gaze solemnly, the shrewd eyes hooded, and then a smile quirked the corner of his mouth. "Really, my dear. You shouldn't do that. You were so like your grandmother just then, I was transported thirty years backward and nearly forgot where I was."

I waited, watching the smile on his mismatched features fade to resignation, then determination.

"Child, I have not spoken of this issue to you, as it really had no bearing on your life at Stranwyne Keep, and you were so little disposed to venture out. . . ." He glanced once at Mary, breathing heavily in her sleep against the upholstered wall. "I am speaking, of course, of Lane Moreau."

I looked back out the window.

"Do not be offended, my dear. There are few in England who could understand the circumstance of Stranwyne as I do, or the worth of the young man in question. His importance to the well-being of your uncle can never be undervalued. But the fact remains that Mr. Moreau was a servant in your house, that Alice Tulman owed you a particular grudge for the crime of inheriting the estate, and that she was well aware of the relationship before she went back to London. I believe it has made for . . . interesting conversation in certain circles."

Memory flashed brilliant through my mind, the dim light of Stranwyne's kitchen corridor, my fingers in Lane's hair and his mouth on mine, and the small, tight smile on the face of my aunt. I had never imagined that Aunt Alice would actually reject an opportunity for revenge against me, especially one so temptingly within her grasp. But facing the malicious gossip of proper ladies was a very different prospect in this Parisian carriage than when viewed from the faraway peace of my bedchamber in Stranwyne. "Then you are saying, Mr. Babcock, that my reputation is ruined, and that my sullied state, so to speak, will follow me to Paris."

Mr. Babcock looked unhappy. "Perhaps not right away. You were relatively unknown in London society, but it will soon come out, and to be perfectly honest with you, my dear, I would call your reputation at this point less 'sullied' than 'infamous.' Hence the need for starting from a place of ladylike quiet and normality. But I am not proposing some scheme to rehabilitate your standing in society, Katharine. I am thinking of your uncle. We must avoid drawing any more attention to the house than can possibly be helped. For his sake."

I nodded yet again, trying to digest this newfound vision of myself, my eyes glancing away from a black-bearded gentleman who was much too short. Mr. Babcock cleared his throat.

"And, Katharine, that should also include any odd ramblings far from home or visits to remarkable places."

My head whipped around to face him. He meant I was not to go looking for Lane.

"Ah! Now you are angry! But it must be said. I agreed to this mad plan of coming to Paris because of the unavoidable need for speed, your grandmother's preparations, and because the sheer idiocy of bringing your uncle here contained a certain potential to baffle both sets of our enemies. But you, Katharine, are what stands between Frederick Tulman and what is certain to be harmful to him. You are his only protection. You must look after the living, not go chasing after the dead."

I turned back to the window. "You do not know that he is dead."

When the little lawyer's voice came again it was tired. "Lane was doing dangerous work. Work he chose to go and do, Katharine."

I closed my eyes. Yes, Lane had chosen to go. But not for the reasons that Mr. Wickersham had wanted him to, no matter how much Mr. Wickersham now tried to deny it. He'd wanted to be certain that Ben Aldridge no longer breathed, to make amends for Davy's senseless death, and to avenge Ben's treatment of me. Information about French naval preparations would have been far secondary to Lane Moreau.

"Katharine, my child, Mr. Wickersham may not be what I would call an honorable man, but it is unlikely that he is making a pronouncement without reason. He has no motivation to do so. It is best that we face that fact. No matter how we might wish it to be otherwise."

"He has shown no evidence to me," I snapped. "And he is a liar. If all was as Mr. Wickersham says, then Lane would have written. He is not an idiot. He would have found a way to communicate with me, as he did before. And if he has not written it was because he has been prevented, and that would be long before Mr. Wickersham's ridiculous story about being drowned in the Seine." The carriage bucked once, as if in response to my mood, and I kept my eyes stubbornly on the streets. "Lane could swim, Mr. Babcock. Very well. He has been prevented. Hurt or . . . detained . . . but not . . ."

I let my words trail away. There had been a time in my life when I had thought I was going mad, before I learned of Ben's subtle drugging of my tea. How I had hated not being able to believe what was before my eyes. Now I had to trust in what was not before my eyes, because the alternative was unbearable. I looked back across the seat to where Mr. Babcock remained silent, his misshapen face cast down. I reached out and took his hand.

"I will take care of my uncle, I promise you that. I will keep him as safe and happy as I am able. I will eat biscuits and have uninteresting conversation with ladies I dislike. I will conduct myself like a model of English gentility. Like a novice nun, if necessary. But I will look for him, Mr. Babcock."

Mr. Babcock patted my hand awkwardly. "Really, my dear, I expected no less."

CHAPTER EIGHT

*I*t was not long after this conversation that the carriage turned onto a small, narrow street marked RUE TRUDON and jerked to a halt. Mary's eyes flew open and once again we competed for the view from the window. Before us was a house of stone, four stories high, intricate wrought iron decorating the lower half of the windows. Two red-painted doors marked an entrance at the level of a narrow sidewalk. The houses continued on either side, as if rectangular blocks had been stuck together by a playing child, all in differing sizes and hues, making for a changing, yet unbroken, line of dwellings in both directions to the end of the street.

Then I saw that there was a girl on her knees before the red doors, her scrubbing of the paving stones interrupted by our arrival. She was a blue-eyed, yellow-headed, fair-skinned angel of a thing with dirty hands and a sodden apron. She stared at the carriage for a bare second before leaping to her feet. The water bucket tipped, a sudsy pool slowly surrounding the forgotten scrub brush as one red door slammed shut behind her.

"Hmph," Mary said, eyeing the mess as Mr. Babcock climbed stiffly out of the carriage. He put his cane under his arm, telling our drivers to wait before handing us out. I looked back over my shoulder, at the wagon with the steamer trunk looming large in its back. A few people had slowed to gawk at our entourage, one man in a bright blue vest watching openly as he slouched against the iron post of a streetlamp. I turned away, but I could feel his eyes on my back. We stepped up to the doors, avoiding the puddle, and Mr. Babcock rapped lightly with his cane.

"We've a smidge more than fifteen minutes, Miss," Mary whispered, shutting the pocket watch with a *snick*.

Hinges creaked, pulling my attention from the watch to the red doors, and the woman I saw standing in the widening space made me positively start. She was tall, skinny to the point of emaciation, skin the color of bleached muslin, made even more severe by the ebony of her dress and hair, both of which shared the same puritanical style. She looked like a corpse. An imperious corpse.

"Lord!" Mary breathed.

The woman stared down her nose at us. *"Puis-je vous aider?"* she said slowly.

"Parlez-vous anglais, Madame?" replied Mr. Babcock.

Her nostrils flared imperceptibly. "Yes, I speak English," she said, heavily accented. "What do you want?" Her bone-white hand remained firmly on the doorknob, blocking our entrance.

"I would like to present Miss Katharine Tulman to you, Madame," he said, indicating me with an elegant gesture. "Miss Tulman is the mistress of this house."

She looked me over, a brief and somehow dismissive appraisal, her gaze going right back to Mr. Babcock. That would not do. I gathered up my wrinkled skirts and pushed past her restraining arm, forcing her to release the doorknob. "And this is Mr. Babcock, my London solicitor, and Mary Brown, my maid. I take it you are Mrs. DuPont?"

I found myself in a narrow foyer, all creams and pale blue and tiles and gilt, in something of the style that Stranwyne's ballroom had been, elegant stairs with iron railings winding up from the center. I turned briskly back to the door. "Did you happen to receive our telegram, Mrs. DuPont, or perhaps our letter? Is the house in readiness?"

The woman's arm had resumed its place, causing Mary to duck beneath it, but her dark eyes were now where I wanted them: fixed on me. "The house, it is not ready," she said. "Come back tomorrow."

"Oh, I think that won't be necessary, Mrs. DuPont. We shall just make shift until it is ready, that's all." Mary was trying to catch my eye, tapping a finger on the case of the pocket watch. "There is quite a bit of luggage to be brought in. Do you have a man that could help with the unloading? No?" I turned back to the door. "Mr. Babcock, would you see if someone can be found to help the drivers unload? I will inspect the house and decide where our . . . things should be deposited."

Mr. Babcock nodded his understanding and hurried back toward the street.

"And our other luggage," I said, resuming my conversation with the corpse, "it was sent on before us. Has it . . ."

"A man brought boxes, too many boxes. They are upstairs, Mademoiselle." Her face remained expressionless.

"Very well. Then if you would show me the house now, please, very briefly. I will make a more thorough inspection tomorrow. And you may refer to me as Miss Tulman, if you please, Mrs. DuPont."

The woman gave me a cool little curtsy. "I will show you to your room, *Mademoiselle*," she said, emphasizing the last word. I raised a brow.

"You will show me the house, Mrs. DuPont, and then I shall choose my room. And please call me Miss Tulman. Come, Mary."

I took a few quick steps across the tile floor and opened a large sliding door that disappeared into the wall, like a hand into a pocket. Mary peeked over my shoulder into a dim, dust-sheeted room with draped windows that would overlook the street.

"The ladies' salon, Mademoiselle," said Mrs. DuPont, very deliberate. But I did not remark on her refusal to use my name, as I was already hurrying to an identical door on the other side of the foyer.

"The salon for the men," she announced, coming up behind me. I would have called it a library. The furniture here was also dust-sheeted, the curtains closed. "The room for dining, it is behind this," continued Mrs. DuPont, "and the pantries, and the kitchen. You could wish to sleep somewhere else, Mademoiselle. It is not a comfortable house."

I stopped halfway to the stairs. "And what rooms are behind the other parlor? The ladies' salon?"

"There are no rooms there, Mademoiselle," said Mrs. DuPont.

Mary looked up from her watch and snorted. "Well, that ain't right. Why would a body be building one side of a house a different size than the other? I never heard of such a foolish . . ."

Other than a slight flare of the nostrils, Mrs. DuPont's face did not change. "Those are for the other lady. The other English lady."

If Mrs. DuPont's face was expressionless, her voice was not. She said the word *English* as if it were something filthy. Mary's nose wrinkled and she drew a breath to argue, but I put a hand on her arm. "I believe Mrs. DuPont means that the rooms behind the ladies' salon do not connect to this house, that the space is used by the house next door. Is that correct, Mrs. DuPont?"

The woman gave a tiny nod, and I glanced up at the ornate chandelier above my head, gilded cherubs looking down at me, each of their fat arms holding up a cut-glass globe. If the interior walls had not been respected, then I could better understand how one might hide a set of rooms in a rectangular block of houses. "I will see the upstairs now, Mrs. DuPont. Starting with the top floor going down, please."

I moved quickly up the stairs. The plaster wall decorations became less and less grand as we ascended, each set of steps narrower than the last. On the first landing, we passed the enormous stack of trunks and boxes that Mr. Babcock had sent ahead from Stranwyne; on the second, a halo of blonde hair that bobbed once before flying away to the lower floors, a book tucked beneath her arm. Mary turned to watch the girl who had been scrubbing the sidewalk descend. "Who is she?" I asked Mrs. DuPont.

"She is my child, Mademoiselle, Marguerite."

"I see," I said, though I was mentally gaping. Nothing about Mrs. DuPont's looks, age, or demeanor could have possibly suggested such a daughter. "And please remember that I have asked to be referred to by my name, Mrs. DuPont."

At the top of the third set of stairs, we stood in an unpapered, unpainted hallway beneath a sloping ceiling, one oval window overlooking a jumble of foliage below. There was a railing around the stairwell, a row of three doors to the right, and on our left, only one. I took a quick look at the empty chambers on the right — for servants, most likely — then opened the single door on the left. Behind it was an uninviting room, plain lathe and plaster, the wall opposite covered in unused shelving. One high window, cut into the slope of the ceiling, showed a square of cloudless sky, leaving a corresponding block of sunshine on the scarred wooden floor. But it was the shelves that had drawn my attention.

"This shall be my particular room," I declared. "To be used for matters of business."

For once, Mrs. DuPont seemed neither angry nor dead, just rather bewildered. "But it is only a room for the storing, Mademoiselle!"

"It is quiet and private, and will therefore suit me well. I will have much to attend to over the next few weeks." I heard Mary's fingernail tapping insistently on the pocket watch. "And now that we have that settled, I shall go back downstairs. I am perfectly capable of viewing the other rooms on my own. You and your daughter are free to go home, Mrs. DuPont, but if you would be so good as to come back in the morning, to discuss our further arrangements, that would be most appreciated."

"But —" Mrs. DuPont began.

"Half past ten will do. Please leave whatever keys you may possess on the table in the foyer. Knock, and we will let you in."

I turned and nearly ran back to the staircase, Mary trotting close behind me, leaving Mrs. DuPont to make of this what she might.

Downstairs I found a grimy young man I'd never seen before setting one of our boxes onto an already precarious pile of similar packages, while Mr. Babcock was coming backward through the front door, directing the steps of both of our drivers as they hauled in the steamer trunk.

"Careful!" I said, hurrying over to flatten the wrinkles in the rug. "Set it down gently, please." I motioned Mr. Babcock away from the others and whispered, "I've found where the entrance must be, it is just as described, but I have not yet been inside. Three flights up, I'm afraid."

Mr. Babcock considered. "How long before he wakes?"

"Perhaps five minutes. Ten if we are fortunate."

"He will need another dose?"

"Yes, I think we shall have to. He shouldn't wake until we have gotten all his things into the room. This is going to be difficult either way, so we might as well start with all our advantages. The boxes from the workshop are on the first landing. I've sent Mrs. DuPont and her daughter home until —"

But my thought was interrupted, cut neatly in half by a high voice, falsely cheerful, saying my name from the doorway.

"Katharine Tulman!" the voice said again, and in an instant the years had melted and I was back in my aunt Alice's morning room, pouring miserable tea in a gray worsted dress. The feeling of suffocation was so overpowering I had to clutch Mr. Babcock's arm, making certain I had the capability of breathing, before turning around.

And there she was, smiling beneath a garish feathered hat, complete with overlarge bosom and the inevitable pince-nez perched on her nose. One of the dearest, truest friends my vile aunt Alice ever had.

"Mrs. Hardcastle," I replied.

ary dropped the stack of hatboxes she'd been holding and ran pell-mell across the foyer, past Mrs. Hardcastle, and sat herself abruptly on my steamer trunk. She lifted her chin and then crossed her arms, swinging her dangling feet. Mrs. Hardcastle gave her and the now-ruinous pile of scattered bonnets a thorough going over through the pince-nez spectacles, and then swung them around to examine me.

"Katharine," she said, "this is indeed a pleasure. It has been too long. Too long, my dear. You are looking well."

I smoothed back a chunk of wildly curling hair that had escaped my pins. "Thank you, Mrs. Hardcastle. How pleasant to see you. May I present Mr. Babcock? Mr. Babcock is my solicitor." My eyes darted to the steamer trunk, where Mary was gesticulating wildly and incomprehensibly at me while Mrs. Hardcastle and Mr. Babcock both inclined their heads.

"I believe I have heard your name before, sir," said Mrs. Hardcastle. She turned back to me, grinning hugely. "What a head for business you must have, dear, to bring your lawyer with you all the way to Paris."

"I assist Miss Tulman in all things, Ma'am," said Mr. Babcock, his ugly face the picture of calm. "Shall I have your trunk brought upstairs, Miss Tulman?"

"Yes, thank you, indeed." I leaned my head close and whispered, "Three flights, a single door on the left. Mrs. DuPont has not come down, and the daughter is running about somewhere, too."

He gave a brief nod and then lifted his hat to Mrs. Hardcastle, who was gazing through the pince-nez, watching us whisper. "Your servant, Ma'am," he said, and hurried out the front door. My glance brushed past Mary, and then remained there. Mary's eyes had gone very wide, her chin jerking repeatedly toward the trunk. Mrs. Hardcastle followed my gaze over her shoulder, and Mary's expression became instantly nonchalant. I dug my nails into my palms. I wasn't sure what Mary had heard, but Mrs. Hardcastle had to leave. Now.

"Well, this has been lovely," I said quickly, "but as you can see we have only just arrived. We are all rather tired and shall be going straight to bed."

Mrs. Hardcastle faced me once again, still smiling, brows raised slightly, causing the spectacles to fall, bounce, and then dangle from their chain over her bosom. "The journey from England is wearisome in the extreme," she said. "Enough to make anyone wish their bed at half past noon, I'm sure. This is why, of course, I came to invite you to dinner this evening."

I opened my mouth, to make an excuse of I knew not what, and then I heard what Mary must have: a distinct *thump* from inside my trunk. Mrs. Hardcastle whirled about to see Mary staring at the chandelier like an imbecile, absently swinging her feet, as if her boot heels might be striking the leather-covered wood just behind them. "Would you like to see the ladies' salon?" I blurted.

Mrs. Hardcastle turned about again, her head cocked a little to one side. "Why, certainly, Katharine dear, if you would like to show it to me." I stepped around the fallen bonnets and indicated the still-open doorway on my right. Mrs. Hardcastle entered the room with the pace of a royal, lifting the pince-nez. I slid the pocket door closed behind her as quickly as decency would allow, immediately plunging us into an almost complete darkness after the sunshine of the hall.

"Oh," I said in confusion, "I am so sorry. Let me open a drape." I bumped into a sheeted chair, looking for a window, then fumbled for the tassel to pull the curtain back, only to discover the window to not only be draped, but shuttered as well. I was feeling about for the latch when I heard a familiar *hiss* and *pop*. Light leapt across the room, a globed, gilded sconce now glowing yellow with flame. Mrs. Hardcastle stood below it, her hand on the turning key.

"Won't you sit . . ." I stopped speaking. There was not a chair uncovered.

"Yes," said Mrs. Hardcastle, looking about. "A very nice room, I am sure."

I clasped my hands behind my back. "I apologize for not being able to properly receive you, Mrs. Hardcastle. As I said before, we have only just arrived. I cannot even offer you a cup of tea."

"Old friends should never stand on ceremony," she said, wandering over to examine a watercolor through the pince-nez.

I could recall no time when I had considered Mrs. Hardcastle a friend. "I do thank you for the dinner invitation, but . . ."

"Yes, yes. We shall have just a few guests, three or four courses, nothing too fancy. Eight o'clock is our usual hour. I do so look forward to introducing you, Katharine. Very much, indeed."

I narrowed my eyes. There had been genuine enthusiasm in that last statement, and why would that be? I thought of Mr. Babcock's words in the carriage, and all that Mrs. Hardcastle must have heard at Aunt Alice's tea table. My lips pressed together. Mr. Babcock, as usual, had been perfectly correct. My reputation had found me. His only mistake was that the process had not taken weeks; it had taken exactly five minutes. But I had no intention of being Mrs. Hardcastle's item of curiosity for the night. I straightened my back.

"Please accept my apologies, Mrs. Hardcastle," I said, without the slightest hint of regret, "but I must decline your invitation."

Mrs. Hardcastle opened her mouth in surprise, her head cocking once more to the side. With the feathers on her hat, it made her look like a very plump chicken.

"Perhaps you are not yet aware that I am in mourning, Mrs. Hardcastle. That — and the newness of my arrival — make it impossible for me to accept invitations at this time."

"Mourning?" she repeated, the pince-nez now taking in the significance of my clothing colors.

"Yes. My uncle, Mr. Frederick Tulman, he is . . . gone." And, as luck would have it, this is exactly what I hoped was true. I could hear low voices and movement in the foyer.

". . . had no idea, my child. Is Alice Tulman aware of the circumstance?"

"I am not certain, actually. My aunt and I . . . are not on speaking terms."

"No, I daresay you are not." Mrs. Hardcastle's breath whooshed through her nose. "Well, that is all the more reason to come, dearest child. No one stays inside the house in Paris. You must let our little party help you forget your troubles." She smiled at me. "We dine at eight."

The presumption jumped right beneath my skin, where it prickled. "The idea is out of the question, Mrs. Hardcastle. Another carriage ride today would be most unpleasant. Come to tea tomorrow, if you like, but for now I will stay in my own house and tend to my own affairs." I took a breath. "And I would be most gratified if you would address me as 'Miss Tulman.'"

Mrs. Hardcastle's face wore an expression I remembered from Aunt Alice's morning room. A smile, but one that hid something ugly, like the prettily embroidered cloth that covers a casket.

"Why, of course, Miss Tulman. I hope I did not offend. I was merely eager to hear more of you and your intended stay in Paris."

I inclined my head, thinking I would not mind knowing the same of her. I had been too busy dealing with the fact of her presence to even question why it should be here.

"But please," she continued, "do not think me so rude as to wish you to traipse about the city on the very day of your arrival. I assume you know the Reynolds family? They are set up just next door. Mrs. Reynolds is my husband's second cousin and I am with her for a several months' stay. I had the good fortune to witness your arrival from the drawing-room window."

I stared back at her, trying to process this information, the knot that had become a permanent feature of my insides pulling agonizingly tight.

"Good day to you, Miss Tulman. I do hope we will be favored with your company soon."

I returned her curtsy, and then, waking slightly from my shock, ran to the pocket door, getting there just in time to block her exit. I cracked the door, saw that the foyer was devoid of trunks, and only then allowed her out. She chose not to comment on my bizarre behavior, but swept from the salon in an elegant rustle, stepping over the fallen bonnets. The front door closed, and less than a half minute later, still standing in the salon, I also heard the faint close of another door, outside and down the sidewalk, just beyond the shuttered window I had tried to open.

I closed my eyes. No one but I, Katharine Tulman, could run across land and sea to hide a supposed-dead uncle from not one but two governments, only to move next door to one of the most blatant gossips on the continent. I really wasn't sure why I was surprised. And then I remembered my uncle. I picked up my skirts, hurried through the empty foyer, and ran up the stairs.

On the second landing, I passed our two drivers, going down with a heavy tread, one of them rubbing his arms. They tipped their caps, otherwise ignoring me. I assumed this meant they had been paid and continued my dash for five more steps before I met Mrs. DuPont coming down with a smooth, almost unnatural glide. I stopped.

"Have you not gone home yet, Mrs. DuPont?"

"The house, it is full of English," she hissed.

I squeezed past her on the stairs, in too much of a hurry to consider the sense of this comment, the question of what she might have been doing on the upper floors all that time more prominent in my mind. Light footsteps clacked down the steps and the girl Marguerite blew past me in a streak, another book, larger this time, tucked beneath her arm. She maneuvered around her mother and across the landing, her clamor sinking lower into the house.

I had twisted my head to watch her go, sure I'd already seen her descend once before, and when I turned back again I was facing yet another figure, this time a man I'd never seen. He was short and gray-headed, lines and wrinkles on his cheeks, though the muscles in his chest were still hard, wiry with strength. I could see all this very clearly, as he was wearing no shirt. I stopped dead on the stairs.

"Who are you?" I demanded.

Mrs. DuPont said something in French that I thought might be angry, but the man did not answer either one of us, just kept the pace of his downward tread.

"Excuse me," I said, "but why are you not . . . clothed?"

"Ah," he sighed as if the world were a sad place indeed, "*Napoléon est mort.*" He shook his head. "*Napoléon est mort.*"

I found myself pressing against the wall to let him pass. He joined Mrs. DuPont, who was sputtering rapidly in French, and then I remembered my business and ran to the fourth floor, where I found Mr. Babcock. He immediately took my arm, steering me toward the little storeroom.

"Are they gone?" he asked.

"Mrs. Hardcastle is," I replied, panting from the climb, "but I met a man on the stairs without . . . well . . . when I inquired about his clothing, I believe he told me that Napoléon was dead."

"Ah, yes," said Mr. Babcock. "That would be Mr. DuPont. He informed me of Napoléon's demise as well. The first Napoléon, I assume, not the current one." He pulled a ribbon from beneath his shirt, a key hanging on its end. "A helpful man, quite correct in his assertions, though his information appears to be limited."

I shrugged a shoulder in agreement with this as Mr. Babcock shut the storeroom door and locked it behind us. The trunk was now in the middle of the floor, its contents quiet, and Mary was running her hands over a section of shelves on the far wall.

"You gave him a dose?" I asked Mary, joining her to examine the shelves.

"Had to, Miss. Is the old bat gone?"

"Yes." I chose a section of the dirty wood and felt carefully, looking for a latch or anything that might be out of place. Mr. Babcock got with difficulty onto his hands and knees at the corner of the room, where the shelf wall began, and peered upward. "We have to get Uncle Tully out of that trunk soon," I said. The worry was returning, eating at my stomach like an ulcer. "Dr. Pruitt said much longer than this would be unwise, and he's already been several hours without water."

"I know it, Miss. And I'm not looking forward to the cleaning of that trunk, if you don't mind me saying. It weren't so nice when I opened the lid, though I suppose he can't be helping it, and them old dresses is only fit for the fire. . . ."

"Here!" cried Mr. Babcock.

We both turned. He was reaching below a shelf, a shade lower than the height of my waist. A latch clicked, and the shelf swung out and into the storeroom, creaking a bit on its hinges. It was just a door, I saw, half my height, a thin layer of plaster spread over its wood and with shelves built across it, matching the other sections in the room. The whole thing was so simple it made me nervous, though I supposed there would be no reason to think that what lay beyond the wall of shelves did not belong to the next house. Still, I was glad I'd told Mrs. DuPont this room would be mine. The storeroom door would have to stay locked.

Mr. Babcock stuck his head through the resulting doorway, and then crawled through. Mary went next and I bent down and followed, surprised when I needed to step upward once; the wall between the rooms was much thicker than I would have anticipated. I got through the door and straightened, straining to fill my eyes with everything at once.

It was a very comfortable room, not large, but airy in its sense of space. The ceiling was high, with the same slope as the storeroom's, but instead of one small window and the resulting corner shadows, here the roof was cut by a row of five of them, tilted to the sky, sending a bright swath of light through the air to the carpeted floor. A long roll of pink cloth was set along the top of the windows, a system of crank, pulleys, and thin rope ready to let the cloth down or roll it back up again, to block the sun as wanted.

I left Mary and Mr. Babcock to explore and went to the back wall, past a little stove tapped into a chimney of bricks, and through another door. Behind it was a tiny bedroom, windowless, with a cot and a door on either end. The first door was locked, bolted, and painted shut, but the second opened easily. I shook my head, surprised, and yet not surprised. It was a bathing room. The convenience was not as modern as the one my grandmother had put beside her bedchamber in Stranwyne, but there were pipes connected, a copper tub, and a faucet hanging over a large shallow bowl. I turned a tap, and watched the water run.

"Look, Miss!" I heard Mary calling. I came out of the little bedchamber to see her standing beside a workbench — though I'd hardly recognized it as such, it being so clean — searching noisily through a box of tools. There was a box of metal parts, I saw, and a few dingy tin toys. Other trunks and boxes lined the walls, which instead of being painted or papered were covered in a pale pink cloth.

"There's most everything Mr. Tully would be needing in here," Mary was saying excitedly, "though I'm not seeing his hot pen, Miss, what he uses for making them bits of metal stick together. Did we bring this with us? I'm thinking we did but everything was done in such a tearing hurry, I can't be sure. . . ."

"Mr. Babcock," I said, "is all well?" He was standing perfectly still in the middle of the room, hands clasped behind his back, staring up at nothing, his belly when left in that position looking amazingly close to the shape of his head. He smiled.

"Oh, yes, my dear. It's just your grandmother . . . she did a rather good job of it, didn't she?"

I knew what he meant. I'd felt it, too, the same presence as in my bedchamber at Stranwyne, one that I suspected my uncle also sensed in places like his clock room. My grandmother's stamp was indelible, and the thought made me long for home. But I only replied, "And she's managed to get water and pipes up here, too, though I can't imagine how."

Mr. Babcock smiled again, and then we both jumped violently at a sudden crash, as if every pane of glass above us had burst into a thousand shards. I spun on my heel to see Mary, wide-eyed at the workbench, holding the ripped lace of her sleeve, the full box of tools now a scattered mess on the floor. "I'm sorry, Miss, I —"

"Shhh!" said Mr. Babcock, holding up a hand.

We waited in silence, listening to three sets of breath. I hadn't had time to think of it yet, but I realized that what had to be below us was the house next door. The house, it came to me suddenly, where Mrs. Hardcastle was living. I held my breath and heard nothing, not even the noises from the street, and then I understood the raised, carpeted floor, and the thick, cloth-covered walls. The sound in this room had been deliberately deadened. But how much so? If my uncle woke frightened, unable to find the familiar, could this room possibly conceal one of his tantrums from whomever might be directly below?

When the silence continued, Mr. Babcock slowly lowered his hand, closing his eyes for a moment in relief. But I could not be certain that relief had a foundation. How quickly would rumors of strange noises in the house next door get from Mrs. Reynolds to Mr. Wickersham? Or even to the French? We could not allow my uncle to stay here without knowing. I would not. I ran a hand along the side of my head, smoothing the curls that were springing their way out in the warm attic air. I felt infinitely weary.

"What time is it, Mary?"

She snatched up the pocket watch hanging on its chain, and then paused, nose wrinkled. "But I said I've already been giving Mr. Tully his —"

"What time?"

"Not quite a quarter past one, Miss. Why?"

"Because I think we must hurry. We need to unload Uncle Tully's things, have this room ready as quickly as possible, and get him out of his trunk before I have to go."

"Go? But where do you have to be going, Miss?"

"Dinner," I said. "With Mrs. Hardcastle."

If I had exchanged the words *dinner* and *firing squad*, I think my expression might have been the same.

CHAPTER TEN

By a quarter past eight I was ready, or as ready as I was going to be. The three of us had worked feverishly, dragging the cases and trunks up the stairs and into the storeroom, handing through the hidden door my uncle's floor pillows, his teacups, a smattering of clocks, and the tools, pieces, parts, and half-finished automatons from the workshop at Stranwyne, all his comfortable familiarities I'd told Mr. Wickersham had been melted. I pronounced the mattress on the cot in the bedroom unusable, so Mr. Babcock ransacked the house to find another while Mary warmed water, scrubbed, swept away mice droppings, and brought out the linens.

Then carefully, and with a struggle, we brought my sleeping uncle out of the trunk and got him through the little door. We laid Uncle Tully out on the floor and cleaned him — no time for modesty — dressing him in his usual nightshirt before putting him on the bed with a new mattress and fresh coverings. He was thrashing some now, groaning and speaking the nonsense of dreams, not asleep but never truly awake either. Dr. Pruitt had told us to expect this, a certain time of grogginess and weakness after the prolonged anesthetic, and that my uncle would become himself again given time. But it hurt me to see it. Uncle Tully drank half a glass of water, eyes closed, before I laid him back on his pillow.

"Are you sure you'll be all right?" I'd asked Mary in a whisper, helping her tighten the blankets around his kicking legs. Lane had discovered this, cocooning Uncle Tully in a blanket when he was upset, a trick that had always seemed to give my uncle security. It was doing nothing for him now, and the guilt of leaving him was nearly intolerable. But for his own safety this task had to be done, the quicker the better. And short of burglary, I could not see how it was a task that could be performed by anyone but myself.

"We'll be just fine, Miss," Mary said softly. "I'll be taking care of Mr. Tully; he's used to finding me with him. It's Mr. Babcock that'll have to be staying away, but I've sent him off to be getting us a bit of bread and honey for toast, as I've already got Mr. Tully's tea. I'll be keeping Mr. Tully wrapped up tight, but if he's waking up proper while you're gone, then I'm thinking I should be giving him a time for your coming, Miss, so he can look at my watch. And I'll explain how we've all been doing just as Miss Marianna said, and let him wind up the clocks."

I considered. "No, I think perhaps have the clocks wound already, if you can possibly manage it, Mary. Seeing them stopped will make him upset. Though I daresay he's going to throw a tantrum once he understands his surroundings, no matter what we do."

"But, Miss, if Mr. Tully does shout his head off, and if you can be hearing it from next door, and the others can be hearing him, too, what are you going to do, then, Miss?"

83

What we would do, I thought, was pack our things again and take my uncle out of this place. I had not the first notion of where we could go. The knot inside me twinged with familiar pain as I glanced guiltily at Mary; there was nothing about my life lately that did not involve guilt. "I had thought to tell them that my maid was . . . prone to nightmares. Do you mind?"

"Lord, what would I care, Miss?" she replied, tucking in the last corner of blanket. "'Tis no skin off my nose, as they say."

I wondered what I had ever done in life to be blessed with the likes of Mary Brown. "Then let's try to keep him calm," I said, "but if he shouts, he shouts. And be sure and move about normally. I need to understand what can be heard from the other house. But you're perfectly right about giving him a time. Let's say eleven . . . no, we'd do better to say half past. Mrs. Hardcastle mentioned four courses, and I'll need time to look about the house." Only heaven knew how I was going to manage that.

Mary shook her head, a dark smudge beneath each eye. "Well, don't be a minute after, that's what I'm saying, Miss. There'll be the devil to pay if you are. Is there anything fit after being stuffed in your trunk — your dresses, I'm meaning, Miss, not your uncle, and I'm meaning your real trunk, of course, the other one — and are you needing any help with your hair?"

I'd told her that I could find something to put on and do my own hair. And I did, my appearance scarcely being a priority. But the deep brown silk rustling at my toes suited me well, and under artificial light should be dark enough to be taken for proper mourning. It was a far cry from a gray worsted dress, I reminded myself. I touched the small, healing cut on my neck, pulled some wisping curls around my face, hoping to lessen the effects of fatigue I could plainly see there, turned from the gilded mirror of the foyer, and shut the red doors quietly behind me.

It was nearing full dark and the streetlamps were lit. I pulled a patterned shawl tighter around my shoulders, more against the strangeness than the slight chill. Rue Trudon was mostly residential, it seemed, with only a boy, whistling, moving leisurely to what was likely his last destination of the day. I could smell cooking that was not like London, could hear the *clop* of horse hooves from the cross street, oddly muffled on the smooth, black pavement and, from an open window, a conversation I could not understand. Seven days and eight nights had passed since the Frenchman had died in my uncle's workshop, and since then I had buried a stranger in my own family plot, told more lies than I could count, bribed a sea captain and a bevy of French officials, committed what I suspected might be treason against the British government, and left behind the only place in the world I had ever known as home. It seemed blatantly unfair that dinner with the likes of Mrs. Hardcastle had to follow. I sighed, walked thirty-two steps to Mrs. Reynolds's door, and knocked.

A servant answered, very formally attired in a black frock coat with silver buttons. He stared at me without the slightest hint of welcome, brows raised in inquiry.

"Miss Katharine Tulman," I said to him, "acquaintance of Mrs. Richard Hardcastle. I believe I . . . am expected to dinner." I only just kept the question mark from my sentence. I'd sent Mary flying next door with a note accepting Mrs. Hardcastle's invitation several hours earlier. Surely it had been received? The door opened a bit wider.

"Come in, Miss," he said, "and I will summon my mistress."

Vaguely uneasy, I stepped inside a foyer the same size and proportions as mine, only much more sumptuously furnished. It was all knickknacks and portraits, fringed velvet hangings and thickly woven rugs. Stuffed birds, eyes sparkling in the gaslight, peered down at me from glass-domed perches on the walls, and I felt instantly sorry for whichever maid had the misfortune of dusting. The black-frocked man disappeared through a green velvet curtain to my left, its edges leeching the light and the sound of voices, many of them, male and female, while I ran my gaze over the gently curving stairs.

Just as in my grandmother's house, the stairwell rose upward through the center of the foyer, while to my right there was a closed door. A room, I surmised, that must share a wall with my ladies' salon. It would be important, then, to see whether the top floor had any rooms to the right of the stairwell. I suspected that it did not, that my uncle Tully was currently occupying that space. The longer I looked, the more each step seemed to lure my feet, enticing them to climb, to run all the way to the top, find what I needed, and then dash back down and out the front door again before anyone was the wiser. This fancy was cured by the unmistakable tremolo of Mrs. Hardcastle as she flung aside the hanging velvet.

"Oh!" she said, the pince-nez in the act of falling from her nose. It swung crazily on its chain, bouncing against a dress of salmon-striped taffeta with gigantic, poofing sleeves. "Katharine, my . . . Forgive me. Miss Tulman, what a lovely surprise! I am so happy you decided to accept my little invitation!"

I cringed inwardly at her use of the word *surprise*. "Did you not receive my note, Mrs. Hardcastle? Truly I would not have . . ." I took a breath. "I would never have meant to . . ."

"Your note? Oh, of course, my dear. Your note! Think nothing of it. I merely forgot to notify Hawkins is all. Silly mistake." She turned back to the servant in the frock coat, who I assumed must be Hawkins, and said something in his ear. He took my shawl, bowed, and then left the room in a dignified hurry, to have an extra place set at the table, more than likely.

Mrs. Hardcastle took my arm. "Now do come and meet everyone. I simply can't wait to introduce you." She pulled me firmly through the curtain, and when it fell shut behind us I froze for just a moment, like an animal trapped, eyes as wide as those of the company staring back at me.

I was in a room full of skirts, huge, billowing, in shining pinks and yellows and pale greens, with lace and flowers and trimming of every sort from head to hem. Necklaces, bracelets, and earrings winked, and there were also pure-white cravats and neatly trimmed whiskers, coal-black jackets against waistcoats of satin, gloves and handkerchiefs, and beribboned shoes. This was not the sort of clothing I would have worn to a dinner. This is what I would have worn to a ball. Or an audience with the queen. I smoothed my brown silk. I might as well have been back in the gray worsted. Mrs. Hardcastle beamed.

"Gentlemen and ladies, may I present Miss Katharine Tulman to you, lately of Devonshire, previously of London." I barely managed the bending of my knees. "Miss Tulman has only just arrived today in Paris."

I saw a young lady with flowers in her blonde curls speaking surreptitiously to her companion behind a gloved hand. An older woman, perhaps in her sixties, stepped forward with an enormous pile of gray hair and a beaded bodice of magenta. "I am Mrs. Reynolds, Miss Tulman. Welcome to Paris." But her expression did not say welcome, rather it seemed to ask Mrs. Hardcastle what she could mean by bringing me here.

Mrs. Hardcastle said quickly, "Miss Tulman is in mourning, Caroline, as you can see. She has recently inherited a large fortune and estate, and is now mistress of the house next door."

Now both the young lady with the curls and her companion had their mouths behind their gloves, eyes demurely pointed to the floor. Mrs. Reynolds's features softened just slightly.

"I will look forward to making your better acquaintance, Miss Tulman."

"Thank you, Ma'am," I whispered.

What followed next was a blur of exactly seventeen more faces, most of them English with three or four French, and other than the occasional title of *Sir* or *Lady*, very few to which I could later attach a name. I did note that the whispering young ladies were part of Mrs. Reynolds's household, her nieces, both of whom were named Miss Mortimer. The eighteenth face presented to me belonged to a young man, French, dark hair slicked, and with a pencil-thin mustache. Instead of a bow or even shaking my hand, he leaned forward and, before I knew what he was about, had kissed both my cheeks. My face blazed first with shock, and then anger. Mrs. Hardcastle laughed heartily.

"For shame, Mr. Marchand! Miss Tulman has only just arrived and is not yet accustomed to your French ways."

"Forgive me, Miss Tulman," he said, his accent light, brown eyes sparkling with amusement. "I hope I did not offend."

I murmured something unintelligible, and the sparkle in his eyes became a gleam.

Dinner was something of a nightmare, as the table was obviously made to accommodate twenty, and my presence made twenty-one. I was crammed at one end, where I sat around the corner from a bearded gentlemen — one of those whose name began with a *Sir* — and directly beside a matronly woman who was the wife of someone I could not identify. Both were more interested in the food than my person, so I was left to eat in silence. The room was stuffy and hot beneath the gas chandelier and all my petticoats, the steaming dishes and flaming candles on the sideboard adding to the lack of air. I pushed at the food on my plate, feeling curls fly loose from my hair knot under the influence of the heat.

During the second course, I caught a lady in gold satin looking at me. Her gaze went instantly to her lap, where she fussed with her napkin, ceasing her low conversation with one of the nieces of Mrs. Reynolds. But I had caught the last word she spoke, watched it form, ugly on her lips. The word was *lunatic*. And as the dinner progressed, I noticed a similar undercurrent, a whispered conversation running beneath the acknowledged one, smooth ripples of gossip, neighbor to neighbor, flowing like a tide toward me.

I knew what they were discussing: the young heiress who had so scandalously and unrepentantly carried on with a servant in her uncle's household, who had chosen to live with a lunatic rather than put him properly away in an asylum. My temper warmed like the hot air. I tried to put my thoughts on Uncle Tully, to think about rooms and walls, to lay the plan of Mrs. Reynolds's house clear in my mind. Then I tried to take my mind away from my uncle, confused, ill, uprooted, and without me; the thought left me nearly unable to swallow. Fourth course, and I realized the table's open conversation had turned to the war.

". . . preposterous," a man was saying. "Whipped like puppies when we had the Russians outmanned and outgunned. The shame of the Royal Navy. Admiral Price shot himself and no wonder. Fought like schoolgirls, they did."

I raised a brow, thinking this man must have had a very limited experience with schoolgirls to make such a statement, but I also pricked up my ears. Mr. Wickersham had mentioned this defeat of the navy in my morning room.

"But do you not think, Monsieur Fortescue," said Mr. Marchand, the impertinent young Frenchman, "that the shame of your navy is the age of its boats, and not its captains? If your English ships had fought with the power of steam instead of waiting for the winds, if your Royal Navy could have had the use of ironclad batteries to bombard the shore, like the French, do you not think the British would have defeated these inferior Russians?"

Mr. Fortescue spluttered indignantly. "Floating batteries of iron, you say? And you think Russian cannon shot will bounce right off them, do you?"

The young Frenchman grinned, stretching his tiny mustache. "Like so many rubber balls. And neither shall they catch fire, as your English ones do."

Mr. Fortescue turned red in the face, evidently interpreting this remark as some sort of slight to his nation. "Gentlemen, do enjoy your pudding," Mrs. Reynolds suggested, which did nothing to lessen the man's color.

"I think, Monsieur," Mr. Marchand continued, leaning back in his chair, "that the country that builds these ships of steam and of iron from which the shot will bounce, I think this nation will need a new name for its monarch. Which do you think it shall be, Monsieur? 'Queen of the oceans'? Or shall it be 'emperor of the seas'?"

The man threw down his napkin, blowing out his breath in outrage, but before he could speak, Mr. Marchand half raised his glass, his light French almost a purr. "To allies, sir," he said, "and the ingenuity of both our countries." And just before he drank, he looked straight at me and winked.

Every head at the table turned, instantly distracted from the political squabble. I looked away from the staring eyes, from Mrs. Reynolds's rising brows, frowning at my place settings. How dare he treat me in such a familiar way? Did he think my character so tainted that I would tolerate such behavior, and in front of all these people? And who were these people to judge me, in any case, and who was I to care for their judgment? I sat up straighter in my chair, and turned to the bearded gentleman next to me.

"And what think you, sir?" I said loudly. "Will England and France continue to be allies, or will the Emperor Napoléon use these new iron ships to start a war in Europe and spill the blood of thousands of Englishmen, as his late uncle did?"

One rattle of a spoon disturbed the charged silence that now reigned in Mrs. Reynolds's dining room. Not only had I spoken out, I had spoken on a subject that was not in a lady's province, spoken of it rudely, and in such a way that one half of the guests was like to be set against the other. Good. I took a slow bite of my pudding, enjoying a moment of satisfaction as I waited politely for the poor man's reply, his expression now that of a gasping fish. Mrs. Reynolds folded her napkin deliberately, set it beside her plate, and stood, her austere face thunderous.

"Ladies, we shall leave the men to their port. Coffee is served in the drawing room." The only thing lacking from her statement was the command of "*Now!*"

I dabbed the corner of my mouth, all my pleasure transforming into shame. So much for the demure young woman I'd described to Mr. Babcock, the one who had promised not to draw undue attention. I would be the talk of several drawing rooms tomorrow; I might as well have put an advertisement in the papers. I filed out with the other ladies, crushed among the bell-shaped dresses, careful to give the impression that I had not noticed the grinning young Frenchman once again half raise his glass to me. Never had I seen Mrs. Hardcastle look so amused.

CHAPTER ELEVEN

I was the last through the velvet curtain and into the foyer. The ladies were disappearing through the door I'd noticed before, the room I thought shared a wall with my salon, and I saw a little maid in a starched white apron pressed flat against a cabinet, eyes on the floor as the tittering conversations passed. The clock in the foyer said three minutes past eleven, and my heart squeezed. I would have to hurry. When the last skirt had been squashed through the doorway, I approached the maid.

"Excuse me, but can you tell me if there is a . . . retiring room, for ladies?"

The little thing looked at me quizzically, and I was afraid that perhaps she only spoke French, but then her face unclouded and she said in a bright, brass British accent, "Oh, you'll be wanting the WC, Miss? Is that it? The water closet?"

I nodded, glancing at the open door to the drawing room. I hoped none of the ladies inside were hearing this conversation. Then I changed my mind and hoped they were.

"Well, you just go straight up the stair thataway, Miss, and be looking for the little door on your left."

"Thank you, indeed," I said, well pleased. She scurried off, and with one quick look back, I picked up my skirt and went noiselessly up the stairs, though I did not stop at the first landing. I took the next flight up, and then the next, pausing only to catch my breath. There was a small oval window straight ahead, looking into a bit of garden, the same as on our fourth floor, and surprisingly there were also two doors to the right of the stairwell, where I had thought there should be none. I tiptoed to the first door on the right, found it unlocked, and peeked inside.

The room was being used for storage, dim, dusty, and windowless, but in the light from the doorway I could see that it was shallow, not nearly as long as I might have expected. Leaving the door open, I tiptoed around piled boxes to press my ear against the only clear patch of peeling plaster I could find along the far wall, the rest being covered with cast-off furniture and stacked trunks. I could hear nothing, no voices, no movement. But I also could not be sure that Uncle Tully's rooms were actually on the other side of this wall. I shut the door to the room as gently as possible, brushed off my skirt, and opened the next.

A plain bedroom, and just as shallow as the storeroom, though it had the sloped ceiling and one of the high windows like Uncle Tully's new workshop, the moon shining down onto the floor matting. I stole quietly across the room, passing shapes in the dim that it took me several moments to realize were easels, cloths thrown over their canvases. I tried to imagine Mrs. Reynolds in a paint-spattered smock with a brush in her hand, ignored the urge to peek beneath one of the cloths, and again pressed my ear to the far wall.

Silence. Encouraged, I closed the door, hitched up my skirt and padded down to the next landing, pausing just a moment to listen for nonexistent noise. The dinner party seemed to have left the upper floors completely deserted. Directly below the rooms I had just visited, there were again two doors beside the stairwell. I chose the one closest to the front of the house, twisted its knob, and slipped inside.

The gas was on, and I saw a large bedchamber, more than double the length of the rooms above. I smiled. Then Uncle Tully must have been on the other side of the walls I had pressed my ear to, and there-fore, had to also be just over the farther half of this room. I stood underneath the far section of ceiling, white plaster roses and ivy vines twisting out from the chandelier in its center, listening for noise or a *thump* or the sound of a footstep. I hoped Mary had not unintentionally nodded off. If she was asleep and so was my uncle, then this little exercise would have to somehow be repeated, and after my behavior at dinner, I was not expecting any renewed invita-tions. I saw the same proliferation of doilies and figurines and pictures as downstairs, as well as three separate beds, a pair of curling tongs near the fire, the same circumference as the blonde cylinders bounc-ing on the head of Mrs. Reynolds's whispering niece. The wide, feathery hat Mrs. Hardcastle had been wearing that afternoon was perched grandly on a hat stand. *Both nieces must be sharing with Mrs. Hardcastle,* I thought. I wondered if any would come out of the expe-rience unscathed.

Two more minutes without hearing the first squeak of a floorboard above me, and I decided to be satisfied. I smiled to myself and had taken two steps toward the bedchamber door before it swung open to reveal Mrs. Reynolds. She stood framed in the doorway, as if she were posing for a portrait, beaded bodice winking in the gaslight, her wrinkled face stony.

We exchanged a long look. I put what I hoped was an expression of apology onto my features and said, "I am so very sorry, Mrs. Reynolds, but I'm afraid I was in search of the WC . . . forgive me, the . . . water closet."

I watched her brows go up, much as they had at dinner, and being rather large and prominent eyebrows, the effect was considerable. "The facilities for your convenience are on the next floor down, Miss Tulman."

"I am sorry," I repeated. "I must have misunderstood your maid. And actually, I hope you will not think me rude," — *too late for that, I thought wryly* — "but I will use this opportunity to take my leave of you."

I watched the woman's eyebrows merge with her swooping piles of hair.

"I am quite exhausted from my trip and feeling rather ill." That part had not even been a lie. "Thank you for an excellent and enjoyable dinner, Mrs. Reynolds."

"Really, Miss . . ."

I gave her a small curtsy. "Please do give my regards to Mrs. Hardcastle and the rest of the party." And I walked right past her, moving as fast down the stairs as my pride would allow. I reached the bottom close to a run, hurried across the foyer, and let myself out the front door. The clock had read twenty-two minutes past eleven.

The streetlamps were out, but the dull yellow light from heavily curtained windows and the moon were sufficient to see the sidewalk. I moved quietly past the glow of Mrs. Reynolds's drawing room, where the ladies had gathered, and turned the knob of the red door. It did not move. I tried the other, then tried it once more, then rattled the door in its jamb. The doors were locked, and I'd never even thought of bringing a key.

I knocked again. Mary would be on the upper floors, I mused, taking care of Uncle Tully, and if Mr. Babcock was not trying to assist, he was very likely near, to be of help, or perhaps even deservedly asleep. The worry I'd been suppressing all through the ghastly dinner hit me now with full force. I had six, perhaps seven minutes before I was late, and nothing upset my uncle more than not keeping to his clock, if he was not already in a full-blown tantrum. I knocked harder, then ran my fingers all around the doors and the house stones. No bell.

My jaw set. I turned away from the doors and began to walk briskly down the deserted street, my footsteps echoing on the sidewalk, craning my neck through the dark to see where our block of buildings came to an end. There would be a way around to the back, to that bit of garden I'd seen through the upper window, and surely a door.

One, two . . .

I counted the silent doorways, so I could do the same to the rear entrances when I circled around, and identify my own door. The cool night air tickled the bare nape of my neck. I'd forgotten my shawl, but

I did not even consider going back. Mrs. Reynolds could keep it. My arms crept up, crossing over my chest.

As I passed the fourth door something caught my eye, a movement, slight, and on the other side of the street. I slowed, staring into the blank shadows opposite. The stillness was unbroken, wedges of deep black night cloaking my vision. I walked faster, feet keeping pace with my heartbeat. Never had I been on a city street at night and alone. After the fifth house, I saw it again, a moving silhouette against the murky light of a curtained window, across the street and just a little behind me. I could also now see the cross street at the end of my block of buildings. I turned left around the corner, glancing once over my shoulder, and caught the dark figure of a man slipping quickly across the pavement.

As soon as I was out of sight, I picked up my skirts and ran. I could not see what I was looking for, the entrance to an alley that might run behind the houses, and I had no time to find it. A double doorway was just ahead on my left, one of the doors slightly open, a small beam of light shining onto the street. I ducked inside without slowing my pace, neither knowing nor caring whose house it might be. But in the blur of my running, I saw that I was not in a house; I was in a stone tunnel, one glass-paned oil lamp hanging down from a chain in its middle.

Twelve more running steps and I came out the other end, feet hitting gravel in the moonlight. I could see trees and waving shadows and planting pots, smell the scent of green. Stone walls and curtained windows, muffled light in some of them, rose three and four stories high on every side, lighting the branches and leaves below in wavering patches. I fled for a space to my left, black and sheltered beneath low-hanging limbs, realizing that the garden was a courtyard, shared in the open center of a triangle of connected houses; the stone passage had run right beneath one.

I inched farther beneath the trees, panting, as footsteps rang down the passage, not running, just heavy and deliberate, booted, maybe. Another two steps back and I bumped into the stones of a house, edging as fast as I could along the wall, stepping alternately on soft, squelching ground or leaf-strewn paving stones. I passed one door in the stone wall, and then another.

Ten, eleven, twelve came the footsteps, and I banged my shin on a flower pot. Four doors I had counted on the street before I turned the corner. One more now and the next should be my grandmother's. The footsteps changed to the crunch of gravel.

I crouched down behind a statue in a dark corner where the building changed its shape by thrusting out a wing, clutching at the heavy vines that climbed the house wall. I could see the door I wanted, a little flame of gaslight in a lantern-like frame mounted right beside it. I tried to control my wheezing breath, afraid it could be heard over the fountain that was tinkling somewhere in the courtyard.

The boots stepped along a graveled path, unhurried, and then the man stopped, standing in the light that was flooding from what I thought must be Mrs. Reynolds's kitchen window. He was thin and slouching, wearing a bright blue vest. My eyes widened, blood beating a thudding rhythm against the prison of my chest. It was the man who had been leaning on the lamppost that morning, watching as I stepped out of the carriage. And he must have been there still when I came out of Mrs. Reynolds's, waiting in the darkness. Whatever this meant, I could be certain it was not good for me or my uncle.

The man slunk about the garden, poking among the clipped roses, vaulting them with surprising agility when the path did not suit. But always moving closer to me, and to the door I had my eye on. And then a latch clicked and a strip of light, brilliant in the night, reached out, illuminating the man's shadow for only a moment as he slid behind the pedestal of a statue of Cupid, eyes on the opening door.

The beating in my chest skipped and fluttered. The man was not ten feet away, his statue the twin of mine on a little stone patio, not one obstacle between us. I couldn't understand why he hadn't seen me already, and then I remembered the dark brown silk, and thanked heaven for mourning. But if he turned his head — when he turned his head — even a quick glance, I was going to be caught.

Water splashed onto the ground, dishwater or some other such being thrown out of a pan, and then the door — Mrs. Reynolds's, if all my guesses were correct — shut, and the shaft of light was gone. The man behind the statue rose up warily, eyes still on the just-closed door, and he stepped away from the statue, leaping easily back over the foliage. I let out a slow, silent breath. And I waited.

Leaves crushed in my hands, staining my fingers, and my legs had begun to cramp before I heard the booted footsteps moving back down the stone passage. I rose, surveying the silent darkness, still guarded, wincing as I stretched out my legs. I was not going back the way I had come. I would have to get inside from here, and then the tight place inside me seized, making me gasp. I was terribly late. What was happening to Uncle Tully?

I hurried to the door I thought was my grandmother's and pushed down on the latch. Locked. I stood back from the door, only just resisting the temptation to kick it, eyeing one second-floor window that was dimly lit, a small lamp or perhaps a single candle behind a curtain. I began to scavenge the gravel path for rocks, scouting for the largest, and when I had four or five, I weighed the selected stones in my hand, wondering if I had the strength or skill to attempt this. I wondered if I even had the right house. I threw the first stone.

It was more of a pebble, really. It hit the masonry with a sharp *snick* and disappeared into the bushes. My aim had been to the right of the lit window, and too low. The knot in my insides was a throbbing, sickening place. I threw again, this time with more strength. Still too far to the right. Once more, and I hit the window glass. I smiled, almost yelled in triumph, but no face appeared at the window. Teeth clenched, I took the next stone, a little larger, turning its heft in my hand before I threw it, hard. The windowpane shattered, a few bits raining down into a flower bed, the rest I am sure, all over the floor of the room above.

"An excellent shot, Miss Tulman."

My body jerked in surprise, hand jumping to my throat as I spun around. But instead of a blue vest and a slouching frame, I saw an orange glow in the air, just beyond a clump of rosebushes. The glow grew steadily brighter, showing dark hair and a thin mustache before it dimmed again, obscured by a sudden cloud of cigarette smoke. It was Mr. Marchand, the impertinent Frenchman, casually watching me throw rocks at my own windows. I straightened my back, but was saved from speaking when the broken window above me was thrown violently open.

"Katharine, my child, is that you?"

Mr. Babcock's odd round head disappeared from the window before I replied, obviously needing no other confirmation. I walked with affected dignity to the back door of my house, willing Mr. Babcock's short legs to run faster down the stairs. When I turned back toward the garden, the cigarette beside the rosebushes was where it had been, silent and still glowing. I could smell the thing now, overwhelming the sweet odor of the plants.

"I hope you find the rest of your evening just as enjoyable, Mr. Marchand."

My voice had been acid, but he chuckled. "Oh, I do not think I shall, Miss Tulman." He shook his head. "No, no. I do not think I shall."

He was still laughing when the lock turned and Mr. Babcock pulled me unceremoniously into the house.

CHAPTER TWELVE

*J*ust move a trifle more quickly, my dear," Mr. Babcock panted, pulling me down the corridor toward the stairs. "You are wanted." And as soon as we had climbed the stairs and the shelf door was opened, I could hear the yelling, though the noise did not sound like one of my uncle's tantrums; it did not sound like any noise I had ever heard from him before. Tired, hoarse, and beyond panic, like an animal that has fought to the point of exhaustion.

"I will remain here," said Mr. Babcock. "I have tried to help Mary, but my presence, it seems, is as distressing to him as the lack of yours."

Mr. Babcock was in a state, I saw, his beloved face creased with worry, and the workshop was not much better, a mess of spilled tools and overturned chairs, toys, and mechanical body parts flung here and there, one piece of ripped pink cloth folding down from the wall. And then I became aware of thudding, something heavy and slow, making the room shudder. I ran across the workshop, faster than I had just run down the street, dodging the debris, to the bed-chamber door.

At first glance I found Mary, tears running streaks down her face, her back pressed tight against the wall, and then I saw my uncle. He crouched on the floor in the opposite corner, and he was bloody, crimson ribbons streaming from his head and from the knuckles of both hands, his white nightshirt covered with it. The noise I had been hearing was his head, rhythmic as it banged against the wall, a brown-red smear staining both his hair and the pink cloth.

"Uncle!" I yelled, running forward to stop him, hearing Mary's warning of "Wait, Miss!" too late to avoid the arm that was instantly flung out as I reached for him. The blow twisted my neck, heat blossoming across my cheek. I took a step back and, through raised fingers, saw the wrench that was still clutched in Uncle Tully's hand. He wasn't looking at me; I'm not certain he even knew I was there. He yelled, his head lifted, and then slammed against the wall.

I felt Mary trying to pull me away but I shook my head, and again approached my uncle. This time I was ready for the hand. I caught it as I knelt down beside him, prying the wrench from his fingers, the weakness of his grip frightening me much more than the blood. I let the tool clatter to the floor as Uncle Tully wailed. The wall shook again with the impact of his head.

"Uncle, stop!" I pleaded. I risked inflaming him further and put out a hand to cup his skull, cushioning it, trying to think what to do. I'd only ever once glimpsed my uncle having a fit like this, and it was Lane who had calmed him. Lane had known how to restrain him, and in a way that reassured rather than punished, allowing no harm. Physically I did not have that capability; I could only use what I possessed.

"Uncle Tully," I said, still loud, but this time with authority rather than fear. He tried to hit his head again, instead crushing my hand. I flinched at the pain, but did not remove my hand.

"Open your eyes," I commanded. "Uncle, Marianna says to open your eyes."

The drooping lids fluttered, then half opened, their usual blue now a dull, clouded sky. I gave them time to focus.

"What is ninety-seven times one hundred and three, Uncle Tully?"

He lifted his head to bang it again, but the movement was slight, and my hand took only a glancing blow. One of the wounds on his temple oozed but had almost stopped bleeding. He had been doing this a long time, while I had been next door, eating a four-course dinner. My guilt squeezed inward, tightening like a vise.

"Look at me, Uncle Tully. Ninety-seven times one hundred and three?"

"Nine . . ." his voice was croaking, ". . . thousand . . . nine hundred and . . . ninety, plus one."

"That's right." There was no need to know the answers; his numbers were always correct. "Do you know who I am, Uncle?"

He hit his head again, and I bit my lip against the hurt. He said, "You are Simon's . . . Simon's baby."

"That's right. Your little niece. Twenty-seven times twenty-four?"

"Six hundred and forty-eight." His face crumpled as if he might cry. "I . . . little niece . . . I don't know where I am!"

"I know it, Uncle."

"I can wait in the wrong place for twenty. I waited for twenty. . . ." His voice rose to a yell again, rasping as his sentence trailed away. He lifted his head to bang it, and behind him I saw the clock Mary had put on the bedside table, chosen because it was a particular favorite of my uncle's, all its cogs and gears exposed rather than hidden inside a cabinet. My hand took another hard blow.

"Uncle Tully," I said, "listen, do you hear the clock?" His head twisted in my hand, telling me no. "Listen, Uncle Tully, listen. What is the clock telling you?"

Uncle Tully finally went still long enough to hear an audible *tick*, and when he did, he froze. I held my breath. Mary must have been doing the same because the room went deathly still, the *tick, tick, tick, tick* like a mechanical heartbeat. My uncle's eyes closed, his battered face intent.

"What is it telling you, Uncle?" I whispered.

After a long time he said, "It says that it is right, that its pieces are working, and that the when is now."

"And the clock is working even in a different place, isn't it?" He moved about in my hand a little, but he was not trying to hit his head. "I told you that when you woke up, that we would have done just what Marianna said to. Do you remember that, Uncle?"

"I waited . . . for twenty . . ."

"But you don't have to wait for twenty here, Uncle, because this place is not wrong. It's a place Marianna made for you. We did just as Marianna told us."

My uncle frowned. "But Marianna said that when the men come that . . . that I am to wait . . . in the tunnel."

I looked hard at my uncle, watching his short, panting breaths. Every now and again he was capable of remarkable penetration, as if a light had somehow beamed through his fog. "Yes, Uncle," I said softly, "that's exactly right. Only this time the men knew all about the tunnel. So Marianna made another place, a place where you could make new toys and where they would be safe. That is where we are now. And you can hear that the clocks are ticking."

Which to my uncle meant that the world was still turning on its axis. I waited, hardly daring to draw breath, to see if he would accept this explanation. If he did not, I had no other plan. His mouth turned down again, ready to cry. I was ready to cry with him.

"But . . . where is . . . the house? And Mrs. Jefferies? The girl is here. . . ." I chanced a glance back at Mary. She had sunk to the floor, her back against the wall. "Did the water take it all away? Like before? I don't understand. . . ."

"The water didn't come this time, Uncle, and it's all right to not understand. I'll stay with you until you do. But now you are very tired. Would you come with me and lie down, and have some —"

Uncle Tully's eyes snapped open. "Will I get too tired, Simon's baby? Will I go away? The forever kind, like Marianna?"

I paused, my uncle's head still cupped in my hand, his white hair and white nightshirt stained with blood, pale skin stained with coming bruises. And he was searching my face, puzzled, the mind that could confound the best the scientific world could offer, asking if someday he would die. The thought filled me with a pain that I could not show him.

"I don't want you to go away, Uncle. I want you to stay with me. But if you did . . . if you did get too tired, then we would not forget. We would remember. Always."

Uncle Tully sighed. "It is right to remember," he said, eyes dropping. "That is what Marianna said."

He was relaxing now. I slowly took my hand away from his head, before he could realize it was there, letting his bleeding temple rest against the wall. "Would you like to come with me, Uncle Tully, and look at Marianna's new place, and all your things that we've brought?"

He winced, eyes remaining closed. "My head hurts, little niece."

"Yes. And it has gotten very dirty. Will you let me use the cloth on it? The cloth will touch, not my hand."

Mary brought a warm cloth, and my uncle allowed me to not only clean his head but his face and the backs of his hands as well. He tottered upright and we helped him to his bed, bloody nightshirt and all. The slowness of his movements woke all my slumbering alarm. But he drank his tea and ate a piece of toast, and I wrapped the blankets tight around him, sitting beside his bed while Mary sponged the bloodstains from the walls. And the last thing I remembered was watching the rise and fall of my uncle's chest, up and down, up and down, counting each precious breath.

I sat up, startled, a blanket sliding down from my shoulder. I was on the floor of my uncle's bedchamber, heart beating hard for no reason I could name. One gaslight flickered in the windowless room, and in the glow I could see that my head had been on a pillow, though I had no memory of it being put there; I had no memory of going to sleep. I blinked, then spun about to look behind me. My uncle was right where he should be, beside me on the little cot, still wrapped tight and sleeping heavily, as he often did after being upset. He looked terrible in the gaslight, but at least this sleep was natural, nothing like the forced unconsciousness I had subjected him to.

When the clocks in the next room began to strike — a soft noise in this sound-deadened place — I stopped watching my uncle, got to my feet, pushed my own wild hair out of my face, and wandered out of the bedchamber. I felt each and every ache earned from a night on a hard floor, but those pains were nothing compared to the seething hot guilt in my middle. Lane had taken much better care of him.

I paused, adjusting the clock that had been just a bit behind the others, and looked about the room. Ten o'clock in the morning, but the light from the high windows was barely there, the sun a mere thought behind low-hanging clouds. Someone — Mary, I supposed — had been cleaning since last night; the toppled chairs were righted, spilled tools back in their boxes, and the automaton pieces organized by body part on the tables and against the walls. A bit of metal shone out from beneath a cloth at my elbow, bright in the room's dimness, and beneath the wrapping I found the flower of brass, one of my favorite things Uncle Tully had ever made. The metallic petals alternated buffed dullness with a high polish, the bloom narrowing at the bottom to the point of a stem. It was nothing grand or spectacular, no engines or steam, just a small piece of wonderment that fit in the palm of my hand.

Glancing once over my shoulder — I knew better than to be caught touching my uncle's toys — I set the flower on the workbench, one finger on the top to hold it upright on the narrow stem, and gave a quick jerk to the string that had been threaded between the petals. The string came free, a wheel softly whirred, and when I removed my finger the flower was spinning, slow and unaided on the tiny stem point, the petals opening and closing with soft clicks. Mr.

Wickersham had held this flower once, examining not its beauty but the spinning gyroscope in its center, the same mechanism that was in my uncle's fish. I watched the flower turn, a thing perfectly and unnaturally balanced. Could there really be something inside this little flower that could sink an ironclad ship?

The little toy spun on and on, never losing momentum, a bloom perpetually losing and then finding its sun, and suddenly I knew that I was homesick, not just for the Stranwyne I'd left but for the Stranwyne I'd known before. For the grandeur of Uncle Tully's workshop, and Lane at a workbench, smelling of smoke and paint, for the summer sun on metal and the steam engines thrumming and my uncle's joy when he wound up his toys. The sheer injustice of the loss twisted all my melancholy into anger. How I wished I'd shot Ben Aldridge when given the chance. Lane and I had that in common.

I stopped the flower's spin with one finger, its gyroscope coming abruptly to a halt. My uncle's vibrant, spinning world may have been shrunk to the size of this attic, but I would extract every drop of happiness from it that he could possibly have. I would live away from my home, tell every lie that was needed, and be the lady Mr. Babcock required. And I would bring us Lane. If we could not have our life at Stranwyne then we would build our old life here, cog by cog and stone by Parisian stone. This I would do. Somehow. Would not rest until it was done. For my uncle. And for myself.

I straightened my back in the would-be workshop and carefully covered the flower, letting it wait for its sun.

CHAPTER THIRTEEN

I stepped through the shelf door into the dingy storeroom, where my empty steamer trunk sat, and crept down the stairs of a still and silent house. On the next landing, I discovered a large bedroom with shuttered windows, an unmade bed, and one of Mr. Babcock's tall hats, and across from it a smaller chamber, bright yellow with white trimmings, containing Mary's trunk and her knitting basket. I shook my head as I shut the door, the soft noise almost startling. The yellow room was obviously for guests, but who was I to deny Mary, who had left home and family for the sake of my uncle and me? Quiet pressed against my ears and I began to hurry down the steps. Where was everyone?

On the second floor, I found a small room with a convenience, the curtain moving slightly with the breeze that came through a broken pane of glass — poor Mr. Babcock, I must have given him quite a start — and then I found my room. There was no question that it was mine, because it had so obviously been my grandmother's. The furniture was dark, tall, and heavy, nothing like the airy style in the rest of the house, the wallpaper only slightly brightened by the lighter shades of pink in a pattern that tended closer to red. My trunk hunched neatly at the foot of an enormous canopied bed, thick with fringed hangings, the noise of a French gilt clock on the chimney-piece rather loud in the silence. A small pile of papers sat beside the clock, pinned beneath a stack of French books that looked like fairy tales. A note in Mr. Babcock's hand was propped upright on the top. I snatched it up, squinting in the dim.

Dearest Katharine,

Have gone to see to our passports, so the French shall have no need of the guillotine where we are concerned. Please find the fruit of my early morning labors below this note, with my compliments. I have put it forward that you are interested in charitable work and wish to study these institutions for the benefit of your own estate.

With my most sincere regards,
A. Babcock

I traded the note for the papers and flipped curiously through the stack.

Documents of differing sizes, all French, with various inks and signatures, gold foil emblems, official-looking insignias, and embossed shapes on each. I dropped onto the rose velvet chair beside the hearth. The word *prison* was the same in English and French, it seemed, and *hospital* could also be easily deciphered. These were invitations, permissions to visit places where a young man might have lost himself in Paris, and very probably, if I knew Mr. Babcock, certified license for me to pry into their every dark corner.

I bit my lip, water stinging just behind my eyes. Mr. Babcock had done this. He thought my search for Lane foolish and hopeless, and yet he had done this. For me. Such an obvious show of trust and affection was almost puzzling to me, would probably always be puzzling to some deeper part of myself, while at the same time a very different something inside me had been set loose, taken flight, and soared. My way was clear, the road smoothed. I would start as soon as I could be certain my uncle was settled. I riffled through the papers again, wondering if any of these places might be within walking distance of Rue Trudon. If I could only get a map of the streets, I could . . .

And then I froze. For the first time in many hours my mind went to the time before my uncle, to the man slouching against a streetlamp, and the short walk home that had become a chase. I'd been so distracted, so preoccupied, I hadn't even mentioned the man to Mary or to Mr. Babcock. And where were they now? The clock on the chimneypiece ticked in the silence. I leapt from the chair, dropped the papers where I'd been sitting, and hurried to tug the drape back from a window that was nearly twice the height of my head. I jerked open one tall, louvered shutter, and a watery, gray light half lit the bedchamber.

The houses across the street were nearly identical to one another, only an extra space between window rows showing their delineations, and I saw a flower seller hurrying past, pushing her brightly laden cart at a trot beneath the heavy sky. Everyone was scurrying down the street or along the narrow sidewalks, making for the nearest shelter. All except for one. The man in the blue vest leaned against his lamppost, hands in pockets, unmoving, watching the doors of my house.

I stepped back, out of sight, the fear of the night before crashing down so that I could hardly stand. I whirled, ready to run down the stairwell, vaguely planning to yell until I found Mary or Mr. Babcock, but I stopped short, one hand jumping to my throat, only just holding in my gasp. A tall, thin shadow stood stock-still in my doorway. After a moment, the silhouette stepped forward, and the pale face and severe hair knot of Mrs. DuPont came into the window light.

"What are you doing here?" I snapped, a bit too loud.

Mrs. DuPont took another slow step into the room, black eyes sweeping over the still-made bed, my untamed hair, the muddy and wrinkled, garden-stained dress that I'd obviously slept in. Her sharp gaze lingered on my face and the hand on my throat went quickly to my cheek, feeling the soreness beneath my fingers. I'd forgotten the blow from the wrench. I wondered if I had a black eye. I dropped my hand and clasped them both behind me, returning Mrs. DuPont's stare.

"Your pardon, Mademoiselle," the woman said, expressionless. "Mademoiselle said to come to her at half past ten, so this is what we do. I have come to tell Mademoiselle that we wait for her in the salon."

Rain struck suddenly on the window glass behind me, and I clasped my hands harder. I'd completely forgotten my meeting with the DuPonts, though I saw no reason for her to know it. "Yes, thank you. I will come as soon as I am ready. Our meeting will not take long. Until then, please remain on the ground floor. On the ground floor only, please," I said again, for emphasis. "And, Mrs. DuPont . . ." I lifted my chin. ". . . I do prefer to be called 'Miss Tulman.'"

She met my gaze, and a strange, miniature war was waged then, a silent battle as we stared. I had not the first notion what we were fighting about, but it didn't particularly matter; this unpleasant woman would be dismissed as soon as I could go downstairs. Mrs. DuPont ceased fire first, and had just deigned to nod when my brows came down.

"Who let you in the house this morning, Mrs. DuPont? I'm certain I instructed you to leave your keys."

Her corpse-like face almost seemed to smile. "There was no need of the letting in, *Mademoiselle*," she said, particular emphasis on the last word.

I would have said something further had she not at that moment been nearly run down by Mary, who came careening into the room with a tea tray. They circled each other, and Mary waited until Mrs. DuPont had glided away like a bird of prey before plunking the tea things on the table and looking me up and down.

"Well, Lord, Miss, what a mess you're looking and no mistake. You could've been rolling in the gutters, as my mum would say. Is . . ." She gave a quick glance toward the open door and lowered her voice to a whisper. "Is Mr. Tully waking? I'm guessing he ain't or you wouldn't be down here. Have a cup a tea, Miss, till you're giving them DuPonts the boot, then we —"

"Where is Mr. Babcock?" I asked.

"Here, my dear."

Mr. Babcock appeared in the doorway, red-faced, winded, and in a frock coat dotted with rain. His short arms were stretched wide to each side, holding up a large, wooden crate that was obviously crushing his round middle. I allowed my curiosity free rein for about one second before blurting, "Last night the door was locked and a man chased me down the street and into our courtyard. He was here yesterday, when we got out of the carriage, and he's outside now, watching the house."

Mary turned from her progress toward the door, mouth open as Mr. Babcock gave me a sharp look. "Chased, you say?"

I nodded and he sighed once before he set the crate down with difficulty in the hall, coming into the room with a careful step, as if an improper haste might mar the sanctity of Marianna's bedchamber. He peeked around the shutter. The windowpanes were running with rain.

"I noticed our new friend just this morning, I'm sorry to say. But the rain seems to have driven him in. For now." Mr. Babcock blew out a breath. "I am not so much surprised by the event as the speed in which it has happened. He could be an agent of Wickersham's, which would be the most logical, though if so he seems remarkably indiscreet. But we must also consider the possibility that this man could be visiting us on behalf of the French."

I frowned. "But to be here before we even arrived, Mr. Babcock? How is that possible?"

"I think we must assume, my dear, that just as Lane was in France —"

"*Is* in France," I corrected. I tried not to notice the look exchanged by Mary and Mr. Babcock.

"Your pardon. Just as Lane Moreau is in France, passing information to the British, one could assume that there are his counterparts in London, passing information to the French." Mr. Babcock closed the shutter and shook his head. "He could also be nothing more than a common footpad, waiting for a young lady of means to step away from her door. It is a possibility." None of us believed it. "Well, well. Until we know more, I think the wisest solution is to do nothing of interest on which he may report. And I must insist that neither of you young ladies leave this house alone. Can we agree upon that?"

Mary began a mumbling protest, but my gaze was pulled straight to the papers I had left in the chair. I had been planning to leave the house just as soon as possible.

"No need to look like that, child," said Mr. Babcock, coming to pat me awkwardly on the shoulder. "I quite understand the difficulties, and I did not bribe half of France to not get any of the benefits. I shall take you first thing in the morning, or as early as you can be ready. Will that do? Assuming your uncle can be made comfortable, of course. I have brought him some things I hope will prove sufficiently distracting. . . ."

But whatever else he might have said was cut off by the kiss I planted on his sagging cheek.

"Well, well," he said again, reaching down to straighten the buttons of his waistcoat. I knew he was pleased. But I also saw a shadow of sadness pass across his face.

I sent Mary to my uncle, to be certain he still slept, and ascertaining that I did not have a black eye, merely a bruise along my right cheekbone, shockingly purple, I made myself decent and left Marianna's bedchamber. I counted each step as I descended, twenty-two from my landing to the lowest floor. That would make sixty-six stairs between the DuPonts and my uncle's lair in the attic. It did not feel like enough.

The DuPont family stood assembled along the front wall of the salon, as if awaiting inspection, Mr. DuPont, I was happy to see, wearing all the clothing he should be. The dust sheets were gone, the window shutters opened to the steady drizzle, and a small coal fire glowed in the grate. It was a nice room, I thought, very bright and new looking, but I missed the dignity that came with Stranwyne's dark and ancient shabbiness.

They must have arrived quite early to clean it, I thought, watching Marguerite stare dreamily at the gilded designs on the ceiling, hair floating about her head like a fluffy blonde cloud. I wished her elsewhere. Mr. Babcock had suggested I be gentle with the DuPonts — I was, after all, depriving them of what must have been an easy and welcome addition to their income — and I planned to be as just and reasonable as was possible. But the child did not need to listen while I dismissed her mother. Perhaps she did not speak English. I turned to ask, but Mrs. DuPont stepped forward before I could speak.

"You cannot send us away, Mademoiselle."

I closed my mouth, and then said, "Mrs. DuPont, I most certainly —"

"*Napoléon est mort,*" Mr. DuPont interrupted, hat in his hands. I raised a brow in his direction.

"You will not send us away, Mademoiselle," Mrs. DuPont repeated. "You will need the cooking and the shopping —"

"*Napoléon est mort.*"

"— and I am a fine cook."

"Mrs. DuPont, I have no intention of —"

"And your salon, is it not pretty, just as the English like?"

"I —"

"We are good workers. Everyone says that we are. . . ."

"Then I am certain you will have no difficulty whatsoever in finding another position," I said firmly, putting an end to the argument. "You will receive an excellent reference and a full month of wages, as agreed, so you may —"

"*Napoléon est mort*," Mr. DuPont said loudly. I saw Marguerite, utterly unperturbed, reach up and take his hand. I softened my tone.

"— so you may begin elsewhere. I wish you all the best of luck. Please leave whatever keys you have let yourself in with and I will bid you a good day."

"I think," Mrs. DuPont said very slowly, "that what Mademoiselle wishes the most, is for the privacy. Is that not so?"

I stiffened slightly, a little frown on my forehead. I was certain her sharp gaze had not missed it. "Mrs. DuPont, I thank you for your time here, but your services are no longer required. Please leave your keys on the table in the foyer. Can I be more clear?"

"But I have already done so, Mademoiselle. Last night, as you instructed, before retiring to our rooms."

I stared, uncomprehending, and then I caught the barest tilt to one corner of her mouth, a smug lift in an otherwise expressionless face. "Mrs. DuPont," I said slowly, "exactly where are your rooms?"

She nodded just slightly, as if acknowledging the arrival of a long-awaited question. "In the servants' quarters, Mademoiselle," she replied, "across the hallway from the kitchen."

I stood mute, drawing in five full breaths before I accepted the truth, and then my temper flared, as I was sure she'd meant it to do.

Mrs. DuPont had never actually left the house. The DuPonts lived in the house. Without anyone's knowledge or permission. I filtered through the memory of our conversations. Had she told me she was leaving or had I assumed? What had been said and done last night when we thought the house was empty? A wave of hot fury was spreading outward from my chest, but there was a cold, cold fear bubbling just beneath it. What might this woman have already seen? Or heard?

Mrs. DuPont waited quietly, unmoving, her black eyes watching me think all these things. "You will need servants, Mademoiselle," she repeated.

"And tell me why," I said deliberately, "I would retain a servant who has breached her contract with my estate, who has lived in my house without permission for . . ." I tilted my head, leaving the question in the air.

"Five years, Mademoiselle."

"For five years," I said. The flush of anger reached my cheeks. "Can you explain why I would keep such a servant, Mrs. DuPont, instead of bringing the police?"

"Because, Mademoiselle, I think you will wish for the servant that does not ask the questions. Am I not right? I think the servant who can hold her tongue will be what Mademoiselle requires."

If Mrs. DuPont's expression remained unchanged, I'm sure mine did not. All my fury was cooling, icing over with dread.

"Mademoiselle will need the servant who will not mind the comings and goings, who will not mind that they stay on the lowest floor. And we . . ." She indicated the man and child with a wave of her bony hand. I'd nearly forgotten they were there. "We can be very quiet, Mademoiselle. We know how to hold our tongues in the street.

When Mademoiselle pays a good wage, we can all hold our tongues very well."

Again we stared at each other, and if before there had been a battle between our eyes, this time it was not even a contest; Mrs. DuPont had all the weapons.

"I think we shall be very happy together. Do you not agree, Mademoiselle?"

We all turned to a sharp tap from the window. Mrs. Hardcastle was peering in from the other side of the smearing glass, pince-nez on her nose, an umbrella over her enormous hat, other indistinct bodies pressed around her. She was grinning, pointing meaningfully at my front door.

"You have visitors, Mademoiselle," said Mrs. DuPont. "Marguerite, *prend leurs manteaux, amèner les ici.*" And to her husband she said, "*Disparais!*" He vanished without a word while Marguerite bounded toward the front door, where someone was already rapping. "You will need tea and sweet things," Mrs. DuPont said gravely, her black eyes dancing at me. "I will prepare it, Mademoiselle."

"Miss Tulman," I whispered at her back. She looked over her shoulder and nodded once, her face as satisfied as a death mask could be.

CHAPTER FOURTEEN

*M*rs. DuPont left the room with the rustle of raven wings, only to be replaced by Mrs. Hardcastle, charging through the same doorway like a stampeding bull.

"Miss Tulman! Good morning! Good morning!" Mrs. Hardcastle grabbed both my startled hands, shoving a bundle of cloth into them. "Do accept our apologies for barging in, but the rain has quite ruined our trip to the Madeleine and I told the Miss Mortimers that we could just pop over to bring your shawl, and that you had invited us to tea anyway and would not mind in the slightest." She looked over her shoulder. "See, girls, Miss Tulman doesn't mind in the slightest!"

I managed a small smile as the two nieces of Mrs. Reynolds came sideways through the door, so as not to crush the dampened frills on their enormous skirts. They gave a small, tandem curtsy, expressions saying clearly that they were the ones who minded this visit if I did not. I wondered if Mrs. Reynolds had mentioned finding me creeping about their bedchamber. And then I saw dark, slicked hair and an impudent smile beneath a thin mustache.

"And of course you remember Mr. Marchand," said Mrs. Hardcastle. "Of course," I mumbled. This one had watched me throw rocks at my own windows. His smile widened at my confusion. My gaze leapt past him to the window and the empty lamppost beyond it, my mind on Mrs. DuPont, the unexpected assemblage in my salon, and the sixty-six stairs that lay between all of this and disaster. Then I realized that we were standing about, and that we were standing about because of me.

"Won't you sit down?" I said quickly. I discovered my shawl in my hands and tossed it to a table before finding the edge of a brocaded chair, one that afforded a good view of both the street and the stairs, while the others found places to be comfortable. The Miss Mortimers squished their skirts together on the settee to make room for Mr. Marchand, but he selected the chair beside mine instead. Dark whispering commenced behind gloved hands, and I was careful not to look in his direction. I remembered my promise to Mr. Babcock and attempted a pleasant expression.

"Mrs. DuPont will bring us tea," I ventured, "and some . . ." I did not finish. I had no idea what else she might bring.

"Well," said Mrs. Hardcastle heartily, peering through the pince-nez, "you were perfectly correct, Miss Tulman. This is a lovely room. Quite a lovely room after all."

Generous, I thought, considering I'd practically dragged her in by the heels to look at the dust sheets. But I only smiled and said, "Thank you," while Mr. Marchand sat quiet, playing with a coin in one hand.

"And where is Mr. Babcock today?" she asked.

"Oh!" said the first Miss Mortimer, the one with the bouncing blonde front curls. "Are we acquainted with Mr. Babcock? I believe Aunt Reynolds knows a family by the name of Babcock in Surrey." Her round cheeks glowed with interest.

"Mr. Babcock is my solicitor," I replied. "He traveled with me to Paris."

Both the Miss Mortimers' mouths formed silent Os as they exchanged one darting, and yet significant glance. How interesting, I reflected, to watch the seeds of a rumor germinate; I could almost see the story sprouting in their fertile minds right before my eyes. All at once I was quite looking forward to introducing these young ladies to Mr. Babcock. I hoped he would be wearing his flowered waistcoat.

". . . quite well, Miss Tulman?" My gaze jerked to the second Miss Mortimer, with the brown frizz sticking out from beneath her blue bonnet. She was frowning at me.

"I am so sorry. What did you say?"

"I was inquiring after your health, Miss Tulman," she said stiffly. "Aunt Reynolds said you weren't feeling quite yourself last night."

Mr. Marchand examined the coin as it flipped across the back of his fingers. "What the young lady wishes to ask and will not, Miss Tulman," he said, voice slow and lazy, "is what in the name of the Holy Mother you have done to your face?"

I blushed — I could not help it — and only just kept my hand from creeping up to my bruised cheek. Mrs. Hardcastle laughed. "Oh, really, Henri," she cried. "You are too much, truly!"

I arranged my face and sat a little straighter in my chair. "It's nothing. I am not yet acquainted with the house, and I'm afraid I just . . . walked into a door. In the dark. That's all."

Mrs. Hardcastle clucked and had begun relating one of her own misadventures when Mr. Marchand leaned close and said, "And I had thought your aim in the dark better than that, Miss Tulman. It seemed so last night. Tell me, is that cut on your neck also from a door?"

A shadow moved across the entrance to the salon. "Ah," I said. "The tea is here."

The ladies stared, dumbstruck as Mrs. DuPont came with her severe hair and silent tread to set a tray with teapot, cups, sugar, cream, and a plate of wafer-thin biscuits that I was unfamiliar with on the table between us. She slid out the door like the living dead and I began to pour, counting sugar lumps and stirring with spoons, using the opportunity to think. How likely was Mrs. DuPont to keep her mouth closed, and what exactly did she know? How soon would my uncle wake, and what would happen if I was detained when he did? Would he try to leave the attic? I decided to take control of the conversation. Perhaps if I made myself sufficiently obnoxious they would all go away on their own. I set down my spoon.

"Miss Mortimer." Both the blonde curls and the brown frizz looked around. They had been craning their necks, stealing glances into the foyer. Hoping for a glimpse of Mr. Babcock, I surmised. I said, "The Madeleine is a very fine building, I hear. Perhaps your aunt could recommend a course of study on Parisian architecture during your stay. I'm sure you would find it improving."

I was pleased by an expression of disgust from one and a look of dismay from the other. "Aunt Reynolds doesn't care a fig for fine buildings," the blonde curls sniffed. "She has been very cross and out of sorts of late. I'm sure you must have noticed it at dinner. It makes one wish to visit the seaside or go somewhere else pleasant."

"Like the emperor's ball," sighed the brown frizz.

Mr. Marchand had set down his cup and was playing with his franc again, letting it travel from finger to finger in a way that was rather astonishing. I deliberately kept my gaze away from him as I turned the conversation where it was least wanted. "Is Mrs. Reynolds politically minded, then? I had thought she was perhaps disturbed last night by the dissenting opinions on the war."

The blonde Miss Mortimer almost snorted while her cousin gaped. Mrs. Hardcastle chuckled.

"Miss Tulman, my dear cousin Reynolds has likely never thought of politics in her life," she said. "I fear that she is rather undone by the loss of her protégé."

"Ah, the protégé!" said Mr. Marchand, snatching the coin from a flip through the air. "I hear of nothing else."

I looked at them all blankly. "I'm afraid I don't understand the term."

"Why, Miss Tulman, having a protégé is quite the thing!" said the brown-frizzed Miss Mortimer.

"It shows your dedication to culture and the arts," explained Mrs. Hardcastle. "My cousin was supporting a painter. . . ."

"Jean-Michel!" sighed one of the young ladies.

"Yes, Jean-Michel, whom she thought to be quite promising. He lived in a small studio upstairs, where he was developing his talent.

But nearly two weeks ago, well . . . he just disappeared, I'm sorry to say. Left the house one morning and never returned."

I thought of the room in the upper floor with the covered easels, my eyes darting reflexively toward the window, and when I did I nearly choked on my tea. The slouching man was back at his lamp-post, a dripping newspaper held over his head, watching my house in the rain. I cleared my throat and said, "Have the police been consulted, Mrs. Hardcastle?"

"That part was rather thrilling," confided the brown frizz.

"Don't be horrible, Jane," replied the other. "I can hardly think of something terrible happening to Jean-Michel. Such clever fingers when he painted . . ."

"You perceive my annoyance," said Mr. Marchand, once again leaning close to my chair. I did not respond, hoping he would perceive mine. I glanced again at the man outside the window. Mr. Marchand began switching the franc from hand to hand so quickly it was difficult to follow with the eyes.

"Paris," he pronounced, the coin moving back and forth, "is a city full of people." The coin moved in a blur. "And where there are the people, then . . . poof!" He spread his hands with a sudden flourish, showing only empty palms. "Things, they disappear. It is the way of the world, is it not?"

Mrs. Hardcastle and the Miss Mortimers set down their cups and clapped, but not with so much amazement as to make me think they had never seen Mr. Marchand's tricks before. He turned to me and said, "The protégé is not the only one with clever fingers, n'est-ce pas?"

"Very . . . dexterous," I said.

He smiled, and I saw that his eyes were not just brown, but many colors, shot through with yellow and green, impossible to say which might be dominant. His hands gave another flourish and the coin reappeared between two fingers. He laid it in my palm, still smiling. "For you, Miss Tulman, so you may hire a guard to walk you to the next door."

Mrs. Hardcastle laughed uproariously at this, but my gaze went again to the window before landing back on Mr. Marchand. He was teasing me, but I could not tell if there was anything of substance behind his grin. And then I heard the squeak of floorboards from the ceiling. There were footsteps moving over my head. Someone was walking — no, running — through my bedchamber. I threw a startled glance through the salon door, where I could just catch a glimpse of the stairs. Had anyone thought to lock the storeroom?

"Shall you come to dinner again tonight, Miss Tulman?" the blonde Miss Mortimer was saying rather halfheartedly, her eyes on the franc in my hand. She was pouting. The noise of feet moving back and forth pattered above my head, and I looked again out the window. I needed these people to leave. Quickly.

"Thank you," I replied, "but I have . . . engagements, early in the morning. And actually, I have much to accomplish this —"

"Oh!" said the brown Miss Mortimer, setting down her cup, "do you have other acquaintances in Paris, Miss Tulman?"

I saw Mrs. Hardcastle's face perk with interest, and gave myself a mental kick. The floorboards groaned with the hurried steps. "No," I said, a little too fast. "No, my visits tomorrow are . . ." My mind raced, searching for anything that would be dull to the present company. ". . . of a charitable nature. I plan to tour several public institutions, to improve what is offered to the villagers on the Stranwyne estate."

I was gratified by the look of repugnance shared between the two young ladies, and the slight boredom of Mrs. Hardcastle.

"But this is noble, Miss Tulman!" said Mr. Marchand. "I have an interest in such things myself. Allow me to escort you on your tour."

That captured the room's attention. I felt three sets of eyes swing to me, waiting for my response. "No need to trouble yourself, Mr. Marchand. Mr. Babcock plans to escort me."

"But he must be a man of much business, while I have nothing so worthy on which to spend my time. And we have already established that Paris can be unsafe." He smiled again, stretching the tiny mustache, and all the eyes moved in tandem back to me. I felt my temper rising.

"I have already made my plans, Mr. Marchand, and I am sure I do not need an escort to go anywhere." This was not remotely true; at the moment I would not have put a toe outside my own front door. But hearing one of the Miss Mortimers give a soft gasp was pleasurable.

I opened my mouth to speak, but was saved from saying anything more rude by a deafening crash from over our heads, a thundering cacophony that shook the ceiling and shocked the room. We all looked up, Mrs. Hardcastle through her pince-nez, and watched the chandelier pendants jiggle and clink. Then the footsteps started up again, just as frantic as before. Mrs. Hardcastle turned the pince-nez to me.

"Is there some sort of trouble upstairs, Miss Tulman?"

A row of curious faces looked back at me, waiting for me to speak. I opened my mouth, struggling to bring any sort of plausible explanation to my tongue, when with no warning Mrs. DuPont appeared in the doorway.

"Your pardon, Mademoiselle," she said, her black eyes canny, "for the terrible noise. Marguerite has dropped a tray."

"A tray," I repeated slowly, "dropped by Marguerite."

Mrs. DuPont's face did not change. "Yes, Mademoiselle. I will speak with her about her clumsiness. A thousand pardons to your guests." She looked at me again, a bit triumphant, dropped the hint of a curtsy and left the room with a *whoosh*, as if she'd sucked all the air out with her. I knew Marguerite had not gone upstairs. I would have seen; I'd chosen my seat for the purpose. What a game the woman was playing.

"But what of our plans, Miss Tulman?" said Mr. Marchand. "I have a relative on the side of my mother, in the Hôtel des Invalides. The hospital there is one of the finest in France. And the tomb of the great Napoléon, it is there, as well. You cannot resist such an offer as that."

I put my eyes on Mr. Marchand, and what I resisted was a very strong urge to suggest that he escort Mr. DuPont instead. "Mr. Babcock has already made up a list and secured my invitations, Mr. Marchand. I will await his pleasure."

His friendly smile widened. "Then I will stop at the same time tomorrow, Miss Tulman, and if you wish to see the Hôtel des Invalides, I shall be happy to serve. If no, then I will not disturb you for the world."

"Well!" said Mrs. Hardcastle, making me start, "I daresay the rain is slowing. Do you think we shall still have time to make the Madeleine, girls?"

I found the Miss Mortimers staring at me from the settee, teacups halfway to mouths, their faces a blend of mortification and incredulity that both flattered and insulted. The slouching man outside was folding his wet newspaper, and I heard the footsteps above my head move toward the landing. The thought of who might come running down those stairs had me instantly on my feet.

"Well, thank you so much for visiting, Mrs. Hardcastle, Miss Mortimer, Miss Mortimer, Mr. Marchand." I gave them each a brief nod. "Do come again."

Cups were set down in haste and Marguerite appeared from nowhere, showing everyone to their damp wraps and umbrellas. The Miss Mortimers peered up the stairs as they were ushered out, looking for the elusive Mr. Babcock, and I ignored the tip of Mr. Marchand's hat after it went onto his head. As soon as Marguerite had shut the door and trotted off toward the kitchen, I ran up the stairs to my bedchamber.

There was no Uncle Tully. Only Mary on her knees in the middle of the floor, wrestling with an armload of clothing, my trunk lid propped up, the wardrobe gaping wide. From the tall chest, various drawers were hanging open, one of them pulled right from its slot to the floor, a jumble of candlesticks and small ornaments scattered where they'd fallen. I let out a long breath, and Mary looked up from her skirmish with the petticoats, freckles invisible beneath her irritated flush. The petticoats seemed to be winning.

"Are they gone, Miss? Well, that's a relief and no mistake. Mr. Tully is awake and had his tea, but it's playtime, Miss, playtime like you've never seen. He's got that box of Mr. Babcock's open and you know what it's like when he's got something new to grab hold of. There's no reasoning with him, though he don't look near ready to be out of a bed, if you're asking me, which I note you ain't. You're meant to come upstairs at noontime on the dot, Miss, so mind your time, 'cause Lord knows I'm not going back up anytime soon. Mr. Tully yelled like the devil for me to be on my way and I locked the door — you forgot to do that this morning, Miss — and came down to do a quick spot of unpacking, and instead dumped a drawerful of candlesticks and I don't know what else on the floor."

She gave up her attempt to fold and wadded up my petticoats. "I don't know how a body's supposed to be doing their job, or how we're supposed to be keeping ourselves to ourselves when it's worse than the London Bridge about this place, people in and out, in and out the whole day through. And what with men on the sidewalk and that DuPont woman hanging about like a crow on a limb, it's a miracle we ain't done for already. And what's to happen to Mr. Tully, then, Miss? And to you? We won't be lasting out the week at this rate. . . ."

I sank into the velvet chair, not bothering to dam Mary's flood of words. Mostly because they were true. Every last one of them. This was becoming less a matter of whether Uncle Tully would be found or not, and more of a race to see who would be the first to make the discovery.

I closed my eyes, and for one moment, for a fleeting second, sitting in that chair behind the darkness of my eyelids, I wished that I was empty-headed and vapid, with an over-trimmed dress and nothing more pressing than rain on the way to the Madeleine.

What I truly wished was that Lane was here, telling me what I should do.

CHAPTER FIFTEEN

$\mathcal{J}$ dreamed of Lane that night. Maybe because of the search I would start the next morning, or maybe because of the afternoon I had spent with my uncle, watching him "play," as Lane and I had done together so many times before. Though I doubted even Lane had ever seen the state my uncle Tully had been in that afternoon. The contents of Mr. Babcock's box — coils of wire, jars of hazy fluid, and other things I did not understand — had my uncle's attention at such a fevered pitch, an almost manic intensity, that I wasn't certain Uncle Tully ever fully realized I was there. In any case, I dreamed of Lane, as I often did, but this was a dream that felt more like memory, though I knew it wasn't real.

"*Fais attention,*" he was saying, "*aux femmes déterminées.* That's what my dad always told me."

We were in my green morning room at Stranwyne, and Lane had his elbows on the back of my chair, toying with one of the small curls below my hair knot. He was unshaven, uncombed, and just a little annoyed with me, but I did not move away or reach for the stack of ledgers that lay waiting on the desk.

"You know I don't speak French," I replied, deciding to feign petulance. He knew I was pretending.

"He said to 'beware of strong-blooded women.' And good advice that was, too. Don't you think that was good advice, Miss Tulman?" I smelled the outdoors and molten metal. I'd never been aware of scents in a dream. "Come with me now. Work's done for the day."

I was pulled from my chair in mock protest, and I saw that it was not annoyance but mischief glinting in his eyes, like sun on a choppy gray sea, and with the current running high. I allowed myself to be led out the morning-room door, not quite successful in hiding my smile, past the stone stairs, through a gaslit corridor, around the corner, and all the way to one end of the dim and silent drawing room. Lane dropped my hand and left me at the bottom of the wide, curving staircase, his long legs taking the steps two at a time. He stood for a moment at the top, grinning down at me, straddled the banister, and then he slid, very fast and quite gracefully — though I would not tell him so — back around the curve and to the bottom, where he leapt off, dark hair now wild from the brief burst of wind. I crossed my arms.

"You are not going to get me to do that." But we both knew he was going to get me to do that. "I'll get my dress dirty."

"Oh, no."

"I'll fall off and break my neck."

"My, my. Just make sure you fall off on the side with the stairs. Are you going up or not?"

"Do I have a choice?"

His smile was wicked. "Not really."

And inevitably I was sliding, the wind of my speed rushing past for a few precious seconds before I hopped off lightly at the bottom. He laughed when I ran up to do it again, and the next time I slid down he caught me, still laughing, and put his mouth on the bare place just beneath my ear.

When my eyes opened, it was to the dark of a bedchamber in Paris, my neck still warm and tingling.

I was ready to go early, too early, as the sun was not quite high enough to allow me to pin up my hair without a gaslight, though far enough along to let me ascertain that no one waited outside beside the lampposts. Mr. Babcock had reassured me again, advising me to be cautious, but not fearful, that this was most likely a quest for information, not my person, and that he would take care of the situation in due course. I wondered what that could mean. What could he do if the slouching man was from the French government, or if he was from the British, for that matter? I shoved in the last pin. Whatever it was, I was certain it was for the best. I'd never known Mr. Babcock to do otherwise.

I stood up from the dressing table and examined the mirror. The bruise on my cheek had lightened, the cut on my neck hardly showed, and I had a bag with me that matched my dress, a dusky slate blue, holding my passport and all the French documents Mr. Babcock had given me. Proper or no, I did not plan on finding Lane in a mourning dress. The silver swan glistened dully in the gaslight, and my grandmother looked down on me from her portrait, now hanging on the wall beside the bed. Eighteen months of being powerless to affect my situation, and today I was stepping forward to change that. My feet fairly flew up the stairs to the next landing.

But Mr. Babcock's bedchamber door was still shut, and there was no sound when I pressed my ear to the door. So I went downstairs alone, ignoring the temptation of the banister, set my bonnet ready on the table in the foyer, and went through toward the dining room, where I stopped, openmouthed, in the doorway. The crystal and gilt chandelier was sparkling, reflecting brilliantly on the carved surface of the sideboard, where a feast had been set: scones, croissants, marmalade, tea and chocolate, bacon, sausage, boiled eggs, kidney, and I knew not what else under the silver dish covers.

I sighed. Mr. Babcock had had some sort of talk with Mrs. DuPont, to "make matters clear," as he put it, the result of which had been to pat me on the arm, say that all was "understood," and that he had given Mrs. DuPont seven days to find other accommodations with the strict stipulation of remaining downstairs. I suspected that a substantial chunk of money might have gone with this. Mr. Babcock was the shrewdest man I knew, but his heart did have its soft places; I trusted him to deal with governmental spies more than I did the wily Mrs. DuPont, who was nobody's fool. Dinner last night had been exotic, delicious, and overabundant and, like this morning's breakfast, told me without question that she planned to play every card in her hand, to make herself indispensable and intimidating all at once. I would have to put a stop to it; the waste was a crime. But I decided to do so after I'd eaten.

Thankful there had not been a single soul to see how I stuffed myself, I stole quietly back upstairs, four scones wrapped in a napkin.

The sun was bright now. I could hear horse hooves and French noise coming from the street, and a peek through the shutters showed me an empty lamppost. When there was still no movement from Mr. Babcock's room, I set aside my growing impatience, continued up the stairs, unlocked the storeroom, and slipped through the shelf door.

The workshop was beginning to look like a workshop now, littered with the debris that was the hallmark of my uncle Tully's presence. He sat cross-legged on his floor pillow, white head hunched over some sort of paper, the epicenter of a metallic explosion that had scattered tools and little bits to every corner of the room. Mary came out of the bedchamber, folding a blanket.

"Ain't you gone yet, Miss?"

"Mr. Babcock is still asleep, I'm afraid. Here, I've brought Uncle Tully some scones."

"Well, good luck to you getting him to eat them," Mary commented. "It's playtime."

"I can see that." Uncle Tully was intent on his paper, a pamphlet called *Philosophical Magazine*, which he held exactly one inch from his battered face. I had watched him examining this for a good part of the afternoon yesterday, but now he had some sort of wooden box beside him, not clockwork as far as I could tell, but with two small poles sticking up from the top on either end, wires connected to four of the fluid-filled jars I'd seen the day before. I frowned at his wrinkled jacket. "Has he been doing that all night?"

"Most of it, I'm thinking, Miss. He's needing rest, but he's all out of schedule, and you know there's no talking sense to him when —"

"Little niece!" Uncle Tully called suddenly. He had looked up, his eyes bright globes of burning blue, shining out over the blackened bruises beneath. "Come here! Quick! It is ready! Come quick!"

I went to my uncle and crouched down beside him.

"Look, Simon's baby. You must watch carefully. It is not out of my head. This is from someone else's head, but it is splendid, just the same. . . ."

He had a clock key connected to a little lever, almost like a telegraph key, with wires running from it to the wooden box. I could not imagine what this key was for, but when he pushed it down, suddenly there was a spark, a strange crackling, and blue flame shot between the two poles on the top of the box. I jumped back, nearly sitting down in my surprise as Mary shrieked. My uncle let go to clap his hands, and the blue flame disappeared.

"Is it not right?" he cried. "Is it not just so? It is lightning, Simon's baby! A machine that makes lightning!"

He pushed the key down again, held it, and an even bigger flame sparked and shot between the poles, the noise like insect wings, or meat sizzling on a hot pan, or maybe the crinkling of dressmaker's paper. Or perhaps all of them at once. I stared at the sparking blue fire that almost hurt my eyes. It really was lightning, I realized, electricity in a box. Where had Mr. Babcock procured the parts to make such a thing? "Did you build this yourself, Uncle?"

He shook his head. "The pieces were in the box, and the pictures were in the book. This is from someone else's head. But I made it different. When you make it different, the lightning is . . ."

His words trailed away, and I saw that he was gone from me, lost in the smoothly ticking mechanisms that were inside his head. I stood up slowly, so as not to disturb, and went to set the scones on the table. Mary was still standing where she had pressed herself at the sight of the first spark, flat against the wall.

"That ain't natural, Miss," she said, her eyes on the little wooden box.

"Oh, I don't know, Mary. Perhaps it's as normal as rain, only we've just been raised in a desert."

Mary peeled herself from the wall cautiously, nose wrinkling. "What can you be talking of, Miss? When have you ever been going to the desert? That's nonsense, that's what my mum would say."

"Never mind," I said, before I got an earful of the wisdom of Mrs. Brown. "Run down to the dining room before I have to go, and get yourself some breakfast. There's a king's feast set up in there. And if Mrs. DuPont says a word about you eating at the table, tell her she'll have Mr. Babcock to deal with. I'll stay with Uncle Tully. He looks like he'll be busy for a good while."

Mary nodded. "That's the truth and no mistake. You'll be gone for the day, then?"

"Yes. As soon as Mr. Babcock wakes up."

"You're looking right nice today, Miss," she said suddenly. "I hope you . . . I'm hoping it all goes the way you'd be wanting it to."

"Thank you, Mary," I said, but my smile went away as I watched her inching her way past Uncle Tully's machine. The words had been kind, but they had also been laced with tiny threads of pity.

Forty-seven minutes later, Mary returned and Mr. Babcock had still not emerged. So I went downstairs, found Marguerite, gave her some coins, and with my smattering of French and a strange game of charades, succeeded in sending her out to buy me a map of the city.

As eager as I was, I hated to wake Mr. Babcock. He was not young, and had been working tirelessly on my uncle's behalf since this entire business started. I wondered what he had left behind in London, and when he would have to leave me to my own messy affairs and return to his own.

Marguerite gave me some change and a curtsy. I smiled and put the change back in her hands — she couldn't help having her mother, after all, any more than I could help having Aunt Alice — and spread out my new map and the official invitations on the tea table, trying to ascertain where I actually was and where I wanted to go. Someone knocked at the front door, and my heart sank. I'd thought to be long gone before Mr. Marchand came, or hoped that he might forget his fancy and never come at all.

I stood, smoothing two or three errant curls, and went to peer out the window. The red doors were not in sight, the angle was too sharp, but what I did see was the slouching man, hands in pockets, propped against the stones of the house that was directly across the street. I stepped back from the window. No matter how Mr. Babcock tried to soften my fear, the man had my pulse throbbing against the tight material of my dress. And then Mr. Marchand was in the salon.

"*Bonjour*," he said, bowing formally, sleek and preened as always in an immaculate suit. "You see how I am behaving, Miss Tulman. No kisses today, though you are looking so very beautiful."

I closed the shutter with an angry *snick*, hiding away the sight of the slouching man. How Mr. Marchand could manage to find the exact words that would irritate me every time he opened his mouth was a mystery. He must have seen me bristling because he turned to my maps and papers, still spread out on the table.

"You are planning your day, Miss Tulman? And where is your escort, this Mr. Babcock?"

"He will be ready shortly, Mr. Marchand. I'm sorry to have caused you an unnecessary trip, but I did say there would be no need. Please stay and have a cup of tea if you like, but I'm afraid I must say good day to you. I have several things to attend to."

And before he could respond, I had given him a curtsy, hurried out the door, and away up the stairs. Exhaustion or no, Mr. Babcock needed to wake. The morning was wearing on, and he would want to know that the man was once again outside, watching the house.

I knocked softly on his door. "Mr. Babcock?" When there was no response, I turned the knob, peeped inside, and then threw the door wide. The room was empty, the bed neatly spread up, Mr. Babcock's coat, hat, and cane all missing. I had been waiting all this time and Mr. Babcock had been gone, perhaps since before I got up, and without even the courtesy of a note.

I bit my lip, disappointment flowing bitter and out of all proper proportion. The morning was mostly gone, and perhaps the one institution I would not now get to visit was the one that actually held what I sought. And despite my saucy declarations during yesterday's miserable tea, how many of these places were actually going to allow a woman inside unescorted? Not many. Perhaps none.

I marched back downstairs and into the salon, the bonnet I'd left on the foyer table now snatched up and in my hand. Mr. Marchand dropped my map and jumped to his feet.

"I accept your offer, Mr. Marchand. Would you mind if we left by the courtyard?"

CHAPTER SIXTEEN

The next on your list is Charenton, Miss Tulman. Would you prefer a carriage, or . . ."

"Walking is fine, Mr. Marchand, as long as we do it quickly."

He grinned. "I think that wheels will get you there faster than your feet, Miss Tulman, though you do walk with such a hurry."

I relented, ignoring his amusement — everything I did seemed to amuse him — and we boarded an omnibus, climbing up to the open second story. I paid little attention to our direction or Mr. Marchand's occasional comments as the horses pulled us through the rain-washed maze of the city streets. But I did look at the faces around us, noting each in my memory. So far I had seen nothing that would make me suspicious, no one in the same place twice, no one that seemed particularly interested in my person. I looked carefully all the same.

We had visited two hospitals that morning, one for those who could not pay, little better than a street gutter, and one for those who could, a fine building with swept floors and nurses that wore white aprons and served red wine. Though when it came to the end of a life, I was no longer convinced that the misery for those in clean beds was very less than for those in the filthy. It was all death, disease, and pain, and it had sickened me. But there had been no sign of Lane. The idea of finding him immediately, on my first day of searching, was ridiculous, of course. The practical side of me knew this. But the illogical half, growing larger by the minute, could not help but be disappointed.

"Come, Miss Tulman," said Mr. Marchand. I saw that the omnibus had stopped. He steered me out of my seat, down the narrow set of stairs, and onto the sidewalk. I looked behind as we walked, but if we were being followed, I could not see it.

Mr. Marchand led us up a narrow road that climbed a small cliff, dropping off to a creek and then a river below, stone buildings rising up on our other side. We reached a wrought-iron gate, and Mr. Marchand rang the bell. A burly man unlocked the gate, large and oxlike with his white sleeves rolled up — he gave me a twinge of homesickness for my gentle Matthew — and I silently handed him one of Mr. Babcock's papers. A quick glance and he ushered us through a pleasant courtyard of orderly trees and summer flowers at the end of their season, then into a grim building of stone.

I was struck by the smell as soon as we stepped inside, much as I had been in the other two hospitals, the overpowering stench of human bodies and waste, here overlaid with a perfumed soap that was nothing more than a translucent veil. We were in a long corridor of closed doors, iron bars across their tiny windows. And then I became aware of noise, a constant jabbering like a pack of worried dogs, punctuated by the occasional yell or scream. I kept my eyes in front of me, feeling the knotted place inside me twist. This was not a hospital. It was an asylum.

The burly man was replaced by a tiny nun, head and body swathed in white and black, a crucifix swinging gently from her belt as we followed her down the hall. Mr. Marchand translated as we went, something about the numbers of rooms and classes of patients and bowls of soup, but I hardly heard. Through the bars of the fifth door, I saw a man in a bare room with grotesquely twisting limbs; behind the seventh, another systematically pulling out chunks of matted hair; and in the twelfth cell, a man tied to a chair obviously made for the purpose, his shrieks a large part of the disturbance in the hall.

My feet moved on down the hallway, my breath coming in shallow gasps. I thought I had belonged in an asylum once, for a time had thought I was going to one. And I had never even known how much I should fear it.

After twenty-four doors, we left the hall and stood in a garden. People were about in the morning sunshine, all women this time, either busy or indolent, several Matthew-sized attendants stationed around and about, still, but watching. It was more peaceful here, without the noise or smell, these cases obviously not requiring the prison-like conditions I had just seen. A little boy, perhaps four or five, sat in the dirt along the path we were walking, hunched over two piles of small stones. His hair was uncut, a scratch on his arm scabbed and a bit swollen. He did not look up as we passed.

The child's silent play put me in mind of Davy, and the sight of him, alone, and in this place, set my teeth on edge. I tapped Mr. Marchand's arm. "Ask the sister why there is a child here," I whispered.

He spoke, listened to the little nun's response, and said, "The child is *débile*, not normal, he does not speak or let the others speak to him, though she says he is well-behaved when left alone. He was found at the door . . ." He listened again to the nun. ". . . eight days ago, tied in a basket. He will be taken to the Hospice des Orphelins, the place for the orphans, unless the doctors decide it is better to keep him here."

I watched the little boy with his stones, picking them up, putting them down, arranging and rearranging the piles while Mr. Marchand and the sister walked on down the path. I wondered if this was how Davy had been in that London workhouse, before Mr. Babcock brought him to Stranwyne, playing inside a shell of his own making to escape the horror of what lay just outside. I very much wanted to hit something. Or cry. And then I felt a touch on my hand.

A woman who had been sitting on a bench near the path now stood right beside me. She was small and bent, hair that might have once been blonde now graying, and she was lovingly stroking my hand. I suppressed the impulse to step away and instead stayed very still, afraid to upset her. Mr. Marchand and the nun were far down the path, deep in conversation.

"Such a pretty little girl," she said, caressing my hand as if it were a baby. "You should know my Charlie. Do you know my Charlie?" She looked up at me expectantly, smiling, her round cheeks succumbing to wrinkles.

"No," I said quietly, "I don't know your Charlie." And then I realized that this woman was speaking English, very good English, only a trace of French in her words. "Are you from England, Ma'am?"

She just smiled dreamily, staring at my hand. Her arms were covered in long, thin, running scars, disappearing beneath her sleeves. I shivered.

"My handsome Charles-Louis," she said. "He would not come to see his little Charlie, such a fine boy." She lifted two empty eyes to me. "Would you come to see him?"

Before I could answer, the tiny nun was there, speaking soothingly in French, helping the woman back to her bench. Mr. Marchand was at my elbow. "Could you ask the sister who she is?" I said, almost embarrassed by my relief.

He asked, and the nun shrugged. "Her name is Thérèse," Mr. Marchand translated. "She is a . . . a . . ." He thought a moment. "She is unmarried, a woman who claims the father of her child to be Charles-Louis Napoléon. Our emperor," he added, in response to my look. He listened again. "The sister says she is a quiet woman, but cannot be given sharp things and must eat with spoons."

The woman settled back onto her bench, turning her attention to unraveling the threads from her fraying skirt while someone on the other side of the garden cried out in a long stream of gibberish. I looked back to the child, still arranging and rearranging his stones. I would keep Uncle Tully out of a place like this if it took my dying breath. I realized that Mr. Marchand was watching me.

"Do you wish to leave, Miss Tulman?"

I kept my eyes on the child. "Mr. Marchand, would you please tell the sister I do not believe that child is slow. Tell her that he is adding and subtracting, and that someone should give him a slate, and teach him numbers, so that he does not have to use stones." I stood up a little straighter. "And no, Mr. Marchand, I do not wish to leave. I will see every room."

Mr. Marchand spoke quietly to the nun as we stepped back into the dimness of the asylum.

When the iron gate had locked behind us, I pulled my map from my bag, but Mr. Marchand took my arm.

"I will buy you a coffee."

I stiffened. "You shall not. I've no time for . . ."

"You will allow me to insist. I do not escort fainting young ladies about the streets of Paris."

I resented that statement and opened my mouth to say so, but all at once I was not quite sure that he wasn't correct. My head felt fuzzy, my vision swimming about the edges. I allowed myself to be pulled down the sloping street, around the corner, and to a shop with tables along the sidewalk. Mr. Marchand deposited me into an empty chair and took the one opposite, gesturing to a waiter.

"*Deux cafés,*" he said, "*et deux brioches.*"

"I want tea," I said, sounding like a child.

"And yet this time, Miss Tulman, you will take coffee. And while we wait, you can tell me all about this man you look for."

I sat still in my chair, the people on the sidewalk breaking around us like a wave, unconcerned pigeons scavenging beneath the tables. The dizziness in my head became a sharp pain behind my eyes. When I glanced up, Mr. Marchand had a coin in his right hand, making it disappear and reappear. It put me in mind of the Miss Mortimers' delighted shrieks, and for the first time I wondered just how much of this man might be a trick.

"Well, Miss Tulman?"

I had stalled, but my brain had not used the time to supply me with an answer. "What makes you think I am looking for someone, Mr. Marchand?"

He smiled, the little mustache broadening, the wind ruffling the perfection of his slick hair. "You do not like me, Miss Tulman. I cannot think why that would be."

"Because handsome young men should not act as if they know it," I blurted, biting my lip in instantaneous regret. I had been thinking more of the Miss Mortimers' opinions rather than my own. He laughed.

"You are very direct. About some things, that is. About others, Miss Tulman, you are not." Our coffee and a plate with some sort of fat buns arrived. He put the coin on the table and lit a cigarette while the waiter set out the cups and plates. When the waiter was gone, he said, "But I am glad you find me handsome. Perhaps more handsome than this man you search for, yes?"

"I did not say I was . . ."

He blew his foul smoke into the wind. "You look in every room, in every bed. But always, your eyes, they skip over the women, the very young, the old, and the men whose hair is brown or yellow. Tell me who he is then, this dark young man."

I sipped the bitter coffee, pondering the enormity of my mistake in being here with this man. Henri Marchand was not quite the idiot I had taken him for. I set down the cup. "If you wish me to be candid, then why don't you tell me exactly who you are, Mr. Marchand, and why you insisted on coming with me? I would think a young man in Paris might have something better to do."

"Than take a lady to a café? But that is exactly what every young man in Paris wants to do."

I waited, eyes narrowing until he stubbed out the cigarette and shrugged. "What do you wish to know? I am Henri Marchand, and I have just inherited the house of my father, the house that was taken when my family went to the guillotine, returned when France once again had a king. I can only hope we do not lose it again under the regime of the emperor, as others have. I went to school in England, and for now I am what they call the 'man of independence.' I met the two Miss Mortimers at the opera, and the good Mrs. Reynolds wishes me to take one of them into my house, which I will not. In the meantime, she feeds me good dinners. And I meet the most interesting company, like sharp-tongued young ladies of whom I hear the strangest stories, who have the excellent arm for throwing and whose cheeks go pink with anger, as yours are doing now, Miss Tulman."

He bit into a bun while I continued to stare. "So. Have you thought of the morgue, Miss Tulman? The day is ending, and it is on the way, more or less. I do not wish to offend, but it could be the more . . . what is the word? The more efficient place to start. You can look at the records, and rule that possibility from your search. And there is a viewing room for the public, for the latest finds, if your taste tends to such." He shoved the buns toward me. "Here, eat."

I ate, silent, as he knocked back his coffee like a shot of hard liquor, considering the morgue. If I could prove Mr. Wickersham a liar, if I could find no certificate of death, then perhaps Mr. Babcock might be more amenable to escorting me on my search, more willing to stay at home in the mornings. I certainly was not going again with the surprisingly observant Henri Marchand. He pushed back his chair.

"Come, Miss Tulman," he said, making the coin I hadn't even noticed was missing appear suddenly again on the table.

The morgue squatted near the banks of the Seine on a cluttered street, its chimneys belching black, gritty clouds. I did not wish to know what fuel made such a smoke. The tips of the towers of the Cathedral of Notre-Dame could just be seen through the hazy air, while below, people of all sorts milled about the morgue itself, a small but raucous crowd.

"The viewing room," Mr. Marchand explained. "It brings them, like a show."

I said nothing of my disgust. This was not where I wanted to look, to be, or to find. We threaded our way through the crowd and entered the building. A long, wide hallway extended to my left, its ceiling far above me, and I followed Mr. Marchand to the other side, going immediately to a door marked with a title in French that I could not read. Mr. Marchand's knock was answered by a rather scruffy man in an ill-fitted suit, and after a few moments of explanation, during which the man's replies took on the sound of irritation to my ears, we stepped into a small, paneled office smelling of stale cigars. I was thankful it smelled of nothing worse.

A long conversation ensued, the particulars of which I was not privy to. Several of Mr. Babcock's papers were laid out and perused on a large, scratched desk, the scruffy man's hands were thrown up in exasperation, and eventually he stormed out the door. Mr. Marchand grinned at me. Two minutes and the man was back, slamming a leather-bound book with brass clasps onto the desk. He marched back out again. I looked to Mr. Marchand, inquiring.

"It is the record," he replied, "of the bodies brought for the past sixteen months." His smile broadened as I immediately scooted my chair close to the desk and undid the brass clasps. "You would like my help, Miss Tulman?"

"No, thank you," I said primly, unwilling to give him the name that I knew was all he wanted.

I opened the book, then briefly closed my eyes, stung by my own stupidity. The book was in French, of course. I looked down the page, at the paragraph-like entries, and then flipped to the back, where the pages were still blank. "Are you sure this is all? It doesn't seem like much, for an entire city."

Mr. Marchand went to the door and asked a question of someone outside. He came back inside, brows drawn together. "Only the bodies that have no name," he said, "that is what is brought here."

He shrugged once, as if to say, *"How would I know?"* and I frowned down at the book. Then this would prove nothing to Mr. Babcock and was a waste of my precious time. I saw Mr. Marchand watching me sidelong, waiting for me to give up or ask for help. I turned my attention stubbornly to the pages, studying their arrangement. I was here now and might as well make the best of it.

The column on the left gave the date — I could manage that much with the French I knew, while to the right a paragraph was written. I could not pick out much of this, though the writing was quite neat, but as I looked at the next stiff page, and the next, I saw that at the end of each paragraph there was a name, sometimes in a different hand or a different ink, and sometimes instead of a name, there was merely *"non identifié."*

I smiled to myself. That was easy enough. With my smattering of French for colors and numbers, I could simply run through the names looking for either "unidentified" with its accompanying description of age and sex, or the name *Moreau*. The thought of seeing Lane's name in that horrible book made me dread the turning of each and every page, and I had to remind myself over and over that this was only for whatever little good it might do me with Mr. Babcock, and for my pride in front of Mr. Marchand. That I would find nothing in this book because Lane was alive.

I sighed when I got to the end of the entries, slumping down slightly in my chair. I had thought the book small, but so much recorded death was difficult to comprehend. There had been only one "unidentified" that was a possibility, and that only because of hair color; I doubted Lane could be mistaken for a man of fifty.

I stretched, feeling pleased with my failure. Mr. Marchand was gone, I saw; I hadn't noticed exactly when he had succumbed to boredom. And then I realized that the noise outside the office had gotten louder. Much louder. I left the book on the desk and stepped out the office door. The hallway was absolutely stuffed with people, a river of humanity flowing into the building, filling the long, wide space I'd noticed on my way in. I would have thought there was some sort of panic in the streets if it hadn't all sounded so jolly. I craned my neck, trying to look over the shouting, laughing crowd for the scruffy French official or Mr. Marchand, when a woman in a stained purple bonnet gave me a good-natured shove from behind. I was jostled, pushed, and then swept away as if I'd stepped into a running tide.

I was surrounded by bodies, mostly cheerful, but also too hot and too unwashed, children darting disconcertingly past my feet. The noise was overwhelming. I could not see around the heads and shoulders, but I quickly learned that my elbows were useful and employed them, murmuring insincere apologies as I forced a path sideways through the crowd. What could be happening to bring such a surge of people?

Finally I found the wall, and began scooting back along it toward the dingy office. A few people were going my direction now, peeling from the front to give those complaining behind them a turn, and I finally grasped what they were here for. The entire end of the hall was spanned floor to ceiling by a wall of glass. The viewing room. There must be something sensational behind that window, I surmised, some murder made infamous in the papers. I could see none of it, thankfully, only three sets of clothing, displayed high on a rope behind the glass.

And it was this, of all things, that pulled my gaze, drew it as unwillingly as my body had been swept through the crowd. I moved, back the way I'd just come, pushing my way past arms and backs, stepping on feet, ignoring grumbles and curses in French. Someone knocked my bonnet from my head, and it was lost beneath the tramping feet. But I did not stop until I was pressed into the little iron fence that separated me from the glass.

Three bodies lay on display, slabs tilted to the crowd and heads propped up for our inspection. What the people had come to see was undoubtedly in front of me, a woman, bare-chested and cruelly cut. The part of me that was aware knew I was horrified by this, but the rest of me could comprehend nothing, because the body to her left had turned me into something made of stone, stone that melted in an instant from a rocklike numbness to fiery, liquid pain.

My chest squeezed, my throat clamped closed; I wanted to cry out, and could not. A woman in the crowd jostled me from behind and I pushed her back, hard, barely aware of what I was doing. All I could think was that I knew the head, the arms, every feature of the swollen, blue, and now lifeless face that lay on the slab behind the glass. I knew every flower of the horrible waistcoat, now mud-stained and dripping water to the floor from where it hung.

It was Mr. Babcock.

CHAPTER SEVENTEEN

*I*t was late when the hired carriage rolled to a stop before the red doors.

"We are arrived, Miss Tulman," Henri Marchand said. I nodded and sat up straighter, trying to rouse myself enough to climb out of the carriage without his help. I'd made a scene in the morgue, given the crowd their money's worth, I'd wager, until Henri Marchand found me and took me back to that hateful little office while we waited for the police. Mr. Babcock had been found in the Seine, in the "dead nets" as they called them, strung across the river to keep the city's rubbish from flowing downstream. There were no signs of violence on his body, so his death was being considered an accident, but I knew better. Mr. Babcock had never done anything "by accident." Someone had taken his life from him, and the noisy grief I had suffered in the shabby morgue office was as much about the utter wrongness of it as the pain of losing my dearly loved friend.

Obviously Henri had thought to send a note ahead because, before he had finished speaking to the driver, the red doors burst open and I was in Mary's arms. Mary got me inside, locked the door behind us, and then took me up the stairs, her own eyes red and swollen. She turned to me on the landing, my hand still in hers.

"You've got to be going to the attic, Miss," she said, holding her voice low. "Mr. Tully is —"

"Is he all right?" I was late. Horribly, horribly late. Again. I had been consumed with my own grief when I should have been worrying about my uncle. "Has he hurt —"

"No, Miss. He's angry, but he ain't hit his head or the like. It's strange. It's still playtime, been playtime ever since you was gone, Miss. He's all out of sorts and can't think of nothing else. But he does need you, Miss, and I'm sorry you can't even be taking a moment, but first . . ." She drew a deep breath. "You have to be telling me. Do you know? Do you know who . . ." She couldn't finish.

I shook my head. I was frightened almost out of my wits, and I still didn't know exactly whom I should fear, other than everyone. I put a foot on the next stair, but Mary's hand pulled me gently back.

"One more thing you ought to know, Miss. Mostly I've been with Mr. Tully today, you understand, but I've been keeping a sharp eye to the window, and that man, the one by the lamppost, well, he was leaving sometime in the afternoon, and then sometimes I was downstairs, Miss, and . . ."

"Of course, Mary." I didn't expect her to stay above stairs every hour of the day. She dropped her voice to a hoarse whisper.

"Well, I was in the kitchen, getting Mr. Tully some things to eat, and that little Marguerite was there, and Mr. DuPont, Lord love him — that little girl is a wonder with the man, Miss — and I told them I was that fond of toast, which is why I was making so much, and . . ."

"I understand."

"And I noticed a young man, Miss, at the back door, talking real low with Mrs. DuPont, and . . ."

My body jerked. "What do you mean? What sort of young man, Mary? English or French?"

"I weren't certain, Miss, and when I was asking the old bat when she came into the kitchen — she acts like I ain't allowed in the place, Miss, which sets my teeth on edge, as you can —"

"What explanation did she give?"

"She said it were the boy delivering groceries, only I didn't see no groceries, Miss, so when I was back upstairs again I just took a peek through that funny little window, you know, Miss, the round one that looks out over the back into that garden what belongs to all the houses, and there she was again, Miss, talking to a man, only this was a different one than the first time. And she gives him a little package and off he goes."

"A package?"

"That's right, Miss, and it happened again, only with the same man what didn't have the groceries before. And again later in the day. I'm not knowing how many times I didn't see, Miss. But I thought you was needing to know." Mary's lip trembled slightly. "Whatever are we going to do, Miss?"

I didn't have the heart to tell her or myself that I just didn't know.

"Late!" my uncle shouted. "You are late, late, late, and late!"

He was standing in the middle of his workshop, his fists clenched, all glare and shadow from the light of the gas lamps. I was struck suddenly with the impression of a nursery, only with hammers and files and pieces of metallic humans instead of tin horns and toy soldiers. I listened to Mary carefully locking the storeroom door behind me, and tried to pull myself together. It was amazing that Uncle Tully had not gone into a full-blown tantrum when I missed my appointed time that evening. He'd taken apart several of the room's wooden chairs, but that appeared to be the worst of it. I could not let him see the terrible state I was in lest he decide to reverse his progress and have a tantrum now.

"I'm very sorry, Uncle," I said, straining to find my normal voice. "Sometimes it is hard not to forget."

He considered this as I pretended to straighten my skirt. "That is true, Simon's baby," he said. "Sometimes I forget. But I waited already. And the girl was unhappy." I glanced at Mary, wiping her cheeks as she shut the bookshelf door and hurried away toward the little stove. "I waited for twenty, and then I waited more. . . ."

"I know you did, Uncle. You are so good at that now. I think it is splendid that you were able to wait so long. Marianna would be so pleased."

He fidgeted while he thought about this, plucking at the jacket. I watched him waver, then all at once tip to the side of contentment. "That is just so, little niece. Just so. But come, come here quickly. Hurry up!"

I followed him over to the box that had made the blue "lightning," created from the parts that Mr. Babcock had brought him. I turned my face just slightly away, so my uncle would not see the fresh pang of grief the thought had brought me. Uncle Tully was bouncing on his toes.

"It is a new toy! A new toy, Simon's baby! Now watch," he demanded. "It is new. Watch!"

I stood obediently while he pushed his little clock-key lever; the blue fire shot between the poles as before, and then, suddenly, a bell began to ring on the other side of the room. I spun, startled, thinking Mary was behind us, but there was no one. Mary was still at the stove, kettle in hand, her mouth slightly open, staring at a little bell that hung from a panel on the workbench. Its clapper was going back and forth, as if a hand were shaking it. Only there was no hand. There was nothing at all. My uncle let go of his lever, and the bell went still. I turned to look at him, my mouth a similar shape to Mary's. Uncle Tully clapped his hands.

"Is it not just so, little niece? Is it not just right?"

I did not understand. Down the lever went again, and tendrils of blue electricity snaked between the poles, buzzing and crackling, oddly mesmerizing. I reached out a finger.

"No!" my uncle bellowed. "No, no!"

I jerked my finger back, again wracked with guilt. I really was not myself. I knew better than to touch one of Uncle Tully's things. He was panting, his eyes very bright, but all he said was, "No, Simon's baby. The lightning will hurt. You do not touch the lightning. Never, never touch the lightning."

I put my hands behind my back while he made some minute adjustment to the wires and pushed down his lever. The bell rang instantly, and this time I hurried over to examine it while it rang, waving my hand in the air in front of it, looking for some kind of tiny string. But all I could find was a small wire, attached to one of the clear fluid-filled jars, the same sort of jar that was attached by wires to the lightning machine. And there was nothing else; the bell was ringing alone.

"How . . ." I stopped myself. Uncle Tully did not tolerate questions on "how" any better than he did touching. But somehow he was making that bell ring, making that blue spark fly through the air unseen. I wished Lane was here, seeing this. I wished I could have described it to Mr. Babcock. Once again, Uncle Tully had created something unbelievable, almost magical in its proportions. And this, I thought, was why Mr. Babcock had died. Because of Uncle Tully's wonderful and astonishing mind. I held an arm across the ache in my stomach, and then I realized that the bell had gone quiet. Uncle Tully spoke from just behind me.

"You are not splendid, Simon's baby, and neither is the girl. Did I do it wrong?"

I glanced back at Mary, who had been watching the bell with a handkerchief pressed to her mouth. I tried to smile, and then on second thought turned my face away. "You did it just right, Uncle Tully. The new toy is so very splendid. Where did you get the bell?"

"From the boat in the box with the other things."

I remembered seeing that now, the box of tin toys in the corner. There had been several boats with bells, much like the one we'd found in my grandmother's library at Stranwyne, the one Uncle Tully had made balance on its keel. Having the boats must have been important to him at one time, if Marianna had made sure to have them in Paris. But she was gone, just as Mr. Babcock was gone, and Lane was not here to help me either. How could I protect my uncle? How could I take care of everyone? So far I had taken care of no one at all. The knot in my insides was now an agonizing weight, the tears

I could not prevent rolling freely down my cheeks. The clocks in the room struck a multi-note clang, marking the half hour. I felt a feather-light touch on my sleeve.

"Here, Simon's baby," said Uncle Tully. I looked down to see the brass flower sitting in his palm. When I waited, he pushed it into my hand. "Here. You like the flower."

I took the intricate, shining thing, amazed at this freedom, feeling its weight like a bloom of pure gold in my hands. And Uncle Tully had given it to me to hold. He might as well have told me he loved me.

I woke once in the night, the moon shining down, making strange shadows in the workshop. A light shone from my uncle's bedchamber, dim, and I could hear him puttering around inside the room with soft, metallic clinks. Mary had made a sojourn downstairs for nightgowns and spread us a pallet of blankets on the carpeted floor — we'd both deemed it safer in the hidden workshop than on the lower floors — and I could hear her heavy breathing from just beside me, feel her warmth on my back, immeasurably grateful that she was with me. I lay awake a long time, staring at everything and nothing, tears wetting my loose hair and the pillow. Never had I felt so alone.

A touch on my shoulder and I sat straight up from the pallet on the floor, clutching hard at the blanket, the sun streaming in from the high windows making me blink.

"I'm that sorry to wake you, Miss, but you'd best be coming downstairs right away. There's a sight to be seen, Miss."

I stumbled upright, a bit stupid with sleep, feeling a heavy ache behind my eyes. I pulled the blanket around my nightgown, running a hand over my wild hair, which I'd neglected to braid, and forced myself to keep up with Mary's pace. She was fully dressed and in a hurry.

"Tell me what's the matter," I said, waking up enough to be frightened. But Mary only shook her head.

"Down here, Miss," she said, leading me down sixty-six stairs and into the salon, where she went to the hearth and stood, arms crossed over her apron. I could not understand what was upsetting her until I saw that there was something new on the wall, a piece of wood, screwed firmly into the plaster on one side of the chimneypiece, little white shavings all over the floor. I touched the wooden plank. It was part of a chair. A small box was attached to the wood, and from the bottom of this box hung a brass bell, just like I had seen last night on Uncle Tully's workbench. I turned to Mary in horror. Surely not. Surely Uncle Tully had not put that bell here? Mary's face was grim.

"Did you go out of the storeroom last night, Miss? 'Cause I know I was locking the door."

"I didn't, Mary, I swear it. And I remember that you locked it." I looked again at the innocent little bell. If Uncle Tully could make bells ring by themselves, I don't know what made me think a simple lock and key could keep him in. I looked down into the open top of the box and found the clear jar and the wire, just like last night. But Uncle Tully couldn't make this bell ring, not all the way downstairs? Could he? I looked to Mary, and her large eyes confirmed that he had, and he could.

"There's another one in my room, Miss, and in yours, one in the dining room, and one next to the convenience."

I dropped onto the settee. "Is he . . ."

"Sleeping like a lamb, Miss."

"But have you . . ." I ran a finger over my temple and lowered my voice. "Have you seen the DuPonts?"

Mary's voice followed suit. "That Mr. DuPont was creeping about early this morning, Miss, as soon as I came down the stairs."

"Do you think he could have seen Uncle Tully? Was he acting normally, Mary?"

Mary rolled her eyes, and I acknowledged the idiocy of the question with a shrug. "Well, if he was, Miss, then Mr. Tully will be all caught up good and proper on the state of that first Napoléon's health, that's all I've got to be saying about it. We . . ."

Mary fell silent as Mrs. DuPont came into the salon, her expression unaffected by the sight of me sitting downstairs in my nighttime dishevelment. "Your breakfast is in the dining room, Mademoiselle."

"Miss Tulman!" I said sharply, in no mood for niceties. Her mask of a face did not change as she held out a letter. I came to take it, she curtsied, and shut the salon door.

"Bat!" Mary blurted. "If it wasn't for the girl I'd say toss her on her backside, that's what."

I ripped open the letter and began to read.

"And what are we going to be doing about them DuPonts, Miss? Mr. Babcock was the one that had all that in hand, and you know that man is about by his lamppost this morning, Miss, watching our doors as bold as brass, shiftless as you please. How to even be taking a bit of air without . . . What is it, Miss?"

I looked up from the letter. "Mrs. Cooper says someone has dug up Uncle Tully's grave. She is quite upset about it. It happened during the night, two . . . no three days since. They've filled it back in again."

"Lord!" said Mary.

I dropped back into my spot on the settee. We thought this would happen, but now that it had, what did it mean? Did Wickersham know my uncle lived, or no? I pushed a finger against my throbbing temple. Seeing Mrs. Cooper's writing, like a little piece of Stranwyne in Paris, had left me shaken for other reasons as well. Mr. Babcock was to have been steward of the estate while I was away. How was I to safeguard my uncle and Mrs. Cooper, and manage the entire village as well, now that he was gone?

A noise interrupted my thoughts. The front door was opening, and I could hear Mrs. DuPont's French, and a deep male answer. I jumped up from the settee.

"She knows you ain't dressed, Miss, even she wouldn't . . ."

But Henri Marchand was through the salon door before Mary could even finish her thought, hat in hand, preened as always, stopping mid-stride at the sight of me. He did not smile, though his brows went up slightly, and he took me in from head to toe for a trifle longer than was strictly needful. I snatched up the blanket I'd left on the settee, wrapping it about myself like a shawl while Mary's hands went to her hips. She was bristling like an angry cat.

"A gentleman," she said loudly, "would turn himself about and be going out the way he came!"

If she had hissed and spat at the man, I would not have been surprised. Henri opened his mouth, undecided, took one step backward and that was when the bell beside the hearth rang, sudden and shrill.

I jumped, but Mary merely scrunched her freckles, her face a picture of pained resignation. Bells were ringing all over the house. I straightened my back.

"Mr. Marchand," I said over the noise. He pulled his gaze from the bell to my face. "I'm very glad you came. I wonder if you would mind escorting me next door?"

He opened his mouth, as if to ask a question, only to shut it once more. I could see him trying not to let his eyes wander.

"If you would be so good as to wait while I make myself decent? I shall take care of those bells and won't be a moment. Marguerite is having a bit of a joke with the bellpull, I suppose. I promise not to take more than a few minutes of your time."

I held the blanket ends together as I passed by his gaping face, Mary flanking me like the palace guard. I paused and turned around in the doorway. "Or wait in the dining room, if you'd like. I'd bet ten francs there's a breakfast in there fit to feed the emperor."

CHAPTER EIGHTEEN

When Mary ran upstairs to my uncle, the bells went quiet. I dressed quickly, pulling a brush through my hair's length from crown to waist, hoping Henri was focused on eating rather than any lack of strings on my uncle's bells. I needed to get next door without incident. There was at least one small safeguard I could accomplish today, one small something within my power, but it was going to require a humbling I dreaded. But doing anything, even something that would humiliate me, was better than sitting in wait for the next disaster. Mary flew in the door, breathless.

"He's up, Miss. And making his own toast, if you can credit it. But he was getting a bit of honey on the sleeve, and that's what the bells was for. I reckon he's thinking to push on his little key and make them bells ring every time he's needing something and we ain't there, heaven help us."

Heaven help us, indeed. She came over and pulled hard on my corset strings. And what in the world could Mrs. DuPont be thinking of all this? They would have to go today, if I had to find them rooms myself and pay for it. Then I paused in my planning and bit my lip. Mr. Babcock had taken care of all my money in Paris. At the moment I didn't even know where it was located. I'd had to borrow the price of his body from Mr. Marchand. If Mr. Babcock had not already paid Mrs. DuPont, there might be trouble much sooner than I was prepared to deal with it. When Mary tied the strings, I jerked on a dress, hurried to the desk in the corner, and began to write.

"Do you have any money, Mary?"

She looked up at me in surprise. "I ain't sure, Miss, I . . ."

"See if you can scrape up the price of a telegram. I need to get word to Mr. Babcock's offices. Look in my bags. Perhaps Marguerite will know how to get it sent?"

I scribbled out the last words. "And Mary, I need you to do another thing for me, just as soon as you send the telegram. Go to Mr. Babcock's rooms, box up all his things, especially his papers, and bring them in here . . . no, maybe up to the attics. The police are going to come and "seal" his possessions, or that's what they called it, because we are not relatives. We'll get them to the right person in due course. . . ." I realized I had no idea who that would be. "But he was bribing officials, Mary, and I don't know who to trust with his paperwork. And he's got all my money somewhere — I'm certain he never got it to a bank. And on second thought, do that first, before the telegram. Leave them a few clothes for show." I kissed Mary's cheek, for once not letting her get a word in edgewise, and went downstairs to find Henri shoveling eggs from plate to mouth. He stood at my appearance, dabbing the little mustache with a napkin.

"Miss Tulman, I am sorry to —"

I cut him off. "It's no matter at all, Mr. Marchand. Do you mind if we just go?"

I stayed rather close to Henri Marchand, even though he smelled strongly of cigarettes. The slouching man was at his lamppost, just as Mary had said, in his blue vest today, eyes following us. I'd forgotten my bonnet, and felt naked for it as we moved down the sidewalk. I knocked on Mrs. Reynolds's front door, feeling horribly exposed, and with my heart beating hard, making my headache worse. Henri shifted his feet.

"Miss Tulman, I wish to say that . . ."

"Do hush, Mr. Marchand. It was all my fault and there's really no need."

He hushed, and Hawkins opened the door, looking down on my bare head dubiously.

"Miss Tulman and Mr. Marchand to see Mrs. Hardcastle," I told him. "I shan't take up but a moment of her time, so if you would be so kind." I did not wait for an invitation, but came right past the startled Hawkins into the dim, overfilled foyer, letting Henri follow. "Shall we wait in the drawing room?" I opened the door myself and went into the drawing room before the poor man could say a word about it.

I sat down on the settee, hands in lap, while Hawkins went to inform Mrs. Hardcastle, and Henri opened the drapes, letting in the morning sun. He observed the street and then he sat as well, hat on his knee, regarding me.

"Are you well today, Miss Tulman?"

"Not particularly," I answered. He tilted his head slightly, acknowledging this likelihood.

"And you are in the midst of some trouble, no?"

"Oh, I am in the midst of some trouble, yes," I answered. I looked about the room. It was nicer, I thought, than the other rooms in the house. Perhaps Mrs. Reynolds had paid less attention to it, or had just not had the opportunity to fill it to capacity. I got up to examine the watercolor behind me, too restless to sit. I did not look at Henri when I said, "I do want to thank you, Mr. Marchand. Most sincerely. For your help at . . . and with the police. I was extremely . . . distressed."

"Miss Tulman, I . . ."

We both turned to the noise coming from the foyer, and then Mrs. Hardcastle, Mrs. Reynolds, and the two Miss Mortimers entered the drawing room in such an overabundance of taffeta I wondered if the ladies were having some sort of contest about who could wear the most. As they rustled through their curtsies and bows, Mrs. Hardcastle came immediately across the room and took me by the shoulders.

"My dear, what dreadful news. I am so sorry to hear of Mr. Babcock."

"Oh, indeed!" said the brown-frizzed Miss Mortimer. "What a shock for you, Miss Tulman. To have your heart broken yet again!"

She grimaced hard as the blonde Miss Mortimer stepped deliberately on her foot before flouncing down onto the settee beside Henri. He shot me the impertinent grin, the brown eyes amused, almost sparkling, one brow slightly up. Mrs. Reynolds gave me a cold nod and then smiled as she joined them, well pleased, evidently, by the seating arrangements.

"Mrs. Hardcastle," I said, voice lowering, "I would speak to you for a moment, if I might."

She raised the pince-nez, following me to two chairs arranged companionably together in front of a cabinet of curios. We sat, the two Miss Mortimers doing an excellent job of filling the other end of the room with chatter while I prepared to set aside my pride. Mrs. Hardcastle watched me expectantly.

"I will spare us both and be direct, Mrs. Hardcastle. I know we have not been friends, but I need to ask a favor of —"

I saw her give a start. "And why, Miss Tulman, do you think we have not been friends?"

I stared at her frank face, uncomprehending. Surely she couldn't have forgotten all that tea in Aunt Alice's morning room? Those moments were some of the most painful in my existence. Mrs. Hardcastle chuckled.

"Well now, don't look at me like that, my dear. If there was no friendship between us, it certainly wasn't on my side."

I blinked. This conversation was nowhere near the topic I had intended, but I could not let this pass. "Mrs. Hardcastle, for years you visited my aunt's home and showed her every consideration, tittering and laughing behind your cups while she treated me abominably, and you visited Stranwyne Keep — on her request, I remind you — and started the proceedings to have my uncle committed to a lunatic asylum. How exactly would you perceive such behavior as 'friendship,' Ma'am?" I could feel my cheeks burning, pent-up emotion boiling up hot from my chest. Mrs. Hardcastle raised her eyebrows.

"Why, whoever laughed at you, child? Alice's behavior was so ridiculous it was an absolute lark. Why do you think we ever came there? We were all waiting for the day you would stand up and tell her to go to blazes but apparently you did it without us, more's the pity. I'd quite looked forward to that."

I was so angry I could scarcely see straight. "And how was I to tell her to 'go to blazes' and still feed myself, Ma'am? Had you thought of that? Or did you think her incapable of putting me on the streets?" I'd nearly shouted this last, and the conversation on the other end of the room faltered for just a moment before resuming, though not without glances thrown our way.

"Miss Tulman," said Mrs. Hardcastle, moderating her voice, "let us be calm. How could Alice have turned you out without losing the income on your father's money, the money for your upkeep? You didn't really think Alice Tulman would have turned her back on those pounds to make a point to you? When the woman threw away money right and left? Ridiculous! Really, my dear, I would have thought you had more intelligence than —"

"Mrs. Hardcastle . . ." I leaned forward. ". . . I was not aware that I had one farthing from my father until I inherited Stranwyne Keep."

Mrs. Hardcastle sat back in her chair, the pince-nez plopping onto her bosom. "Really!" she said. "Well!" And then, inexplicably, she chuckled, and then she laughed. "Why, what a poisonous little toad that Alice Tulman is! Truly! She didn't tell us about that after you left, my dear, not by half!"

Though she'd told them plenty else, I'd wager.

"Well, that does explain a good bit," she said, sighing through her laughter. "You see . . ." She scooted forward to the edge of her chair, as if about to confide a secret . . . "I enjoy folly, Miss Tulman, in all its forms, not excluding my own. There is nothing more amusing than observing the foibles of others. It makes the day pass faster. And my, but didn't your aunt Tulman provide plenty to be amused about! I daresay I might have behaved differently had I known the true situation, though I'm not certain what good it could have done. To be honest, I've never considered Alice Tulman far beyond the occasional letter and our little morning teas. . . ."

Her gaze wandered over my head for a moment, then she smiled at me again. "But I must say that your uncle looked as if he belonged in an asylum to me, my dear. When he threw that hammer I can strictly promise not to have run so fast before or since. Another bit of fun I must thank you and your aunt for! Now . . ." She tapped me lightly on the knee. "I'm so glad we got that settled to satisfaction, Miss Tulman. What is it that you wished to speak to me about?"

It took me several moments to stop staring at Mrs. Hardcastle, to give up contemplating the result of living a life in which nothing worse had ever happened than a wrongly colored ribbon or a particularly vexing maid, a life so vain and pampered that the pain of others was nearly indecipherable. I clasped my hands together, reformulating my view of my childhood. Mrs. Hardcastle was not an evil woman, I decided, but her mind had the depth of a Parisian puddle, and it occurred to me that sometimes the result could be the same.

"Miss Tulman?" Mrs. Hardcastle prodded.

I took a breath. "It is my aunt I wished to speak to you about, actually. I was hoping to ask you for . . . a favor."

Her little eyes lit up behind the spectacles. "Anything!" she replied.

"My aunt Alice was afraid of Mr. Babcock, legally speaking, and she had good reason to be. I think as soon as she hears of his death . . ." I paused. "I think that she will seek to prove me incompetent and take Stranwyne Keep. On behalf of her son, of course."

Mrs. Hardcastle nodded her understanding.

"It may be some time before I can return to London and talk with anyone in Mr. Babcock's offices, and my affairs there could be in some disarray. I wanted to ask if you would keep up a correspondence with my aunt, and if . . . if you would not mention our meeting here in Paris. If you would be so good as to inform me of any plans or proceedings that are moving forward, I would be most grateful."

Mrs. Hardcastle grinned hugely, as if I had presented her with some sort of delectable tart. "Why, I would love to, Miss Tulman. Of course! I told you I relish folly, and a regular correspondence with your aunt is a veritable treat! And now that I am aware of some of the truer circumstances, I shall relish it even more!"

I smiled, perhaps the first genuine smile I'd ever given Mrs. Hardcastle. I had expected to beg, crawl, and flatter to win her to my side, and the relief of not doing so was intense. But even as the smile came, the expression froze on my face. My eyes had wandered to the little curio cabinet I had noticed before, just beyond Mrs. Hardcastle's shoulder. On the top shelf, behind the curved glass door, the light from the open curtain had caught on a collection of silver. Little animals, palm-sized, carved in intricate detail.

I leapt up from my chair, reached over Mrs. Hardcastle, and pulled open the curio's glass door, rattling the porcelain figures that stood precariously on top. I touched a silver dog in a dreaming sleep, a raven, a lumbering bear, and in the back, a fish. The posture of the fish was stiff, not natural like the others animals, as if its model had been made of metal plates. I grabbed it up. Tiny, minute rivets ran down the edges, levers entering the body from the fins. Not a replica of an animal, but of a machine.

I whirled about, facing the other end of the room. They were all watching me, the girls openmouthed, Henri with his forehead wrinkled, Mrs. Reynolds offended. Mrs. Hardcastle looked back and forth between us through the pince-nez. I held out the fish.

"Where did you get this?" I demanded of Mrs. Reynolds. When she did not answer, I looked at them all, my voice rising. "Where did you get these?"

"Whatever is the matter, Miss Tulman?" said the brown-frizzed Miss Mortimer at the same time her cousin was saying, "The little silver animals, you mean?"

I pounced on her question. "Yes, the animals! Where did you get them?"

Mrs. Reynolds's gaze on my face was a thing that could cut flesh. "Those works of art were made by Jean-Michel, Miss Tulman."

"Who?"

"The protégé!" cried the blonde Miss Mortimer. "Don't you remember? We told you all about the . . ."

The protégé. The artist who painted with clever fingers. The man who had not returned home.

I dashed from the room, throwing open the drawing-room doors to run up Mrs. Reynolds's stairwell, my mind moving much faster than my legs could. I was remembering my search through the house that first night in Paris, the room with the easels and cloth-covered canvases, on the top floor, second door to the right. I burst through the door, panting, the fish still clutched in my hand, slamming it behind me and turning the lock before I ran to the first easel and yanked off the cloth.

It was a painting of Stranwyne, the northeast side of the house, the brown stones blushing rose and orange in a dawn rising up from the moor hills. I pulled off the second cloth, and it was the village church with the graveyard beside it. The third painting was stones and rocky hills, a ruin I recognized at the top of the tallest one, but in the foreground of this picture stood a woman, her back to the painter, skirts and curling auburn hair blown wild by a strong north wind. The woman in the painting was me.

I raised the fish to my mouth, clutching it hard as I closed my eyes. Mrs. Reynolds's protégé had been Lane Moreau.

CHAPTER NINETEEN

I heard feet on the stairs but I ignored them. Instead I ransacked the drawers, also choosing to ignore the knocks, calls, shouts, and then thudding *bangs* that accompanied my search. There were shirts here I recognized, and the red cap, and the smell, I knew it. It made my heart quicken, both in recognition and fear. Wherever Lane had gone, he could not have taken much with him. I stripped the bed, where I found nothing but blankets and sheets, and then got on my knees to look underneath. A box with odds and ends, mostly painting supplies, and in the back corner, hiding from the maid's broom, a scrap of paper. I got two fingers on it before the door splintered around its lock. I caught a glimpse of four female faces peeking in before Henri stepped inside and casually shut the broken door behind him. It would not latch. He observed me in my position on the floor.

"Did you know it is very painful to do that?" he asked, rubbing his shoulder.

"It took you twelve times," I commented.

"I must practice, I think."

I remained on my knees, staring at the scrap of paper in my hand. It was torn and dirty, only part of a scrawled word visible, but the handwriting belonged to Lane. It said *Tuiler* and that was all. The paper was torn, the rest missing.

"So, who is he?" Henri Marchand asked, strolling across the floor to examine the paintings. He stopped before the third canvas, the one of me with my hair down and said, "Ah," as if I had answered his question.

I stood, eyeing the room. Other than the paintings, there was nothing else to look at, no other things to go through. I held out the scrap of paper to Henri.

"The Tuileries, perhaps?" he said after a glance. "That is the imperial palace. Or one of them."

He handed the paper back to me as the door creaked, and then Mrs. Reynolds was standing in the room with us, hands clasped in front of her. She opened her thin mouth to speak, but I spoke first.

"When was he last here? What day, exactly?"

"Ten days before you came to dinner, Miss Tulman. We had notified the police exactly one week before that."

Ten days before I came to dinner, so almost two weeks ago now. And only three days before the Frenchmen tried to kidnap Uncle Tully. "And what did the police say?"

"Nothing at all. They were of very little help, though he was a Frenchman."

"Half French," I said absently. "His mother was English."

"I think not, Miss Tulman," Mrs. Reynolds replied, voice taking on a wintry frost. "Jean-Michel barely spoke passable English."

"He was born in England, Mrs. Reynolds, and had never set foot in France until last year." She stared at me a moment, then her eyes roved about the room, as if seeing it anew. "How did you meet him?"

She put her gaze back on me. "He was working in a silver shop, not very far from here, around the corner from the Opera. I had already bought several small pieces. He was leaving his position. . . ."

"Leaving? What do you mean?"

Mrs. Reynolds frowned, but after a glance at Mr. Marchand, she said, "I mean that he no longer wanted to work in a shop, of course. Jean-Michel wished to pursue his talent rather than waste his time with trays and spoons. When he showed me his paintings, I offered to support his work."

"And he lived here how long, Mrs. Reynolds?"

"About seven weeks," she replied. "Only seven weeks."

The wistfulness in her voice made me almost like her. "Thank you, Mrs. Reynolds." I glanced about the wrecked room. "I do apologize for the . . . consternation I caused, and for the state of your door. I will arrange to have it repaired. Would you . . ." I hesitated, then held up the silver fish, the replica of the "toy" that had caused Uncle Tully, Lane, myself, and two governments no end of trouble. "Would you allow me to keep this?"

I think she heard my thinly veiled plea. After a long moment, she inclined her head and I left the room, stepping around the gaping Miss Mortimers, curtsied to Mrs. Hardcastle, and then turned and walked right back in again. I marched past Mrs. Reynolds, snatched up the red cap, this time without asking, and took to the stairs. I was halfway down before I realized that Henri was with me.

"I wonder if you would tell me, Miss Tulman," he said quietly, "if Mrs. Reynolds's Jean-Michel was ever a servant of your house?"

I would not dignify the question with a response. But my lack of answer must have been the same as an affirmative, for he replied once again with an "ah."

"And I think, perhaps," he continued, "that this Jean-Michel was also a young man with dark hair, yes?"

I did not answer this either.

"Well. Then I think that this time you will come with me, Miss Tulman, and let us see if we cannot continue the work of the morning."

He took me by the arm, bringing me down Mrs. Reynolds's stairs at a trot and out the front door.

The day was growing warm and fine, but instead of turning left to the red doors, Henri let go of my arm, stepped into the street, skirted around a slow-moving carriage and made a beeline for the opposite sidewalk. The slouching man straightened when he saw him coming, his unshaven face registering the danger rather late, as he had only taken one step away before Henri had him by the arm. I felt my mouth open slightly.

The man struggled once, but Henri was larger and his grip must have been strong, because the slouching man went limp and decided to go without a fight. He allowed himself to be led back across the street, and I hurried down the sidewalk, just in time to follow them both through the red doors and into my foyer.

Mrs. DuPont was there when we entered, watching, cadaver-like, as Henri pulled the man inside the house.

"Where?" Henri asked, eyes on me.

"Dining room," I said quickly. "The door locks."

He had begun to move in that direction when Mrs. DuPont said, "The police were here to see you, Mademoiselle, and to take the things of the little man who is dead. I told them I can say nothing, that I know nothing of you. . . ."

"*No gendarme!*" the slouching man yelled. "*No gendarme!*"

I thought I could glimpse the beginnings of an actual expression on Mrs. DuPont's face, a slight widening of the eyes before I shut the pocket door of the library and went through to the dining room. Henri put the man in a chair at the table while I set the red cap and the little slip of paper carefully on the sideboard, beside the covered remnants of breakfast. The key hung from a string on the door frame. I used it to lock both doors, and then sat, the fish still cradled in my hands.

Henri leaned back in his chair, playing with a spoon. The slouching man watched him warily. "*Parlez-vous anglais, mon ami?*" Henri asked.

The man's eyes shifted back and forth between us. He was a bit older than I had thought, with gray in his hair, and the lined face of a laborer. "A little English," he said carefully.

"Ask him why he chased me into the courtyard four nights ago," I said. He watched me speak, then looked to Henri for the translation. When he understood the question, his words came quickly, low and earnest. Henri turned to me.

"He says he did not chase the young woman, that he wished her no harm. That the lady could not get into her house, that she was on the street alone with the lamps out, and that he followed to make certain she found her own door."

The man's gaze again darted, trying to decipher the English and my reaction to it. I shook my head, disbelieving. "Ask him why he has been watching my door at all, then?"

This was done, and the man frowned. He stared down at the little sugar spoon traveling through Henri's fingers, and then up at my face. He spoke quietly, making Henri lean forward to hear.

"He says he is waiting for a man, that this man was to have come six days ago, but that the man has not come as he was meant to. He says sometimes it takes days for the man to come, but not this many days." The slouching man spoke again, and Henri said, "He says he is waiting, and then a young lady arrives in a carriage — that is you, Miss Tulman — and that he knows her face. He thinks he has seen it before." Henri asked a short question in French, and his dark eyes swung back to mine after the man's response. They were dancing. "He says that he has seen your face in a painting."

I met the eyes of the slouching man, who was studying me intently, as if by staring he could break the barrier of language between us. I raised my hand from my lap and placed the little silver fish I'd held tight to my palm between us on the table. The man's face transformed, lines curving upward in a smile. "Jean-Michel," he said.

I leaned forward, hands pressed flat on the table. "Where is Jean-Michel?" I said, taking away the man's grin.

The slouching man also leaned forward, our faces just a few feet apart before he began to speak. Henri said, "He was hoping you would tell him. That you would know. He is worried."

"Then if he doesn't know where he is, ask him how he knows him, why he was waiting to speak with him. Ask . . ." I had to stop the questions from tumbling from my mouth. Henri spoke, and the slouching man returned with a sharp question of his own.

"He says that he knows who you are, he knows your face. But he wants to know if I am trustworthy."

"Are you?" I asked.

Henri's shoulder went up elegantly, the insolent smile at one corner of his mouth. "Of course."

I thought of the twelve ramming thuds of his shoulder against Mrs. Reynolds's attic door, looked back at the slouching man, and nodded once. The man stared thoughtfully at the table, then the words began to flow in a smooth rhythm. Henri kept up a simultaneous translation.

"His name is Joseph LeFevre. He is a metal worker, and met Jean-Michel thirteen months ago in a silver shop on the Rue Basse-du-Rempart. And yes, Miss Tulman, that would be rather close, as Mrs. Reynolds told you. Joseph says that Jean-Michel was able to do him a favor at one time, a favor that meant much to him, and in return, he was able to find out things that Jean-Michel wished to know."

Henri paused, listening. "He says he has much family in Paris, brothers and cousins, all men that can close their mouths — he means hold their tongues, Miss Tulman — and that Jean-Michel pays for little jobs to be done, finding out about things, about the buying and selling of metals and certain . . ." Henri hesitated. ". . . chemicals, and the building of ships, and that this has put bread on the tables of his nieces and nephews. He says that Jean-Michel has no love for the emperor, or this war. . . ." The translation halted as Joseph sighed. "But always, he says, Jean-Michel is searching for a man."

I did not have to ask the name of the man. It was Ben Aldridge. "And what did Jean-Michel find? Ask him that."

Henri listened to the man's response and said, "He does not know. He says Jean-Michel never tells him why, or what his information means. . . ." Henri smiled at the flow of French coming from the slouching man, his eyebrows rising slightly. "But he says that if Jean-Michel asked him to fight another Waterloo, then he would fight another Waterloo, and sing while he did so, and that his brothers would do the same. Because Jean-Michel, he is like them, but he is not like them. He is *noble*." Henri put his dark eyes on me. "That must have been a very large favor your servant did, would you not agree, Miss Tulman?"

I didn't answer. I was watching Joseph, who was still speaking, his eyes on mine. "He says after Jean-Michel left the silver shop, they were to meet regularly at Rue Trudon, but now Jean-Michel is not here. And he says there are men watching the house."

I drew a quick breath. "English or French?"

"French," Joseph replied directly. "They are . . . *discrets*."

"The men are discreet," Henri translated. "*Combien?*"

"*Trois,*" the man answered.

Three Frenchman watching the house. The emperor, then, not Mr. Wickersham. I retrieved the slip of paper I'd found beneath Lane's bed, sliding it across the dining-room table until it lay beside the fish. "Does this mean anything to you?" I asked.

Joseph glanced at it and shook his head, pushing it back toward Henri, who told him what it said. The man frowned. "*Soyez prudent, Mademoiselle.*"

"He says you should be careful, Miss Tulman," said Henri.

"Ask him if he saw Mr. Babcock," I said. "The small man who arrived in the carriage with me."

When he had finished asking, Joseph spoke quickly. "Yes," Henri replied for him. "He left with two of the men who had been watching. Early in the morning, the day before yesterday."

I let out my breath. Mr. Babcock left with two Frenchman. So that crime was at the hands of the emperor, too. The fury that had accompanied my grief stretched out for the idea of Napoléon III like Uncle Tully's snaking blue electricity was drawn to the next pole. Obviously the emperor must believe the weapon my uncle could produce was powerful indeed, much more valuable than one lawyer's life. But how could he know that my uncle was not dead? Unless it was French agents that had opened Uncle Tully's grave, and not Mr. Wickersham's men?

Joseph was still talking. Henri interrupted with a quick question, listened, and then said, "He says it did not look like an unfriendly meeting. But he did not see the little man come back. I do not think he knows your friend is dead."

Joseph's face blanched at the word. "*Mort?*" he asked, looking back and forth between us. Henri spoke, evidently explaining while Joseph shook his head. When Henri had finished, the man spewed forth French at such a speed that I could not catch a word.

"He says your business is dangerous, that he worries for his family and Jean-Michel, and that he and his brothers will watch no more." When Henri stopped talking, Joseph gave me one more long look and held out a calloused palm.

"He wishes you to give him the key, Miss Tulman," said Henri.

"Wait. Ask him where we can find him, and will he come to us if he hears of Jean-Michel?"

This was done and Joseph said, "Rue Tisserand," as he nodded. I put the key to the dining-room door in his hand. He said something quickly to Henri, unlocked the door, left the key in the lock, and after another moment I heard the front door slam. The slouching man was gone.

I turned to Henri. "What did he say? At the end?"

"He said that I should watch out for you, for Jean-Michel's sake. That Jean-Michel used to talk of your beautiful hair."

I got up and went to the sideboard, to see if the tea might still be hot, but mostly to keep Henri's teasing eyes away from my face. I touched the red cap that sat there.

"Such amusing times I spend with you, Miss Tulman. Truly, it is never dull."

I did not find it amusing in the slightest. Henri lit a cigarette. I let go of the hat, but did not turn around when I said, "Mr. Marchand, would you take me to the Tuileries? Are there public rooms?"

He blew out smoke. "I might take you, perhaps. If you are truthful with me."

I turned around. "You think I am dishonest?"

"Maybe you do not lie, and yet you do not always tell the truth."

"I can go to the Tuileries on my own."

"No, Miss Tulman," he said, teasing set aside. "No, I think you cannot."

I thought of Mr. Babcock, canny and shrewd in his horrible waistcoat, and felt a sharp ache in my chest.

Henri asked, "Who are these Frenchmen that watch your house?"

"I don't know."

"Yet you thought they were perhaps English."

"It seemed a logical question."

"And who is this man Jean-Michel was looking for?"

I saw Ben Aldridge as I'd last seen him, his look of curiosity as I aimed the rifle scant seconds before his boat became a fireball. "He is no one. A dead man."

Henri smiled as he blew a puff of smoke. "And you were also looking for a dead man, Miss Tulman. And now you seem to have found him."

I had found nothing. Nothing that had brought him to me. I grabbed a handful of the red cap. Ten days since Lane had not returned to Mrs. Reynolds's house, seven weeks he had lived there before that, and Mr. Wickersham had informed me of his death nearly two months ago. What had happened? He had left British employ and become the protégé of Mrs. Reynolds at about that time, that much was certain. But to what purpose? Certainly not to "pursue his art." I knew Lane better than that. Could he have been arrested quietly, as a spy? Is that why Mr. Wickersham could or would not claim him? And yet Joseph had said he was to meet Lane six days ago at Rue Trudon, and Lane had been gone from Mrs. Reynolds's for ten. Had he left on purpose? And if so, what had happened since? Joseph had not seemed aware of Lane's ties to Britain or Mr. Wickersham, or anything concerning my uncle at all, but perhaps this was calculated as well. All Joseph had admitted was Lane's dislike of the emperor, the man who had killed Mr. Babcock.

My thoughts swirled in confusion, and I felt the tears once again threatening my eyes. *I do my utmost for the house of Tulman,* Mr. Babcock had once said. And as Uncle Tully was at this moment sitting safe in his attic, that must have been exactly what Mr. Babcock had done. To the very end.

I looked up to find Henri watching me closely. All this time I had been still, squeezing the knitted yarn of the red cap. "Will you take me to the Tuileries?" I asked again. A flimsy clue at best, but it was all I had.

But before he could answer, Mrs. DuPont flung open the dining-room door. She was animated, flushed, actually suffused with a pale pink color that made her look distinctly . . . alive. I felt my eyes grow wide as she hurried to the table and handed me an envelope. Large, made of thick, pale ivory paper, and with a very official-looking seal pressed into red wax. I cracked the seal, looked over the contents without comprehension, and silently handed the letter to Henri.

He ran his eyes over the words and said, "I think there will be no need to escort you to the Tuileries today, Miss Tulman. You are invited there tomorrow. To the emperor's ball. And you are invited by Napoléon himself."

Mrs. DuPont erupted into excited speech that seemed to be for no one but herself while I looked again at the invitation. I saw my name now, formally inked in the midst of the print, and I felt the chal-lenge, just as clearly as if I had been slapped on the cheek by my enemy's glove. I had been called out. And then Mrs. Hardcastle was in the dining room, breathless, barely able to utter her words.

"Saw the royal messenger from the window, my dear. Is it so?"

I handed her the invitation. Henri stubbed out his cigarette and immediately pulled out another.

"It is so!" cried Mrs. Hardcastle. "Oh my, but won't the Miss Mortimers be jealous! But what shall you wear, my dear? I'm certain you don't have a thing. We'll have to call in a seamstress, immediately, this very morning, or . . ."

I sat down at the table, trying to sift what I knew, to order, to sort, to calculate. What could I gain by facing the emperor? And yet, now that the enemy was clearly defined, what else was there? Despite all my best efforts, despite all that had happened, Uncle Tully was not safe, none of us were, and Lane was as lost to me as the day he left Stranwyne. And what of Uncle Tully? What if I left this house and did not return, like Mr. Babcock? Like Lane?

"Shall you go?" asked Henri, his voice low beneath the chatter. Mrs. Hardcastle was now discussing my clothing possibilities with Mrs. DuPont, of all people. I glanced at the invitation still in her hand, fluttering about as she talked, at the over-fancy, overconfident script that said my name. Nothing would be resolved by sitting at home. And I had been challenged. I turned to Henri.

"Will you escort me?"

He sighed, exhaling smoke. "I think I had better, Miss Tulman."

And then the bell in the dining room rang, shrill and insistent.

I leapt to my feet. "I wonder what Mary could want," I said over the ringing, snatching up Lane's things and my skirts to go.

"Do you always run when your maid rings a bell, Miss Tulman?" Henri asked. I straightened my back.

"Almost always, Mr. Marchand. She's a very good maid."

I left him to chuckle in his self-imposed cloud.

CHAPTER TWENTY

$\mathcal{F}$or the next hours, my activities were polar extremes. I received a reply by telegram from Mr. Babcock's offices, arranging for the transport of his body to the family burial plot in Westminster. And I was fitted for a dress, my perceived social standing high enough to gain me credit for the cloth. Mrs. Hardcastle, Mary, and a tiny French seamstress became an unlikely team, united in the common purpose of making me fit for an emperor I heartily despised. I could only hope the dress wouldn't be the cause of my new life in a French debtor's prison.

"Would you like to trade places with me, Marguerite?" I asked the child. She was sitting in the corner, one of the French fairy-tale books I'd found in my room propped open in her lap. I'd realized that these must be her books, that my grandmother's room was a place she came often, but she was not reading this time. She was watching, wide-eyed, as I stood, arms over head in my underclothes, having swaths of cloth pinned all over me, listening to a frank discussion on certain aspects of my figure as if I were an interesting piece of horseflesh. "They'd never notice," I whispered to her. I was rewarded with a giggle.

I'd never asked Mrs. DuPont about the comings and goings at the courtyard door — too many other worries had intervened — and she had never asked me about the bells that rang all over the house about once every hour when I was not above stairs. Curiosity seemed to be sadly lacking for the both of us, until on my way to the attic room after my fitting, I happened to glance out the round window on the upper floor. Far below, I saw a young man talking with Mrs. DuPont at the courtyard door. I watched as he put something slyly in her hand, perhaps a letter or something folded in paper.

I hurried down the stairs and around the landings, through the foyer, and into the back corridor. But Mrs. DuPont was no longer there, and there was no one at the door. She wasn't in the kitchen either, only Mr. DuPont, staring dreamily at the wall, eating a bowl of porridge. I ducked away before he could see me and start one of our bizarre one-sided conversations, and found myself staring at the closed door to the servants' quarters.

I was not actually lacking curiosity, far from it; the door to Mrs. DuPont's room was a terrible temptation, even more so than the time I had succumbed and opened Lane's. And this time I knew the house belonged to me. I reached out a hand for the door latch. For all of our posturing and squabbling over names, for all of her glorious dinners, hoping I would choose ease of service over actual authority in my own house, I was frightened of Mrs. DuPont. I did not understand her, could not make out where her allegiances lay except with the Bonapartes. Was her enthusiasm that of a loyal subject, or a more personal devotion? If she knew enough to lead the emperor's agents to my uncle, surely she would have already done so? I put my hand on the latch.

Of course, she also might be choosing an income over the emperor, and there was the nexus of my fear. I was afraid of what Mrs. DuPont might do if she thought I couldn't pay. And despite having searched through many of Mr. Babcock's papers, the location of my money in Paris was still an enigma. I dropped my hand from her latch, and instead stepped out the back door and into the courtyard.

The sun was lowering, sinking down behind the steeply pitched roofs, and I could hear children in some other part of the garden, behind a screen of hedges, but that was not what captured my attention. I had come to see if there was any sign of the young man, and there he was, just a little way down the path, a large, strapping sort of lad with his pants tucked into his boots. But he was not with Mrs. DuPont. He was with Mary, and Mary was giggling in a way that showed perhaps one-third of the sense I knew her to possess.

The young man took one of Mary's hands and kissed it before leaning forward to whisper in her ear. I felt my eyebrows rise. Mary Brown had always held strong opinions about her proper duties as my maid, but the role she'd felt most keenly was that of chaperone, a rather prudish, overprotective one, in my opinion. Mary would snap like a disgruntled goose if Lane's skin ever brushed anything other than my hand. Not that we hadn't outwitted her. Often. But we'd certainly never done so in public.

Mary caught sight of me and yanked her hand away, pushing the young man from her ear. The boy looked over his shoulder, grinned, made a motion as if he was tipping an invisible cap, whispered one last thing in Mary's ear, making her giggle, and then trotted away down the path. I walked out to meet her, and Mary tossed up her chin, despite the fact that her freckles were disappearing beneath blotches of pink.

"Robert is a right nice young man," she said with no preamble. "And you don't say 'Robert' when you're French, you say 'Ro-bear' like there's a big, furry animal on the end of it. He brings the groceries to Mrs. DuPont, and he's good to that Mr. DuPont, even though the man ain't much of talker, if you take my meaning."

"I thought you said there weren't any groceries, Mary."

"I said there weren't any groceries that time, Miss. He's a nice boy," she said.

"I'm sure he is," I replied carefully. "Does Robert . . . does he speak English?"

"Not so much. But he's teaching me French, and I can't be spending all my years up in the attics, Miss."

"I wouldn't expect you to." Part of me wanted to laugh, the other was aware of a great, empty void in my chest, a reminder that I was full of echoes. "But, Mary, surely . . . you couldn't have known Robert very long, could you?" The last I'd counted, we had been in Paris for exactly four days.

I had thought this quite gentle as far as a remonstrance went, but Mary's brows came down, still on the defensive. I took her arm, and she let out her annoyance in a little puff of air. Then she leaned her head on my shoulder, and we began walking back to the house. This was not the way a lady was supposed to walk with her maid, I supposed, but then again, I did not have a history of correct behavior with the servants. I wondered how she would feel if tonight went badly, if I decided we had to take Uncle Tully and flee from Paris. It seemed that any move I made — or didn't make — was bound to hurt someone. My feet felt heavy in the gravel as we approached the back step.

"Miss," Mary said suddenly, straightening up. "I've been thinking on this for a while now, Miss, only I hadn't said, but . . . that Lane Moreau, now." My arm stiffened slightly in hers. "Before you was coming to us, he didn't go about with any of them other girls in the village, not a bit of it, and he could've, Miss, Lord knows he could've. Mostly he was with Mr. Tully, of course, and we're both knowing what a job that is. But when you came, you was the only one I saw turning his head, and you turned it proper, if you don't mind me saying. But, Miss, if all that's so, and if he weren't dead these months, and was just next door only now he ain't, then why in all this time wasn't he writing to you, Miss? Not even a line or two, not using his name?"

Every muscle inside me was now clenched and tense. Mary, in her usual way, was putting her thumb "right on the sore spot," as her mother would have said. I didn't know the answer to her question.

Mary went on. "Unless — and I hope I ain't hurting your feelings none, Miss — but, unless maybe he was finding somebody else? He's been gone a long time, and there's lots of girls running about Paris, I've noticed, girls that ain't so far above him. But what I'm really wanting to know, Miss, is . . . do you think they'll all be changing their minds someday?"

I'd been so focused on my own worries that I hadn't seen the direction Mary's thoughts were taking. I turned my mind from my own conundrums and squeezed her arm.

"I'm not certain, Mary. But I would guess the shorter the acquaintance, the more changeable a mind could be. Wouldn't you agree?" I tried to smile at her serious face.

"Well, Miss," Mary said, "if we're swapping advice, and if you don't mind a dose of it from me, I wouldn't trust that Mr. Marchand, Miss. Not for a minute, Miss. He looks at you like a fox in a chicken coop what's got only one hen."

I attempted a smile for the second time, but I couldn't summon it. It wasn't Henri Marchand or Mrs. DuPont or even the emperor of France I was afraid of this evening. The name of my deepest fear was Katharine Tulman, and whether tonight she would once again be making a terrible mistake.

At nine o'clock, I stood in front of the mirror in Marianna's room, fidgeting. Uncle Tully was well, his bruises more faded, the upstairs attic now resembling a mechanical nest. My bruise was almost undetectable, but the small cut, I feared, was going to leave a scar. I had a bag packed beside the door of my room, and one of Dr. Pruitt's little brown bottles on the chimneypiece, just in case the night went badly. I had not yet mentioned the idea of fleeing Paris to Mary, but I saw her eying the bottle and guessed that she was drawing her own conclusions.

But my hair was done, my dress almost so, the poor little French seamstress still on her knees at my feet, frantically stitching. There had been no time for complicated tucks and flounces, so Mrs. Hardcastle had suggested we rely on simplicity and the beauty of the material instead. I was enveloped in layers of rich velvet in an emerald green, yards of it, heavy and hot where it was not too breezy.

There were places that were much too breezy. Mary stood behind me, fumbling with the buttons.

"Good heavens, Miss!" she fussed, giving me a light whack on the exposed skin of my back. "Will you stop your moving about?"

The seamstress looked up from her last line of stitches, scandalized. I managed to stand still for three more buttons before surrendering again to my nervousness. It was just like the night before my eighteenth birthday, another night when I had wholeheartedly regretted my choice of clothing, mostly because the girl looking back at me had not resembled Katharine Tulman. Then I had been remarkably pretty. For me. Tonight I was all eyes and pale skin — too much pale skin — and cascading curls made red by the color of the velvet. I was not remotely pretty; I was exotic, and I wished I could stay home, for more reasons than just my wardrobe. The seamstress pulled the final stitch, Mary did up the last button, and we all stared at my reflection in the mirror. My stomach squeezed.

"Fine," I said to the alien creature in the mirror. "Let's get this over with, then."

I soon discovered the difficulties of getting through a door while wearing an enormous hoopskirt, and then the dangers of negotiating stairs when one could not catch a glimpse of her own feet. I took the steps slowly, feeling for each solid surface beneath my slippers, which must have made my entrance downstairs rather dramatic, because Henri Marchand, who was waiting in the foyer, nearly dropped his cigarette. Mrs. Hardcastle was there as well, ogling the scene through her pince-nez, gathering some juicy bits of news for the girls next door, no doubt. I breathed out my relief when I made it safely to the bottom of the stairs.

"My!" said Mrs. Hardcastle, patting my arm fondly. "I wish Alice Tulman could have been here to see that, I daresay. What a face she would be making! Have a lovely time, my dear."

I tried to say something in reply, but nerves had made me mute. Henri did not smile, either, insolent or otherwise. He had a white rose in the buttonhole of his black coat. He said nothing, just offered his arm. I took it.

In the carriage, Henri was quiet, looking thoughtfully out the open window as he smoked. It was a cool evening, but I had decided the smoke was a greater evil than the cold.

"This invitation," he said, breaking the silence, "it comes from the emperor himself, or from the empress, or someone high in their circle of friends, yes? Do you know why this is?" I was thinking how best to answer, but before I could he turned his face to me and said, "And if you did know, Miss Tulman, would you tell me?"

I sighed. "No. I probably wouldn't. I'm sorry."

He laughed, but there was no humor it. I could see the lack of it in the light of passing streetlamps. I truly was sorry. I felt guilty, putting him to so much trouble without explanation.

"There is a purpose to the evening," I said, "of that I am certain." It was what I found so frightening. "My thought is to just remain as unobtrusive as possible, and see where the night leads us. I'm sure all will become clear."

He laughed again. "Miss Tulman, in case you do not know, you will not remain 'unobtrusive,' as you say, in that dress."

"Don't be impertinent," I said, holding back a smile.

"Just stay close to me," he said, not impertinent at all.

Light blazed at the Tuileries, eclipsing the stars. From every door and window, and from the dozens of bonfires set along the drive, showing the way for the carriages. We drove through an enormous stone arch, life-sized statues of horses on its top, through a gate, and followed the line of fires to the doors. I had elected not to wear a wrap even with the slight chill, not having anything near fine enough, and when we were shown inside, I was glad. The crowd was dense, the heat of so many bodies sweltering even with so much of my upper half exposed. We ascended a very grand staircase, one with the crowd, moving with them through a columned gallery, past guards standing motionless in their finery, and then from room to ornate room, deeper and deeper into the palace, not speaking to each other or to anyone else, but eliciting stares nonetheless.

I'd been wrong, I realized, that first night at Mrs. Reynolds's, about what people wore to a ball. The extravagance of satin, lace, curls, and glittering gems was beyond anything I could have imagined. But it was the heads I was watching again — I could not help it — eyes searching for one that was tall and dark. There was no reason in the world for Lane to be here, I knew that; it made no sense for him to be. But that one partial word written in his hand had me looking all the same.

We entered a large, open hall, even more crowded, two stories high with a balcony, and after a quick count, exactly one dozen arched windows. The hall was all marble and statues, candelabras and gilt, so much gilding that the entire domed ceiling was covered with it, dully reflecting the crystal chandeliers. The walls were thick with portraits and flowers, the scents mixing with the many different perfumes in the air. It was dazzling, the noise of French voices and skirts and shoe heels and laughter and the clinking of glass all too much to listen to. But everywhere I did listen, I could hear the same name, and everywhere I looked, in brocade, on the tapestries, emblazoned in pieces of silver, there was the large letter N. Napoléon. Everything was Napoléon.

I clutched Henri's arm and whispered, "If you see the emperor, you will point him out?"

"I do not think I shall have to, he will . . ."

The man in front of me stepped back, treading on my skirt, and I realized that the front of the room was clearing, the crowd pressing backward. Violins began to play, and the noise subsided. Over the shoulders and heads I saw four large contraptions being wheeled into the now open end of the room, each tall, light brown, and with the same fat, cylindrical shape. Black-and-yellow papier-mâché insects were attached to them by thin wires, floating and bobbing as they came to a stop. They were supposed to be beehives, I decided, one giant bloom of a purple violet set between them.

The music swelled and I jumped as women burst from the bee-hives, breaking through the brown paper, dressed in stiff, short, black-and-yellow skirts showing all their legs and wearing bodices that looked like nothing more than corsets. I was a bit shocked by this, though no one else seemed to be. Wire antennae were attached to the ladies' hair knots, and they immediately began to prance about, spinning on their toes, little skirts bouncing, stretching arms and kicking legs. But always they circled the enormous violet, adoringly, as if it were the sun of their universe, or a god they were compelled to worship.

"The bee," Henri whispered, "it is the symbol of the Bonapartes, and the violet their chosen flower. The emperor, he is very superstitious about such things. Did you hear the ladies behind us, speaking of the spiritualist in the palace? He . . ." Henri must have taken a moment to look at my face because he paused his story. "Have you never been to the ballet, Miss Tulman?"

I shook my head, unable to take my eyes from the spectacle. It was the single most ridiculous thing I'd ever seen in my life. I heard Henri chuckle. The girls finished their dance, hop-trotting away to thunderous applause, the beehives were pushed aside, and the noise fell away to low muttering. The servants stationed at each doorway suddenly and simultaneously hit their staffs against the marble floor, creating a resounding crack. The room fell silent.

"*L'Empereur . . . et l'Impératrice . . . de la France!*" one of them shouted, exaggerating the words.

The emperor appeared beneath an archway of crimson hangings, his arm outstretched to hold the hand of the empress, walking perhaps two feet to his side. The couple paused, and then entered their ball. We watched them walk, the entire assemblage, all our eyes together, as they made slow progress toward a raised platform with gilt chairs set upon it.

The Empress Eugénie was a rather average woman, pale, but with a belt made of what I assumed were diamonds, and a grand pile of blonde curls topped with a sparkling diadem. But my gaze only glanced over her, landing firmly on Charles-Louis Bonaparte, Napoléon III.

Not as tall or as imposing as I might have thought, despite an extravaganza of medals on his red uniform and an impressively waxed mustache. But his smile, his little nods to acquaintances here and there while we stood, the entire assembly listening to each of his footsteps, struck me as self-satisfied. Smug. How I hated him. For Mr. Babcock, for John George, and for what he had done to me, my uncle, and possibly Lane. Even I was surprised by the violence of it.

"Miss Tulman?"

I looked up to see Henri Marchand's dark eyes on me. I think it was the second time he had said my name.

"Perhaps we should dance, yes? That would be the easiest way, I think, to search the room."

So he had seen me looking on our way in. Was there anything he did not notice? I had not even realized that the orchestra was playing. The emperor was seated on the platform now, one leg thrown out inelegantly, kissing a lady's proffered hand, and then Henri's voice was in my ear: "And if you do not stop looking at the emperor like that we will be removed by the guard before we can."

I pulled my eyes away from Napoléon and smiled wanly as I took Henri's hand, though I could not feel it through my glove, a bit shaken by my own anger. It wasn't until we reached the edge of the dance, where black-suited men spun the ladies with their twirling, swishing skirts, that I had the sense to panic. I looked up at Henri. "I . . . I don't actually know how to do this, you know."

"No?" He kept my left hand in his, lifting it in the air, then used his other arm to place my right hand on his shoulder before taking me by the waist. "You have never danced with a young man?"

My curls moved slightly as I gave my head one tiny shake. When Lane and I had gone to a ballroom, we'd rolled about on skates. Henri leaned forward again, whispering in my ear. He smelled faintly of spices and strongly of cigarettes.

"Follow my feet, three steps in a square, the fourth step a turn and we begin once again. Leave it to me, and you watch the faces."

Two times through the steps and I had it. Or had it well enough. It was mostly counting, after all. Rolling had been harder, but significantly more fun. I dared not look up, lest I see a teasing smirk, so I began to watch the crowd, not really knowing what I was looking for, other than the tall, dark head and gray eyes to go with it. I thought of those eyes in all their moods: storm, stone, or waveless sea. I wondered what their mood would be when they once again looked at me.

Three more turns with these thoughts, and I realized that there were indeed eyes on me, though they did not belong to Lane. I could not look at any one person without either catching their glance, or seeing their gaze invariably turn my way. And it was not just me that was attracting the attention. The women especially, I saw, gave me a quick glance up and down before settling the rest of their interest on my partner. I looked up at Henri, a little startled. I'd almost forgotten he was handsome, though the fact had evidently not escaped him. He was returning each of these coy little compliments with a smile that was deliberately dashing.

He looked down, saw my raised brows, and grinned like a little boy. Then he leaned close again and said, "Do you see the Englishman with the champagne glass, standing to the left of the emperor? That is Cowley, the British ambassador, and the man he speaks with is the son of Napoléon I, though not the son of any of Napoléon's wives, of course. He resembles his father, no?"

We turned, and turned again, and when I was facing the right direction once more Henri continued. "And the man on Cowley's right, that is the brother of the first Napoléon, who the emperor has made his heir until he has children, and the other, with the bald head, that is Charles de Morny, the emperor's half brother, the illegitimate son of his mother. And that man," Henri said on the turn, "do you see him, with the big woman? That is the illegitimate son of the emperor's father."

I eyed the man, dancing rather well with a stout woman in a startling shade of salmon, and tried unsuccessfully to process the Bonaparte family entanglements.

"And that woman there, who sits chatting with the empress, she is rumored to be the emperor's most recent mistress."

I turned to see what Napoléon III might think of this, but he was not noticing the empress, I saw, not in the slightest. He was staring, directly and unwaveringly, at me. I was jarred by his look, by the absolute single-mindedness of it, as if there were no others present in this ballroom, only the two of us, watching each other across a space of maybe twenty feet. And there was something in this, the intensity, the penetration, giving nothing away, that rang recognition deep inside me, a faint noise like Uncle Tully's bells; I could hear the ringing, and yet was unable to identify the power that made them chime. How I hated him.

Henri and I spun about in the dance, the crowd closed in, and the shared gaze was broken. I was looking back over my shoulder, wanting to know if those inscrutable eyes were still on me, when I realized that we had stopped dancing, that Henri was stepping back politely, letting me go, that someone had tapped his shoulder to take his place. There was another hand in mine, another hand on my waist, the music playing on. And when I looked up, I was three inches away from the beatific smile of Ben Aldridge.

CHAPTER TWENTY-ONE

I did absolutely nothing. I just stood there, letting him hold me close, then responded to his lead as we began to dance. The strings played and inside my head there was nothing but confusion, a dissonant swirl of *hows* and *whys* and *wherefores*, as if each instrument had started its song on a different page. But the discord lasted only a moment or two before I began to hear the inklings of harmony. Deep down, I must have known, or at least suspected. And Lane must have known it, too. He wouldn't have stayed in Paris if he hadn't.

Ben was not much changed. The round boyish face, the blue eyes, the neatly trimmed side whiskers were all there, but he was paler, not sun-pinked and tanned as he had been during that hot summer at Stranwyne, and he was a little thinner, more polished. The biggest change was the fact that in my imagination he had been cold, drowned, and dead, and the man now swinging me through the dance was very much alive. And smiling hugely.

"My, my, Miss Tulman, you are all eyes. I believe I am flattered." We made our first turn. "But you are looking extremely well. Paris will not know what to make of you."

"What are you doing here?" I whispered.

"Is that a philosophical question, Miss Tulman, or are you speaking more practically?"

"Why are you alive?" I clarified.

He laughed merrily. "Well, it's no thanks to you, I must say."

I thought of the opium-laced wine he'd nearly killed me with. "I suppose I could say the same of you, Mr. Aldridge."

"Now, now, Miss Tulman, the name is not Aldridge here. We don't use —"

"So it's Arceneaux, then?"

He looked pleased. "Fancy you knowing that. And it's Charles, by the way. That's what my mother called me. 'Charles Arceneaux,' or no one will know who you're speaking of." He swung me around, making the hoop under the green dress swirl. "But we were speaking of being alive, Miss Tulman. Let me heartily recommend that you learn to swim. It's a very useful skill, even with a broken arm and a knock on the head."

My eyes went reflexively to the hand that held mine. Of course it was not still broken, but I saw a bandage there, a strip of snowy-white cloth around the wrist, disappearing beneath the black sleeve of his jacket.

"Yes," Ben said, seeing where my eyes had gone. "I daresay we are even for past wrongs, you and I." His smile remained the same but his voice lowered slightly, the grip tightening on my hand. "Burns can be extremely painful, can they not?"

My brain was still sluggish, picking its way through a mire of new facts, but I could see the night in my uncle's workshop, the oil lamp in my hand, the smash of glass, the burning jacket being ripped away from the body of a man in a mask. My eyes darted upward. "You?"

"It's rather a shame we got the wrong door. I wouldn't have disturbed your rest for the world." I thought of that crude map in the pocket of the dead man, with my corridor marked. Made by someone who knew the house, of course. But I kept silent, unwilling to increase his enjoyment with my shock or my words. "Though I don't suppose we're even in the matter of our servants," he chatted on. "Your little maid split my man's skull."

He was still smiling outwardly, but I could feel the fury bubbling just below the surface, tightening the arm around my waist, his hand now squeezing down so hard on mine that I had to hold in a gasp. If I could sense the heat of his anger, I wondered if he could feel the bitter, freezing bite of my hatred. He leaned close to my ear. "I should have shot her. But since I did not, I think you rather owe me a favor, don't you?"

I'd had enough. I struggled once in his arms, trying to shove him away, and we faltered in the dance. He jerked me back into position.

"Temper," he chided. "Don't make a scene. We are being observed." I followed his eyes straight to the piercing ones of Napoléon, slowly twirling the pointed end of his mustache, sphinxlike as he watched us dance. "The emperor will take it as a personal insult if you — or your current watchdog — offend me."

I caught a glimpse of Henri, frowning as he followed us surreptitiously around the edge of the dance, never quite letting me out of his sight.

"Marchand, wasn't it?" he continued. "You seem quite good at picking up protectors, Miss Tulman, but I must say that was fast work, even for you. It took you much longer to convince Lane Moreau to step into that position."

I was done being baited. "What do you want? I assume it was you that had me invited here tonight for this nasty little chat? Wouldn't it have been easier to knock on my door? I daresay you know where I live."

"So charming," Ben said pleasantly. "I invited you here tonight, dear Miss Tulman, so you could view where I live. Or where I will live very soon. Welcome to my future home. It is rather grand, is it not?"

I felt my brows come down, feet moving automatically to the count of the dance as if they'd been wound with a key. Ben had gone truly insane.

"But as for you," he continued, "in that regard my wants are very simple. I merely want you to tell me where your uncle is."

"My uncle is dead," I said immediately.

"Really?" He smiled. "A most conveniently timed death, I must say. But why then, Miss Tulman, have you been visiting hospitals and asylums?"

I said nothing, heart slamming against its tight casing of ribs and green velvet, my insides in a tangle. I had never considered that my search could take on such a connotation. He leaned in close, whispering in my ear. I shuddered.

"Bringing him here was bold, but it was stupid, Katharine. Very stupid. Mr. Tulman is an old man, and I would be most gratified if you did not endanger his health. Is he well enough to work?"

"I told you that my uncle is dead."

He sighed sadly, breath moving the long curls that were brushing my neck. I wanted to scream, to thrust him away, to run, kick, make him stop touching me, but then he did move away of his own accord, and I realized the dance had ended. Couples were breaking apart with smatterings of gloved applause. Ben let go of everything but my wrist and began to pull me from the dance floor. I dug in my heels, but he turned quickly and said, "Come. The emperor is beckoning to us, and believe me, Miss Tulman, this is not a man you would wish to offend."

I looked over my shoulder as I was dragged away, tripping a bit over the enormous skirt. Henri was still watching us from the edge of the dance, hanging back now that he saw where we were going. He would not be able to help me. I turned back to Ben.

"And if this emperor is a man one would not wish to offend, Mr. Aldridge," I hissed, voice dripping venom, "then tell me why I should not inform him that you are a liar and a murderer, and that you are holding me against my will at this very moment?"

We stopped, and those hard blue eyes locked on to my own. "Because, dear Katharine, we have a bargain to discuss. One that I think you will wish to hear." He smiled at me. "And because he will not believe you."

"And why in the world not?" If I did not know what was behind Ben's beautiful smile, I might have been charmed.

"Because, Miss Tulman, he is my father."

And before I could think or react, I was jerked forward eleven more steps, and found myself wrapped in the enigmatic gaze of Charles-Louis Napoléon Bonaparte, emperor of France.

Ben bowed, pulling me down into a curtsy beside him. "*Vos Majestés Impériales,*" he said, "*je vous présente Mademoiselle Katharine Tulman?*"

My head was down, but I was stealing looks at the emperor, trying to understand how what Ben had just told me could be true.

"Does the young lady speak French, Charles?"

I lifted myself up to see the ivory-skinned empress smiling sweetly at us. Whatever Ben's relationship might be to Napoléon, it was clear that the Empress Eugénie was not his mother. She could not have been much older than Ben. Her glance slid once over my tightly gripped wrist, and Ben instantly let go of me, smiling stiffly. "I believe she does not, Your Majesty."

"Then where are your manners, Charles? Let us speak English for the new acquaintance."

He bowed formally and said, "This is Miss Katharine Tulman, Your Majesty, lately of England."

I curtsied again, and the empress inclined her head before she said, "So you must have known Charles in England, Miss Tulman. He talks so little of his time there."

I stared at the empress, a large diamond winking from the center of her tiara. I had no idea what any of them knew about Ben's past. For that matter, neither did I. "He is a . . ." I began. *Liar? Poisoner? Murderer? Thief?* "He is a remarkable man," I finished lamely.

"And so thoughtful," said the empress, beaming. "Only last week, Charles brought me a gift of my favorite claret, just because I happened to mention my fondness for it."

"You are too kind, Your Majesty." Ben gave her his smile, all charm, while I prayed that the empress would drink nothing from the hand of Ben Aldridge.

"Is this your woman?"

The voice had been high and distinctly German. We all turned to look at the Emperor Napoléon, whose gaze now rested fondly on Ben. The question had been directed at him, but it was me that he had been speaking of, as if inquiring after a pet.

"No, Your Majesty," I said clearly, and a little too loud. "I most certainly am not."

There was a pause in the surrounding conversation. Napoléon's gray eyes bore back into mine, like a tunnel where no one else could intrude or interrupt, and again I was struck by the sound of distant bells. Then his waxed mustache twitched.

"You must dance with her some more, Charles, I think, if you wish to make her so."

Everyone laughed politely, including Ben at my side, as if the emperor had just concocted a very witty joke. Ben said, "Then with Miss Tulman's permission, we shall take our —"

"Is the woman a Pisces?"

Again there was a lull in the conversations surrounding us. Ben hesitated, turning to me, and the empress said quickly, "The emperor is so very interested in his horoscope." She caught my eye and gave me one tiny shake of the head.

I had no idea what any of this meant, or what sort of superstition I was playing into, but I said, "No, Your Majesty, I am not a . . . Pisces."

"Then I am safe to dance with the lady, wouldn't you agree, Your Majesty?" Ben said. The emperor waved a hand, while the empress smiled, seeming relieved.

Ben bowed yet again and, remembering late, I curtsied before he took my arm, steering me — without my permission — away from the royal couple. When we were swallowed by the crowd, I pulled my arm loose, but he grabbed it again, jerking me sideways through one of the arched doorways. I heard a few male chuckles. There was another grand room here, smaller, with upholstered chairs, fine cabinets, and one or two trysting couples, and then we were through another door, in the dark, and I was pushed up against a wall. The room was large, I could feel that, and empty, but it wasn't until my eyes adjusted to the moon shining down through the window that I saw the dais containing two thrones. I made a move toward the doors but Ben had me in a grip of iron, bruising my upper arms. He pushed me back into the wall.

"You forget that we have a bargain to discuss," he said. "Something I want for something you want."

"You have nothing I want," I spat.

He came close to my face, crushing the hoopskirt. I leaned back as far as I could, hands splayed against the wall. "Are you certain of that?" he whispered. "And what if I offered you Lane Moreau?"

I went still.

Ben smiled. "Well, that got your attention, I'd say. Poor Mr. Marchand."

"Where is he?"

"This is a bargain, Miss Tulman."

"Is he alive?"

"At the moment. But I cannot guarantee that he will remain so."

I turned my head away. The velvet was so hot I could hardly breathe. *Alive.* I had been so sure, and yet it was my relief, not my corset, that was going to suffocate me.

"Give me the location of Frederick Tulman," Ben said gently, his grip on my arms still painful, "and I will give you the location of Lane Moreau. That is our bargain."

I took three shallow breaths that did me no good before I said, "I told you that my uncle is dead."

"Oh, dear," said Ben. "I do hope for Mr. Moreau's sake that you are a liar, Miss Tulman. If you have nothing to trade, then I simply have no use for my guest." My face was turned as far away as it could be, but he was so close now that his breath tickled my cheek. "And what do you think I do with things I have no use for?"

I remembered Davy's small body making a curving arc through the air as he was thrown from Ben's boat.

"Do you think I will hesitate?" he said. "Did I hesitate with that annoying little lawyer of yours?"

I turned to face him then, letting the truth of this settle into me. Whether Mr. Babcock's death had been with or without the emperor's knowledge I couldn't be sure, but some of my earlier hatred twisted about, finding its proper place. I stared back into Ben's eyes, a clear blue void of nothingness. No, he would not hesitate. But the mention of Mr. Babcock had let loose a rivulet of my pent-up rage.

"I take it you don't know how to make the gyroscope work, then?"

His smile disappeared. "All I need is for Mr. Tully to show me," he said. "It's a very simple request."

"And your father will be . . . most grateful, I suppose. So grateful he'll hand over a palace and a kingdom? I had rather thought your father was a sailor, Mr. Aldridge, or that's what you told me at Stranwyne. But I believe the emperor has already named his heir, hasn't he? If the empress doesn't give him one first. She would be quite the forbearing wife if —"

"Shut up!" he yelled, pulling me forward to slam me once against the wall, the words reverberating several more times in the empty room. "That . . . woman," he said, his eyes close to mine, "is a bloody, royal fool. She has no idea who I am, and when my father is done being besotted with her, he will set her aside. But do not dare . . ." He paused, choosing his next words slowly. "Do not dare question his love for me. I will hand him a weapon that will give the Bonapartes more power than they ever dreamed of, and when I do, my father will give me anything I ask. Anything!"

There was a mania in this that frightened me more than anything else that evening. Ben relaxed, but not his grip on my arms.

"Our bargain, Miss Tulman?"

"I told you that my uncle is dead," I whispered.

"I will come to Rue Trudon tomorrow night at midnight to collect him. If you give him to me without a fuss, then I will give you Lane Moreau. Without a fuss. And if Mr. Tulman is not there, dear Katharine . . ." He finally let go of one of my arms, reaching out to twine a finger around one of the curls on my bare shoulder. ". . . then I have a bullet eager to rid me of an unwanted guest. A fair and simple trade. Other than that, Miss Tulman, I don't care what you do." He chuckled at my shiver. "Choose well."

And he left me.

CHAPTER TWENTY-TWO

I jumped when, less than a minute later, Henri Marchand threw open the door to the dark and empty throne room, bouncing it against the wall, laying a bar of bright gaslight across the floor. I caught a glimpse of a ball going on through the open doors of the room behind him, a table with fluted glasses and stacked confections, servants and milling guests, a world I'd nearly forgotten was there. He closed the door, shutting us away again.

"I lost sight in the crowd," he said. "I could not find you, until I saw that man leaving. Who is he?"

Ben Aldridge. Charles Arceneaux. Not dead, but alive, and the emperor's secret son. How could any of that be? I thought of John George's bloodstains on the floor of Stranwyne's chapel, and of dear Mr. Babcock, dewy-eyed at the memory of my grandmother. On whose orders had they died? Ben's, or the emperor's? Or were those orders one and the same? And then there was Lane, dead if I did not hand over my uncle, and Uncle Tully, innocent as a child in all of this. How dare he make me choose between them?

"Miss Tulman?" Henri said.

Bitter cold slid down my spine, not freezing or numbing this time, but bracing, tingling, every corner of my mind awake and alive to it.

"Miss Tulman!"

I pushed away from my leaning stance against the wall and straightened my dress. Henri stepped back. I was angry now, deeply so, the kind that made me cool and calm, the kind that would not let me rest until I'd had my way. Ben always had the upper hand, always left me no recourse but to react to whatever plan he had set in motion. I'd been doing so for more than two years, in some ways. Now it was time for him to react to mine.

We waited outside the Tuileries in the night air, bathed in lights. I was surrounded by history and magnificence, but the plans now filling my head left no room for their appreciation. My neck ached from where I had hit the wall, and I was regretting my lack of cloak or wrap. Henri tugged off his jacket and silently offered it. I hesitated before I took it, but it was warm. I heard the horse hooves, and our carriage rattled up. A lavishly dressed servant opened the door and I was handed in, taking a moment to squeeze the enormous skirt through the narrow doorway.

As Henri began to step in after me I said, "Be so good as to tell the driver we wish to go to Rue Tisserand. Quietly, if you can."

He leaned back out, and I distinctly heard him say "Rue Trudon." I frowned. He climbed in and sat down opposite me, my skirt leaving no room for his feet. "I said the Rue Tisserand, Mr. —"

I saw his hand shoot up in the semidarkness, stopping my speech. "No more, Miss Tulman. No more."

Gravel crunched under the carriage wheels. When we left the gates and began rolling smoothly on a paved street, I said, "Is something the —"

"I mean that you tell me nothing. Nothing!" he shouted. "And yet I am to go with you to Rue Tisserand in the middle of the night. Madness! You will go home as you ought."

He was absolutely seething. Oddly, I liked it much better than when he was flattering. "I am sorry. It isn't fair to you, I know. I will go home first . . ." I saw his shoulders relax slightly. ". . . so I can take Mary with me. She is —"

I was interrupted by what I could only assume was a long and bountiful example of French cursing. "What is wrong with you?" he said finally. "What is wrong with you? I do not know your troubles. You will not say. But the emperor's men, they watch your house, and other men, they disappear around you, poof!" His English was suffering with his anger. "And you say go here, and go there, and you wish to visit slums in the night in a dress that would buy a month of bread, and bring the imperial court right to the poor monsieur's door! Idiocy!"

I was taken aback, mostly because he was correct. I had been letting my own fury get the better of my sense. Of course I was being watched, whether I could see the eyes or not. I could not simply drive up to Joseph's door. I would get the man killed. Henri leaned forward, elbows on knees, rubbing his forehead with one hand. I could smell his jacket all over me.

"I am sorry," I told him again. "The man in the ballroom is . . . He is known as Charles Arceneaux, he is a . . . a favorite of the emperor. He thinks I have something he wants. If I do not produce this thing by tomorrow night, then he says another man will die. I cannot let this man die, but I also cannot produce this thing that he wants. I must speak with Joseph and I have no time to wait until a more proper hour."

There was a long silence, just the *clop* of horseshoes, the echo of wheels on passing buildings. The streetlamps had been put out; the only lights were the ones swinging outside the carriage.

"This man who will die," said Henri finally, "he is the artist. Your servant."

"Yes."

Another string of French came from the other seat, though softer this time, and resigned.

"Send the carriage away when we come to the house. I will get you to Rue Tisserand."

Once inside the red doors, I hurried upstairs, leaving Henri to turn on the gaslights in the ladies' salon and the dining room and kitchen, as if we intended to be awake for some time. The house was very quiet. I passed Marianna's bedchamber, and now that I was alone I hiked the annoying hoopskirt up to my waist and ran the next flight of stairs. I entered Mr. Babcock's room in the dark, closed the door behind me and, leaving the lights off, tried to feel my way to the wardrobe. I nearly screamed when the door kicked open in a burst of candle flame, but let the noise die inside me when I recognized Mary's nightcap silhouetted in the light.

"It's me, Mary," I said, "only me."

Mary lowered the arm with her fireplace poker. "Good Lord, Miss, what are you doing . . . ?"

"Blow out that candle and shut the door, Mary. I need a pair of trousers."

We waited an hour before letting ourselves out the back door and into the courtyard, Henri in his shirtsleeves, jacket left behind, me in Mr. Babcock's smallest pair of trousers, which were both too big and too short all at once. I'd felt ridiculous coming down the stairs, much worse than in the green velvet earlier, Mary shaking her head and giving her opinion freely all the way down. It felt absolutely wrong, like I'd nothing on but bloomers. But I forgot all that in the cool silence of the garden, where the shaking of the dying leaves in the night wind made it impossible to know if someone else might be out there with us. We scooted in the darkness along the edge of the buildings, finally crouching down at Mrs. Reynolds's back door.

"Keep watch," Henri whispered, quietly pulling what I took to be a ring of keys from his pocket. I had my hair braided, pinned up beneath Lane's red cap, and I held it on my head with one hand while I watched the shadows move, wondering why Henri would have a set of keys to Mrs. Reynolds's, then wondering why it was taking him so long to use them. I risked a glance behind me. Henri was not using keys; he was picking the lock.

The lock clicked, the door squealing lightly on its hinges, and I followed him inside. We flitted through the dark house to the foyer, trying not to bump, knock over, or be impaled by one of the myriad ornaments along the walls and in the corners. Henri put his hand on the front doorknob and whispered back to me, "We will walk quickly, and with purpose, like servants sent for the doctor, or . . . I don't know what. Just walk . . . *avec confiance*, with confidence."

I nodded. It did not matter in the least whom the men watching my house thought was coming out of Mrs. Reynolds's, as long as they did not think it was us. Henri opened the front door, we stepped outside, and he closed it behind us with a *bang*, as if we were doing just as we ought, with no need of silence. We moved away down the sidewalk as a light came on in Mrs. Reynolds's second floor.

"Where did you learn to pick locks, Mr. Marchand?" I asked as we turned the corner.

"I am a man of many talents and, *mon Dieu*, stop walking like a woman before you are arrested."

A city at night, I discovered, was an uglier world, where things hidden by the nicety of sunshine dragged themselves out to revel in gaslit music halls and the light of the occasional streetlamp. It was a long way to Rue Tisserand. We avoided noise and crowds, keeping to the dark, but twice we were accosted by women, one painted and bedraggled, the other hardly more than a girl, and once we had to speak to a *gendarme*, or rather Henri did, loudly and with much laughter. I was fairly certain he informed the man that we were drunk. I stood half behind him, mute, thankful for the darkness that I suspected was the biggest component of my so-called disguise. Or maybe the policeman just didn't care.

It was three o'clock in the morning before we arrived, having made several wrong turns after a consultation with a man sleeping on a door stoop. Rue Tisserand was small and narrow, rank with the odor of rubbish and cess. No lights shone other than a dim candle in an upper window, where a baby cried, and a house at the end, where the night-soil men were shoveling. Henri looked closely at a doorway and then knocked on it hard. He turned to me.

"And now . . . how do the English say it? It is your time to 'call the shots,' Miss Tulman."

Footsteps came down the passage, and someone spoke on the other side of the door. *"Qu'est-ce que vous voulez?"* A girl's voice, a little frightened.

"Joseph, please," I replied, mouth close to the door.

"Qui êtes-vous?"

"She wants to know who you are," whispered Mr. Marchand.

"I am here about Jean-Michel."

The door flew open.

We sat in a clean kitchen, which smelled of cabbage, with scrubbed pots hanging from the ceiling. Joseph, face creased from his blankets, leaned on his elbows on the opposite side of the table, seated beside a younger, longer-haired version of himself, a man who introduced himself as Jean-Baptiste, one of Joseph's brothers. The young woman that had opened the door — rather healthy in all her curves, I'd noticed — heated coffee at the stove while Joseph and Jean-Baptiste listened to everything I said, interpreted as necessary by Henri. Joseph rubbed his stubbled chin, pondering, as the young woman set down our coffee. I was grateful for it. I'd been too anxious to eat all day, and I was feeling the lack. After a long time, Joseph spoke rapidly in French, and I elbowed Henri's attention away from the girl to tell me what he said.

"If the man is high in the imperial court," Henri translated, "then there will be a heavy price to pay if we are caught." The girl's smile had vanished.

"Tell him that all they need to do is get the information and hold the man at my house. If they remain masked, then there is no need for the man to know who anyone is, and we only need to hold him long enough to free Jean-Michel and get a head start out of Paris. I have . . ." I glanced away from Henri. "I have a secure place to keep him. But also tell them that I believe this man will tell no one at the imperial court, that he will not risk admitting a failure. They can leave the door unlocked and slip back to their streets, and we will be out of Paris before he even knows he is free."

After the translation, we waited, listening to the rasp of Joseph's chin against his palm. Henri lit a cigarette. When Joseph spoke again it was soft, and Henri lowered his voice as well. "He says Jean-Michel was very good to Marie, his sister . . ." We all glanced at the curvy girl, who was flushing prettily. ". . . that he helped her out of a . . . a bad position."

"Did he?" I replied, eyes narrowing. I'd hoped this Marie was Joseph's wife.

Henri was still listening to Joseph, who was speaking with an occasional soft addition from Jean-Baptiste. Henri's expression became surprised. "He wants to know if you know who trained Jean-Michel in silver, and the names of his parents."

It was my turn to be surprised, both by the question and by the realization that I had no idea where Lane had learned his trade. I'd never thought to ask. The bodies around the table were still, waiting for my answer. "He must have learned it from someone in the village," I said, "or perhaps from his father. But his father was a French soldier."

"Moreau?" Jean-Baptiste asked after Henri's translation.

"Yes, Jean Moreau. His mother was English, of the name Jefferies. Why . . ."

Henri didn't bother to repeat this for Joseph and Jean-Baptiste, as they seemed to understand enough already. They consulted, their like heads close together. The pretty sister stood against the wall, chewing a nail.

"We will do it," Joseph said in English, "for Jean-Michel."

I only knew I'd been holding my breath when I let it out in relief. "And you can make him speak?" I said. "You can make this man tell you where Jean-Michel is?" This was essential, but I wanted no part of it.

"Yes," Joseph said after Henri repeated my question, continuing the rest of his thought in French. When he was done, Henri's dark eyes turned to me.

"He says that it will be a small blow to the emperor, but it will also be justice, for the old man."

I nodded at Joseph and held out my hand. And though he was French and I was a woman, we shook like Englishmen. When we were done, I said to Henri, "Two more questions. Joseph said before that he had helped Jean-Michel find out about certain chemicals. Ask him if he can get me this." I held out one of the little brown bottles Dr. Pruitt had given me, now nearly empty. "To make someone sleep."

Joseph took the bottle while Henri spoke, sniffed the contents, and put one tiny drop on his tongue. He slipped the bottle into his pocket, muttering, and Henri said, "He says he will find out."

"Also ask him what Jean-Michel wanted to know, what he has

been waiting by the lamppost to tell him. Was it news of the man we've been speaking of?"

Henri asked, and then listened to the response. "He says no, it was not about the man, but a woman. Jean-Michel wanted the name of a woman in the hospital at Charenton." Our eyes met briefly. It was the asylum we had visited. "He says he found the name."

"And what was it?"

Joseph did not wait for a translation, but merely replied, "Thérèse Arceneaux."

·CHAPTER TWENTY-THREE

*W*e made our way back in silence. The back alleys and boulevards had become sleepier in the hours before dawn. I
followed at Henri's heels, counting the repetitive motion of putting
one foot in front of the other, a calming process that could be used
as a background for sorting my thoughts. Lane had asked Joseph to
find the name of a woman in Charenton, and the name had been
Thérèse Arceneaux. I could not help but think of the woman who
had stroked my hand, talking of her Charlie and Louis. The nun
said she claimed the father of her child was the emperor of France,
but she was a madwoman. Wasn't she? There was certainly one man
who believed it: Ben Aldridge, also known as Charles Arceneaux.
And the emperor did not seem to be discounting the possibility
either. I wondered what had led Lane to Charenton in the first place.
He must have known that Ben was alive for some time.

I looked up and realized we were slipping through the street door
of the courtyard, the sky the luminous sort of blue-black that comes
just before the sun, the smell of earth and green a welcome change
from the gutters and rubbish heaps of the city. We seemed to be

alone but for a prowling cat, so we opened my back door, tiptoeing in like sneak thieves, and let it shut softly behind us.

Someone was in the kitchen, rattling the stove lids. "Go on through," I told Henri, "I'll see about getting us something to eat." He nodded, rubbing his heavy eyelids, and moved down the corridor while I opened the kitchen door.

Marguerite stood at the stove, her head wrapped in a kerchief, her spoon dropping into the pot with a soft clatter when she turned to see who was behind her. The kitchen smelled of hot chocolate. Mr. DuPont, sprawling untidily in a chair at the table, seemed to wake up at the sight of me. "Ah," he said cheerfully, "*Napoléon est mort.*"

"Good morning to you, too, Mr. DuPont," I replied, coming fully into the kitchen. I ignored the fact that he was once again not wearing a shirt. "What are you doing up so early, Marguerite?"

Marguerite lowered her eyes, turning away from me to fish her spoon out of the pot. She really was a lovely little thing, extraordinarily so.

"*Bonjour, Mademoiselle.*"

Mrs. DuPont stood behind me in the doorway, a shawl around her nightgown, her hair hanging in a tight braid down her back, not a single strand out of place. "Marguerite," she said in the calm, even way I found intensely irritating, "you have not spoken to Mademoiselle properly. Apologize at once, and then you will scrub the front sidewalk after breakfast."

I glanced back at Marguerite, saw a slight twitch to her shoulders, and was stung to anger. No child deserved to be chastised for not responding properly to a lady dressed in Mr. Babcock's pants. "Mrs. DuPont," I said, "Marguerite is always polite, which frankly is more than I can say for you most of the time. And I'm quite sure my sidewalk is just as clean as it needs to be."

Mrs. DuPont's white face remained expressionless while Mr. DuPont shook his head. *"Napoléon est —"*

Mrs. DuPont cut off this statement with a sharp, *"Tais-toi!"* a phrase I assumed meant, "Be quiet!" since that is exactly what Mr. DuPont did. I shot another look at Marguerite's twitching shoulders, and realized that the child was not crying; she was trying not to laugh. I raised a brow, decided I had no time to decipher the intricacies of this inexplicable family, and turned back to Mrs. DuPont.

"I'm glad you're here. We need to speak about —"

"Can I offer Mademoiselle some chocolate? Or a bun?"

"No, thank you, Mrs. DuPont. And please refer to me as 'Miss Tulman.' Tonight I will —"

Mrs. DuPont drew herself up tall in the square frame of the doorway, the grim reaper in a nightgown. "Have we not served you well?"

"I —"

"Do we not keep our peace?"

"You —"

"Do you not eat the hearty, English breakfast?"

I sighed.

"And where will you find such clean windows? Such shining glass —"

"Tais-toi!" I said. "Please," I added. Mrs. DuPont closed her mouth. "I am not asking you to leave. Or at least not yet. But I am asking you to leave the house for tonight. Do you have somewhere you can go? For one night?"

She looked at me for a moment, then her eyes slid toward the hallway, where Henri Marchand had gone, and back to my frankly bizarre choice of clothing. And she smiled. It was not a nice smile. "As I said, Mademoiselle, we can keep secrets. You will find no others that can keep secrets so well."

"*Napoléon est* —"

"*Tais-toi!*" she hissed. "Perhaps Mademoiselle would like to give us some money," she said, still smiling. "For the hotel?"

A small silence fell, and Mrs. DuPont's black eyes stared back significantly into mine. I had no time for this. Or funds.

"Actually, Mrs. DuPont, perhaps you would like to tell me what you are selling at my back door? That is what you're doing, is it not? I would think those profits might be plenty for one night at a hotel."

All I could hear was the bubbling of the chocolate. One of Mrs. DuPont's bone-white hands crept up to adjust the shawl around her shoulders.

"I think you'll find that I can keep secrets, too, Mrs. DuPont. Do we have an understanding?"

The quiet in the kitchen stretched until there was one tiny nod from Mrs. DuPont's chin.

"Good. Please be out of the house by the time the sun goes down, and you may come back in the morning. Maybe at that time we can continue the discussion about your future arrangements." I wondered if it was too much to hope that we'd be gone from Paris by then. "Thank you very much, Mrs. DuPont. Good day, Mr. DuPont. Have a lovely morning, Marguerite." I started to the leave the kitchen. "Oh, and I would happily accept your offer of chocolate and buns. If you could bring them into the dining room, as soon as is convenient? There is no hurry."

I glanced at the clock in the corridor, feeling satisfied as I walked down the hall.

We had nineteen hours, forty-two minutes until Ben Aldridge came.

Five men came at intervals during the day, Jean-Baptiste and four of his cousins, all entering through the courtyard with milk or bread or some other supply to "deliver," and then never actually leaving again. The day had turned gray and cool and there was a fine rain falling, darkening the house stones. If anyone was observing the courtyard, it was from the interior of one of the other houses. The last to come was Joseph, a bag of tools at his side and a hammer in his belt for a disguise. Mary spirited him up to Mr. Babcock's room, where his male family members awaited, well provisioned with the remnants of the ridiculously vast breakfast Mrs. DuPont had prepared. I really should have known better when I asked for "chocolate and buns."

Mary had been very somber as she packed our things. She'd said nothing of it, but I'd seen her in the garden again with the boy Robert, and I felt rather sorry about it. She scowled at the little bottle Joseph had supplied me, green instead of brown, sitting next to its fellow on the chimneypiece of my bedchamber.

"Are you thinking that will be enough, Miss?" she asked. "Last time it was taking ever so much more."

"Yes, there will be enough," I replied grimly. I had more stashed away for Uncle Tully. The ones over the fireplace were for someone else.

When I came through the shelf door, Uncle Tully was waiting for me in his favorite frock coat, rocking back and forth on his heels. He looked almost like his old self standing there, the white beard spreading wide when he saw me.

"Little niece!" he shouted at me. "You are two minutes not late for playtime!"

Which meant I was one minute early. I smiled absently, coming back to the reality of the coat that hung loose on his frame and the space he had been confined to. So much had been taken from him. But tonight he would sleep, and when he woke we would be back at Stranwyne with Lane, and he would play and we would find a way to keep up the illusion that my uncle's only home was now the cemetery on the hill. Heaven knew what I was going to say to Mrs. Cooper, though surely bringing Lane with me would help. I saw that Uncle Tully was now plucking at his coat.

"You are not ready," he said. "You are not thinking of clocks."

I snapped back to attention and smiled at him. "Of course I am, Uncle. I came especially to help you wind them." Nothing could have induced me to miss my uncle's clock-winding, not when I was about to spin his carefully constructed world out of balance yet again. The clocks chose that moment to strike four times. Eight more hours until Ben Aldridge came. "See, they have said it's time. Which shall we do first?"

We began, alternating the privilege of turning the winding key, always clockwise, of course; my uncle would not have had a clock that wound otherwise, if such a thing existed. He knew precisely how many turns each one of them required. The last clock fell to me and, as it was on the floor, we sat there, too, my uncle cross-legged and me in a poof of skirt, both of us mentally calculating the turnings.

My uncle shook his head and said, "There are not enough, Simon's baby." I paused in my twisting of the key.

"Is this one not thirty-seven?"

"No, no! Not windings! Clocks!"

I turned the key again, the tick of the mechanism soft in the sound-deadened room. The clock room of Stranwyne had held hundreds of clocks, the ticking alone a noise one almost had to swim through. We had only brought ten of those clocks to Paris, all we'd had room for, small ones, chosen in haste. It would give me much joy to see my uncle back with his clocks. Uncle Tully was still shaking his head, muttering.

"Shall I? Shall I tell her a secret? Should I? Shall I?"

I finished the thirty-seventh turn, returned the key to its place inside the clock, shut the glass door, and then folded my hands to wait while Uncle Tully argued with himself. This was a common enough debate, and one that almost always meant he told. He lifted his bright blue eyes to me for the briefest moment and then whispered, very loudly. "I went down the stairs."

I nodded, thankful it was nothing worse. "I know you did, Uncle. It's all right this time, but we —"

"No, no!" he said, voice rising. "It is not right! No!" He pulled on his coat sleeves. "The rooms were wrong, and the floors did not squeak where they should, and there were things outside, not the right things. . . ."

"What things? You didn't go outside, did you, Uncle Tully?"

His head was in a permanent state of shaking back and forth now.

"No, no. Not outside. They were all the wrong things. There were other places, not hills, not grass, and there was no Mrs. Jefferies. Where has Mrs. Jefferies gone, little niece?"

I kept my voice calm. "Mrs. Jefferies is Mrs. Cooper now, do you remember, Uncle? She is at Stranwyne, keeping your things tidy, just as Marianna told her to." He rocked slightly in his position on the floor. "Just like we are doing what Marianna told us. Do you remember? But, Uncle, I want you to think about something. Sometimes we like one thing better than other things, isn't that right? I like the flower best, and Marianna liked her piano, and you like your bells and the box with the lightning right now. Isn't that so?"

He frowned, mulling this over, and I continued before he could find an objection.

"And sometimes we like one place better than another place, yes? We both like to be at Stranwyne, and would rather be there than here. But, Uncle, even if I like one place better than another, what I like best is when you are in it. If you are there, then I think that place is right. Do you understand?"

Uncle Tully's face was screwed up, his mouth puckered, as if he were studying the complexities of a very tiny engine. Finally he looked up and said, "I think a place is better with clocks, little niece."

"Yes, Uncle," I said, smiling.

"Will Lane ever come? Or did he get tired and it's the forever kind of gone now?"

I paused before I said, "He will come, Uncle Tully. I'm certain of it."

"You always know, little niece," he sighed, some of his distress ebbing. "You always know what we should do, and Lane always knows what is right. You always know what we should do, little niece, like Marianna said."

How I wished that were true.

His words were still running through my head when I stood before the mirror in my bedchamber, Marianna's portrait watching me from the wall, the silver fish now sitting beside the swan on the bedside table, trying on first one dress and then another before carefully arranging my hair. I had to believe that Lane was coming here just as much as my uncle did, and that Lane would know the right thing to do. That some of this weight inside me would lift, and that I would have to make no more of these decisions alone.

There were two more hours until Ben Aldridge came.

I turned down the gas, all the sconces dark except for two, leaving the salon in a soft yellow light, almost like candles. The shutters were latched, curtains drawn, the clock pointing to three minutes until midnight. Our stage was set. One of Joseph's cousins waited on the upper landing, two were with Joseph in the library, and one with Jean-Baptiste in the cabinet beneath the foyer stairs, ready to block the doors as soon as Ben Aldridge and whoever came with him entered the ladies' salon. I had not asked how they planned to subdue him or get the required information, but when Joseph shut the door to the library I had heard the distinctive *click* of a gun being loaded.

Henri leaned on the chimneypiece, smoking, his dark brows pulled down. He had spent part of the day napping on my settee while I did the same in my bedchamber, and I'd been too busy the rest of the time to pay much attention to his doings. I had not asked him to be here and he had not asked to stay, so we just didn't speak of it. Mary fidgeted on the settee, playing with her apron as if she wanted to find something to scrub with it. I sat down beside her, nerves jangling, wondering what I had put in motion, and where it all might end. We watched the clock hands move.

A carriage went by, and our three heads jerked in unison toward the front of the house. But the rattling moved on down Rue Trudon, fading with the seconds. I smoothed my skirt, touched my knot of hair, feeling my pulse beat hard in my neck. The clock struck and I jumped.

Henri looked quickly away from my face, throwing his cigarette into the hearth, while Mary, who had been frowning at Henri, flipped out her pocket watch to adjust the time, a bit of tongue sticking out between her teeth. Eleven more times the chimes rang, and half an hour later they struck again, and then once more on the hour. Three more times this happened. Two thirty in the morning. The room was silent, the street outside was silent, and we sat like people in a sepulcher.

I stared down at my hands, still and folded in my lap, mildly surprised to see the tiny splashes of water dotting my fingers. He wasn't coming. I counted the drips, *five, six, seven, eight,* as they fell from my cheeks. Something had changed. We had been too obvious. For whatever reason, Ben had decided not to trade. I heard his voice again in my ear, whispering, *"And what do you think I do with things I have no use for? Do you think I will hesitate?"*

My chest heaved, and heaved again, but no matter how hard I tried to fill my lungs, I was still short of air. I was suffocating. I stood, pushing away Mary's hand, turned away from Henri Marchand, half hidden in a haze of smoke, and walked out of the salon. I passed the open door of the library, startling the half-asleep men inside, and then ran down the back corridor. Still struggling for air, I threw open the door into the cool green smell of the courtyard.

I needed to be thinking, laying out a plan. But I could not. I hurried down a graveled path, wiping my cheeks, until I was leaning over the edge of the fountain, letting the spray wet them again. The bricks along the fountain pool's edge were loose, the mortar crumbling beneath my hand, like everything was crumbling. I didn't know how to correct this. I didn't know how to find Lane, how to take care of my uncle, how to provide for Mary and Mrs. Cooper and the village and Stranwyne, or even what to do when I went back to the house. It was like the numbers had no order, as if one no longer proceeded to two and three and four, leading in circles instead of straight, honest lines. The knot of pain returned to my middle, doubled in intensity; I couldn't stand straight against it. I had failed them. All of them. I had, and I alone.

And almost as soon as this revelation came, I had two others: The first being that I was not alone, not in this garden, the second that I was very, very stupid. The water splashed and played and I heard the noise again, a sound that could not be made by wind or a falling branch or even the paw of an animal; it was the soft crunch of gravel beneath a foot, near, and directly behind me.

Now my mind was moving, thoughts shooting like the crackling blue electricity. I considered the speed of the unhurried footsteps, the nearest path and how fast I could get there, the brick that was cold beneath my hand, loose in its mortar. The sound of the footsteps disappeared, masked by the paving stones surrounding the fountain and the splashing water, but I felt the presence. Maybe it was the change in the wind or the atmosphere, or maybe I could almost hear breath. But the presence was there. And then I felt a touch on my shoulder.

I spun, swinging my hand as if delivering a slap, only my hand now held the brick. The brick connected with flesh, there was a grunt, and the tall figure that had been standing behind me staggered back a step before falling to the paving stones. And there he lay, rolled onto his side, hands clutching his head where the brick had done its job.

But I did not run as I'd meant to. I stood still as the man on the ground moaned once and sat up, still clutching his head, murmuring some of the same curses I'd heard Henri use in French. But even in the darkness, in the wrong time and place and in the wrong language, I knew that voice, and the long fingers, the way the elbows were now resting on his knees.

I knew the sound of my name when his low voice said, "Katharine, was that a brick you just hit me with?"

CHAPTER TWENTY-FOUR

I stared at Lane like an imbecile, my mind as blank and numb as the brick in my hand. He was thin, sitting in a pale square of light from a moon I hadn't even noticed, his hair long and several days' growth of beard on his chin. I tried to set down the brick, but I could not remove my gaze from what was in front of me. It fell with a watery *thunk* into the pool. And then Lane was on his feet. I'd almost forgotten how quickly he could do that. Lithe, like a cat.

"What in God's name are you doing here?" he said, keeping his voice soft. One of his cheekbones was darker than the other.

"You're bleeding," I said.

"Where did you come from? Are you next door?"

"What?"

"Get back inside, Katharine."

"But —"

"Go! Quick!"

"But —"

He repeated the French phrase I had heard a few seconds earlier, his low voice both familiar and new, then grabbed me by the arm and I was trotting after him, away from the fountain and across the paving stones, where he thrust me straight into a clump of ornamental trees. I squeezed into the damp, leafy space, the branches snagging at my dress, the ground beneath my feet soft with moisture and uneven roots. Lane pushed in after me.

It was very dark. I sensed rather than saw the motion of his finger going to his lips, stopping my questions. We stood still, listening. I heard the wind, the fountain, my heaving breath, and far away, the howl of a dog. I could make much more sense of those things than my thoughts at that moment. Then I heard a little hiss of pain as the long fingers I loved so well began exploring the side of his face.

"Katharine," he said, his voice barely a whisper, "why did you just try to kill me?"

"I wasn't trying to kill you, I . . . you were sneaking up behind me."

"I didn't reckon on it being that dangerous," he murmured, trying to see the stickiness on his hand in the dark. I bent down, feeling beneath the hem of my dress for the seam of my petticoat.

"Don't . . ."

I got my teeth on the edge, and ripped a piece of thin muslin away from the lace.

"Katharine . . ."

I finished tearing away a vaguely rectangular piece of cloth and reached up to press it on his wounded cheek.

"Katharine," he said. "I had a handkerchief in my pocket."

I pressed hard on the wound. Either I was standing in a hole or he was taller than I remembered. I couldn't think of a thing to say. All I could think was that the blood soaking through the cloth was warm on my fingertips, the skin beneath my hand present and real. Here, solid, not gone, not dead. With me. My breath caught as I held the torn cloth, and I realized it was because I was crying.

I heard him sigh again, and then the space between us went away. My wet cheek was pressed against his chest; there were hands on my back and I was being held tight, tucked beneath his chin, his mouth in my hair. Long fingers steadied my head, kisses working their way from my forehead to my cheeks to my ears and around to my mouth, where I tasted the saltiness of my own tears. I had no knowledge of what had brought him to this courtyard, no understanding of anything, really, except that for the first time in so many days and months that I could not remember, something was as it should be. The ever-aching knot inside me loosened, relaxing its grip.

After too short a time he reached back and unwound my fingers from his hair, put my arms around his waist, and rested his chin back on top of my head. I became aware of the garden again, of the quiet, the branches poking my back, and the heartbeat beneath my ear.

"You have a beard," I whispered.

"Razors have been scarce."

"Where have you been?"

"Locked up," he replied. "Unofficially. What are you doing here?"

"Looking for you."

He leaned back and I tilted my chin, his face a frame of shadow. I felt the tension drawing inside him, like a coiling spring. "But what about Mr. Tully?"

"He's here, safe. In the attic."

I felt him flinch. "In Paris?"

"Yes, he's —"

"What? How did . . . Is he —"

But then his fingers went to my lips, shutting them, as if it had been my voice rising above a whisper. The darkness became charged, strained with listening, and then I heard what he had. Voices in the garden, male, speaking very quietly in what I thought was French. He pulled me in close as two figures passed not ten feet from our hiding place, avoiding the gravel paths, moving quickly through the foliage toward the street door.

We listened to them go, to the faint footsteps in the stone passage, and the quiet returning. I felt Lane's body relax, and risked a whisper. "Who are they?"

"I don't know," he replied in my ear. "Just watching, maybe, or more likely looking for me. I have to go, Katharine. I only came to get my things."

"From Mrs. Reynolds's, you mean? What were you doing there? And where are you going?"

"Shhh."

"Lane, where do you have to go?"

I could feel him shaking his head. He was pushing me away now. I held on to his arms.

"Listen to me, Katharine. Get Mr. Tully out. I don't know how you managed it, but he can't stay here. Ben Aldridge is here, and he needs him. He . . ."

"I know it. He came to take him from Stranwyne. . . . I had to . . ." I searched for a way to explain, to keep him from bolting away from me. "They all think he's dead now. The village, Aunt Bit . . . We told them that so we could —"

"You told my aunt Bit that Mr. Tully was dead?" The note of con-demnation I heard there made me stiffen.

"And what else could I have done? Let Mr. Wickersham have him?"

"No, but you could have . . ." He paused.

"Could have what? Did you have a better plan? If so, you really should have written and told me of it. You've let Aunt Bit worry that you were dead for months." I felt hurt creeping into the words. "And why didn't you? Why didn't you write? One word to . . ."

I felt the muscles of Lane's arms go tense beneath my hands. He stood ramrod straight, looking over my head, gaze fixed on the house. Color blushed faintly on his face, on the leaves and the rosebushes, as if the first rays of dawn had reached over the rooftops. But it was too early for the sun. I spun around. The kitchen window of my grandmother's house was glowing, as was Mrs. Reynolds's, and it took a long moment to realize that the rosy flicker was not the light of gas or even candles.

It was fire.

Lane broke from the little clump of trees and ran down the grav-eled path, while I untangled my skirts from the branches and went after him. His long legs reached my back door far ahead of me, smoke billowing as he threw it open.

"Stay here!" he yelled over his shoulder before rushing inside.

I did not slow my stride, even for the back step, dashing into a thick cloud in the back corridor. I glanced to one side and through the smoke saw Lane throw the bucket of kitchen water onto the fire that was licking the wall behind the stove, and when I turned back to what was in front of me I nearly collided with Mary.

"Out the back," Mary managed to say, coughing, pushing me backward, "the front room's on fire!"

"So is the kitchen!"

We paused for a mere second, then ran in opposite directions, Mary presumably for the back door, while I dashed into the dining room and through to the library. The curtains were a flickering pattern of orange and yellow fire. Joseph and a cousin were pulling them down, trying to stop the spread of the flames, while Jean-Baptiste picked himself up from the floor, rubbing his jaw. I hurried into the foyer to fling open the front door, took a few quick breaths of the cleaner air, and then ran into the empty salon to unlatch the windows and draw out the smoke.

I saw the lights being lit in the house across the street, people pouring from Mrs. Reynolds's onto the sidewalks, nightgowns and bed caps and hair tied in rags, mistresses and servants indistinguishable in their confusion and dishevelment. I caught a quick glimpse of Mrs. Hardcastle in a dressing gown before I pushed the last window open, hiked up my skirts, and ran for the stairs.

Smoke rose through the central stairwell, thinning as I climbed above the cloud. *Twenty-eight stairs, twenty-nine, thirty . . .* My body demanded more breath, but the smoke burned, like it had that night in the workshop, the night that had changed everything. *Fifty-two, fifty-three . . .* I reached the final landing, coughing and sputtering.

The smoke was very thin here, barely noticeable beyond the stairs, but all I could see was that the storeroom was unlocked and open, giving me a straight view to the bookshelf door, also swinging gently on its hinges. I burst into Uncle Tully's workshop in an explosion of sooty skirts.

Most of the toys were still there, but Uncle Tully's lightning box was gone, his bench turned over, the tools in disarray. And Henri Marchand stood coolly in the middle of the room, hands in his jacket pockets. He turned his dark eyes on me, but I had no time for him.

"Uncle!" I yelled. "Uncle Tully!"

I ran into the little bedroom, but it was empty, and so was the bathing room. The other door, the one that connected with Mrs. Reynolds's, was unbolted, slightly ajar; the painted cracks had been slit with a knife. My insides wrenched, so hard I thought I might be ill.

"Uncle Tully!" I screamed, stumbling through the door. The large chest that had been blocking the way in from Mrs. Reynolds's was now toppled on its side. I scrambled over it and through the debris of the silent, dusty storeroom. "Uncle!"

I went like a demon down Mrs. Reynolds's stairs, and there was no one anywhere, nothing, not even a fire, each landing, each bedchamber soundless and empty, the overstuffed foyer quiet in a smoky haze. Whatever had caused the glow in her back windows must have already been put out. I stood still in the hushed gray air, panting, not heeding the pandemonium I could hear on the other side of the front door. Uncle Tully was gone. I had been outmaneuvered. Ben had played his hand skillfully indeed, and now my uncle was paying the price.

I heard the commotion outside growing, and the clanging of a distant bell that was not Uncle Tully's. Someone must have sent for the police or the firemen. I turned and flitted up the stairs, back the way I came, and into the storeroom. I righted the overturned chest with difficulty before going through to Uncle Tully's bedchamber, dragging the chest as best I could across the open doorway. I barred the little door behind me, kicking something in my haste, and a green bottle went rolling across the carpet, empty. I picked it up, clutching it tight in my hand.

Henri Marchand was still amid the mess and broken chairs of the workshop, gazing at the unfinished automaton of a singing bird at his feet. He had one hand in his pocket, the other fingering a brass wheel that had been left behind, one of the gyroscopes my uncle had taken apart. I had no idea how he'd gotten here, or what he thought he was seeing, and at the moment was beyond caring. But his next words jolted me awake.

"So this is where you kept him?" he said quietly. "Locked up. Like an animal."

There was real disgust in his voice. It lit a fury beneath my fear. I marched up and snatched the wheel from his hand. "Do not ever," I said slowly, "touch my uncle's things."

His brows contracted, then the sound of running footsteps came across the storeroom, and Lane slid through the door. It was the first time I'd seen him in proper light: gaunt, soot-stained, unshaven, and with a bleeding cut beside his eye. He looked terrible, but I could not help the illogical feeling that his presence was going to put all this right. I squeezed the little brass wheel until it threatened to break the skin of my hand as Lane took in Henri Marchand and what was obviously an empty workshop.

"Is he gone?" Lane said, his voice very low. There was no need to ask who he meant. I nodded.

Lane took four strides across the room, pulled back a fist, and hit Henri Marchand in the face. I gasped. Henri dropped straight to the floor, as if his body had suddenly chosen to obey gravity rather than the reverse, a short scream ringing out from somewhere near the door. Mary must have come in just behind Lane. I took a step toward Henri.

"Stay away from him, Katharine!" Lane said.

I looked up at Lane, shaking the reddening knuckles of his right hand, his skin flushed even darker with rage. Lane's temper was nothing new to me; more than half of the time, I was the cause of it. But I had never seen him give way to actual violence. He turned his gray eyes to me, chest still heaving.

"He works for Wickersham."

My lips remained parted for a long moment before the shock of the words finally closed them. Always Henri had been there, every time I looked up, sticking to my side without question through the bizarre events that had circled me like vultures. And I had trusted him. I wrapped an arm around my stomach. Why had I trusted him? I took a small step closer to Lane as Henri sat himself upright, ruefully rubbing his jaw.

"Well met, my friend," he said almost cheerfully. "You rule the day."

I needed no translation to know exactly where Lane had told Henri Marchand to go. At that moment, I wished exactly the same.

CHAPTER TWENTY-FIVE

I left Mary in the salon with the police and hurried up the stairs. The fires in both houses had been deliberately set, of course, and two *gendarmes* found it their duty to inquire as to why. While I feigned fright and illness like a proper sort of lady, Mary acted the part of a heroine. She was speaking much faster than the poor Frenchman could possibly write, using her best British Cockney, filling her story so full of nonsense I was surprised he had not already given up and gone home, especially when a more coherent statement could be had next door. Mrs. Reynolds's recitation of events was nearly the same if one could sift through the chatter, except for the five strangers hurrying down her stairs in the confusion — "burglars" she'd called them — two with a large box between them, two more supporting an old man who appeared to be either ill or asleep. The thought of this made my feet move faster as I went softly up the steps. I locked the storeroom and ducked back through into my uncle's workshop.

Joseph slouched against one wall, silent and with his hands in his pockets. His cousins had made themselves scarce before the *gendarmes* came, but his brother, Jean-Baptiste, sat against the wall, trimming his fingernails with a short, sharp knife. Lane straddled one of our two unbroken chairs, elbows propped on its back to face Henri, who was tied to the other one. His jacket strained at the shoulders where his arms were pulled tight behind him, each ankle bound to a chair leg.

A quiet conversation in French had been going on between the two of them, but they stopped when I entered, two dark heads turning to look at me, one with his sleek smugness only slightly ruffled, the other tan-skinned, gray-eyed, still bloody, and not a little wild. He was calm, I saw, but fighting his temper; I knew that set of jaw and the stony quality of his eyes. I wondered what sort of infuriating things Henri had been saying to him, but mostly I thought that the person Lane actually needed to be having a conversation with was me. I had no notion how he fit into what was happening here at all.

Lane stood and came across the littered floor to meet me, as if he did not want me near the man in the chair. I opened my hand and showed him the empty green bottle in my palm.

"They will have given him this," I said, ignoring the feel of Henri's eyes watching us. "If they got it all down him, then we have five, perhaps six hours. Last time he . . . he did not wake well."

Lane took the bottle, rolling it in his fingers. "This is how you got him here?" I nodded, and he turned his body just a bit, partially blocking the view of the man tied to the chair. "Is Mr. Tully all right? Has he been . . . well?"

"Well enough," I replied. We both knew Uncle Tully was not well now. "What are we going to do?"

Lane put a hand on the back of my head, kissing me once on the forehead before he went back to Henri, sliding easily into his backward position on the chair. I met Henri's dark eyes and the impertinent smile playing about his mouth, and suddenly had a very good idea of the sort of thing he'd been saying to Lane. That peck on my forehead had been about more than affection, and we were all aware of it.

"Tell me what you know about Ben Aldridge," Lane said to him. We were speaking English now, I noted.

"If you are meaning Arceneaux, you should be asking that question of her, my friend," Henri replied, eyes still on me.

I saw Jean-Baptiste's knife slow as he watched the proceedings intently, waiting for the word to intervene. Though a brew of anger and betrayal simmered just beneath my rib cage, I was also silently willing Henri to stop being an idiot.

"Or perhaps you have not had much time for talking," Henri continued, smiling at me. "That blood on your face is not your own, is it, *chérie?*"

My hand jumped to my cheek. Of course I had Lane's blood on my face, which would explain the way Joseph had stared, and Mary's offer of a handkerchief. And since when had Henri ever called me his "darling"? I dropped my hand and lifted my chin. Henri probably deserved whatever he got.

But Lane only said, "I will ask you again."

He had not even changed his position in the chair, yet there was something behind his words, something that riveted the attention. From the corner of my eye, I watched Joseph straighten and Jean-Baptiste's knife go still. There wasn't a man in this room that was not going to do exactly as Lane said when he spoke like that, including Henri, I realized, and the revelation startled me.

Henri shrugged against the ropes. "I was told to find out about his background, to mingle in his society. But he was a man favored by the emperor, high in the imperial circle. . . ."

"Then you knew him," I said, "before the ball." This hurt me. I could not help it. "And Mr. Babcock? Did you know about that, too?"

Lane looked back at me. "Is Mr. Babcock here?" Before Henri could respond or I could think how to answer, Joseph started speaking rapidly in French. Joseph almost never spoke in English, but it was good to remember that he understood his share of it. I watched Lane's face darken and, when Joseph had finished, Lane said, "I'm sorry, Katharine."

I took a breath against the pang in my chest and looked back to Henri. "Did you know? Is that why you took me to the morgue?"

Lane's gray eyes slid between us, but Henri was looking directly at me. "I swear to you I did not. And I did not intend to lose sight at the ball. On the grave of my mother."

"And what did you intend?" asked Lane.

Henri grinned. "Why, to find you, of course. Wickersham said she would lead me to you if she could and so she did, though the lady is not the talker. But I am guessing you know this. You should take her dancing more, *mon ami*."

I held my breath as Jean-Baptiste watched Lane, waiting for a sign. Nothing came. But I had seen the muscles in Lane's back tightening. I came to stand just behind him. When the low voice spoke again, it was dangerously quiet.

"And what did you find about Ben Aldridge?"

"Nothing at all since my assignment was changed." Henri's eyes went sly. "Since Wickersham asked me to find the traitor who had left our ranks."

By "traitor" he meant Lane, and then my own temper was igniting. "That is quite a word coming from you, Mr. Marchand." I nearly spat the words. "Remind me what country you were born in again?"

"I am no traitor to France," he replied, once again serious. "I do not betray France if I wish to see the emperor overthrown."

"You favor the royal line, then?" Lane said.

Henri lifted a shoulder. "I would see a king in France."

"So you help those that are the enemies of France?"

"I aid the enemies of Napoléon," he corrected.

Lane smiled. "I sympathize. But you are not helping the enemies of Napoléon."

"Allies or not, England will see the emperor overthrown," Henri said. "She must."

"England may. But Wickersham will not."

Again Lane had not moved, or significantly changed his voice, but somehow the entire room had fixed its attention.

"Let me explain," he said. "When you have information you are to write to Wickersham's secretary, Mr. Johnson at the British Embassy, in English, with a particular wording that tells Wickersham when and at which of your chosen places you are to meet. Am I right?"

Henri remained silent.

"I know I am right," he continued, "because those were the instructions I followed for over a year. Until the day I arranged my meeting, and Wickersham didn't come. My information could not wait. It was so important, in fact, that I boxed up a silver service and took it to the embassy, said it was to be an imperial gift, that the order was late and that I'd been instructed to put it directly into Mr. Wickersham's hands. In short, I made such a nuisance of myself that they showed me to Wickersham's office. Only the office didn't belong to Wickersham." Lane spoke directly into Henri's gaze. "It was Ambassador Cowley's office. Wickersham was his secretary, unexpectedly sent to London for a few days. And the man Johnson, our contact? Always taking down Wickersham's notes? Wickersham's valet."

He paused, letting the words sink in. I shook my head in confusion, and he reached up to find one of my hands, absently rubbing a thumb across the back of it. Henri stared.

"It explained a good deal," Lane said. "Like why we were not allowed to take Ben Aldridge, only watch, even when I told Wickersham what he was buying and what I was sure he was building. And why the British government didn't just come and take Mr. Tully in the first place. And why, the very next day after Wickersham returned from London, I began an annoying routine of having bullets whizz past my ears."

I tightened my grip on Lane's hand.

"My trip to the embassy was unappreciated. A new residence seemed wise. And why would that be, do you think, if all of these doings had the blessing of the ambassador? Wickersham is making a play for power, or position, or both. Or he's working for someone else. Russia, maybe . . . Who knows who he's dealing with, or who he might be double-dealing with? Anyone who wants the weapon for themselves or wants to keep someone else from getting it. I found

Wickersham's rooms. I searched them, and Johnson's. I even watched him meet with you. . . ."

That surprised Henri, I saw.

"But he is careful, and in the end all I knew was the one government he was not working for, and that was the British. He played us all for fools. I don't enjoy being played for a fool. Do you?"

A heavy silence filled the attic, the sound of truth settling in. I thought of Wickersham's brash behavior in my morning room, his ungentlemanly overconfidence. I'd never once thought to question his credentials. I realized that Lane and Henri were now staring at each other, like two dogs circling, Lane's thumb very deliberately tracing the veins of my hand.

"Oh, stop it," I said, jerking my hand away. "Both of you." I saw Henri's brows go up at that. "I don't care who Mr. Wickersham is at the moment. How do we get Uncle Tully back?"

Instead of answering, Henri asked suddenly, "What is the weapon?"

Lane and I glanced at each other before his gaze slid back to Henri.

"Listen to me." Henri's voice was grave. "I do not know this man, this Mr. Tulman, except for what Wickersham has said, that he was a lunatic caged and badly treated by his niece. I can see this lie, and I can see that you are not lying to me now, *mon ami*." This last had been to Lane. "And as for the so-called emperor of France, I think we can find agreement, there, yes?"

Lane did not answer, but the gray eyes held Henri's brown for some time.

"What is the weapon?" Henri asked again.

Lane glanced at Joseph and Jean-Baptiste, still standing ready, and then again looked at me. I gave him one tiny tilt of my head. He turned back to Henri. "It will sink an ironclad ship."

"You are certain of this?"

"Quite certain," I said. I saw him eyeing the discarded brass wheel I had snatched from him earlier, now sitting on the righted work-bench beside us. I didn't need to explain the importance of such a weapon to him.

"Your uncle," Henri said, "he made the bells ring?"

I saw Lane's brows go up. "Yes," I replied.

"And he can make this weapon, to sink an iron ship?"

"Yes."

Henri turned to Lane. "Then I have three questions, my friend."

Lane smiled. Henri was, after all, tied to a chair. "Ask your questions."

"Why did you not leave Paris when your life was attempted? Where have you been these past days, and what was so urgent to tell Wickersham?"

I watched Lane, to see if he would answer. These were all things I wanted to know, too. Lane shrugged, much as Henri had against his ropes. "I don't mind telling you. I did not leave Paris because Ben Aldridge and I have unfinished business between us, business that has nothing to do with Wickersham. Even more so now. And as for where I've been, I was underground. Beneath a crypt in what I think was a wine cellar."

"Ben must have been keeping you for Uncle Tully," I said, suddenly putting this together, "to have you there, so Uncle Tully would work." Which meant Ben would have never traded Lane for my uncle. "How did . . ."

I paused. Lane had straightened, his lazy stance in the chair gone. Jean-Baptiste slid up the wall to his feet. "You said Ben Aldridge was at Stranwyne, trying to take Mr. Tully. You mean he came himself? Into the house?"

"Yes. But they went to the wrong door. It's been so long, he must have forgotten which was the —"

"Which wrong door?" Now Lane had gone absolutely still. "Was he in your bedroom?" I reached down and took his hand back in mine. He let me, but his eyes did not move from my face. I hoped he wouldn't notice the scar on my neck.

"I am not hurt," I said. "I —"

"This is most interesting," said Henri, breaking into our conversation, "but perhaps you can continue your little quarrel at another time? I would like the answer to my last question."

The gray eyes were back on Henri now, and there was a storm in them.

"What was your information that could not wait?" Henri insisted.

"I think I know what you went to tell Wickersham," I said, pulling Lane's gaze back to me. "You went to tell him that Ben Aldridge is the son of Napoléon the Third."

Lane waited a moment before he nodded.

"Ah," Henri said. "Then I am sorry for him. That is an unfortunate dealing of the cards." He glanced very deliberately at my hand, pale in Lane's tan one, the impertinent grin lurking once again at the corners of his mouth. "Would you not agree, *chérie*?"

I only just kept from rolling my eyes as Lane's grip strengthened, his thumb beginning another slow trace of the veins in my hand.

"Yes," Lane said. "That is very unlucky. For him." These words had nothing to do with Ben Aldridge's origins. Lane smiled, the wicked one I remembered of old, and Henri smiled back. Two knowing smiles that might have erupted into a fight if one of them had not been tied to a chair.

"Just stop it!" I snapped, pulling away my hand. "I don't care what you two think of each other, or who Ben's father is, any more than I care about Mr. Wickersham at the moment. We have to get Uncle Tully back! Lane, where were you when you got out of the cellar?"

Henri cut off Lane's answer. "It was the Saint-Merri, was it not?"

Lane tilted his head in agreement.

"So I thought. You must take me there with you."

Lane smiled again. "And why should I do that?"

"Because I know where the man you call Aldridge goes underground. I know where he had you. And . . . I know the back way in."

The skepticism in the room could have been cut with the knife of Jean-Baptiste. Henri tried to lean forward, straining against his bonds.

"You must listen. It is where he has taken him. There is nowhere else. And they will be watching the Saint-Merri now that you are gone, *mon ami*."

Lane stared hard at Henri.

"You will need the back way in."

Lane sought my face and I saw the question there. He did not want to trust Henri, but he was afraid we might have to.

"Why?" I asked Henri. "Why help us bring him back?"

There was no tease in his voice when he replied, "Because if all that you say is so, Miss Tulman, I would not give this weapon to a Bonaparte. We may disagree on many things, but I do not think we disagree on that." He gave an upward glance to the window. "You will have to decide soon. We must leave before the light or wait for the evening."

Lane put his elbows on the back of the chair. "I don't know that I believe there is a back way. But if we go to see, are we clear on who is in charge?"

"Oh, I have always been certain of that, *mon ami.*"

Lane's brows came down, but Henri again stopped his teasing, his face going serious. "I have no wish to see the old man harmed, but I swear to you, I would not put this weapon in the hands of the emperor."

The room was quiet, only the ticking of Uncle Tully's clocks marking the silence. "Untie him," Lane said to Joseph.

All the impudence I was used to seeing on Henri Marchand's face returned full force. Before Joseph or his brother could even move he had sighed with relief and slipped his arms from their bonds, wriggling out of the loops around his wrists, stretching happily before reaching down to untie his own legs. He stood, slicking back his hair, and grinned at me.

"It is easy to be fooled by a magician, *chérie.* Do not forget that I like tricks of all sorts."

"Call her that again and I will hit you twice," Lane said, matter-of-fact. We all believed him.

Henri smiled as he straightened his sleeves. "What an amusing time we shall have."

CHAPTER TWENTY-SIX

I met Mary as I was hurrying down the stairs, she having just rid us of two thoroughly confused policemen. Mary and Lane had already renewed their acquaintance while fighting flames in the kitchen, but I watched her large eyes go a bit larger when he came stepping down behind me. I had not realized just how dead she'd thought he was. After a quick explanation of where we were going and the request that she find Lane something to eat, I dashed back up to Marianna's room to wash the blood off my face, stuff my hair into the red cap, and put on Mr. Babcock's pants.

When I came down again, Henri had surrounded himself with a new cloud of cigarette smoke in the already sooty foyer, watched carefully by a slouching Joseph, who had his jacket on, his pants tucked into his boots, apparently coming with us. Lane was silently finishing two pieces of bread with some sort of meat in between, his hair dripping. He must have dunked his head in a bucket. He caught sight of me on the stairs, and his expression so mimicked Mary's first reaction to seeing me in my ridiculous clothing that the comparison might have been comic had the whole situation not been my worst nightmare. I saw Henri's eyes sparkle.

"Miss Tulman has her own sense of fashion, *mon ami*. Were you not aware?"

I ignored him. I had watched Lane's face change from incredulous to dubious, and now I was observing the stubborn line of his mouth. That he would think I wasn't coming had never crossed my mind. I hastened across the foyer to set him straight.

"I've no time to argue with you," I said. "If they've given Uncle Tully the contents of that bottle, he is going to wake badly."

Lane's scowl deepened. "How badly?"

"The worst I've seen. He hurt himself and, Lane, he hasn't had a glimpse of you in eighteen months." I could have told him it had been five hundred and sixty-three days. "Uncle Tully is going to need me. You're going to need me if you want to get him out, and if we're going to crawl about underground I'll be of no use to you in petticoats."

An expression I couldn't quite fathom passed over his face, and I thought we were about to quarrel the point when a key rattled in the front door. The latch clicked, and then Mrs. DuPont stood looking in at us, swathed in an enormous cloak that was blacker than the paling night behind her. But before I could move or react, both Lane and Mrs. DuPont erupted into a storm of angry French.

I looked to Henri and Joseph, who both seemed as confused as I was, but at one of Lane's last words, something about money, I suddenly understood. I couldn't believe the answer had not come to me sooner. I took a step toward Mrs. DuPont. "You sold him! Didn't you?"

The room went quiet, Mrs. DuPont glancing over the soot stains on the wall before deigning to land her gaze on me. I was so livid I was shaking. How else could Ben have known about the attic room?

"How much did they pay you?" I yelled. "How much?"

Lane took my arm. "That's not what she's selling, Katharine," he said. "Come on."

Mrs. DuPont's bone-white mask looked just a bit aggrieved as she nodded once at Lane, carefully closed the front door, and began to move, bat-like, through the smoky foyer, the two of us following close behind. Lane paused to look over his shoulder.

"Not you," he said, the low voice forceful.

Henri stopped mid-stride, throwing up both hands as if in self-defense, Joseph right behind him with the gun in his hand. We chased after the billowing cloak of Mrs. DuPont, walking fast down the back corridor, the smell of burnt plaster going deep into my nose.

Mrs. DuPont slowed before the door to the kitchen, running her eyes over the charred, wet mess around the stove, then put a key to her door and disappeared inside, leaving it open behind her. I followed Lane into Mrs. DuPont's lair.

It was a plain room, unadorned, two comfortable chairs and a smaller stool arranged around an iron stove, an open door showing a bed neatly spread in the chamber beyond. But the room was also full of crates and boxes in perfect stacks, some reaching to the ceiling, piles of gunnysacks, and a table that was completely covered in exacting rows of brown and white paper parcels. The place looked like an apothecary, or the storeroom of a dry-goods shop. Lane put out a hand, stilling my questions, his gray gaze on Mrs. DuPont.

"Our agreement?" he said.

Mrs. DuPont turned from the table with the packages and silently held out two folded white parcels. He took them, gingerly prying open one corner to peer inside.

"I would not get that on your hands, Monsieur," she said.

I leaned closer to look, but he was already folding up the paper. "And how many did he purchase?"

"*Deux.*"

"This is the rest of it?"

Mrs. DuPont nodded. "And my payment? You are late with my payment."

Lane looked up. "I told you that I could not come sooner. But why don't you tell me, Madame, how much Miss Tulman has paid you already?"

I thought this an extremely good question. But Mrs. DuPont merely returned Lane's gaze and kept a stony silence.

"Well, I reckon you've gotten plenty, then," Lane said. "Close up shop, Mrs. DuPont. Get rid of it all and get your family out."

I looked about the room again, at the crates and boxes, this time reminded less of a shop than of the boat that had carried us across the Channel. And then, finally, the varied cogs in my mind meshed, clicking in rhythm. The mysterious comings and goings at the back door, and Mrs. DuPont's stubborn need to stay. All these goods were illegal, one way or another. Smuggled or stolen or who knew what. And the woman had been selling her wares out of my house. Lane took my arm again. "Come on. . . ."

"No. Not yet. I want Mrs. DuPont to explain to me why I shouldn't send for the police."

Mrs. DuPont clasped her hands together, her bony mask well in place. "You know best, I am sure, Mademoiselle. The police and I would have such a nice talk. About so many things."

I almost laughed, but the feeling in my chest was too bitter. "It's rather late for that, Mrs. DuPont. I'm afraid that game is over." I began to turn away.

"Wait, Mademoiselle!" Mrs. DuPont stepped forward, suddenly animated. "You must believe me! I have sold things, yes, many things, but it is for Marguerite!" She waved her hand about the room. "All for Marguerite, for her school! She shall be a lady! A proper French lady! Please, Mademoiselle! She is . . ." She lowered her voice, as if there might be eavesdroppers behind the sacks. "She is my grand-child. But I do not tell about lunatics, Mademoiselle. Even if they are English ones. I would not do that for money. I would not!"

"And why should I believe a lunatic is something you would not sell?"

She took a step back. "Are you simple? Are you slow? Because I am married to one, you fool!"

I opened my mouth, but then Lane had me by the arm and we were leaving, hurrying down the hallway. I looked back at Mrs. DuPont, standing in her room of contraband, thinking of lovely little Marguerite reading fairy tales in Marianna's room, not one whit afraid of her corpse-like grandmother, or her grandfather. What it said about my own mental state, that I had never even thought to consider Mr. DuPont as officially insane, that I'd seen him as just part of the strangeness of the Parisian landscape, I could not speculate. Normal, evidently, was completely unfamiliar to me.

At the end of the hall, Lane stopped, hand on the door latch to the foyer. The gray gaze was hard, fixed at nothing. "I don't understand. All this time, and I don't understand it."

There were hundreds of things I didn't understand at the moment. I was still amazed by the fact that he was here, in a white shirt gone gray and with his hair uncut, present and by my side.

"I tracked him all over Paris," he said. "Made lists, mapped the places he'd been, where he might go. I know where he bought his base metal, and sulfur and acid, and a host of other things. I know who his father is, and I know why he goes to Charenton. What I don't understand is why Ben Aldridge has been buying arsenic, arsenic that he doesn't have to sign his name for."

He held up the two little white packages, his body coiled up, unnaturally still.

"But whatever he is doing, I will end it this time. Like I should have at Stranwyne. I swear that to you."

I put my hand on his arm. "Let's end it, then, and go get Uncle Tully."

When Jean-Baptiste said he could find no one watching the house, we left him with Mary, who gave me a quick kiss on the cheek and stuffed a bun into Mr. Babcock's shirt pocket, and I slipped into the streets with Lane and Joseph, again following the lead of Henri Marchand.

Henri took us through the back alleys, avoiding the main boulevards, snaking our way through the city as we had on our trip to Rue Tisserand. We moved fast, Lane at Henri's left elbow, Joseph on his right, as if they were escorting a criminal or a dignitary. I trotted a few steps behind, watching Lane. He was shadowy in the predawn light, but a shadow that seemed natural, to belong, turning corners he knew, muttering the occasional word to Joseph in French. He seemed a man in his place, not a man in a place he has carved for himself, as he'd been at Stranwyne. It made me wonder what he saw now when he thought of home. The notion made me uneasy.

Despite our speed, the light grew, and even with a thin, early fog my anonymity was coming to an end. I received a long, penetrating look from a flower seller setting up her wares before Henri led us sliding down a short, steep embankment that ended in a stone wall.

My feet squelched when I landed at the bottom of the wall, the smell of the river wafting up foul from the fog. We were at the edge of the Seine. The water was lower here, or the banks higher; a thin strip of muddy land was just navigable between the river and the wall. We made our way beneath a stone bridge, and Lane hung back, speaking to me for the first time since our conversation in the corridor.

"Marchand thinks that we can't have you on the streets anymore, that we need to go underground a little sooner than he'd planned." A carriage rattled by on the street over our heads, the *clop* of the hooves reverberating against the stone. "He may be right, but until we get to the church, this is where he has his advantage. Stay close to Joseph or to me. Agreed?"

I hesitated. Cold-blooded murder or leaving us lost underground was not Henri's style, I thought. But then again, how could I be certain? It was not as if he'd ever been truthful with me.

"Do you agree, Katharine?"

I nodded. Joseph was bending down, following Henri into a round, bricked, stinking opening in the embankment. Lane stepped toward the tunnel, then quickly detoured to the edge of the river, mud suck-ing at his feet. He emptied the two white parcels of arsenic into the gray water, careful to not let a breeze catch the powder.

I watched him straighten, saw the tension in his back as he looked at the thin paper dissolving in the slight current, and suddenly I won-dered exactly what Lane was not telling me. There was something about this that was more than Wickersham and Ben Aldridge and my uncle; I could almost see the thing, coiled up and waiting, biding its time inside him. *"I only came to get my things,"* he'd said in the dark of the courtyard. And just where had he been planning on going next, when he came upon me beside that fountain? And he had been dodging my gaze ever since we left my grandmother's house, as he'd done once before, just before he left Stranwyne. I felt my own deter-mination set, like silver cooling in a mold. Lane and I would not be going down that particular road again, not if I could help it. He ducked into the tunnel, avoiding both my eyes and the stream of thick brown-ish water running out the tunnel's center. I climbed in after him.

One step inside and I gagged, triggering an almost instantaneous heave in my middle. The stench in the tunnel was so overpowering I staggered, using my free hand to pull Mr. Babcock's collar over my nose. Lane was bent almost double in front of me, nose cradled in the crook of his elbow. The light from the entrance grew fainter as the air grew warmer. I heard the squeaks and scrabblings of rats, and just ahead of Lane, the sound of Joseph rooting through his pock-ets. Henri must have heard Joseph as well because he looked back at us over his hunched shoulders, dark eyes wide over the sleeve he held over his face.

"Pas de lumière!" Henri shouted.

Joseph looked at Lane, Lane nodded, and only then did Joseph put the candle and matches back into his pocket. "Explosion," Lane whispered back at me. I eyed the passing murky water, for a moment unsure if a tunnel of fire could be more of a torture than this sewer of stink. But before the light from the outside world was quite gone, Henri turned right and squeezed himself into the wall. There was a crack there, I saw, a vertical fissure where the bricks of the tunnel had fallen away. I slipped in after Lane, feeling raw, cut stone beneath my hands. The fallen bricks had revealed a passageway, and one that was much older than the sewers.

The passage widened with height enough for me to straighten. I scooted my way in the dark, stone beneath each of my upraised palms, guiding me forward, the ground below angling down. And then the shuffling of feet ahead of me quieted, and I found myself in the open again, though where I did not know. The air was cool, smelling of stone and musty damp, except for the foulness wafting out from the way we'd come.

"Joseph," I heard Lane say, somewhere close to my right, and I listened to him once again fumble with the candles. A match struck, blazing like a star in the dark, blinding until my eyes adjusted to the soft, flickering light. We were in a stone passage, deep beneath the city, the candlelight dancing on dust motes and tan limestone walls. Beyond the light was utter blackness.

"Stay together," Henri whispered, voice enhanced by the stone, "and do not walk ahead of the light. There are sometimes holes, old wells that it would take a very long time to find the bottom of."

We walked slowly, gathered around Joseph's candle, Lane on one side, myself on the other, Henri a little ahead, just at the edge of the light circle, the only noise the occasional drip that echoed in the caverns. The pace was trying my patience. I wanted to run, to find my uncle instantly, and it felt as if we were getting nowhere. The walls were unvarying in their irregularity, endlessly carved shapes of the same-hued stone, sometimes with passages going off to the right and left. Some of these we passed, and some of these we took, but always with the same slow, steady footfalls, and often with a gradual descent.

Lane was evading my eyes, looking away if he caught my glance. Whatever he was hiding from me was still there. I could see it in the way he held his head and his back. I could feel it in the air, too; it was a wonder to me that everyone did not feel it. Perhaps Joseph did, being stuck between the two of us. He had frown wrinkles in his forehead, leaving white lines in the dust that was now covering us. For no reason at all I had an image of his quite pretty and very healthy sister. The knot in my middle was now a living, flaming thing, but it still found room for a little burst of heat directed at Lane.

After he looked away from me yet again, I asked Henri suddenly, "Are these the catacombs, Henri?" My words bounced back and forth above my head.

"No," he replied, "not like what the people used to pay their sous and francs to see. Those are full of bones, put together in patterns, like decoration. They are dangerous and are closed now. You must write a letter for permission to see them. But that is all on the other side of the Seine. We are in places where they *extraire*, they cut the stone." He turned to Lane. "What is the English?"

"Quarry," said Lane. "We're in stone quarries."

"Yes. Where they took the stone away. Maybe it was so with the catacombs as well. But these tunnels are long before France."

"Then how do you know of them?"

Henri grinned back at me, a smile of actual pleasure, with no teasing in it. "I played here, Miss Tulman, with my brother, many, many times. We found a way through our cellar, and it was like another world. We were explorers, we made maps. And all without leaving the house. Or that is how we explained it to our mother, rest in peace. Our explanations were not always so successful."

"And the church?"

"There is a crypt, but it is an old one, below the crypt of Saint-Merri. From the church that was there before, I think, and in there is a door to the tunnels. Very old. I am sad to say that my brother and I were sometimes guilty of using it to steal the priest's wine, which my mother told us was a very large sin. She made us go to confession, but, being a good mother, she took us to a different priest. But twice I have followed the man you call Aldridge to Saint-Merri from the Tuileries, and twice he has not come out again. I do not think he is confessing that many sins, do you, Miss Tulman? He is getting into the tunnels, I think. But I have not been here for many years now, so we shall . . . ah."

We all stopped. The tunnel was blocked by a long, cascading tumble of fallen stone.

"*Donnez-moi la chandelle, s'il vous plaît,*" Henri said softly, and I saw the quick look of permission Joseph got from Lane before he handed Henri the candle. I wondered if Henri knew he was on a leash, and probably a rather short one, if I had to guess. I'd been bumping against Joseph's jacket, and had felt the pistol in his pocket. But I had accomplished what I wished. Lane had met my eyes before we stopped.

Henri put a foot experimentally on the leading edge of the stones. "There is a way," he said, peering up at the pile. "It is not a hard climb. I will hold the candle."

When we had all scrambled through — the climb, in my opinion, not being difficult if you were the height of a grown man — the candle went back to Joseph. Joseph's hand was covered in pale, running drips of hardened wax, and I tied a handkerchief around it before we started off again. He smiled his thanks to me, showing the wrinkles around his eyes.

Twice more we climbed a rockfall, though none as difficult as the first, and then Henri held up his hand.

"What is it?" Lane asked. The stub of the candle showed me all of his suspicion.

Henri was looking about, as if he might be lost, but then his expression lightened, and he motioned for Joseph to bring the candle. There was a wooden door, with no handle or latch, covered in stone-colored dust and therefore barely distinguishable from the walls, not much different than we were. And then, all at once, a long, thin knife had appeared in Henri's hand.

Joseph jumped back, hand to his pocket, and Lane had me instantly behind him, but Henri merely grinned as he knelt down and slid the knife into the crack between the door and the jamb. I waited behind Lane, feeling his tension increase while Henri worked the blade, jiggling it against something on the other side. Henri stood and used all his weight to jerk upward on the knife handle.

Wood rattled and metal grunted on the other side, and Henri, triumphant, let the door swing open into the space beyond it. The knife was already gone, secreted to who knew where on his person.

"Shall I go first?" Henri offered. He stepped into the darkness, and Joseph went next, candle held aloft, hand in his pocket, watching Henri's every step. I followed Lane cautiously.

"This is the crypt you described, is it not?" Henri said, voice echoing. "Where the man Aldridge held you?"

I walked a little way down the flagged floor of a barrel-shaped room, narrow and chill, rough arches forming the ceiling. Long rows of stone shelves ran down each side, as far as I could see in the candlelight, empty of bodies, though a few still contained the ancient webbing of long-dead spiders. I shuddered, crossing my arms over my chest. Lane was talking softly near the tunnel door, Joseph listening intently as he lit Lane a new candle with his stub. The door, I saw, had a very dusty and unused wine rack tacked to it, concealing it from view; I vowed to someday examine every bookcase in Stranwyne.

Lane came down the center of the crypt with his light, then stepped to the side and pushed open a wooden door. He held up the candle and I saw a plain, windowless room of the same stone as everything we'd seen, a dilapidated wine shelf sagging in one corner.

"This was where he held you?" I asked. He did not answer.

"The way to the church is here," I heard Henri saying somewhere farther down, "up this ladder to open the floor of the crypt of Saint-Merri above, where they stored the brooms when I was a boy. I do not know if the priest even knew it was . . ."

Lane had still not answered. "Did he give you a light?" I asked abruptly. Lane shrugged, and I pressed my lips together. And in what sort of place was Ben keeping Uncle Tully? He would have almost certainly woken up by now. I moved my crossed arms to my stomach. "How did you get out?"

Lane waited a moment before he said, very low, "Picked the lock." He looked at me sidelong. "With a sharpened fork." I caught a hint of the wicked smile, and all at once, there was the Lane I knew, so much more than this new one whom Joseph obeyed so carefully and who walked the streets of Paris like a Frenchman. I took a step closer, basking in the cool gray of a gaze that was now examining me with minute attention. I wondered if he could find anything beneath the dirt and dust. He was still grinning.

"Katharine," he said, voice almost at a whisper. I had to lean even closer to hear. "Is that my hat you're wearing?"

I had the sudden urge to laugh, and then his brows came down, face darkening as if a storm wind had blown through the bright place inside him.

"What is that cut on your neck?"

I touched the scar, trying to think of what to say, but then Lane turned. Henri was standing behind us.

"Twice I followed the man Aldridge to this church," Henri said, "and yet he was not inside. I searched, and stayed until the priest unlocked the gates. And yet the dust would say that the door to the tunnels has not been opened in some time. Do you not agree?" This last was directed at Lane.

"You let your man slip past you, I think," Lane said.

"I think not," Henri replied. "I . . ."

Joseph called softly from the other end of the crypt. He was near the tunnel door, and a bit to one side, meticulously dripping molten wax into a soft pile on the stone flags. He lit a new candle and stuck it in the hardening wax as we approached. Lane squatted down beside him, and then all four of us were staring at the same thing: a pool of bright new light showing a small, half circle of iron set into the flag seams, only just sticking out above the level of the stones. The crypt had a trapdoor.

"This, I did not know about," Henri said.

I looked to Lane. "If he wasn't coming out again, and he wasn't using the tunnels, then it must be here."

Lane nodded at Joseph, and Joseph got one finger through the ring and stood, jerking hard on the flagstone. He must have been expecting something heavier or more difficult to open, because the piece of floor sprang upward, much thinner than the other stones. I looked down into a dark, dank hole, where I could just make out the first rung of an iron ladder. But it was what I heard, not what I saw, that made me draw a sharp breath. Distant yelling, putting me immediately in mind of Charenton, echoing up from somewhere far below. The noise formed into words as I listened.

"No, no, no, no, NO!"

It was the sound of a grown man having a tantrum, and that could only be my uncle Tully.

CHAPTER TWENTY-SEVEN

The yelling faded, then immediately rose up again, the cries more intense. I turned to Lane.

"How many men came to feed you? Here, in the wine cellar. How many different men?"

Lane's brows came together. "No way to know."

"There were four last night, plus the two in the garden," I said.

"There will be more of them than us," said Henri, "of that we can be certain. Is he not expecting you, *mon ami?*"

That quieted everyone, because it was so obviously the truth. It was almost more than I could stand to sit there, hearing my uncle's distress and being able to do nothing about it. I looked up.

"Then let me go. No," I said, cutting off Lane's protest, "listen to me. I'm the one who can calm Uncle Tully, and get him out if he can be convinced to go. Maybe he's alone down there, and if so, two strangers and someone he hasn't laid eyes on in a year and a half are only going to hinder me. I will see what can be seen and come back, either with my uncle or without. If I do not come back, then you will know what the situation is, or at least better than you do now, and there will be somebody left to do something about it. If we are expected and outnumbered, then to have all of us walk in and offer ourselves up is stupidity."

On the surface my words had been for everyone, but my real conversation was happening with Lane. He was silent, elbows on his knees, considering while Henri muttered in French, my uncle rambled on below, and Joseph kept a sharp eye on all of us. I watched Lane thinking. We had often disagreed, fought even, but he had never yet dismissed me.

"I can do it," I said.

"I know," he replied. "I've always known that." The gray eyes met mine, not looking away. "One hour, and we come after you both."

I nodded while Henri leapt up, hands going to the back of his head, gesticulating wildly as he protested in French. But he did not try to do anything about it, I noticed. So far, he had teased and he had been insolent, but he had also not crossed Lane. I swung my legs into the hole as he ranted, my feet finding a firm hold, testing the first rung of the ladder.

"Not right, NOT RIGHT!" My uncle's voice drifted up to join in with Henri's. Lane handed me his candle.

"Be careful," he said. His voice was very low.

"He won't hurt me, not when he needs to control Uncle Tully."

"I know."

"But you will come?" I'd not wanted to ask that.

We both looked up at the metallic double click, and saw that Joseph had the pistol pointed at Henri, who in his rambling objections had gotten too close to Lane from behind. Henri threw up his hands in frustration.

"In one hour," Lane said.

I looked down, readying my feet to find the next rung, and then there was a hand on the back of my head and Lane's mouth had found the corner of mine. He held me only for a moment before letting me go.

I gave him a small smile. "Try not to shoot each other." And I lowered myself down one rung.

It was awkward, climbing down a ladder with a candle, and this candle was fitful, unable to illuminate more than a small space around me. I couldn't see how far down I had to go. But either way, this was a deep hole and I schooled myself not to think about the tons of rock and earth that must be over my head. Lane's face and the square of light above grew smaller, as did the sounds of Henri's protests. I was concentrating so completely on feeling for the next thin rung beneath my foot that I was a long way down before I looked to the side. When I did I held in a gasp, or perhaps, had I not clamped my mouth closed, it would have come out as a shriek. I hooked one arm securely around the iron rung, and stretched out the other, holding the candle at arm's length.

The ladder was descending through bones. Legs, ribs, arms, skulls, and spines, some intact, some just chunks and parts. The faint light showed rusted metal, and a bit of cloth with a tarnished button, but mostly they were pieces, human beings gone yellow-brown and shiny with age, piled as far as I could see on both sides of the ladder. Something glittered at me from an eye socket and then scuttled away, making the bones rattle. I measured my breaths.

"Katharine?" Lane's voice came down from above.

He must have seen that the candle wasn't moving. I tilted up my head. "It's only bones," I hissed, though the words left out much that could have been said. These people had been tossed down a hole to rot by the hundreds.

"What?" he called.

"Bones," I said slightly louder, and held out the candle again, hoping he could see what I did. The words echoed more than I'd wanted, probably more than either of us wanted, because we both chose not to speak again. And then I realized that all around me was silence; Uncle Tully had gone quiet.

I stepped down eleven more times, faster now, the bone piles growing closer and closer on each side, and then I was at the bottom, trying to let nothing touch me. The candle glow showed a few feet of narrow path between the disarticulated bodies, extending only in one direction. I walked as quickly as I was able, feet crunching on a fine, gravelly surface that I chose not to contemplate, instead wondering if my uncle Tully had seen this. Would it have frightened him, or would he think of the bones as merely parts, cogs and wheels broken loose from their machines?

The bone piles tapered down and then away, ending in scattered bits, and the tunnel turned left into a dark, much narrower passage. Uncle Tully had been silent for some time now. I prayed he had not wound down, as I thought of it, as he'd been known to do before, like a clock that has not had its key turned. He would need to be carried out if that had happened, and I was not going to be capable of that.

I wanted to hurry but I remembered Henri's warnings and moved quietly down the passage, watching where each foot hit the ground. Surely Uncle Tully had to be close, but the underground of Paris seemed to be a maze, not only side to side, but up, down, and in depth as well; the proximity of noise might be deceptive.

The candle dripped wax on my hand, a brief, intense burn that faded almost instantly as the molten liquid hardened, and then I discovered a glow that was not my dripping candle, an unnatural shining in the tunnel far ahead of me. It was gaslight, coming from a passageway on my right. I became aware of a *tink, tink,* as I drew closer, a noise I knew to be a hammer hitting metal. I approached the lit passage, the tunnel beyond it noiseless and dark, and slowly craned my neck into the opening.

It was a cavern, huge, with a round, domed ceiling soaring at least thirty feet in the air, where the limestone had been quarried out, but it was also a workshop, the likes of which I had not seen since I first went to Stranwyne, blazingly lit with hanging gas lamps. Cut shafts shot upward through the ceiling, gas pipes running down from the surface and across the walls, tacked straight into the rough stone, both rock and pipes dripping with condensation. I blinked, disbelieving, at the steam engine, quiet at the moment, its brass gleaming with polish, and the many tall conglomerations of greased pulleys and iron wheels that I knew were machines for shaping metal. How many people walked above us, not knowing what was beneath their feet?

My eyes gathered all this in a few precious seconds, just before they became riveted to the very center of the room. There, propped up on a stand and stretching the length of what must have been a ten-foot table, was a fish. It had almost none of its metallic skin, was mostly cogs and guts, but I knew exactly what I was seeing, just as I knew the white head bent over the table it sat on. I flitted into the room, threading my way around worktables and a stack of brass bars and little piles of metal shavings and scrap.

"Uncle?" I whispered.

He did not look up. He was on a stool, and to my surprise he was working feverishly, assembling a mass of incongruous parts on the table, working as if his life depended on it. Perhaps it did.

"No, no, NOT!" he shouted suddenly. "That is not right!" His voice bounded off the walls, but there was no movement in the room besides the two of us. Now that I was inside the cavern, there was a faint whiff of something chemical, something putrid. I knew the smell; I could never forget it: guncotton.

"Uncle Tully?" I said, hunching down next to him, sheltering from the sight line of the entrance behind the metal fish. I was relieved to see that he hadn't bloodied himself. His face was deep red, veins popping out in his temples, frightening if you did not know him, but that was not what had my breath coming hard, my pulse skipping madly in my veins. Uncle Tully was in a tantrum, a full-blown tantrum, and he was working. Never had I seen him do both those things at once. But if Uncle Tully was working, that meant I was expendable. It was time for us to go.

I avoided touching anything near him and whispered, very calmly, "Uncle Tully, would you like me to take you away from this place? If we go right now, I can take you."

"Go away, Simon's baby. It is not the right day."

He was using his hot pen, a curl of smoke twisting up as tiny bits of lead melted beneath it, and his hands were a little shaky, probably from the contents of the green bottle. My internal clock said that maybe half my time had gone. "Uncle, do you know who is waiting for us right now? It's Lane. He's come back, just as he said he —"

"NO!"

I paused, unsure whether he had been responding to his work or to me. "He came back, just as he said he would, Uncle. He'd like for you to come and see him."

"Go away. This is not right, little niece. It is never the right day. Never the right place. You said it would be right and it wasn't."

I agreed with him there. "No, Uncle, it isn't right," I replied, darting a glance at the empty entrance to the cavern. "But I'm trying very hard to fix it. Do you remember how some days it is right to wind all the toys, and see what is needed? It is a time like that right now. Time to fix things, just like when one of your toys isn't working properly. Let's go back and fix things, and get Lane, and some tea, and find all your toys. Marianna says —"

"The fish wasn't working."

I looked up at the smudged, oil-spattered monstrosity on the table, and saw with relief that the chamber for the guncotton was empty. Something this large would not just blow a hole in an iron-clad ship; it would obliterate it. "This fish doesn't need to work, Uncle Tully."

"NO!" he shouted, his fingers never slowing. "It must! It should! Toys should work!"

"But this toy could hurt someone, Uncle." I tried to hold my voice low. "Marianna says we shouldn't make this one work."

"Clocks should be wound and people should be splendid! Go away, little niece. It is not the right day."

I could feel desperation creeping around the edges of my words. "I would be splendid if you could come with me now, Uncle. It would make me very happy. You like to —"

"And yet it would not make me happy, Miss Tulman, to be deprived so soon of your company."

I straightened. Ben Aldridge was coming across the cavern, almost to the other side of the table that held the fish. He was elegantly dressed, as if he'd come from a party, his blond hair combed back, the side whiskers neat. I searched again but I could see no other entrance. Had he come from the crypt, or from the other direction, farther down the passage? Uncle Tully's fingers did not slow, and he did not acknowledge Ben's presence.

"I thought it must be you," Ben was saying, sounding pleased, as if I'd happened to drop in for tea just when he wanted me for business. "But where is your entourage? Don't you keep a string of suitors about you these days? Or have you discouraged them all by running about in caps and trousers?"

I did not answer, just watched him warily as he came around the fish to my side of the table. I had no idea what to do, other than stay alive until my hour was up. At least Ben seemed to be alone. The room was deeply quiet beneath the hiss of gas and my uncle's distracted muttering. I backed into the table as Ben reached around my neck and pulled off Lane's cap, clucking in disapproval as he tossed it to the table.

"Oh, no, no, no," he said, reminding me weirdly of Uncle Tully. "Never braids, Miss Tulman. I liked you better as a wood nymph, like the last time, when you came to my cottage all dirty and wild and with leaves in your hair."

Thankfully he did not touch my hair.

"You quite impressed my father the other night. The emperor was rather taken with you, I think."

"Do you have guncotton in here?"

"Oh, I do apologize. Such a shame about the smell. But I'm finished with the production process, at least for now. The barrels behind you there are full of the stuff. Quite watered down," he said, "so not to worry. Unless you fire a rifle into it, of course. But you demonstrated the danger of that rather well, didn't you, Miss Tulman?"

I saw the six large barrels behind me. If the tiny amount from before had blown Ben's boat to smithereens, and if the empty chamber before me held enough to destroy a ship, then what would six barrels do to the shops, streets, and houses above us? Ben smiled as he ran his hand along the spine of the enormous fish. "She's a beauty, don't you think?"

I had no response. My uncle moved, reaching for a spool of wire, and then a *clank* near his feet drew my eyes downward. Uncle Tully had a shackle around his left ankle, linked to a ring driven into the stone wall by a length of heavy chain. A trickle of rage ran down my spine, the cold kind. I lifted my eyes to Ben Aldridge.

"I think my father will be more than pleased with his surprise. How shall he honor the son that hands him victory in the Crimea? And that should make you happy, too, Miss Tulman. You'd like to see Britain win this war, wouldn't you? But it will be the Bonapartes that dominate the seas, in the end. And who will stand against them then?" He patted the fish. "Your Uncle Tully really is a marvel. Aren't you, Mr. Tulman?" His voice rose on this last question, as if my uncle were hard of hearing. "Thank goodness I didn't let you lock him away. All the trouble I've gone to, more than a year of work in the strictest of secrecy, all without making any headway at all, and Mr. Tully had the dashed thing fixed in less than five minutes."

My eyes darted to the fish, and then back to my obliviously working uncle, the burning, flaming knot inside of me growing heavy with dread. *Oh, no, Uncle Tully. No.* Ben chuckled, reaching one finger inside the fish to swing a little strip of dangling metal back and forth.

"A pendulum, Miss Tulman. A pendulum! Of all things. Creating perfect balance. Just like a clock. So simple, childlike simplicity, and yet sheer, unadulterated brilliance. Yes, I think my father is going to be very pleased indeed."

I was breathing, trying to stay calm, trying not to think of iron-clad ships exploding into ragged bits and the thousands of bodies that would be the result, like the bones I'd just walked through. Trying not to think of the disgusting shackle around my uncle's ankle. But the most immediate danger was that my uncle was working, and I was not needed, and Ben was telling me everything. I needed to live for at least fifteen more minutes, until Lane came.

"Miss Tulman," said Ben, smiling hugely, "you've had a trying time in Paris, and you seem . . . rather distressed. Do sit with me a moment. I've some things I'd like to discuss."

He indicated a wooden box behind me as if it were a brocaded chair, waiting politely for me to sit first. My uncle chattered on, incoherent. I stayed where I was.

"I desire that you would sit," Ben said, his voice gone cold. I sat, and when he had done the same, he said, "Miss Tulman, this enmity between us accomplishes little, don't you think? Have you ever considered that there is much to be gained with our understanding?"

My lips parted in disbelief.

"Katharine," he said gently. It made me shudder. "Have you ever considered that I can give you everything you have ever wanted?"

"You know nothing of what I want."

"Don't I? What if I told you that your uncle could have a workshop like this, a much better one than this, better than anything he's ever had, that he could live out his days making every brilliant thing that pops into his head?" He leaned forward, boyish face serious. "What if I told you that I could make sure that Mr. Tully never sees the inside of an asylum?"

I stared.

"I can make that happen, Miss Tulman. And you can be with him, no thought of separation. I can set you up in Paris, in luxury you've never known. Infamy is of no concern when there is power behind it, and the emperor likes you. You would be perfectly independent, doing exactly as you wished. Bring Lane Moreau with you, if you can find him. I care not. Or if Paris is truly not to your taste, then by all means take your uncle to Stranwyne and we will build his workshop there. Have you thought of a proper hospital for the village, with the newest treatments, or teachers that are not the outcasts of society? The place would be the model of England, and how life would be improved for those who live there! Perhaps you would like to repair the house, to bring it back to its glory days in the time of your grandmother? A steward to run it for you?"

I sat on my crate, hair in braids and wearing absurd trousers, my uncle murmuring nonsense behind me, a man spewing nonsense in front of me, and a weapon of incredible destruction to my side, all in an underground cavern that would defy common belief. And for one moment, sitting there, I tasted the sweetness of what was offered me. Respect, independence, the freedom to do and even marry as I pleased. A complete and lifelong protection of my uncle, who would live in a world of unblemished happiness. It was utterly charming. Ben smiled.

"I would do it all, Miss Tulman, every bit. Happily, and all I would need is the result of your uncle's work. Can you imagine what other wonders reside in his head? He has already won a war for two countries. What might he do next for mankind?"

My uncle muttered on about clocks and their turnings, the chain on his ankle clinked, and I was back in my reality. These lies were mirrors and bright light, honey and ambrosia, pretty words whispered in a glittering, gilded, velvet cage. I rejected them. I would not live like Mrs. Hardcastle. And then, just on the edge of hearing, I thought I heard an echo from the tunnel. "Did I tell you that I met your mother the other day?" I said quickly.

The smile on Ben's face froze. "Then I'm sure you heard many interesting things."

"Oh, yes. She told me all about her Louis. She said he never came to see you, though you were such a handsome child."

"He sees me now, Miss Tulman. Do we have an agreement?"

"But what about the empress? I am still rather concerned about what she will —"

"That woman has nothing to do with me. Nothing!"

He was getting agitated now, but words were the only weapons of distraction at my disposal. "But will she stand aside, do you think, while Napoléon makes another woman's child his heir to —"

"You think he will not?" Ben yelled, leaping to his feet. I felt my uncle jump a bit behind me, but he kept on working. "You think the emperor will ignore me? He will have no need to look further than me! There will only be him and me!"

He went still, breathing hard, and I thought for a moment he was calming until he hit me hard across the face with the back of his hand, spinning me around and down behind the wooden crates that surrounded my uncle.

And that was when a shot rang out in the tunnel.

CHAPTER TWENTY-EIGHT

*L*ights danced behind my eyes, the gas jets above my head sparkling. There was wood beneath my hands, and I heard the
grunting, crashing noise of men fighting. I blinked, tasted blood in
my mouth, and pushed myself upward in a daze. Beneath the table, I
saw a jumble of thrashing legs, then the legs seemed to sort themselves and the bodies stilled.

"Bloody fool!" Ben was screaming.

I heard Lane say my name.

"Shut him up," Ben yelled.

"Katharine?"

I stood shakily and saw Lane, disheveled but unhurt, his hands up,
palms out, and then Henri with rumpled hair and a bloodied nose,
tense and still, a pistol pressed to the back of his head. The man at
the trigger was Robert, Mary's Robert from the courtyard. My heart
skipped and sank. Not Mrs. DuPont, then, but Mary. No wonder
they'd known where to find Uncle Tully. What had she said to
Robert, and did she even know she'd done it? I glanced at my uncle,
who had evidently never stopped working. His fingers were flying,

coiling wire, and he was muttering, repeating the same words over and over, "Not to touch, not to touch . . ."

". . . told them to watch the church!" Ben was still yelling. "No one to come but her!" He swung around to Lane.

"You! Why did you come back here? This has nothing to do with you anymore!"

"I disagree," Lane said quietly. "This has everything to do with you and me."

"Shut him up!"

These directions were being yelled at Robert, who had at least some English, because he was trying to do as Ben asked. The gun swung its aim from Henri's head to Lane's. Henri let out a breath.

"Not to touch, not to touch, not to touch," Uncle Tully muttered.

I met Lane's gaze, my head humming. He was dusty and dirty from the tunnel, making his skin even darker, and in contrast his eyes were almost startling, beautiful and possibly dangerous, like the sea. He held me with his look, as if the cavern had narrowed to the size of the tunnel, as if there were no one else in the room, and then his gaze slid once to the side.

"Shut him up!" Ben ordered, only now I realized he was speaking of Uncle Tully. Robert didn't seem to be sure where he should point the gun. I looked hard at Lane. Where were Joseph and his pistol? The gray eyes made the movement one more time, and I realized with a start that my body, the body of Mary's young man with the swiveling gun, and the entrance to the cavern all made a straight line. And that there were six barrels of guncotton directly behind me. I gave Lane one almost imperceptible shake of my head.

Henri was staring at my uncle as if transfixed, his nose bleeding freely, but he'd slipped one small step closer to Robert, who seemed to have settled on Lane for his target. I remembered the knife he had somewhere in his clothes.

"Not to touch, not to touch, not to touch . . ." Uncle Tully muttered.

Lane had turned back to Ben. "It's time to settle this." Ben actually laughed, and the gray eyes caught mine, and again slid to the right. I shook my head.

"Settle what? Do you want a share of the money? A sliver of the glory? You should talk to dear Katharine. Ask her what I've offered." Ben glanced once at me, grinning like a shark. When he did, Henri took another small step toward Robert, whose eyes were trained on Ben, waiting for instruction. "Tell him what I am giving you, love," he said.

I didn't answer, my uncle's voice mixing with the humming in my head and the blood pumping in my ears. I shook my head again at the movement of Lane's eyes, wondering if he could somehow tell Joseph not to shoot.

"I'm going to give her everything. And what can you give her?"

The gray gaze bore back into Ben. "Nothing much."

"That's right. I am going to give her everything that you can't, and she will take it. . . . Stay where you are!"

Lane had taken two quick steps forward, risking Robert's shaking hand. Robert had followed and Ben stepped back, while, unnoticed, Henri moved closer to Robert. It was like watching a mad dance, a dance that had nearly gotten Lane shot. But it had taken me out of what I guessed must be Joseph's line of fire. I slid back, again aligning myself with Robert and the entrance. If Joseph's shot hit the gun-cotton, we were all going to die, perhaps along with the people in the streets above us. I saw Lane's gaze take in my movement, then lift to the barrels behind me.

"Not to touch, not to touch . . ." said Uncle Tully.

"If he moves again, shoot him!" Ben said. "Do you understand me? And make him be quiet!"

This last order had been to me. My uncle worked frantically, paying no mind to any of us, deep in his own world. I wiped the blood from my mouth and, keeping my eyes on the scene in front of me, curled the fingers of my other hand around a small wrench. It would not hurt anyone, not much, but it might cause a distraction if needed. Ben was straightening his jacket, adjusting the cloth around his neck to its position before the scuffle.

"I don't know exactly what either of you think you are going to accomplish down here, Mr. Moreau. You're not getting them out. In fact, I think it rather likely that Miss Tulman will not go. She might ask you to stay, though. You'll have to decide what to do with Marchand. Wait and see if she . . ."

Lane moved forward, two quick, long steps that again had Robert following and me gasping in terror. But Robert did not shoot; I could see the fear all over his face. Who he should have been fearing was Henri. Henri had again moved closer, deliberately staying silent, still out of reach, but now with something gleaming held just below his right shirtsleeve. Lane was going to have to risk that move again to get Robert out of line with the barrels of guncotton.

". . . not to touch, not to touch, not to . . ."

"What I expect to accomplish," Lane said, deadly calm, "is making certain that bloody machine and nothing like it ever sees the light of day . . ."

"Not to touch, not to touch . . ."

". . . and to leave this place with all of them. The question is whether you wish to be alive or not when I do it."

Ben grinned, stretching the arms of his well-cut suit, looking heavenward in mock exasperation. "You realize I'm about to have you shot, don't you?" I glanced at the gun shaking in Robert's hand. "You know that I will be the one walking out of here with Mr. Tully and his niece? And that she is going to come willingly?" I gripped the wrench in my hand. "Because she knows I can give her what I promised."

"You can give her nothing that's good enough," Lane said, his voice very low.

"Not good enough? Not good enough!" he yelled. "That, coming from you, to a Bonaparte? You are nothing! What can you do that I cannot? Name one thing I cannot give!"

"Not to touch, not to touch, not to . . ."

The gray eyes were all for Ben now, and they were stone. Lane put his hands in his pockets. I think he'd forgotten everything else, including the gun pointed at his head. "Give her Davy back," he said. "And Mr. Babcock."

"And John George," I whispered.

"Not to touch, not to touch . . ."

"Give her back the last eighteen months. Can you do that?"

"Not to touch, not to touch, not to touch . . ."

"Shut him up!" Ben screamed.

"Give Mr. Tully back his old workshop, and all the things he made there. Give me back the Lower Village."

It was as if the world had again narrowed, making it impossible to look away. Lane was furious, and there was something mesmerizing in the evenness of his rage.

"It is you who are nothing," he said. "You were always trying to make it not so, even when we were children. Only it still was."

"Stop it," Ben said.

"Not to touch, not to touch, not to touch . . ."

"Everything you've tried to accomplish, every foul thing you ever did, all to fawn over a man who will not even give you his name, and instead of more, you were less."

"Shut him up!"

"And you are still less."

"Not to touch, not to . . ."

"So I ask you, when we leave here, do you wish to be alive, or not?"

"Stop it! And shut him . . . What is he doing?"

I broke from my trance and looked properly at my uncle. And suddenly I knew exactly what he was doing. The crate beside him, full of his things from the attic workshop, the wires running down to the glass jars in the crate, the hum that was not really in my head. And Uncle Tully, repeating and repeating his odd phrase at the parts that had taken shape on the table beside the fish, the blue-white spark reaching up and between two spindles. And then I saw Ben's body tilting forward, straining to see over my uncle's creation, the blue, empty eyes wide as he spotted the strange flame; and I saw Lane's brows coming down, his hand coming up, and the wires now connected to the fish's metal frame. I watched Lane's arm stretch, and Ben leaning, both Ben's hands coming down toward the fish.

"Stop!" I screamed. And Lane did.

There was a blinding flash and Ben's body convulsed, crackling, eyes unblinking, staring straight at my uncle as he shook, stuck to the fish as if to a magnet. Smoke went up, a corona of purple fire and light blazing from his hands. A part of me realized that there was screaming, that it was coming from my mouth, and that the word I was screaming was "No!" Robert had dropped the gun and was reaching for Ben, to wrench him away from the fish and, as soon as he touched Ben's body, he was thrown violently, almost supernaturally across the room, hitting the metal press before he fell to the floor. Ben dropped as Robert did and the crackling stopped, leaving only the smaller hum of the blue flame between the spindles.

Uncle Tully let go of his little switch, and the electricity was gone. "Not to touch, not to touch, not to touch . . ." he chanted.

I sat down hard on a crate, learning the smell of burnt flesh. I saw Henri's bloody face staring downward, horror-struck, the same expression on Joseph's as he rose up from behind a workbench near the door. His pistol was still cocked.

"Stay where you are, Katharine," Lane said, but there was no need. I could see Ben's dead body from underneath the table. His hands were charred, blackened stumps.

As soon as Lane had picked the lock on Uncle Tully's shackle, we led my uncle out and a little way down the passage, distracting him from the sound of the hammers inside the cavern, where Joseph and

Henri were destroying Ben Aldridge's fish. It was uncertain whether Robert had died from the electricity or from the blow of the metal press, but either way, my uncle had examined the two bodies curiously and carefully. It was seeing a machine taken apart that we were not sure he could stomach.

We set him in a chair from the workshop and he folded his hands in his lap. "I am ready to go now," he said. "And I wish to go to the old place, not the new one." He was supremely confident. I was amazed, stunned, and also horrified, unable to feel anything properly. "This place was not right, was it, little niece?"

"No, Uncle," I whispered.

"I said not to touch. I told him so, didn't I, Simon's baby?"

"Yes, Uncle."

"And now he's gone away, the forever kind. Isn't that so?"

I nodded, biting my lip.

"He was not splendid. He touched my things. And he hurt my little niece. You should not hurt. That is not right. He made my niece not happy."

Lane crouched down, elbows on knees, so my uncle could see his face. "You did well, Mr. Tully. I reckon Marianna is proud of you. She would have said you did just right."

I was not at all certain how I felt about this logic.

"Lane knows," Uncle Tully said cheerfully. "Lane always knows what is right. He always knows. And Lane came, didn't he, little niece? That was not the forever kind."

"Just like I said I would, Mr. Tully." But his voice had been very quiet when he said it.

"I want to go to the old place."

"Yes, Uncle. I know. But first we have to wait for twenty. You know you can wait for twenty."

He instantly closed his eyes, counting the seconds, a thing he was rather good at as long as he was reminded to stop. Lane stood slowly. I wondered when he'd last slept. He held the candle up to my face, examining my bruising mouth while I tucked my hair back into the red cap, and then he leaned against the wall, breathing in and out, making the light waver in crazed patterns along the wall while the hammers struck metal in the cavern. He glanced once at Uncle Tully, and then let his back slide down until he was sitting. I saw the war being waged beneath his skin. I got onto my knees and sat in front of him.

"You need to tell me something," I stated, though it was really a question.

Lane wouldn't fully meet my eyes, and the burning knot in my middle became a cold, lead weight. He might need to tell me, but I wasn't sure if I wanted to hear it.

"When Ben took me . . ." He ran a hand through his hair. "It was . . . because I let him."

I waited for him to go on, and the hand in his hair became a fist, pulling.

"Months I'd been at it, Katharine. Months! And with nothing to show for it but a bullet hole in a wall beside my head. And Ben had put himself right in the middle of a fortress with the imperial court. Untouchable. Joseph had heard he'd been buying arsenic, and then there was Mrs. Reynolds in the shop, her address right there in the book, and there's not a smuggler in France that doesn't know Mrs. DuPont, or that's what Jean-Baptiste says, and he is one. So I painted her some things and got myself taken in by the Reynolds family, and Joseph made sure Ben heard that Mrs. DuPont was selling. Only Ben didn't come himself; he sent his manservant. I don't know what's happened to him since. . . ."

"Mary killed him," I said. Lane lifted his head to look at me. "In Stranwyne, with a hammer. We buried him on the hill and pretended he was Uncle Tully." He reached out and put one long finger on the scar on my neck. "Yes," I said, responding to the question he had not asked. Lane closed his eyes, silent, his jaw working in and out while the hammers rang. He continued.

"I paid Mrs. DuPont to tell Ben Aldridge exactly where I'd be, and let him take me. I just didn't think they'd hit me quite so hard."

"But how did it help you, to be locked in a wine cellar?"

"Because I was locked in a wine cellar with my picklocks in my boot. And one of them did at one time happen to be a fork, Katharine, in case you were wondering." I smiled just a little, but he didn't see; he still had his eyes closed. "I wasn't in that room for more than a day, and as soon as I learned the routine I was only there when they came to feed me. I've been all over these tunnels. I told Joseph where the trapdoor was. And I knew exactly where I was sending you. I couldn't believe it when Marchand opened that door. I must have passed it dozens of times without seeing it."

I glanced at my uncle's silently counting lips. "But why not just tell me, then? And if you were here, then . . . why didn't you just destroy the fish when you had the chance?"

"You're asking the wrong question." He was coming to it now. I could see whatever it was building to a crisis. "What good would it have done to tear the thing to pieces? He would just build another.

It's the idea, Katharine, that's what's so hard to stop. It was the idea that had to die."

His eyes were open now, his gaze on the candle flame. "Three times I was in there with him, under the bench with the canvas. Three times I could have done it. Twice with a knife, once with his own gun. Not a soul down here to stop me. If he had found me, fought me, I think maybe I could've. But he didn't. He just whistled and went about his business, and . . . I didn't. Couldn't. It's what I came here for, all those months ago, and I couldn't, not for Davy, and not for you. If I had, he wouldn't have gone to Stranwyne and you wouldn't be here with a scar on your neck. Maybe Mr. Babcock would be alive. Mr. Tully was the better man, in the end."

I stared at Lane, at this wretched bitterness I did not understand. He sighed.

"I was never going to tell you this. Any of it. I didn't want you to know. But now . . . I think maybe it's best that you do." He was completely avoiding my gaze now.

"So when you saw me in the courtyard . . ."

"Leaving. Getting out of Paris. I wasn't doing any good here."

"And where were you going?"

"It doesn't matter."

I felt my eyes narrow. It mattered to me. The hammers had slowed in the cavern, and I could hear Henri and Joseph talking. Uncle Tully would be done counting soon. "Lane, where does the tunnel go?"

"Beneath the Tuileries. A straight passage, with little branches coming off, all the way through. We should probably go that way. I think we'll be risking morning mass if we go through the church, and the passage is stairs rather than ladders, easier for Mr. Tully. Ben spent most of his day socializing with the court, and the boy Robert . . ."

I had a pang for Mary.

". . . and the manservant were the only other ones I ever saw down here. We shouldn't have any other company."

I watched the tension inside him coiling as he talked, tightening, closing him to me, and it had nothing to do with our way out of the tunnel. There was still something else, a deeper layer that he had not told me, and I could not yet see.

"I'll get Marchand and Joseph to come back with me tomorrow," Lane was saying. "We'll take care of the bodies and see if the place can't be sealed off. I doubt the emperor knows about these tunnels, since they're here, and I don't know how long it will take for him to notice who's missing, or even how much he knows about what Ben was up to. But I'm thinking Mr. Tully needs to be on a boat no later than day after tomorrow. To be safe. Can it be managed?"

"I think so." He was right; we would have to get out of Paris as soon as possible. But I dreaded sending Uncle Tully back into that horrid sleep.

The gaslights went off in the cavern then, leaving us only with the candle flame, and Joseph and Henri came out, both a little sweaty, Joseph carrying the crate that now contained my uncle's lightning box. Lane was suddenly on his feet, and Uncle Tully's eyes snapped open. He put his intense gaze directly on Lane, making sure not to notice the other two men. "Fourteen, and fifty-two," he announced. "Take me to the old place now."

Lane took the crate from Joseph, quickly, before my uncle could notice who had been holding his things, and I saw Joseph look over at Lane and frown, then glance uneasily at me. Lane did not look at me as he said, "The new place first, Mr. Tully, just for a bit. Then the old place next."

I could not tell if that meant Lane was or was not coming with me.

CHAPTER TWENTY-NINE

"Two hundred twenty-two, two hundred twenty-three, two hundred twenty-four, two hundred twenty . . ."

I helped my uncle count the steps while we crept quickly beneath the Tuileries. The passage had already climbed several times, filthy with cobwebs and dust rather than the dirt and the grit of stone, though only about its edges; the frequent travel this passage had gotten recently had kept the center reasonably clear. Again we were walking in the circle of light from one candle, our last candle, and the closeness was difficult for my uncle, but as merely "difficult" was so remarkably better than the "impossible" it would have been even two days ago, I felt a rush of pride. He was careful not to look at either Joseph or Henri, and to keep his mind on his counting.

"New place first, Uncle Tully, then the old place next. That will make it right."

Whatever had happened in my absence from the crypt beneath the crypt of the Saint-Merri, rather than shooting one another, it seemed, the three men had instead found common ground in their distaste for the emperor. They were having a conversation about him now, in whispered English and animated French, all about elected officials that crowned themselves and seizure of property and unfair laws and how giving the merchant class the vote while taking away any power that vote might have had was meaningless. Every now and again, Lane stopped the soft conversation to listen to footsteps or the murmuring of voices above us. Then as soon as the noise had died away, they would start right up again.

I was not particularly focused on their political views. What Lane had said outside the cavern bothered me deeply. He had things the wrong way around, in my opinion, and this avoidance was exactly the way he'd worked himself up to leaving Stranwyne the last time. *"I didn't want you to know. But now . . . I think maybe it's best that you do."* He hadn't asked me what I thought was best, and he hadn't told me everything, either. Of that I was certain. I wished I could ask my mother, or Marianna, or even Mrs. DuPont, someone at least partially successful in the management of a man. The more I dwelled on it, the more infuriated I became. The name *Eugénie* from the conversation in front of me broke into my thoughts.

"What did you just say?" I asked. Uncle Tully kept on counting.

Lane whispered his reply without looking at me. "I was talking about the stairs up ahead. They go to the Empress Eugénie's apartments."

Henri's little mustache spread wide in the candlelight. "And I said that if more of the kings and queens of France had known what was down here, then perhaps we would have some of them left, yes?"

Joseph added something in French, and we kept moving, but again my mind was not on the conversation just ahead of me. I was thinking of dead queens, and the imperial ball, and how charming the empress had thought Ben Aldridge, so considerate with his gifts, and how he had secretly despised her. *"There will only be him and me."* How could Ben have been so certain the emperor would have no need to look beyond him for an heir?

I looked up the stairs to Eugénie's rooms, the center of the worn stones without dust or cobwebs, and suddenly instead of stairs I was seeing those little white packages of arsenic in Lane's hands, and pale, ivory skin beneath a glittering diadem, and a bottle of claret, pouring purple into the glass in my hand. My feet stopped moving, and Uncle Tully paused in his count. The other three had gotten a little ahead of us.

"Uncle Tully," I whispered, "wait for ten. Can you do it?"

He instantly sat himself on the first step and closed his eyes. I flew up the narrow stone stairs.

At the top of the stairs was a wooden door, the slightest bit of sunshine leaking in from a crack along its bottom edge. I ran my hands over it, the planks of wood wide, hard with age, the iron fittings thick and much more roughly made than the modern ones. I touched the hinges, and my fingers came back slick with oil. I knew, just as certainly as if I'd read Ben Aldridge's confession.

My mind began racing. Uncle Tully could not stay in Paris, and after what had just happened in the cavern below, my being seen again at the palace was unthinkable. And how to even get in without an invitation? And if I could get in, who to talk to? Who would begin to believe me? How would I even explain such a fantastic tale?

I glanced back down to the tunnel. Uncle Tully was exactly where I had left him, and Lane had exchanged the crate for the candle, one foot on the first step. Henri and Joseph looked over his shoulder.

"Katharine!" he whispered.

I thought of the empress's pale skin. Ben had bought the first of those little white packages weeks ago. I pressed my ear to the door. Silence. If it was morning mass, surely an empress would need to be seen there?

I looked again down the stairs. Lane was shaking his head back and forth, the word *no* forming silently on his lips. I had not come this far to root out the plans of Ben Aldridge, only to leave some of the seeds to grow. I turned the latch, and the door cracked open.

My head was behind a tapestry. I pushed it aside, saw a small but empty room done in bright yellows and gilt, slipped through the door, and shut it soundlessly behind me. I was in a parlor or sitting room of some sort, a little tumble of needlework lying discarded on a silken settee, a large, impressive-looking portrait of the emperor staring down at me from over the chimneypiece. I tiptoed to an ornate cabinet, quickly and quietly opening one door and then the other, glancing through the contents. I was looking for wine.

In the third cabinet, I found it, three bottles of claret, only one of them unsealed. It was clever of Ben, I thought, waiting for her to break the seal herself. I wondered why he'd always chosen claret. A personal preference, or did it just obscure the taste? I grabbed the bottle, shut the cabinet door without noise, straightened, and then jumped at a burst of feminine giggling coming from behind the door of the next room.

My heart leapt irregularly in my chest, my body tingling as I hurried back to the tapestry and pushed it aside. But there was nothing. No doorknob or latch visible. The door had disappeared, perfectly disguised by the wainscoting.

I set down the bottle and felt all over the cream-and-yellow-papered wall, searching for some type of spring or latch, appalled to see that I was leaving dirty handprints on everything I touched. I wondered if Lane had come up the stairs and was on the other side of the door, if I dared knock or make a noise. More giggling from the other room. I shot a glance over my shoulder, and found not only the portrait of the emperor staring at me, but the emperor himself.

I spun about, flattening against the wall, wrinkling his tapestry. We stared at each other, mutually stunned. He had been in the act of knotting the belt of a satin smoking jacket around his bare chest and legs, his hair an unruly mess, and just as in the ballroom before, I was struck by the ringing of distant bells, even stronger this time. It was something in his gaze, which at this moment looked as if he might like to shoot a hole right through my head. Napoléon saw the bottle of wine at my feet, and took a step toward the bellpull.

"Wait!" I said softly.

He paused, then his dark brows contracted, and he pointed. "You are that woman. Charles's woman. Are you not?"

There was no time to correct this or explain. He was moving again toward the bellpull. "Your Majesty," I whispered. "I'm sorry, but the wine . . ."

He put his hand on the rope.

"It belongs to the empress," I said desperately. I picked up the bottle and held it toward him. "It's poisoned!"

"Ridiculous," he said after a moment, hand still on the rope. But he was holding his voice low.

"Please, listen. Ben . . . I mean, Charles, he has . . ." I took a breath. "He has been poisoning the wine." The emperor's piercing gaze held me a moment longer, and then, instead of pulling the rope, he went back to the door he'd just come through, calling out something cheerful in German before he shut it. "How have you gotten in here, and what have you been doing to yourself?"

"There is a door, just behind me. I came through . . ."

"Quiet," he commanded, whispering. I waited until he came closer to where I was standing.

"A door," I said, my voice only just audible. "Ben has . . . I mean Charles, he has been coming through it to . . ." The empress, or I assumed it was the empress, called out something in French.

"Dans un instant!" he replied, then whispered, "Tell me what you are speaking of, you little wench. Now, before I am calling the guard."

I closed my eyes for a moment, trying to think how to quickly explain what I knew to be true. I said, "Is the empress well? Has she been sick?" He did not answer. "Has she always been so pale?"

"She is only a little tired, like a woman, but the doctor, he says . . ." The high voice trailed away.

"Arsenic," I said. "In the claret. You do not drink it, do you, Your Majesty?"

Napoléon shook his head, eyes on the bottle in my hand. "And why . . ."

"He was afraid she would give you an heir." The emperor glanced back at the closed door. "I know he was your son."

"But . . . no. He could not think that. That I could . . ."

"He did think it."

I could see the doubt in the emperor's brows, in the way his head was still slowly shaking. He glanced toward the bellpull. I blurted,

303

"And, Your Majesty, he was afraid to tell you, but . . . secretly, he was a Pisces."

Napoléon stiffened.

"Replace the wine. I was trying to take this one away because it was unsealed, but I would pour all of it out. And anything that touches her skin: powders, lotions, face paint. I think you will find that she feels better. But . . . I really must go. Will you let me go?"

"Where is Charles?" he said slowly.

"He's . . . he is dead. I'm sorry."

I watched the play of emotions on the emperor's face. "How . . ." he began, but he looked me over again and seemed to change his mind. I'd almost forgotten the soreness at the corner of my mouth, and wondered if he could see the bruising. And then he said inexplicably, "His . . . mother . . . she was an actress."

I think my mouth made the shape of an O, though the sound did not come out. The emperor stared at the thick golden rug, where I had left some horrible footprints, thinking. Was there someone trustworthy he could have escort me out, or would he give me time to find the latch I knew must be there?

And at that moment, almost helpfully, the door behind me opened. The tapestry was pushed aside and Lane Moreau had a hand on my arm, ready to yank me to the safety of the stairs. And then he saw the emperor.

If something in Napoléon's expression had rung familiar to me before, now it was as if the bells of Notre-Dame were chiming in my head. How had I not seen? The beard, and the rumpled hair heightened the similarity, but it was the eyes, that same gray, unpredictable stare that could bottle up a moment and somehow keep it twice as long. I gasped, as if I'd been struck. The bodies were different, but I saw the same nose, the same mouth, the same shape of the brows. It couldn't be, and yet it was.

The emperor had taken half a step back, his expression confused, dazed, and then stricken. His own gray eyes sought mine for explanation, and I shook my head, my face possibly more shocked than his. But by the end of this look if we had not reached an exact understanding, we had at least exchanged significant information. I had not known, the emperor had not known, and the man in the doorway still knew nothing. Lane seemed to be vacillating between starting a conversation or a fistfight, or just yanking me straight into the passage and slamming the door. A querulous voice called from the other room.

"Your Majesty," I whispered, "we must go. Please. Board up the door."

He nodded. I moved, glancing again at Lane to mouth, "Go!" He began backing slowly down the stairs, out of the emperor's sight.

"Wait!" the emperor said. I was already down a stair, my hand on the door latch. "Tell me your name. I do not remember. Please!"

I opened my mouth, then shook my head. "Go!" I mouthed again at Lane. Joseph had come up behind him, pulling on his arm.

"Please," the emperor said, lowering his voice even further, "what is his name? Where does he live?"

I hesitated, looking down the stairs. Lane was fighting Joseph's pull, beckoning to me.

"Is it England?" the emperor begged. "Please!"

I turned back to Napoléon and shook my head. The empress's voice was now calling from just behind the other door.

"Here, *Fräulein*! Miss!" He grabbed a polished box from the table beside him and dumped out the contents, pressing something hard and cold into my hand. "Tell me, please! How old? How many years?"

"Katharine!" Lane whispered.

"I'm sorry," I said, and shut the door fast, making the emperor leap out of the way. I knew he would not be able to find the latch.

"What is happening?" Henri asked. We'd come scurrying down the stairs with no explanation other than Lane's order to run. And so we were, stumbling in the light of one candle down the passage as fast as Uncle Tully could go.

"Oh, nothing much," Lane replied. "Katharine just decided to run up the stairs and have a little chat with the half-naked bloody tyrant of France!"

Henri's dark eyes slid to me, as surprised as I'd ever seen them, and Joseph frowned while my uncle panted happily. "I waited for eleven, little niece. Almost twelve!"

I couldn't answer any of them, for the moment I couldn't even explain. My mind was still reeling.

"Can we get out?" Henri asked Lane.

"If they get into the tunnel before we get to the end, they will see the light," he panted, struggling with his grip on the crate. They were carrying it between them. "The passage is a straight line. But if we can get to the end and through, then they might turn the wrong way. I would send men both ways, so I would reckon it depends on whether the emperor bothers to dress himself first."

I comforted myself with the difficulty of finding that latch. But if we were caught and arrested, the result was going to be very different from what Lane expected. Disastrously so. This would be a blow to him, a blow to his very core. I willed Uncle Tully's feet to go a little faster. We needed to disappear. All of us.

A distant *bang* echoed down the tunnel, and then another, and another. *Never mind about the latch*, I thought; the emperor was bashing in his wife's sitting-room wall. Soft French bounced off the stone-lined walls around me, words I guessed would not have been uttered in my presence in English, and then Lane slowed.

The tunnel ended abruptly in a wall of dirt with reinforcing stone, but near the floor there was a low arch that one could slide through. "Where does it come out?" I panted.

I thought Lane might not answer. He was furious with me, of course, but I was in no mood for his temper. I glared at him. "It's a drain," he said, already on the other side, pulling through the wooden box, "just a small jump down. It goes to the Seine. We can climb out from there."

Another, softer boom came down the tunnel.

"Keep counting your steps, Uncle Tully," I said, "and when you jump, that's a step, too."

Lane helped him bend down and through, Henri holding up the candle, and then I remembered that I was still clutching the thing the emperor had pressed into my hand. I glanced down, and in my palm was a ring, a ring with a ruby the size of a dove's egg. I closed my fist again, turned my back, and stuffed the ring down Mr. Babcock's shirt and deep into my underclothes. Uncle Tully carefully jumped through the arch, still counting, pretending there was no one present but myself and Lane. He was doing so remarkably well.

"Eight hundred and ninety-seven!" Uncle Tully yelled. Another crash came down the tunnel.

I followed Joseph and Henri through the arch and said, "Uncle Tully, how would you like to ride in a carriage?"

Henri had money, to our collective relief, and slipped out of the drain to bribe a hired carriage to not only wait while we scrambled up the embankment, but to also not notice our strange and shabby condition. At my request, he also bought the coat off the driver's back, and I put it over the head of my uncle Tully, so he could pretend to be elsewhere during our brief sojourn across a public street. It was a bright Sunday, the market packed, a park fluttering with autumn finery, both on the trees and the people. We ignored the stares and quickly shut the door of the carriage.

Uncle Tully sat on the floor at my feet, out of sight under the coat, his crate beside him. I could feel him shaking. I had him doing multiples of seven while Lane's gray eyes stared at the passing streets, one hand running through his hair. Even after I had explained about the arsenic, he couldn't quite get over his temper. Joseph slouched in his seat with his forehead wrinkled, watching Lane. I was doing the same, trying not to see the telltale traces of an emperor.

"Ah!" said Henri, tossing a newspaper he'd found on the seat into Lane's lap. "The Russians have scuttled their own ships in Sebastopol. Perhaps our navies will not need this weapon after all, if their enemies will do the job for them, yes?" He leaned back in his seat when no one answered, grinning, somehow still managing to look sleek when he was covered in muck and stone dust. "Well, well, my friends, the emperor will now know what is in the tunnel, and also who is dead in the tunnel."

Lane kept his eyes on the window when he said, "Napoléon may be a fool . . ." I winced inside. ". . . but he is not so great a fool that it will take him long to find out who Katharine is and where she lives."

Henri nodded. "You will all three have to leave Paris. Very soon. Is that not so?"

My uncle was up to seven times one hundred and thirty-nine before Lane answered, and then he only said, "There is also the problem of Wickersham."

"Ah!"

"I think it must have been Ben who had the grave opened," I said. I wished I had asked him when I had the chance. "How could he have been so sure otherwise? Or do you think Mr. Wickersham's reach was that long?"

Henri shrugged. "It is probable that it is not, or he would have done more than that, yes?"

"So it is possible Mr. Wickersham will still believe my uncle is dead."

"It doesn't matter anymore what he thinks," Lane said, "because I posted a letter to Ambassador Cowley just as soon as I left the tunnels."

"Did you?" said Henri. "Your 'farewell stroke,' as they say? Well, I think I can be of help to you in that. I am long overdue in paying my respects to the ambassador."

Lane turned his gaze to him, still deliberately not looking at me. I pressed my lips together. Joseph slouched down farther in his seat while my uncle said seven times one hundred and eighty-seven.

"Cowley will want to stay in a good standing with my family. I think with this visit and your letter that Wickersham's work here will be over. What is your opinion, *mon ami?*"

Lane nodded, his gaze back to the window.

"Shall you take Mr. Tulman to his home? Can you continue to keep his life a secret?"

When Lane was silent, I said, "That is exactly what I must do. Thank you, Henri. Truly."

His dark eyes glanced once at Lane and then he smiled at me, but he did not tease.

"*Noble,*" said Joseph, out of nowhere, his tone almost sad. We all looked at him, but it was my gaze he was returning, his one word addressed to me. I remembered our first meeting, when he'd told me that Lane, or Jean-Michel, was noble. I felt my back stiffen. What did he know of Lane's background? Or was he referring to something about Lane's behavior now?

I looked at Lane, his dark and dirty skin betraying no expression, his eyes like two chips of stone on the passing streets beyond the window. I adjusted Uncle Tully's coat and clasped my hands in my lap, my irritation combusting into flame. Lane had come to Paris to settle something, and now I did not intend to leave it without doing the same.

CHAPTER THIRTY

When the carriage stopped at the red doors, Mary burst through them, her tongue running faster than my overly occupied mind could comprehend. But I did note that she was brushed, pressed, and had her hair done differently, with curls in the front. Together we hustled Uncle Tully through the door, coat on head, and I sent him straight up the stairs with Mary for tea and toast and probably his bed. My head was aching and I couldn't remember the last time I'd eaten or slept. I thought I might be surviving on my temper.

Lane, Henri, and Joseph came into the foyer having some sort of heated discussion in French, Henri and Joseph with the crate between them, and then I saw one of the things that Mary had undoubtedly been trying to tell me a few moments before. The salon door opened and Mrs. Hardcastle came out, the two Miss Mortimers and Mrs. Reynolds taking tea behind her. The pince-nez bounced on Mrs. Hardcastle's bosom.

"Good Heavens, child," she said. "Whatever has happened . . ." Her eyes went round. "Jean-Michel!"

Lane froze in the foyer, and I heard the sudden rattling of china and scraping of chairs and squeals from the salon. Joseph left the crate with Henri and scooted to the library, where I saw Jean-Baptiste's head poking out, and then there were four faces in the salon door.

"Oh, Jean-Michel, you have a beard!" exclaimed the blonde Miss Mortimer.

Lane wiped his hands on his pants, smiled, and went first to Mrs. Reynolds, who had come out to greet him. He took her wrinkled hands in his, kissing both her cheeks even though he was filthy, burbling away like a Frenchman. When I saw the eager expressions of the two frilly girls waiting in line just behind her, I'd had enough. I didn't care who he was, or what he thought he wasn't.

"Mrs. Reynolds is perfectly aware that you speak very good English, Mr. Moreau."

Lane's back stiffened just a bit. He straightened, then turned around to face me. "My apologies, Mrs. Reynolds, but that is true," the low voice said. He had spoken to her, but he was looking at me.

The brown-headed Miss Mortimer smiled in delight, not thinking beyond the English, while her blonde cousin stared at me with round, slightly frightened eyes. Probably because of the dirt. Or the pants. Mrs. Reynolds pretended I wasn't there.

"Jean-Michel," she said, her face softening pleasantly, "we are so happy to have you back. Do we have you to thank for this, Mr. Marchand?" Her gaze went straight past my face to where Henri must be standing somewhere behind me. "Do come next door and have some refreshment, Jean-Michel. Your room is waiting for you. Almost as you left it." I caught the edge of her sharp glance. "I will have Hawkins get you settled immediately. Are you in need of a doctor, perhaps, or a glass a wine?"

This little speech was followed by all sorts of agreeable and sympathetic chirping from the girls, though Mrs. Hardcastle was quiet and intent, watching through the pince-nez. I straightened my back and cut through the chatter.

"So, Mr. Moreau, will you go to Mrs. Reynolds's? Will you 'pursue your art'? Is that your choice?"

Lane's gray gaze had never yet left me. His hands came up slowly and slid into his pockets. I heard Henri light a cigarette. "No," he said finally. "No, that is not my choice. I thought I might try America for a time."

"America," I repeated.

He closed his eyes for just a moment. *Noble,* I thought. He believed he was being noble.

"So is that what you want, Mr. Moreau?"

"No," he said. "But don't you think it's best?"

I was so angry I wanted to hit him with another brick. "Eighteen months," I said. "You leave without warning — and yes, I know why you went — but you allow eighteen months to go by without a line or a note. And do not tell me you didn't trust the post. You could have done something to tell me you were alive, drawing breath, and capable of holding a pen. Couldn't you, Mr. Moreau?"

"Yes."

The four ladies' faces swung back to me. "Only you chose to be silent. Is that correct, Mr. Moreau?"

"Yes."

"And for more than two months I held the belief that you were alive despite every obstacle, against the word of my closest friend." I saw Mary sit down on the landing above me. "The word of my solicitor, and what was supposed to be the British government. And then I came to Paris, inconveniencing the livelihoods of eight hundred and forty-nine people, distressing my most dear and beloved relative, traipsing across sea and the continent to find you, and all because you chose not to write. Is that correct, Mr. Moreau?"

"Yes."

"Then explain yourself." I lifted my chin, and the four sets of eyes in the salon door went as one to Lane. I watched him coiling like a spring.

"All right. You want to hear an explanation? I'll give it to you. Do you have any idea, Miss Tulman," he was as deliberate on my name as I had been on his, "do you have any notion at all, what they are saying about you in London?"

I felt myself tense.

"Well, I do. Aunt Bit told me, she showed me letters. Filthy, nasty gossip, and it wasn't just London, it was in the village, too. Tattling ladies at their kitchen windows and men at the docks, the ones that didn't know you, that liked to listen to rumors. And do you know why they were saying those things, dragging your name through the muck? It wasn't because of you, Miss Tulman. It was because of me!" This last had been almost a shout, one finger slamming into the center of his chest. "Me! Not you! Because when I was born, your grandmother paid my father a wage!"

I felt one hot tear slide down my cheek. My grandmother had certainly never paid his father a wage, but Lane would never know that. He was mesmerizing, just as he'd been in the cavern, but this pain was very real, and it hurt me.

"Do you have any idea what it was like to walk down the village lane and hear those things? To have your house pointed out to me in Paris?" He flung out a hand at the women beside him. "Do you know what those ladies said you were . . . in front of me?" One of the Miss Mortimers put a gloved hand to her mouth. "I did not write, Miss Tulman, so you could be free of all that."

"And I suppose," I said quietly, "that you thought the loss of my good name would be too much for me. Would have me flying to pieces and make my life unlivable. Well, thank you so much for making that decision for me, Mr. Moreau. It was obviously my good name I was searching every hospital in Paris for!"

"She has you on that one, *mon ami*," said Henri.

"Mr. Moreau, I am perfectly capable of taking care of myself and continuing on at Stranwyne on my own." And I could, I realized. I had been. "But I believe it is a question of more, rather than less."

He looked up sharply, and I saw that the significance of these words had not been lost on him.

"Whatever you think you should have done and didn't over the past few days . . . I believe that you made a choice, and that it was correct." I would never tell him he'd been contemplating the murder of his half brother. "I know it to have been correct. Someone very wise once told me that you always know what is right, and I believe him. I think to have done differently would have made you . . . less. I do not think you could have lived with less. I, personally, prefer to live with more, and don't care a whit what those ladies over there think of it."

He ran a hand through his hair.

"Do you love me?" I asked.

All heads swiveled to Lane. He closed his eyes, so he didn't have to look at me.

"Do you?"

"No," he said, voice firm. Then he opened his eyes and his shoulders slumped. "Yes. But I have nothing to offer."

"What do you want to offer?"

He cocked his head. "What do you want?"

"What do you think I want?"

The heads of the ladies bounced back and forth in unison.

"Home?" he tried.

"I have that. It happens to be the same as yours. Unless you prefer America."

"Position?"

"No. I don't want that. Do you?"

"Not really."

"Good. We both seem to be fresh out, anyway."

"Family?"

"Mine's rather dodgy." *But not as much as yours,* I thought.

"I've got Aunt Bit."

"She's practically my aunt, anyway."

"Money, then?"

"Hmm. I have property, but possibly not much in the way of cash. You could bring that to the table, if you wished."

A small silence followed this, while Lane considered. After a few moments, he shrugged.

"Then we can proceed on those terms, Mr. Moreau?"

"Yes, I suppose we can."

"Good. Then I have one more question of importance for you. What is your relationship with Marie LeFevre?"

All the heads swiveled back to Lane. "What do you mean, exactly, Miss Tulman?"

"I mean that she seems extraordinarily fond of you and rather . . . robust in her constitution."

A rush of French began from the library doors, from both Joseph and Jean-Baptiste. Henri began translating from behind me.

"The sister of Joseph and Jean-Baptiste seems to have had an . . . entanglement with a boy who Jean-Michel put on a train to Nice before Joseph could do something . . . unfortunate to his person, therefore saving the tender feelings of the sister, and Joseph some time in purgatory." Jean-Baptiste said something else, and Henri said, "And she is so grateful, this sister, that now they meet Jean-Michel on street corners and leave their sister at home, as is best. That is all."

I looked back to Lane, and so did everyone else. A tiny flush was creeping beneath his tan skin. "That seems satisfactory," I said.

Lane raised his brows, and we looked at each other across the marble tiles of my grandmother's foyer.

"So, you're coming home with me, then?"

"Yes."

"And that is what you choose?"

"Yes," he said, "that is what I choose." The corner of his mouth lifted. "Is that what you choose?"

I took a deep breath. "Yes, it is. We'll discuss your plans for making money on the train. Now if you don't mind, I'll just let you all chat for a few moments while I go upstairs and put on a dress." *And take a bath, and possibly cry*, I thought. "I'm certain you will have things to explain to Mrs. Reynolds." I started to pick up my skirts, remembered I didn't have any, and instead walked with as much dignity as I could muster toward the stairs. The gray gaze followed me.

"Mr. Moreau," said Mrs. Reynolds, as if she were trying out the name, "I am so concerned that you would leave Paris. Are you certain you wish to . . . abandon your art?"

Lane did not answer her. Instead he came across the foyer, and before I could protest he had his hands on my head and his mouth on mine, hard. By the time he let me go I was blushing, as he'd meant for me to be.

"Go on, then," he said, his grin at me wicked. But I didn't. I stayed where I was, watching him go gracefully across the foyer to do his penance with Mrs. Reynolds, unable to contain my smile. With Mrs. Hardcastle in the room, Lane Moreau might as well have put an announcement in the *Times*.

I had not yet started up the stairs when I had another hand on my arm.

"I am taking my leave, Miss Tulman," said Henri. "Here, you will allow me to be French just this once."

He kissed me on both my dirty cheeks, a strange feeling, as they were both still flushed from Lane. I glanced once toward the salon, where I saw the gray gaze shooting daggers through the door.

"There! That was not so bad," said Henri, his brown eyes sparkling, "but I think it was not quite the same, no?" He was teasing me, and he knew full well that Lane was looking. But then he became serious. "You should get out of Paris quickly, yes? I would not bother much with packing. Take Mr. Tulman safely to his home and make your young man behave. That will be more than enough to keep you busy."

"You are certain you can go to the ambassador without danger to yourself?"

He made a little *poof* noise that I assumed meant that I should not worry. "I am . . . what is the word? Slippery. Have you not noticed, Miss Tulman? I am going as soon as I can change my clothes. If I do not, I shall have to console the women in your salon. I would rather be with the ambassador, I think."

"Here," I said, putting a hand on his arm, "now you will allow me to be French." I kissed his cheek, gratified by an expression of sleek surprise, and then doubly so to glance over my shoulder and find Lane's face dark with annoyance. I smiled at him, and when I turned back around, Henri was already gone. Joseph slouched in the doorway to the library, and so quick I thought perhaps I had not seen it, he winked. Still smiling, I turned and hurried up the stairs to Marianna's room, shut the door and leaned on it, breathing hard, as if I'd just won a race.

I dismissed the velvet chair at a glance, and instead went to the bed and sank down beside it, hoping I was not too dirty for the floor. Mary, being the wonder that she was, had a tub of water ready for me before the hearth. I needed to wash the dust from my hair, to take care of the myriad tasks that would get us out of Paris in the morning, especially concerning my uncle. But I was so tired. Everything in me ached, except for the one place that had been aching so long it had become a part of who I was; now that place was unknotted, unloosed, wonderfully and blessedly free. I felt my eyes closing, resting in the feel of it.

I jumped when the door burst open. "Lord!" Mary said, blowing through the room like a hurricane. "Ain't you done good, Miss! Mr. Tully, he's gone and made his own toast, brushed his jacket, and put himself to bed, no wrapping up of blankets or nothing."

She tugged me to my feet.

"It's a marvel, that is. But, Miss . . . now I ain't talking about Mr. Tully no more when I say this, Miss, but . . ."

She paused in the act of peeling off my dirty clothes, hands on my shoulders, her eyes as large and round as I'd ever seen them.

"But if that weren't a lesson on handling a man, then I don't know what was!" She stripped me down and gave me a push toward the tub. "I'm thinking you did real good, Miss! Real good. Now if I was able to be going about saying all that in French, then I'd be taking a page out of your book, if you take my meaning, Miss. I'm certain it would be a favor to me. . . ."

I held my second foot over the water, the momentary bliss at the thought of being clean taken away by the sudden memory of Robert's body, lying still and broken on the cavern floor. "Mary, I need to —"

"Talking a man's head right 'round till he don't know where he's at. That's artful, that is, Miss, and I'm thinking 'tis what a young man needs. Now take that Jean-Baptiste, Miss, he's a real nice young man, Miss, settled you know, more mature, not so silly and boyish. Do you know what I'm talking about, Miss?" She guided me into the water with a splash.

"Mary, I —"

"And with a real interesting name. Jean-Baptiste! It's so foreign sounding, ain't it, and it rolls right off the tongue. Jean-Baptiste," she demonstrated, shoving a chunk of soap into my hands. "Jean-Baptiste.

Jean-Baptiste! He was staying here all night and day, Miss, helping me with the packing up and such. I figured we was going, Miss, just as soon as we was able, and him being just as gentlemanly as you please, teaching me some real useful French, and you know what he did, Miss?"

I slid farther into the water and vowed to forever hold my peace.

"He was showing me how to pick a lock, Miss! Now that's real interesting, and real useful . . ."

"Mary," I said softly, "I am terribly glad to see you."

". . . and what do you think, Miss, if he didn't find all your money and a paper or two in the top of Mr. Babcock's second-best hat! So now we can be paying the dressmaker. And he's liking hair curls best, Miss. Has a real fondness for . . . Lord! Or what I mean to be saying is *sacré bleu!*" Mary plucked something from my pile of discarded clothing, and held it up to the light. "Is this thing a ruby?"

I didn't remember if I answered or what Mary said next. I fell asleep in the tub.

CHAPTER THIRTY-ONE

That evening I stood with Lane in the attic room, looking down at my uncle, lying still across the bottom of my steamer trunk. The gaslights were lit, and Lane looked more his normal self: clean-shaven, tan skin behind a plain shirt with the sleeves rolled up, arms crossed, and with a scowl on his face.

"I don't like it, Katharine," he said.

I didn't like it either. The soiled lining had been ripped out and the trunk was clean, ready enough for use, but all my trepidation from the first time we'd done this had come back to me triple force. This plan was madness, once again, with everything to go wrong and everything to lose.

"Uncle Tully," I whispered, "are you truly certain?"

The blue eyes popped open. "Oh, yes, little niece, yes! It is just so. Just so! It is tight, like blankets, and there are holes. Holes to see through, Simon's baby! Lane! Tell my niece there are holes to see through."

The gray gaze turned to me in all seriousness. "Miss Tulman, there are holes in the trunk that Mr. Tully can see through."

"Thank you so much, Mr. Moreau."

"My pleasure."

"Likewise."

"Little niece!" said Uncle Tully, petulant. I tore my attention away from Lane. "If there are holes, then I can see out, but when they are little holes, then no one can see in! Is that not splendid? And this place is better than the other place, and the next place is better than this one, isn't that right, little niece? And you are coming?" This was to Lane. "And you are coming, and the girl is coming?"

"Yes, that's right, Uncle."

His shoulders slumped with relief, then they stiffened again. "And the clocks?"

"Yes, Uncle." I knelt down beside the trunk. "Uncle Tully, do you understand that if you ride in the trunk, you are going to see new places, and new people, and some of them might not be splendid? And if you are frightened, or uncomfortable, or if you want something, or to play, then you will have to wait, and you will have to be silent. That is very important, Uncle."

Uncle Tully sat up in his trunk, his white hair a little wild. "Lane! Would I have to be silent in the trunk?"

"Yes, Mr. Tully. That's so."

"I do not like silence, Simon's baby."

"I know it, Uncle."

Uncle Tully thought hard, muttering to himself. Then he said, "If I count, then the silence is only on the outside. Not inside my head. Not in my head. Only on the outside. I do not mind the outside kind. I can make it go away on the inside."

Lane squatted down beside me, elbows on his knees, and we looked at each other. My uncle looked to us both.

"He is quite good at closing his eyes and waiting now," I said. "Remarkably so."

"Mr. Tully, can you stay quiet, no matter what? Can you do it?"

Uncle Tully was solemn. "Sometimes big things can be little," he said.

Lane sighed.

"All right, Uncle," I said. "You may ride in the trunk."

Uncle Tully smiled, as if day had appeared among the gaslights. "Little niece," he whispered.

"Yes, Uncle?"

"Can I tell you a secret? Should I?"

"I think you should."

Uncle Tully whispered, very loud, "I would like to shut the lid again! Now!"

We got out of my grandmother's house in Paris early, hoping to catch the first train and the earliest possible steamer from Calais. We'd had to hire a wagon for my trunk, but not having the extraordinary skill of Mr. Babcock, there had been no time to find transportation for all that was left in the workshop. We left the boxes on the landing, and I went to Mrs. DuPont's room to give instructions on how to send them on to us, and also to place a ruby ring in her hand. Pink suffused her white skin as she stared down at the ring.

I said, "This house will not be the best place for you, Mrs. DuPont, or for Mr. DuPont."

"*Napoléon est mort!*" he said in response to his name.

"Hello, Mr. DuPont," I replied. Marguerite patted his hand. "Use it to find somewhere that is private and quiet, and for Marguerite, to send her to school. A good school, mind you, not severe. Will it be enough?"

Mrs. DuPont closed her bony fingers around the ring. "Yes, it will be enough," she said.

"And no more selling?"

She thought for a moment, then shook her head.

"Keep your agreement with my estate, if you wish. I plan to maintain the house for a time, in case . . ." I didn't finish. "Or if you wish to work elsewhere, write and I will send a reference."

She nodded, and I'd turned to leave when I heard a small voice say, *"Merci, Mademoiselle."* I looked down to see Marguerite smiling in the exact way every master painter seemed to think a beautiful child ought to smile, and then Mrs. DuPont curtsied.

"Yes. Thank you, Miss Tulman."

I was halfway down the corridor before it occurred to me that Mrs. DuPont had used my name.

In the foyer, Lane and the wagon driver were setting my steamer trunk down on the tiles, Mary assisting by carrying a hatbox and giving an endless stream of instructions on the correct way to get a trunk down the stairs. I was nervous and ready to be gone, half thinking to see imperial soldiers come marching down Rue Trudon, though I knew Joseph and Jean-Baptiste were watching. They had already said their good-byes, Jean-Baptiste causing Mary a few tears, but Joseph was coming with us to Stranwyne, as soon as his sister was settled and his passport approved. I was grateful for this. I wanted another set of eyes on Lane when I couldn't be there.

Lane went back up the stairs for my bags, his long legs taking them two at a time in his hurry, the driver made for the door, and then Mrs. Hardcastle was saying, "Hello! Hello! Good morning, Miss Tulman!" from the open doorway.

I turned in time to see Mary run pell-mell across the foyer, this time holding her hatbox, and sit herself abruptly on my steamer trunk. Mrs. Hardcastle raised the pince-nez, looked at Mary briefly, shook her head, then came bouncing across the foyer, opening her reticule.

"Well, I am so glad I caught you, my dear. I waited to speak to you yesterday, but you never came downstairs after whatever you had been up to. . . ." She paused, hoping I might fill that gap. When I did not, she said, "And as fascinating as that little scene was — and I am not being facetious in the slightest when I say that it was fascinating, my dear — I did have a purpose for inviting myself to several cups of tea, overstaying my welcome, and now barging in on you this morning." She handed me a letter, beaming. "I've not forgotten our agreement, you see. I wrote Alice Tulman the very afternoon of our chat, and heard back at the morning post yesterday."

I glanced once at Mary, but all seemed to be well in the steamer trunk. "I take it this is not good news, Mrs. Hardcastle?"

"Not good news at all, my dear!" Mrs. Hardcastle could not actually stand still for excitement. "Alice has heard all about Mr. Babcock. I'm certain something was in the papers, and . . . Now wait, child! You have not let me finish. You see, I know a solicitor . . ." She lowered her voice even further. ". . . a hopeless solicitor. An imbecile and a drunkard, if you can credit it, with . . ." she whispered the next words, "a history. A history that I just happen to be acquainted with.

So let's just say that Alice Tulman is about to be very badly advised in her legal affairs! Is that not delicious?"

My mouth had opened in utter astonishment, so I closed it, wondering if perhaps Mrs. Hardcastle had ever had conversations with Mrs. DuPont that did not concern my wardrobe. Mrs. Hardcastle was smiling at me expectantly.

"Why, thank you, indeed, Mrs. Hardcastle. You will keep me informed?"

"I am a spy in the enemy camp!" She giggled like a girl. "But take heart and enjoy your trip, my dear, the weather has just been divine." She leaned close, whispering dramatically, "And you've made the Miss Mortimers so abominably jealous that I shall have fun for days!"

Mrs. Hardcastle bustled happily out the door, and Mary slumped off the steamer trunk in relief.

We made our train, miraculously, without noise or incident, paying for a private compartment just in case, and even more remarkably, we managed to catch our steamer in Calais. I wondered if Uncle Tully had his eyes closed, counting out his waiting, or if he was actually watching, and if so, what he thought of real life from the view of a peephole.

The steamer was extraordinarily empty, only a few French officers, perhaps on business to London for the war, and the lack of loading and unloading quickened our departure. This also meant a first-class cabin was available, so Uncle Tully could come out of his trunk. Mary had pulled strips of pink cloth from the workshop, bringing them to hang and create a set of walls my uncle could sit inside, along with a broken clock to repair. I stayed on deck while Lane and Mary got him settled, the steam engines chugging, watching the waves and the wake the boat created as it slowly pulled away from France. Hopefully the fresh air and wind would keep me from repeating my lamentable state of health during my last Channel crossing.

I was leaning a bit over the rail, letting the salt spray dampen my face, when someone approached and stood by my side. I straightened, a hand to my bonnet now that I was facing the breeze, and looked into the face of a man, uniformed, a bit short, and vaguely familiar.

"My apologies for disturbing your thoughts, Mademoiselle Tulman," he said.

"Oh, why, I . . ." My voice trailed away, my heart beginning a hard, slow *thump*. Henri had pointed this man out to me at the emperor's ball. A member of the imperial court, and Napoléon III's half brother. Which meant he was Lane's uncle. The thought gave me a start.

"My name is Charles de Morny, Mademoiselle. I can see that you know the name."

I nodded, eyes roving quickly over the deck. We were alone.

Morny smiled, leaning his elbows on the rail. "Your information concerning the empress was appreciated. The emperor has been glad to commandeer this boat to ease your journey back to England."

I stared, all at once aware of the very deep, cold water that was all around us. I didn't even know if I should be afraid. I turned my face to the spray, letting the wind carry our words out to sea. "I'd hoped His Majesty would not find me so quickly. The empress will be well, then?"

"Her wine has been changed and her room purged. Her doctor is of the opinion that the doses were slight, meant to be given over time, and that there will be no lasting effects. The empress will not be informed. She has been told that she was ill, and is now recovering."

I nodded once again and waited.

"The tunnel beneath the Tuileries has been sealed," he said. "But not before it was explored." He looked me square in the eye. "I need you to tell me, Mademoiselle Tulman, what killed Charles Arceneaux and what he was doing beneath the Tuileries."

I pressed my lips together and looked out to sea. The boat dipped slightly, and then rode up a wave.

"Mademoiselle, I am going to be frank and hope for frankness in return. There have been two attempts on the life of the emperor this month alone. And with the discovery of the plot against his wife, and from so close . . . Louis is in constant fear. He has become superstitious, a fanatic with this warning of Pisces. The man will not even eat his caviar."

I closed my eyes for a moment. It had not occurred to me until that moment that Pisces was the sign of the fish.

"Until Louis produces an heir with his name, the throne is insecure."

"Monsieur de Morny, Ben . . . I mean to say, Charles, was obsessed with being of the Bonaparte bloodline, to the point of madness. Whatever he was doing, he did not try to assassinate the emperor." I shook my head at the irony of defending Ben's innocence.

"And in the tunnel, in the big room, what was Charles doing there?"

I held on to my bonnet, willing my voice to sound calm. If the emperor was ignorant of the happenings in the cavern, then surely he was ignorant of Uncle Tully. "I don't know what Charles was doing, exactly. Experimenting, I believe."

"And how he died?"

I had an unbidden vision of purple-tinged fire, and the smoke coming from Ben Aldridge's skin. "Electricity," I said. "That is what killed him. But . . ." I bit my lip. "The contents of the barrels, sir, that is dangerous if exposed to flame, and would be best left where it is." I lifted my chin and looked away. "I don't know anything else."

Morny shook his head. "But I think you do, Mademoiselle." He waited, making me look at him before he went on. "Charles was not the only Bonaparte running about beneath the Tuileries, was he?"

"Please," I said, "he knows nothing of this. He knows only the father who raised him. This news, it would be . . . most unwelcome."

The boat smacked hard into a choppy wave. "Moreau is a name known to us," Morny said. "There was a soldier captured in the war, very loyal, taken to a prison in the south of England — that is where your estate is, is it not? He escaped, but he did not return to France. After Louis's time in London, this man Moreau, was honored, I think, to raise a son of the house of Bonaparte, a boy with the blood of the Emperor Napoléon the First running through his veins. He could not have known that the father of this child would also become the second emperor of France, Napoléon the Third. A double honor. And yet while he accepted the first, a baby still in its blankets, he did not accept the second that was brought to him, an older child, also a boy, whose mother was going mad."

I took a deep breath. Part of me was longing to know more of this, and part of me was longing for him to stop giving me so many things to conceal.

"Will Thérèse Arceneaux . . . will she be taken care of?"

"The emperor pays for her care. This is a thing we also do not tell the empress." He sighed. "I have watched the young man, on the boat and on the dock. He has a strong look of his father." Morny straightened from the rail. "It is a strange thing," he said, "being an illegitimate son. On the streets, you are of the lowest form, while in the court, you become a duke. Our Louis is many things, but his heart, it is soft for his children. We agree with you, Miss Tulman, that it is best for the young man to return to England. The throne of France must be secure. We . . ."

At that moment, Lane came around the deck, jacket collar turned up against the wind. He checked his walk when he saw me with the uniformed Frenchman, and approached warily, like a cat. "Have you been in the wind all this time, Katharine?" he said. His use of my name had been just the slightest bit possessive.

"Mr. Moreau, this is —"

"Monsieur de Morny," the Frenchman interjected. *"Je suis heureux de faire votre connaissance."*

"Moi de même," Lane replied, wrinkling his forehead at the switch to French. *"J'espère que vous allez apprécier votre voyage."*

Morny positively beamed at this reply. It was possible, I supposed, that Lane spoke better French than the emperor. Morny stopped looking Lane up and down like a prize horse and turned back to me.

"It was most pleasant to speak with you, Mademoiselle. I am glad we are of like mind."

"Thank you," I replied with perhaps too much relief, because I got a sharp gray look from my side.

Morny bowed and went belowdecks, and then it was Lane's turn to lean on the rail.

"Mr. Tully's got his cloth hung, and he's playing about with that box. Mary's with him."

I glanced back at the door Charles de Morny had gone through. "Is he locked in?"

Lane looked at me sidelong. "Yes, but the boat's almost empty. You don't have to mother him too much, Katharine."

As Lane's tone showed this to be a point of pride rather than admonishment, I let it go. The sea spat foam in a fine spray. Lane loved the sea. I could see it in his face. I looked at his hand on the rail, the color like creamed tea, such a contrast to mine. That trait had not come from his father. *Could Lane be Spanish?* I wondered suddenly.

"What?" he said, grinning. I snapped awake.

"I was just wondering if you liked the smell," I said.

"You mean the sea? I do. I do like it. Now that we're out of the harbor."

He took my hand that had been on the rail, and held it between both of his. It was so much warmer there.

"So, are you ready to discuss money?" I watched his brows come down.

"I hadn't forgotten."

I proceeded with caution. This whole thing was silly, in my opinion. But if these were the terms he could live with, then so be it. I also knew Lane well enough to guess that the sums in his head were very likely ridiculous. "Did you know that Uncle Tully can make a bell ring with his box?"

He was playing with my fingers now, stretching them out one by one, examining. I tried to concentrate.

"And by ringing a bell with his box, I mean a bell that is in no way connected to his box."

I had his attention now. "How can that be?"

"No idea, of course. But while we were in Paris, Uncle Tully could push his little lever on the box in the attic and make the bells ring downstairs. Without a string, or even a wire."

I'd given a good deal of thought to this, last night in my bed, with the silver swan gleaming in the light of the candle I'd left burning, letting Marianna watch over me from where she sat by the wall, waiting to be packed. I'd imagined bells to summon a policeman, to wake a house in the case of fire, even to call a maid. Putting my uncle's invention to such uses would not only be practical — a welcome change from destructive — but it would also be, I hoped, rather lucrative. Especially with someone who could carve the moldings to make beautiful designs for them. But I would let Lane come to most of these conclusions on his own; probably he could come to better ones. I thought Marianna might be rather pleased with me. The wind blew another cold salt spray, and I shivered.

"Come here, then," Lane said, pulling me into his open jacket. I reached up and untied my bonnet, letting my head tuck beneath his chin, preferring the warmth of him to my hat. He watched the sea from over my head.

"Lane." I hesitated. "You seemed so at home in Paris. Will you be sorry, do you think?"

"I don't say things I don't mean, Katharine Tulman. And my answer was yes, wasn't it?"

·

I nodded. It had been.

"And what about you? Can you live with what you've chosen?"

"Oh, yes. I just won't take tea in London. Or Paris either. I'll just have to go to America for it." I'd made him smile, I could feel it from the way his chin moved on my head. "I'll be the young woman who always takes her steamer trunk to tea. But I'll need a bigger trunk, I think. Uncle Tully only just fits now."

"That's so. If you'd get room for a workbench in there, you might make a world traveler of him yet."

"We could go to Rome, to see the ruins."

"Or the pyramids," Lane suggested.

"India."

"Boating down the Amazon."

"With my trunk in one end of the canoe."

He laughed, a low rumble in his chest; I felt it vibrating through my own. I wanted to tell him that it was a mess at home, that there had been so much to rebuild and repair, that we were overextended, and that without Mr. Babcock I was afraid I would mishandle all of it. That I would not go to Mr. Babcock's funeral, to avoid causing a spectacle. That I didn't know exactly how we were going to hide Uncle Tully, that we might need to hide him for the rest of his years, and that we couldn't continue to deceive Mrs. Cooper. She was going to be so angry, deservedly so, and would Mr. Cooper really keep our secret? I wanted to tell him that I could not stop thinking of that child in the asylum with his silent play, and that I was afraid Aunt Alice's legal advice might accidentally be too good. I wanted to tell him that he was descended from the bloodline of two different emperors.

But then Lane said, "Katharine, tell me more about Mr. Tully's electricity."

I loved the way he said my name. I said, "It really is the most amazing thing. He makes the electricity fly right through the air. You can't see it, but you know it must be there, because . . . well, because the bell rings."

Like everything we'd done, I thought, *throwing unseen sparks into the future, sometimes with spectacular results.* I wondered what spark was flying now.

"Katharine," Lane said, "I think I'll just go belowdecks and talk to Mr. Tully about his box."

He kissed the top of my head, and I immediately missed his warmth as he moved away, disappearing through the door to the cabins below. The wind whipped the ribbons of my hat, overwhelming the noise of the engines. I was alone on the deck, but I wasn't alone at all. I turned my face to the sea and looked toward home.

AUTHOR'S NOTE

Charles-Louis Napoléon Bonaparte, the man who became Napoléon III, was born in 1808 to Louis Bonaparte, brother of Napoléon I, and Hortense de Beauharnais Bonaparte, who was Napoléon I's stepdaughter. After two attempts in his early life to recapture the rule of France, one of which resulted in exile to London and the other in life imprisonment (from which he escaped), Charles-Louis was rumored to have left at least two sons behind him in England when he was elected president of France in 1848. By December 1852, Charles-Louis had dissolved the French Parliament and proclaimed himself Napoléon III, emperor of France, just as Napoléon I had crowned himself emperor forty-eight years earlier.

The uncertainty created by Napoléon III's coronation fueled a French and British race to naval supremacy, even as the two countries allied themselves against Russia in the Crimean War. The war began as a dispute over influence in the declining Ottoman Empire, quickly becoming a full-scale conflict known for its gross tactical miscalculations, one of the most famous being chronicled in Tennyson's poem, "The Charge of the Light Brigade." But it was also the first "modern" war, with the use of steam-powered ships, floating ironclad batteries, railways, and also daily documentation for the public newspapers by telegraph and photography. Florence Nightingale began using modern nursing techniques on the Crimean battlefields, where more men died of disease than of their wounds. The British-French alliance declared victory in 1856. In 1859, the French launched the first steam-powered, ironclad ship, *La Gloire*, after the close of the Crimean War. Britian's first ironclad, the HMS *Warrior*, made its appearance the following year. During the reign of Napoléon III, naval supremacy meant European dominance.

With the advent of steam-powered ironclads also came the race for the ability to destroy them. British engineer Robert Whitehead was the first to design a swimming, clockwork torpedo "fish," the earliest plans of which show a section marked "secret chamber," where the gyroscope was housed. But it wasn't until the addition of a pendulum in 1868 that the fish became a reliable weapon. Filled with the new and volatile nitrocellulose, or "gun-cotton," Whitehead's torpedo could swim a straight line, holding its depth beneath the water to stealthily blow a hole in an ironclad ship. The first torpedoes were purchased by Britain's Royal Navy in 1870, filling the vacuum of power created by the invincible ironclads. The way the balance of power was maintained and naval battles were fought changed forever, not only for Britain and France, but for the world.

ACKNOWLEDGMENTS

When I considered the acknowledgments for my debut novel it was very clear to me that no author writes a book alone. Now that I've completed my second novel, I realize just as clearly that no one publishes a book alone. Thank you, Scholastic Press. What an incredible team I've had behind me! Not only have you come together to make an amazing book, you've done your very best to turn this writer into an author and make me a part of your publishing family. Seriously, why are you people so nice?

For Lisa Sandell, my lovely, encouraging, gracious, and so very patient editor and friend: You've opened your office, your heart, and your home. Thank you for believing that I could do this!

For Sheila Marie Everett, my publicist: Everything's better where you are!

For Elizabeth Starr Baer, Bess Braswell, Emma Brockaway, Jody Corbett, Antonio Gonzalez, Candace Greene, Emily Heddleson, Stacy Lellos, David Levithan, John Mason, Emily Morrow, Elizabeth Parisi, Lizette Serrano, Tracy van Straaten, Jennifer Ung, the fabulous Scholastic sales team, and all the people that have had a hand in getting both the book and myself where we're going: many thanks. And also everyone in Book Clubs, Book Fairs, and the Foreign Rights department: I know you guys do a lot more than I will ever know. Thank you for being my champions.

For Kelly Sonnack, my agent: You know the combination of intelligence, savvy, humor, beauty, and being so darn good at your job is unfair to the rest of us, right?

For the Society of Children's Book Writers and Illustrators, Midsouth Region: If the journey to publication is an upward climb, you gave me a ladder.

All my love and thanks to my writing partners, who continue to teach and hone me: Genetta Adair, Amy Eytchison, Rachel Griffith, Howard Shirley, Angelika Stegmann, Courtney Stevens, and Jessica Young. I would be nowhere without you. And also for Ruta Sepetys, who always manages to show me the way to being a better author and a better person: Thank you for blazing the trail!

For all my family: Your love, support, and enthusiasm have meant so much to me!

For my grandmother Betty Hill: Your résumé has been forwarded to the publicity department. Please watch for that, Sheila Marie.

For Christopher, Stephen, and Elizabeth: You guys would be horrified by all the motherly bragging I do about you while I'm on the road. Sorry about that. I probably won't stop, though.

And for Philip, who has happily done more research, drawn more schematics, become my personal Internet cyber-stalker as well as a minor expert in the business of publishing, and who has dropped me off at more airports, and picked up more slack than anybody should have to. Seven years ago I got a crazy whim, and you are why each and every step toward fulfilling this dream has been possible. You are such a keeper!

ABOUT THE AUTHOR

Sharon Cameron was awarded the 2009 Sue Alexander Most Promising New Work Award by the Society of Children's Book Writers and Illustrators for the prequel to A Spark Unseen: her debut novel, The Dark Unwinding, which was awarded the SCBWI Crystal Kite Award, named an ALA Best Fiction for Young Adults selection, and which USA Today called "utterly original, romantic, and spellbindingly imaginative." When not writing, Sharon can be found thumbing through dusty tomes, shooting a longbow, or indulging in her lifelong search for secret passages. She lives with her family in Nashville, Tennessee. Visit Sharon at sharoncameronbooks.com.